PRAISE FOR EV EHRLICH'S

GRANT SPEAKS

"Ehrlich's prose is genuinely witty... what he has done is clever indeed."
—*L.A. Times*

"Satire of a high order... refreshingly irreverent... good fun."
—*Seattle Times*

"A remarkable tour de force... a writer who lends conviction and humor."
—*Amarillo Globe-News*

"Ehrlich romps... with a wry sense of humor, a telling eye for the times.... He gives us a darn good reason to read a Grant novel—for entertainment. Light a cigar and enjoy it."
—*Providence Sunday Journal*

"A refreshing relief... entertains [with] chapters to relish.... There is much to enjoy."
—*Anniston Star*

"Grant emerges... as a skeptical, humane, and ultimately sympathetic figure... a cheeky lark."
—*Publishers Weekly*

"Entertaining... vividly detailed... Ehrlich gives this Grant a marvelously flexible and sardonic colloquial voice, and enlivens his story with briskly retold heroic tales (the campaigns of Shiloh and Vicksburg are especially well depicted)."
—*Kirkus Reviews*

more...

Also by Ev Ehrlich

Big Government

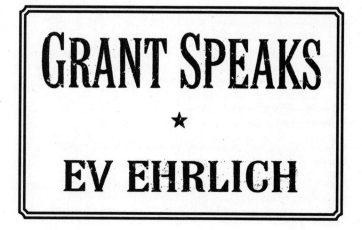

GRANT SPEAKS

★

EV EHRLICH

WARNER BOOKS

A Time Warner Company

Copyright © 2000 by Everett M. Ehrlich
All rights reserved.

Warner Books, Inc., 1271 Avenue of the Americas, New York, NY 10020
Visit our Web site at www.twbookmark.com

(w) A Time Warner Company

Printed in the United States of America

Originally published in hardcover by Warner Books, Inc.

First Trade Printing: May 2001

10 9 8 7 6 5 4 3 2 1

The Library of Congress has cataloged the hardcover edition as follows:
Ehrlich, Everett M.
    Grant speaks / Ev Ehrlich.
        p. cm.
    ISBN 0-446-52387-9
    1. Grant, Ulysses S. (Ulysses Simpson), 1822-1885—Fiction. 2. United States—History—Civil War, 1861-1865—Fiction. 3. Presidents—United States—Fiction. 4. Generals—United States—Fiction. I. Title.

PS3555.H718 G72 2000
813'.54—dc21   99-051680

ISBN: 0-446-67655-1 (pbk.)

Cover design by John Valk
Cover photograph © Corbis

For Donald Marks
(Cpl., Ret., U.S. Army)

GRANT SPEAKS

For Richie —

Garbage in, garbage out —

half a century ago, you saw

the garbage going in —

Much love,

EV · 4.06

The Hartford Courant

— June 15, 2000 —

GRANT MANUSCRIPT
FOUND IN CLEMENS HOME

Workmen Discover Unknown First Draft
of Best-Selling 19th Century Memoir

HARTFORD, Dec. 14 — Workmen renovating the home of Samuel Clemens (Mark Twain) have discovered a manuscript historians now claim is the previously unknown first draft of the memoirs of President and victorious Civil War General Ulysses S. Grant, along with a note from Clemens to Grant, coincidentally dated the day of Grant's death, citing the sensational nature of many of Grant's claims and urging him to destroy the draft.

"It's a shocking text," said Mr. Filbert Manchew, the President of the Hartford Historical Society, who played a major role in authenticating the draft. "Grant's first draft gives us not only a different view of Grant himself, but of most of America's political history throughout the nineteenth century. In his final days, the greatest figure of that period decided to come clean and tell the truth."

Grant's memoirs are widely regarded as a high point in historical narrative. They were a posthumous best-seller of epic proportions, written by the terminally ill military hero and failed President in order to provide an estate for his wife. But this first draft differs substantially from the published one in many respects.

Sources familiar with the draft say that Grant makes a variety of disturbing revelations regarding, among other topics, his use of psychotropic drugs in the Mexican War, Robert E. Lee's character, his impressions of Abraham and Mary Lincoln, and his relationship with the Vanderbilt family. While flattering to such contemporaries as William T. Sherman, Philip H. Sheridan, and E. O. C. Ord, he is sometimes brutally dismissive of such figures as George H. Thomas, William S. Rosecrans, Don Carlos Buell, Ambrose E. Burnside, Henry W. Halleck, and George B. McClellan.

Most controversially, Grant claims to have been an imposter who usurped the "true" Grant's identity only to be confronted with the "real" Grant later in life.

The Clemens and Grant estates are now in negotiations to determine who has legal title to the manuscript.

TABLE OF CONTENTS

INTRODUCTION BY THE AUTHOR,
ULYSSES S. GRANT,
GENERAL OF THE ARMY
AND EIGHTEENTH PRESIDENT
OF THE UNITED STATES OF AMERICA

TO BEGIN WITH, I'm dying.

I first had trouble swallowing a year ago. Now the lump I couldn't swallow is swallowing me. When it was the size of a pea, I sought out my doctor, who sent me to a prestigious fellow proficient in excising pea-sized lumps. By the time that fellow returned from vacation, my pea was the size of an almond, which was larger than his proficiency. Instead, he referred me to a renowned practitioner in New York, who was away in Paris practicing, but who would see me when he returned. By the time he did, my almond was the size of a walnut.

And so a race ensued between the size of the lump in my throat and the stature of the doctors who were unavailable to treat it. In the end, the lump won. Sometimes I think it would be poetic justice if I sought out Dr. Frederick Saveshammer, who already had once saved the life of Ulysses Grant some twenty years before at Shiloh, even if neither he nor Ulysses Grant realized it at the time.

My doctor calls my lump "epithelial in character," apparently the learned term for what you get when you smoke twenty cigars a day for twenty years. I didn't smoke cigars until the capture of Fort Donelson, when a newspaperman (which, as my volatile friend Sherman used to say, is another word for "traitor") took a picture of me, cigar in hand. It wasn't even lit. But it was the first victory of the Civil War, and when people saw the picture, they started sending me cigars, boxes and barrels of them. It would have been wasteful not to smoke the ones I couldn't give away, so I did.

In the end, it was the same old story. My fame killed me.

There's nothing new in that. Every famous person is killed by his fame, one way or another, sooner or later. Look at Lincoln. He was God's Own Yokel, all ears and knuckles and Adam's apple. I remember when he came to visit me at City Point in '64. We were encamped on the James River, laying siege to Petersburg and Richmond. He came off the boat wearing that stovepipe hat of his—at sixty-seven inches, I couldn't have picked a penny off the top of it, not if I'd jumped like a trained monkey.

I thought the wily old goat would live forever. He floated through every public moment, uttering his righteous visions of humanity, and then, in private, would laugh and drawl like the true cracker-barrel sit-about he was. He's dead now, killed by his own fame, although Fate certainly had a helping hand that night. If he'd have stayed home in Illinois and lawyered, he'd have died a rich old man in his own bed. But, like he once told me, once those President grubs start burrowing, they can't be driven out.

Or Lee, the soul of genteel nobility, that sanctimonious little mama's boy. He was the only fellow ever to graduate West Point without a single bad conduct mark. I had 290, a normal lad's share of them, and I was a choirboy compared to Sherman or, for that matter, that lightning-struck farm boy "Stonewall" Jackson, this long before he, too, turned on his country, the dog.

Well, I whipped Lee's hind end like a mule's regardless of what a good boy he was. I shook his hand properly at Appomattox, and they still talk about how magnanimous I was in victory. Why shouldn't I have been magnanimous? I couldn't have punished him any more than he punished himself. Lee was so distraught after he got beat that he moped and fussed and died of a broken heart only five years later. They tell me he was still fighting the war on his deathbed, calling to A. P. Hill to bring his line up. But no matter how often he did, I kept on whipping him. It was more than his overburdened heart could take.

Lincoln, Lee, Jackson, Zach Taylor, my man Rawlins, all of them— I'll be joining them soon. But rather than dying quietly and privately, the way even the simplest man with something *epithelial* gets to die, I'm dying in public view, here in this book, a spectacle. I'm dying this way because I'm broke, busted, just as I always was. My father always said I had no business sense. Even when I was saving the Union, the old jackal probably wished I was a proper merchant instead.

Sad to say, he was right. I never did have a head for business. I lost money in Galena, in Sacket's Harbor, in Alaska, in St. Louis, in Vancouver, in California, on Wall Street—everywhere somebody else was making money, they were making it off me. This book is the only business venture I've ever devised where my downside is covered: I can't lose money as I write. All I can lose is time. But then again, I'm running out of that, too.

Everybody I ever knew saw me as their chance to get something. My Cabinet was a pack of rascals. My brother-in-law duped me into helping him corner the gold market. My father followed my army south to profiteer cotton. Even Mrs. Grant wanted me to run for President a third time simply to get the house back. And when I was stripped of every dime I had, when I had to go to William Vanderbilt, hat in hand, to bail out my good name, he told me the terrible truth— that he had used me, too, used me to send hundreds of thousands of men to die for cheap labor and cotton.

Cheap labor and cotton. That's what they wanted and that's what they got.

I've been a failure, a hero, and a chump. I've seen our nation cleaved in two and bound together again. I've seen men die for nothing and for everything. I've been flat broke and I've toured the world as a king. And what I propose to do in this final hour is to tell the truth—what really happened and who I really am. Let this be my deathbed confession to history—the whole truth and nothing but— with you, the Reader, as my witness.

May God, if my mother was right and He exists, have mercy on me, as He will, I pray, dear Reader, have on you.

CHAPTER I

ORIGINS OF THE GRANTS IN AMERICA—MY EARLY CHILDHOOD—AN INCIDENT INVOLVING USEFUL GRANT—AN ACCIDENT BEFALLS THE OTHER GRANTS—OFF TO WEST POINT

MY UPBRINGING WOULD HAVE BEEN that of any other Ohio frontier boy in the 1820s and '30s, were it not for the fact there were two families named Grant in Georgetown, the town in which I was raised. That there were two such families changed both my life and history itself, forever.

My own family is American and has been for generations, in all its branches, direct and collateral. My fifth great-grandfather, Matthew Grant, came from England in 1630. He was established and prosperous, but not so established and prosperous that he didn't put his wife and everything he owned on a cramped little boat to cross the ocean and take a chance on getting killed by Indians. He settled in Windsor, Connecticut, where he became the town clerk and surveyor. As such, he adjudicated who was entitled to steal what, a position of considerable importance then as it is now. The Grants continued unexceptionally in America until Matthew's great-great-grandson, my great-grandfather, Noah Grant, was born. As was mine, Noah's life was undistinguished until touched by war. He teamed up with the famous patriot Israel Putnam in the 1750s to harass the French and Indians in the war so named. His bravery was rewarded by the Connecticut legislature with a considerable sum of money, which was of great consolation to Noah's widow when he was killed in battle only a few months later.

Now fatherless, my grandfather, also Noah, was as miserable a creature as was ever placed on this earth. After the Revolution, he claimed to take up arms at Lexington and Concord, and rued the fact the war had "spoiled" him. If the war spoiled him, it was only because all the other men had gone to fight it, leaving so much room at the tavern that Noah's access to libation was unimpeded. He chose to pursue a career in life as a drunken farmer. He failed only as a farmer. After a stint in debtor's prison, he sold all of the land he owned—and probably some he didn't—and, in 1790, moved to Pennsylvania, where he married. My father, Jesse Root Grant, was born there in 1794, the first of five children.

Noah soon outstayed his welcome in Pennsylvania and moved to Deerfield, Ohio. But when my grandmother died there in 1805, he found that raising their children interfered with his drinking. Noah's progeny were shipped off to various places and he continued west, where he died a common drunk.

There are people who say I'll die an uncommon one.

My father was pawned off on an older half-brother, who had a tannery in Kentucky. After five years, he moved across the river to Ohio. There he apprenticed as a tanner for a God-fearing farmer named Orvil Brown, who ran a station on what would one day be called the Underground Railroad, with the help of his son John. We would hear more from that corner later.

My father left the Brown house in 1818 and moved to Ravenna, Ohio, where he opened a tannery of his own. He began making money in ample quantities. There he learned of a farming family from Pennsylvania that had moved nearby, and went calling upon them to look for marriageable prospects. The Simpson family had a daughter named Hannah who fit the bill. She was plain and hard in both her features and attitude; quiet, disciplined, a devout Methodist, and, at twenty-three, an old maid. She had a pebble for a heart and a belief that God had a plan in which man played a passive role at best.

My father was uninterested in affection—having received none, he was unfamiliar with it. Instead, he wanted a wife who shared his approach—all business. He now had found one. As for my mother, the fact that Jesse Grant rode a horse out to her father's farm to find her was proof enough he was the man God intended for her—she was all business as well, even if her business was the Lord. Grandfather Simpson didn't take to my father at first, but he soon mastered the algebra of my father's burgeoning tannery bank balance and relented. My parents were married in 1821, moved to the town of Georgetown, and ten respectable months later my mother bore me into the world. I was born Hiram Ulysses Grant—my real name, though that is not how I came to be known—on April 27, 1822, the first of six children. My consumptive brother Simpson followed two years later, then my sister Clara, and then Jennie, who escaped her spinsterhood in 1869 only to trigger the near-downfall of capitalism. My conniving brother Orvil was then born twelve years junior to me, and finally little Mary Frances.

The second Grant family in Georgetown, Ohio—as I mentioned, there were two—was that of Mr. Llemmuel Grant and was not related to ours. In fact, it was not really named Grant. Llemmuel Grant's family's ancestral settler in the U.S. was Velliard Grande, a French reformist who escaped the Huguenot Massacre of 1604, fled to Holland, and crossed over to the New World with Peter Minuit in 1622, where he took the Dutch name Voorhees Grynt.

Voorhees Grynt grew in stature within New Amsterdam until the English defeated the Dutch in 1664 and renamed it New York. Voorhees Grynt was by then well into his seventies and had no appetite for political intrigues. So he approached the English and told them he was not Dutch but French, and as a Reformist whose family had been executed by marauding Catholics, he held a natural affinity for the English. He then made clear his willingness to help finance the new colonial government. Some combination of these statements so impressed the English that they allowed him to maintain his position and standing under their administration. Voorhees Grynt thereupon changed his name to Valiant Grant, which was not a difficult transition since Voorhees Grynt was not his name to begin with, and the other Grant family was now established in America.

Noah Grant cowered before the Revolution; Valiant Grant prospered mightily while waiting it out to determine which side would win. When Cornwallis was beaten at Yorktown, Valiant Grant's family became ardent revolutionists and committed their resources to the new nation by lending it money at a handsome profit.

Valiant Grant's descendants rode the westward expansion to Ohio. There Llemmuel was born and used his family's means to found the Southern Ohio Bank of the United States, which was really the Southern Ohio Bank of Llemmuel Grant.

As founder and principal stockholder of the bank, he elected himself president.

As president of the bank, he created the town of Georgetown and took for himself the position of mayor.

As mayor, he determined the town needed a magistrate and appointed himself.

And so he came to be known in our town as Judge Mayor Grant.

Judge Mayor Grant and my father disliked each other with a passion. If one could have bought the rights to the use of their common name for cash, he'd have done it. Judge Mayor Grant's family gave off an aroma of culture and refinement and looked down at our family, which reeked of the tannery and gave off the aroma of vats of fish oil and offal left in the sun. Judge Mayor Grant attended an Eastern university and married a handsome woman. My father had a few months of schooling, read grammar books so he could write vituperative abolitionist letters to the local newspaper, and lived under my mother's ever-disapproving visage. But the greatest source of friction between our two families was that Judge Mayor Grant *had* money, and my father was *intent on having* money. Judge Mayor Grant's was an "old family," people said.

"What does it mean, to be an 'old family'?" I asked my father.

"It means you're lucky your father was born before you were," my father said, snarling at the memory of his own father all the while.

My father envied Judge Mayor Grant as fervently as Judge Mayor Grant looked down upon my father. My family, as I have noted, was far from poor. My father was one of the few people in Georgetown who was not in debt to Judge Mayor Grant and his bank. He saved to build his home and develop his business and extended his own credit to the many customers who bought his hides. And he was a devout practitioner of Yankee ingenuity, which meant he saw finance, as practiced by Judge Mayor Grant, as a diversion from the august process of creating the wealth he revered. He had everything, it seemed, except the respect that came with Judge Mayor Grant's social station.

The friction between them—Judge Mayor Grant's disdain and my father's envy—was endless. The two of them argued at every available opportunity at the saloon in the local hotel, the Georgetown Inn, where the town's gentlemen would gather to see if "the Judge" and "Jesse" were going at it that evening. Amid the prosperity of the time, they frequently debated such topics as President Jackson's banking policies, tariffs, navigation improvements, or other commercial matters. Slavery was a frequent topic as well. Judge Mayor Grant was attracted to the grand style of Southern plantation life and had no quarrel with the enslavement of the Negro. My father, once Orvil Brown's boarder, opposed it strenuously, although even as ardent an abolitionist as he felt that if slavery *had* to exist, it was reasonable that it was the Negro whom it had been visited upon.

Judge Mayor Grant and his wife had but one son, born only weeks after I. His name was Ulysses S. Grant: I suspect Judge Mayor Grant picked the name to antagonize my father. The curiosity of Ulysses S. Grant and Hiram Ulysses Grant in the same town amused the people of Georgetown, particularly given the contrast between us, which became more pronounced as we grew. Ulysses Grant was articulate, while I was reticent; neat and well tailored, while I slouched and shuffled; facile and outgoing, while I was distant and withdrawn; studious, while I applied myself to school to unexceptional effect (it was only after I was repeatedly told a noun was the name of a thing that I came to believe it); and was focused and outgoing, while I was hesitant and unsure of myself in the face of my father's lofty standards and my mother's divine absolutes.

Given the similarities in our names, ages, and even appearances (we resembled each other to the point that I would often encounter someone hailing me at a distance, only to have them draw closer and say with disappointment, "Oh, Hiram, it's you"), and the differences in our natures, Ulysses and I went through our childhoods as would two horses tethered to the millpole at my father's tannery—tied to each other, but constantly going in opposite directions. Armed with his father's stature and resources and possessed of an inherited ease and command (as well as an inherited disdain for me), Ulysses Grant was at the center of Georgetown's circle of young people. The fact that my father was, by the standards of that time and place, a well-off businessman only seemed to make Ulysses' attitude toward me harsher and less forgiving. My father commiserated with me about it once and told me something I regarded as important.

"Some people are like that, son," he said, sharing the secret knowledge only a father possesses. "They know how to shake hands or cast a knowing look and by so doing achieve great wealth." My father shook his head bitterly. "They look down at an honest man like me not just because I smell like the vats, but because I had to work to obtain what came to them without effort."

As I sat in the tiny parlor of our house—it was a simple two-story brick affair with an interior kitchen my father had added only a few years before to celebrate his success—I found it easy to equate Judge Mayor Grant's easy accumulation of wealth with Ulysses Grant's effortless domination of me and the world around him. My father was right. There were some people who got what they wanted through some mysterious, subtle power, an ability to coax the world into doing their will, while the rest of us smelled of fish oil and worked hard. No matter what we gained or earned or won, it would never be enough to cross the unseen line between us and the other Grants. And, perhaps perceiving my father's unspoken feelings, I found in Ulysses Grant's effortless mastery and resourcefulness a mocking reflection of my own ineptitude.

But if I suffered by comparison in the world of men, I found great consolation, starting at an early age, in the world of horses. A story I was told had me, at the age of two, toddling between the hooves of one of my father's horses, unaware that I was inviting a kicking into the next world. A passerby saw me playing this way and bolted up the two stone steps to our front door, shouting for my mother. She calmly thanked him for his concern. "Horses seem to understand the boy," she explained, and withdrew inside the house.

My mother felt my fate was in God's hands, which must have been large to hold all the things she consigned to them. But she was right. Horses understood me, and I them. Before I could read and write, I rode with only a bridle and set of reins. I was able to do tricks, standing on a horse's back as it cantered through town or racing a horse through narrow trails in the wilderness.

And each moment spent on a horse was a moment not spent in my father's tannery, which was as near to purgatory as I could imagine. Dead animals would be carted to us, breaking wind through their seized, stiff haunches. We first stripped them of their skins, then soaked their fresh hides in lime to loosen the hair and any scraps of flesh still adhering to them. The soaked skins were then laid out and the hair and flesh scraped, a repugnant task. Thus cleaned, the hides were bathed in acid, soaked in a solution of oak bark, and left to sit in vats of fish oil until they were supple enough to be rubbed and softened by hand. There was no escaping all these rude emanations—regrettably, even our house was usually downwind of them.

Is it any wonder, then, that Judge Mayor Grant and his son thought of us as stench-ridden rabble, no matter how successful? Or, for that matter, that from an early age I hoped not to be a tanner? By the time I was ten, I had my own livery business of sorts, carting people around southern Ohio and breaking rebellious horses that vexed local farmers. This left me with a pocketful of coins, enough to hire some other local youth to work in the vile tannery while allowing me to take a team of horses somewhere else instead.

When I was eight years old I coveted a colt belonging to a local farmer named Ralston. I appealed to my father to buy it—when I wasn't using it for my livery, we could hitch it to the millpole. My father was won over by this utilitarian appeal. "Hiram," he said thoughtfully, "it is time to teach you how to be a merchant." I nodded, uninterested in being a merchant, but eager to get on with buying the horse. "What do you think this colt is worth?" he asked.

I quickly did some calculations. "I reckon as much as twenty-five dollars."

"Very good." He smiled, taking off his pinched wire-rimmed glasses and rubbing the harsh red spots they left on either side of his pointy nose. "Go to Ralston and offer him twenty dollars for the colt. If he does not accept, offer him twenty-two dollars and fifty cents. If he persists, offer him twenty-five, but not a penny more, and if he does not accept the twenty-five dollars, then thank him and take your leave. Do you understand?"

I nodded eagerly, delighted to have a strategy. In no time at all I rode to the farmer's house, where I said to him: "Papa says I may offer you twenty dollars for the colt, but if you don't take that, I am to offer twenty-two and a half, and if you won't take that, offer twenty-five."

Well, you do not have to be Commodore Vanderbilt to figure out the final price. When I returned home, I told the story to my father, who promptly whipped me with a switch.

But the story of my transaction shot through town like a winter wind, and my father arrived at the Georgetown Inn that evening to find Ralston telling it to the other village gentlemen, egged on by a jeering Judge Mayor Grant. My father smiled gamely, shrugging his shoulders and saying it was a child's doing, but there was no stopping Judge Mayor Grant.

"A child's doing is right, Jesse," he roared. "And a useless child, at that! You should call him Hiram *Useless* Grant!"

And in the resulting explosion of laughter, it was born. I was referred to as *Useless* Grant from that day until I left Georgetown. Seizing upon the hilarity, the other gentlemen suggested Ulysses Grant be called *Useful* in contrast, and so it was done. We became *Useless* and *Useful*, so much so that my own father would ask me what *Useful* did in school that day, or whether I thought *Useful* would win the races at the Methodist picnic, in each instance oblivious to my implied *Useless*-ness.

And that is how I grew up, as *Useless* Grant.

As I said, Useful Grant was the sun of Georgetown's youthful social orbit, and I was a distant star. Judge Mayor Grant would hold the church youth day at his home, or a maypole party, and as often as not my invitation would somehow not find its way. My father would quietly seethe, and I resigned myself to the obvious: Useful was destined to be a judge mayor himself one day, while I was doomed to be a tanner.

I was sixteen the Christmas of 1838, and it was my last year at the local school. I came home one cold afternoon, the sun low in the winter sky, to see what odious work my father had planned for me, but, to my surprise, there was something else awaiting me—a note from Useful, properly addressed to Master Hiram U. Grant, asking me to attend a Christmas sleigh ride that very evening at his father's house!

Could I have been wrong about the fellow? Probably not, I supposed, but I was overjoyed at long last to be included. I put on the clothes I wore when I could not escape being dragged to church, trying futilely to shake the fish-oil smell out of my coat before I donned it, and headed for Useful's home after supper.

What a home it was! Set upon a fine blanket of newly fallen snow, it looked like a castle. It had a portico with majestic pillars, a parlor as large as most of our first story, and a colossal center hall as well. I entered to find Judge Mayor Grant and his wife smiling at me condescendingly as I gaped at the magnificence of their appointments—paintings, statuary, a library, all of it unique in Georgetown. A portrait of Judge Mayor Grant looked down from atop a large stone fireplace with a roaring Yule log. The town's young people were gathered in the hall, and once a few stragglers arrived we were led out to the largest sleigh I had ever seen, hitched to a team of strong horses that I regarded with envy.

"Magnificent animals, aren't they?" I heard somebody say, and turned to see Useful admiring them, as was I.

"Why, yes. Yes, they are," I said.

"Well, you're the horseman. We're all waiting for you to hitch them up and take us away," Useful said with a smile, patting me on the shoulder to direct me to my task.

I hesitated a moment and then smiled broadly at the realization. My new friend Useful was going to let me manage the team! I climbed onto the driver's bench and turned to see the other boys and girls scampering gaily onto the sleigh—there must have been twenty of them, all dressed smartly and filled with excitement—and I cracked the whip, starting us out.

It was a chilly night, but it was brilliantly clear, and a bright moon shone overhead. I led the team into the snowy woods as Useful narrated. "My father owns these woods," he said. "We imagine a town here and are putting aside capital for its development." I trained my eyes on the path and guided the team silently through the trees. "Perhaps we can even find a new location for Useless's tannery"—Useful laughed—"so its smell needn't offend us any longer." I turned again and saw Useful and his circle all asmile, sharing this humor at my expense. When their mirth subsided, Useful was reminded of his destination and sat up. "Say there, Useless," he cried, pointing off into the woods. "Take this trail off to the right and over this hill. There's a good spot there for finding a Christmas tree!" He smiled broadly at the admiring boys and girls surrounding him. "The Judge Mayor says we can get one as tall as our center hall—fifteen feet high!"

There were gasps of appreciation for the dimensions of this architectural marvel as I led the team onto a narrow trail among the pines and firs, enjoying the chance to run them through the drifts and ignoring the scorn of Useful's barbs. I headed in the intended direction for about a quarter mile when Useful excitedly directed me to stop, a conifer quarry in his sights. The team pulled back and snorted in the dark, brisk cold, their moonlit breath a stream of starry smoke. I hopped down from the driver's seat and shook the snow from a sturdy bough on which to tie the reins when I felt the pat of Useful's hand once again.

"The driver ought to stay with the team, don't you think? I'm sure my father will pay you adequately," he said with hale good nature, and turned away from me to lead his retinue into the piney dark.

The realization stunned me. I had not been invited—I had been hired! I looked down sadly and was listening as Useful's party retreated into the woods when I was startled by a voice coming from alongside me.

"Would you like some company?" the voice said, and I turned to see a girl standing there, a worn shawl over her chilled, rounded shoulders. I recognized her—she was a short, plump, but pleasant girl who was given to sitting quietly in the back of both our school and church, a habit that mirrored my own. She smiled at me and I recalled her name.

"Well, yes, Julia, I guess so," I said with a shrug. She came over and stood next to me.

"It's a nice night," she said, surveying the heavens to confirm her judgment.

"I guess so." I shrugged again and nodded dumbly.

She huddled a bit against the chill and looked off in the direction of the sounds of sawing in the woods. "Useful certainly is full of himself, isn't he?" she said disdainfully.

"I guess so," I said a third time, wishing my limited imagination could offer up something else.

Julia smiled and looked down until both of our attentions were summoned by the sound of a tree trunk shearing as it fell. There was the sound of cheering.

I found myself wishing they all would stay away and turned to my companion, still unsure of what to say, when she spoke up. "He ought to be nicer to you," she declared, then added, "I think you're nice, Useless." I was about to say, *I guess so,* yet again, when what I really wanted to say suddenly occurred to me.

"My name is Hiram."

She put a round little hand to her lips and might have blushed had not the frost already put a rose in her cheeks. "Of course it is," she said. "Won't you forgive me?"

I smiled for the first time and shrugged, this time more good-naturedly. "I guess so," I said, and we shared a laugh around my awkwardness.

Julia sat next to me on the driver's bench of the wagon as we headed back to Useful's house, dragging the felled tree behind the sleigh. Useful narrated all the way home—about the perfect tree he cut, his father, his home, and the like. Julia and I smiled quietly at Useful's self-absorbed prattling as we glided across the snow, when his soliloquy was suddenly interrupted by a thudding noise that forced a "*Hmmph!*" out of him in the back of the wagon, as if he had fallen. We turned just in time to see a second snowball hit him on the top of the head, a few inches above where a first had left a frosty imprint.

One of the girls in the wagon shrieked as a barrage of snowballs suddenly came flying toward the wagon. I turned and there were five or six boys stepping out from behind a nearby ridge on the far side of a frozen creek, their outlines crisp against the snow. They must have seen us head off into the woods and waited in ambush for our return.

"It's those boys from Kentucky!" one of the girls in the wagon shouted.

"Go away, you ruffians!" another shouted.

"Like hell we will!" one of the offending boys shouted in return, his voice heavy with scorn. "We're going to help ourselves"—*t' hep ow-selves,* was how he said it—"to a piece of young Ulysses!" he said.

"Yeah!" shouted a second. "His daddy took our Pa's farm! But you ain't so tough, is you, Ulysses?"

"Go back to Kentucky, you common trash!" Useful shouted at them hatefully, kneeling on the floor of the sleigh. "You're too poor to own a slave and too stupid to farm without one!"

"Oh yeah?" I heard them shout. "We'll see who's stupid, you little sissy!" I watched from the driver's bench as the boys let fly at Useful and his entourage. They must have taken me for a hired hand, just as Useful did, for they spared me. They drew closer as their taunts grew in strength, laying siege to us as smartly as I would Vicksburg years later, bombarding us as mercilessly as Winfield Scott one day would Veracruz.

"This one's for your daddy, the judge!" one of them shouted. "Puttin' men in jail for no more'n bein' poor!"

"An' this one's for your daddy, the mayor!" a second said as he let fly. "Makin' laws that help his own bank!" There was laughter in their ranks as his missile struck Useful's head. Useful glared back at them but then lost both his composure and balance in the face of another barrage.

"Somebody help me!" he whispered tearfully as he lay on the floor of the sleigh, dabbing at a show of blood on his scalp.

I looked at him and felt some unexpected surge of pity. I rose and shouted from the driver's bench, "That's enough!"

"What're you, boy," one of them asked, "some kind of white, up-North nigger? Why don't you just do the drivin' like he pays you and keep your head down!"

He had a point. But that did not give them the license they took for themselves. "You could bury him in snow and be no better for it when you were done!" I shouted back. "If his father's robbed your fathers of their dignity, why let him rob you of yours?"

"Oh, stuff it!" one of them replied. And with that a new barrage of snowballs flew, leaving Useful huddled on the floor of the wagon and his guests cowering as if they were the new recruits who faced their first bullets at Shiloh.

"Get down, Hiram," Julia urged from the bench next to me, but I would not. I looked down at Useful, who now lay curled on the floor of the sleigh behind me.

"Help me!" he cried through fearful tears. "Help me, Useless!"

I ducked a missile that now came my way and resolved to act. I grabbed the reins, the missiles flying around me, and sparked the team's rumps with my whip. The team strained forward against the inert weight of the sled as I prodded them, the runners ground against the snow for an instant, and then we were off. There was some cheering mixed with tongue-clucking in the sleigh as the marauders watched us pull away. I kept my head low and my whip to the lead's rump until we were some ways ahead, then reined them back to a trot.

Useful lay in the center of the sleigh, cradled all around by the other boys and girls like an infant Jesus in the manger. He hazarded raising himself to one elbow and peered over his shoulder to see if the danger was truly passed. Once satisfied, he rose slowly and made his way to the front of the sleigh.

"Thank you, Hiram," he said quietly, the look of fear only beginning to leave him.

"You're welcome," I said, barely above a whisper, and I looked back, expecting to see his hand extended toward me.

But there was none. Instead, he had already turned to the knot of now-hushed merrymakers in the sleigh. "Well, no one but the best driver for us!" he crowed, whereupon a boy in the back started into "God Rest Ye Merry Gentlemen" and the silent night around us suddenly rang with song.

I felt Julia's hand on my arm as I gave the whip a brief snap. The lights of Judge Mayor Grant's house glimmered up ahead.

Useful seemed to tolerate me a bit after that. And in the months that followed, I developed for this girl the feeling that passes for affection in a boy of such an age. She was fleshy like a ripe summer fruit, and her features plain, but she was attentive and soft-spoken, and expected only my own quiet attentiveness in return. We had done no more than some parlor hand-holding, of course, but my ardor for her burned steadily and I began to contemplate marriage so as to consummate our devotion.

Her father objected. He was a farmer, and not too prosperous, and I thought my father's growing affluence would win him over. But he considered my father argumentative and mean-spirited—not without reason, of course—and my own reputation as a lad destined to accomplish little probably led him to think me an unsuitable suitor for his daughter.

The end of our formal schooling came in the spring of 1839. I had just turned seventeen. My father expected me to enter his tannery business, but my desire to do so was even less than my likely aptitude for it. Meanwhile, Useful began his search for an appropriately prestigious college and settled on the United States Military Academy at West Point. Apparently Judge Mayor Grant had gone to some lengths to secure an appointment from our local congressman, a fellow my father had long ago alienated in one of his arguments over President Jackson's banking policies, which favored the common man over the merchant in a way that struck my merchant father as undemocratic.

If there was a moment when I had real feelings of jealousy for Useful's life of privilege, it was when I heard of his admission to West Point. I was never considered for West Point or a career in the military—no one took me for clever enough for any place other than the tannery. But I was envious of the exciting life it offered, and the chance to travel and see the world. If Useful was to go to West Point while I went to work, it was yet another confirmation of my father's views about the world, with its broad division into those who smelled and those who inherited. I began instead to contemplate a business as a livery driver—at least that way I could be near horses and satisfy Julia's father's doubts about me. Anything but a tanner!

Judge Mayor Grant gave a party for Useful the night before he was due to go east. Every young person in the town—all of them, like me, about to enter adulthood as a farmer, tradesman, merchant, or bride to the same—was summoned to see Useful off.

My father allowed me to use our best horse and cart so I could escort Julia in fine array: He would go into town later for an evening of "socializing," meaning arguing and drinking at the Georgetown Inn. I nervously groomed myself and even allowed myself a brief strut before the only mirror my mother would allow in our home. At the appointed hour, I rode out to fetch Julia for the grand event.

She looked wonderful that night bedecked in her finery, and we rode together in happy silence to Judge Mayor Grant's home. We arrived and entered the great hall, where we paid our respects to Judge Mayor Grant's wife. Judge Mayor Grant himself was at the hotel in town, no doubt making sure everyone knew of his son's departure the next morning.

It was a magnificent spring night, and the center hall of the house was crowded with tables, all of them burdened with game and fowl, fruits, nuts, and cakes. Bowls of punch and teas, chilled in the ice house, were laid out before us. A fiddler's band played on the great lawn behind the house, with torches dotting the perimeter. Julia and I sampled the treats and said some quiet hellos to the other young people there, then headed out back to congratulate the object of the celebration.

We walked out to the lawn, and there was Useful, in rare form. He wore a waistcoat and a look of condescension. If he had ever failed to give his feelings of superiority full flight, he would make up for it that night.

"Thank you for inviting us," Julia said to him as we approached.

"Think nothing of it," he answered haughtily. "I want to wish a fond farewell to all of my very good friends," he said, taking Julia's hand in his and pressing it in an unduly familiar way.

"We are pleased for your success," she said politely.

"I'll be starting a whole new life," he responded, engrossed in his own story. "I'm going to be first in my class at West Point and then take a commission among the engineers, which is the army's elite unit, you know. I suspect it won't be long before I end up a general." He turned toward me disdainfully. "Fancy that, Useless, my being a general," he said. "General Grant!"

The paradox of his pronouncement is apparent today, but then I regarded him silently, lest my unmannerliness disturb Julia. Useful scanned me for a reaction and, seeing none, turned his attention to her once again to see if he could raise one.

"There is an excellent life to be lived in the military. You serve the nation, as was done in the conquests of the Black Hawks and Seminoles, and the fellows around you are of a high quality. I have been called to be among the nation's best," he continued, "and it will be a good life for a wife as well, one day."

Now, what the devil did that mean? I wondered, as Julia responded. "We wish you all the best, don't we, Hiram?" she said, prodding me into agreement. "Why, Hiram, perhaps a military life is in order for you! It would please Father to no end!"

"For Useless?" Useful laughed out loud. "I should hope not! Come now, Useless, do you really imagine yourself such a man?"

My temperament was a quiet one, but Useful was pushing me to the limits of my endurance. I was about to respond when we were all suddenly distracted by a lad who ran quite agitatedly toward us across the lawn, shouting over the strains of the band.

"Useless! Useless!" he cried. "Useless, you must come quickly! It's your father!" The boy ran up to us and stopped, gasping for breath. "Hello, Useful," he said politely to Useful between pants, and turned back to me. "He's passed out drunk in the lobby of the Georgetown Inn, Useless! You've got to do something!"

Useful wrinkled his nose and arched his eyebrows in a studied look of revulsion as Julia turned toward me with caring and concern.

"You must go, Hiram," she said earnestly.

"But what about you?" I asked. "How will you manage getting home?"

"Please, Useless," Useful chimed in. "I'll take care of Julia myself. A military man must be the proper gent, you know."

His ceaseless tweaking was irrelevant—I had to go. I excused myself and rode to the hotel, where I found my father collapsed in a chair in the lobby. Just as I later proved to be, he was not a regular drinker, but was ardent when he did, and on this occasion he had carried the torch of abolition so strenuously his thirst overcame him. His eyes were glazed and open and his lips slightly apart—had I run into such a body at Donelson or the Wilderness, I would have buried it before it began to stink.

"Father, it's me, Hiram," I said. He grunted without moving his eyes. "It's me, Hiram," I repeated, and did a bit of what must have seemed like adagio dancing with him as I helped him to his feet and out the front door. I dumped him in the back of my cart and set off for home.

My next concern was that our arrival would awake my mother, who would seize upon my father's regrettable condition to give us another of her never-ending series of sermons about everything under the sun being God's will, except for those things of which she disapproved, such as drinking, which were to be corrected so God's will could once again be revealed as she imagined it. So when we arrived home, I drew a pail of water and flung it over my father as he lay in the back of the cart, to wash him off and revive him and get him quietly into the house.

He propped himself up on his elbows to determine the source of the deluge. He looked down at himself and cognition struggled to emerge from within him, whereupon he beckoned me closer and whispered to me his secret. "I'm drunk, boy," he said, and fell backward with a thud.

"Let's get you inside," I said. I extended my arm under his back and helped him out of the cart and to his feet. "You can lie down in the parlor and you won't have to see Mother until the morning. With some luck, she'll leave for church before you're up."

He nodded in agreement. "That's a good plan, Hiram," he said, and stumbled forward clumsily. "How was Useful's party?" he then asked.

His question lightened the moment. "Useful explained how he would soon be a general."

"Useful!" my father spat. "He wants to be a general, does he? If it was you going to West Point, Hiram, you'd be a general one day, not that little twit."

My father's sanguine if inebriated assessment of my prospects confused me. Did his endless impatience with my commercial ineptitude hide a loving father underneath? Or was this besotted self-pity expressing itself momentarily as affection? I didn't know what to think, but in my confusion I let my guard down and said softly, "I would have liked that," as I maneuvered him through our front door and positioned him on a sofa. "It would be better than being a tanner."

He belched a cloud of evil gas. "Well, Hiram," he said, "that's all I have to offer you."

He spoke the truth. I lay him on a sofa, and a life of acid vats, offal shreds, and fish oil came running up to greet my senses. Was I doomed to be a tanner, as much as I hated it? And if I was, was I doomed to be like my father as well? I sat there forlornly and wondered what the answers were. But when I tried to hear the answers in my own mind, all I could hear was my father's cacophonous snore. So I turned down the lamp, got back in the cart, and started back to Useful's party.

I was riding silently over the back roads and fields to Judge Mayor Grant's home when my horse stopped to relieve itself near an old barn standing in the meadow behind the Grant estate. I looked about at the night sky as the horse released a stream in the darkness. There was only the dimmest crescent of moon, and on this account I noticed a faint light from within the barn.

I thought someone must have left a lantern in the barn, a waste of fuel and a risk of fire. So I snapped the reins and led the horse toward the barn. When we stopped, I could discern voices coming from within and wondered who would be visiting that place at that hour. The horse and I both cocked an ear to listen and were drawn by a familiar quality.

I was listening to Julia.

As I stepped down from the cart, I began to make out pieces of the conversation. Julia was saying something about the propriety of being there when I was shocked to hear the voice that responded.

"But don't you see, Julia?" Useful said. "Useless has run home to tend to his drunken father. And just as I will be a prominent citizen as is my father, so Useless shall be like his father—drunken, temperamental, and abusive—for there is an architecture within us that drives us toward our fate."

My heart pumped with the expectation Julia would champion me.

"His name is Hiram, Ulysses," she corrected. "And he has been kind and devoted to me." It was a defense of sorts, but she had neither accepted nor rejected the argument.

"But isn't it true your father won't consent to your marriage? Don't you see what he's trying to tell you? He's telling you Useless is destined to be the same flimflammer his father is!"

A flimflammer! My father was a conniver, to be sure—he was a concocter, a contriver, a conniver, a bombast, a four-flushing trader in humbug—but he was no flimflammer, or so I then thought. I had a mind to intercede on the old man's behalf when I again heard Julia speak up. "His name is *Hiram*, Ulysses," she corrected once again. "He is not *Useless*. Perhaps he is simple in some eyes, but he has been sweet to me, and I offer him so little, stout and plain as I am."

I might have preferred stronger tones of outrage, but it was a good start. I inched toward an opening in the barn's north wall and saw them sitting together on a bale of hay. The lantern at their feet cast the flickering shadows of bridles and bits against the rough-hewn walls. "You have everything to offer, Julia," Useful responded. "The inner beauty of a woman that can only be the product of a radiant soul that glows with all the colors of the heavens." He shifted closer to her as she, like me, tried to make out what it was he had just said. "Julia, Hiram—if that is what you wish to call him—can offer you nothing. But I can offer you a life of comfort. In four years, I will have my military commission and will soon be a general. You will have servants and the amenities of a good life, just as my mother did when she married my father."

She pulled back, aghast and confused. "Ulysses, what are you saying?"

"I'm saying you must listen to my entreaty and reward me with your affection."

She was as shocked as I was. "Ulysses, I am plain and far from rich. Any girl in this town would be yours. What is it you want?"

Useful suddenly sprang from his seat and knelt before the stunned object of my affection and, apparently, his. "You can give me yourself, Julia. I am leaving tomorrow, leaving as the bell tolls after church, off to serve God and country. Perhaps I shall never return. Perhaps I will be off to fight the Seminoles or the Black Hawks," he said, referring once again to the unopposed extermination of those two peoples, "or be shipped out to fight the pirates in Tripoli." Of course, I didn't know then that he was in no greater danger at West Point than what results from failing to learn the trigonometric tables.

"U-Ulysses!" Julia stammered. "Are you asking for my hand?"

"I am asking for more than your hand," Useful replied with great intensity, and sprang up to embrace her, planting kisses on her face and running his hands over her more intently than a phrenologist explores a skull. I might have interrupted, but I was aghast and appalled, as well as envious that Useful would risk the flames of eternal hell (with which my mother regularly seared my own baser inclinations) for worldly satisfactions. I stood there, immobilized, as Julia fought back, pushing her hands and elbows against his chest and drawing up her knees to stop him. "Ulysses! Please, don't!" she implored.

But there was no holding him back. He wedged a knee in between her legs, his free hand searching and rearranging. "Julia, my sweet, you must now be mine!" he announced.

"But Ulysses, we are not yet wed! I have not responded to your proposal, if that is what it is," she said as she attempted to fend him off. But Useful would have none of it. He reached under the waist of her dress and was drawing down her undergarments, trying to stay atop her as she rolled from side to side. I watched, held in place by both my shock and fascinated curiosity as to what would happen next.

"Julia, I am a gentleman and a military man," Useful pressed on. "My word is my sacred badge of honor. If I vow you shall be mine, it is a hallowed bond between both of us and our Lord!"

I was impressed the Lord was as much a party to Useful's seduction as He was to my mother's dictates. The Lord certainly got around. Julia, meanwhile, was less interested in the Lord than in propping herself up and gaining some leverage, but Useful was overpowering. "Please, Ulysses!" she begged him. "You must give me time!"

"There is no time!" he exclaimed. "We must consummate our love before I go off, perhaps to die."

I steeled myself to burst upon the scene and defend Julia's honor against this affront when Useful suddenly slowed his assault and stared deeply into the girl's eyes, and Julia looked back at him as if transfixed, halting her protestations. I stopped myself and gaped. Lying upon her, he looked down and said, "And now, you shall be mine. Give me your gift," he coaxed.

"Oh, Ulysses," she said, starting to sob, "I am so confused."

"There is no confusion, my dove." And with that, Julia laid back in an attitude of apparent consent. Her eyes suddenly opened wider than I imagined they could. She had surrendered! Was she as pliant to Useful's wishes as everybody else? I watched, stunned, as Useful's motions became more aggressive and lurching—he would receive no points for art—whereupon he twitched spasmodically and made a gurgling sound, then came to a stop, all in little more than thirty seconds at best. Julia squirmed a bit underneath him and cocked her head to regard him. "Is it over?" she asked.

Useful rolled off her and shook his head as if to clear it. A moment passed before he spoke. "Yes, it's over," he smirked, his tone suddenly transformed. He sat up as he fastened himself, never looking down.

"Won't you lie here with me?" she asked.

"I think not," Useful snapped back. "I must be off to my party."

"But Ulysses," she entreated, "I wish to hear more words of love."

He burst out laughing. "Words of love? How about this—you're a plain, stout bag, good for poking and little more. *Is it over?*" he imitated, and laughed again.

Julia started to cry despairingly as she realized how she had been victimized. "How could you!" she exclaimed between deep, heaving sobs. "I shall tell!"

"Oh, shall you?" Useful shot back. "Who will you tell? Useless? Or your daddy? And what shall you tell them? That you snuck off to the barn and I had you without a fight? That you lay down for me like a wanton little harlot? I knew you'd be an easy mark. Do tell them, so we all may have a good laugh. Perhaps they would like to go in front of the Judge Mayor and charge me with defaming your character."

Julia rolled over and began to wail fitfully as I hid against the outside of the barn, anger welling within me. Useful had done this to victimize not only Julia, but me. I suddenly understood he measured himself against me as much as I measured myself against him.

My first inclination was to kill him and flee. There were some implements in the barn that would do the job nicely, a pitchfork among them, although drowning him in a vat of tannic acid—no, fish oil!—

might be better yet. But I then thought my mother would never be able to rest in heaven (where I assumed she was otherwise headed) were her son to take a human life. Of course, I have since taken hundreds of thousands of lives in the most methodical slaughter the world has ever seen. But that was war, which is different, I have been assured.

I then considered consoling Julia once Useful left the barn, which he seemed intent on doing as quickly as possible. But to do so would be to show her I had seen all, which might cause her even greater shame than her actual despoiling. Moreover, she had, once you reviewed it, decided to lie down with Useful after what seemed like only the briefest of arguments.

There was a third option—to go back to the party and make believe I had seen nothing. But doing so would have broken my heart. So that left only one thing to do—go back home, angry and confused, which is what I did.

My mother had already left for church when I woke the next morning. My father was sitting at the pine-planked table in our kitchen, drinking coffee and not looking half as dead as he had only hours before. I felt a pressing need to unburden myself and told him the whole story. He pursed his lips with a look of sober assessment until my tale was told.

"What should I have done?" I asked.

He shrugged his shoulders. "You should have killed the little villain," he offered.

"Maybe," I agreed. "But I couldn't bring myself to."

He nodded. "Son, if you think you love this girl, you must assume this experience will make her wiser. Besides, if it were to happen again, you could kill the next fellow with a clearer conscience. The question is, what do you feel?"

I shrugged. "I don't know."

"Well then, let's go over to her father's farm, like we were apologizing for leaving her there. You can look her straight in the eye and decide."

This seemed like extraordinarily good advice, and we got into the cart and headed north on the main road. We rode for a while without speaking when I saw a carriage heading south toward us. As it drew closer, I could see it held Judge Mayor Grant, his wife, and Useful.

I pointed them out to my father. He told me to be still, which seemed like good advice once again. We slowed down as they neared, in part to greet each other and in part because the road was carved out of a ledge along a rocky hillside so narrow only one team could readily pass. Our carts drifted toward each other until our teams were nose to nose.

"Hello, Judge Mayor," my father said. "Where are you heading this morning?"

Judge Mayor Grant cleared his throat. "We discussed that last night, Jesse, although you might not recall," he answered disapprovingly. "We have come from church, where we were pleased to see Mrs. Grant," he added pointedly, "and we are heading to Cincinnati, where Ulysses will catch a steamboat for Harrisburg and proceed by rail to Philadelphia, New York, and then West Point."

"That's quite an itinerary," my father said, nodding politely to Useful. "I hope your journey will be pleasant."

"We appreciate your wishes, Jesse," Judge Mayor Grant said, his manners failing to conceal his disdain. He tried to get his team to move ahead, but my father seemed unwilling to let him by.

"And we hear you had quite a party last night, Judge Mayor," my father continued. "Tell me, Ulysses, did you have a good time?"

Useful looked up, surprised to be asked. "Why, yes, Mr. Grant, and now I'm looking forward to being off."

"Did you find time to see Julia home, Ulysses? Hiram tells me you promised to do so."

Useful squirmed uncomfortably. "She saw herself home, sir," he replied.

"You sent her walking home?" my father said with a feigned, puzzled tone. "I thought a military man was a better gent than that."

"See here, Jesse," Judge Mayor Grant interrupted sternly. "No need to harass the boy."

"Harass him?" my father said, looking at Useful all the while. "Did I say anything amiss?"

Useful began to sense something *was* terribly amiss. "Let's go, Father," he insisted.

"Stay, Ulysses," my father quickly interceded, "if only for a moment, so we can hear about the life of a military man. I hear the cadets may be fighting the Seminoles or Black Hawks soon, Judge."

Judge Mayor Grant turned to Useful with a frown. "Have you been bragging, son? There's no room for that at West Point." I subsequently learned otherwise.

"Or perhaps the pirates of Tripoli," my father said, and a fearful look of discovery came over Useful. He had been found out, although he obviously could not figure out how. He turned deep red and reached for the whip in Judge Mayor Grant's hand.

"Let's go, Father, right now!" he shouted, grabbing the whip from Judge Mayor Grant's grasp.

"See here now, Ulysses," Judge Mayor Grant blustered. "What's going on?"

"Ulysses, behave yourself," his mother admonished.

"Yes, Ulysses, why in such a rush to go?" my father said, but now Useful was all but fighting his father for the whip. There was a terrible commotion that upset our horse, which was stung by the flailing lash as Judge Mayor Grant and Useful struggled for it. A wooden chest with Useful's belongings rattled in the back of the carriage as they fought, and the cart shifted until its wheels suddenly slipped over the edge of the ridge, rocking all three passengers. They let out a shout that unnerved our horse further and the animal reared in the air, frightening Judge Mayor Grant's team, which began to buck as well. Useful finally wrested the whip from his father and cracked it savagely across his team. His mother shrieked as she reached up to grab her bonnet. They all lurched backward and their carriage's axle teetered precariously over the edge of the road.

"Stop that, Ulysses!" Judge Mayor Grant cried, but Useful lashed furiously in his efforts to depart the scene, and he soon did, but not as he intended: His team panicked and stumbled over the edge of the road, spilling the carriage down the rocky hillside to the sound of screams from all three.

The cart smashed into the steep hillside in explosive caroms and bounces, sending billows of dust and rock into the air. The three Grants stayed inside for a roll or two but were soon thrown away from the wreck. Even before they came to rest, we started scampering down the gravelly slope after them. The carriage shattered at the bottom; the horses' harnesses snapped and the team bolted across the field at the bottom of the ridge and were gone.

"They're over there," I said to my father, pointing to Judge Mayor

Grant and his wife. We hastened to their sides. I've seen bodies stacked from Shiloh to Spotsylvania, but this was a mess. Judge Mayor Grant's cheek was to the ground. He was bleeding profusely from where his nose, mouth, and right eye had been. His wife's head was thrown back at a grotesque angle; my father reached down and closed her eyes with his fingertips. We stood over them, the dust rising slowly into the pale sky. My father and I looked at each other and the same thought came to us—where was Useful?—when we heard a voice from behind us.

"Where am I?" the voice said, and we turned to find him slowly rising to his feet and rubbing his head, which was streaming with blood.

"Useful!" I called to him.

"What's useful?" he asked, looking with shocked detachment at his bloody fingertips. "Who are you? What am I doing here?"

My father cocked his head and put a hand on my arm to stop me from replying. Useful then saw his parents and recoiled in horror. "My God! Who are these people?" he gasped. "They're dead!"

"Don't you know who they are?" my father challenged.

"No, and I'm scared!" Useful said, wrapping his arms around himself. "Please don't hurt me!"

"Hurt you? Oh, a fine story that is," my father spat, and turned to me, hitching his thumb. "This scoundrel is worrying about *our* hurting *him.*"

"No! No! I swear!" Useful protested. "I don't know what you're talking about!" And then I realized what my father already had—Useful had lost his memory. He had not the slightest hint how any of us came to be there.

"You swine!" my father raged. "You assaulted these poor people, tried to rob them!" Useful waved his hands as if to fend off the words. "Don't deny it! We saw the whole thing!"

"I'm not a thief!" Useful cried with a tone of genuine astonishment.

"We saw you!" my father repeated. "You wanted that chest!" Useful turned and saw his trunk, still locked, on the ground—it was making my father's case just by lying there. "And when this poor gentleman and his wife tried to race away, you grabbed the reins and the three of you went over the edge!"

"I did no such thing!" Useful exclaimed.

"Wait!" my father shouted with an affectation of sudden comprehension. "I recognize you! You are the vagabond robber I read about in the notice posted at the general store! 'The Highwayman from Philadelphia!' it said. Didn't you see it, son? McKenna was his name, a little Paddy murderer!"

I looked at Useful and my father and nodded uncertainly, unsure of his intent. "There's a reward for you, and it's going to be mine!" my father said as he started toward Useful.

Memory or no, in only a few seconds Useful realized he was about to be turned in for a reward. He started to back away. "I didn't do anything," he shouted. "I don't remember a thing! I swear!"

"Swear all you like," my father said. "Your words aren't worth dirt. You're a thief and a murderer. You're wanted from here to St. Louis and I'm going to be the one to receive the bounty for bringing you to the gallows!"

"Never!" Useful screamed, and took off across the field as fast as he could. He was a full hundred yards away and still moving rapidly when my father turned to me.

"Quickly," he said. "Help me with the old man." He turned Judge Mayor Grant's body over and reached into his breast pocket. He produced a wallet and some folded papers from the corpse. "Come here, Hiram," he said as he thrust them toward me. "What do these papers say?"

I looked at them quickly. "This introduces Useful to the registrar at West Point. And here's a ticket for the steamboat from Cincinnati to Harrisburg. And a rail ticket for Philadelphia and New York." I looked up and saw the old man at work on Judge Mayor Grant's pockets.

"There's two hundred dollars in bank notes and another fifty in gold coin. Take it," he said, extending a pouch toward me. I froze, horrified at the thought of thievery. "Take it!" he demanded. "Take the damn money and put the papers in your vest. You're the same size as Useful, right?" he asked, turning quickly toward the chest.

"Why, yes, but what are you—"

My father didn't answer. He was already setting Useful's trunk upright. "Help me with this damn thing." He picked up one end as I stood there, frozen. "Come on, Hiram," he commanded. "Pick up the damn chest!"

He spoke quickly as we carried the chest up the hillside. "The old man and his wife are dead, Hiram, and their little peacock will never be seen again. He'll be afraid to talk to another human being for months at least." We slung the chest into our cart and my father took to the lock with an axe. It broke with one blow. A full wardrobe was folded inside, together with some books and more papers.

"Listen to me, Hiram," he said adamantly. "They're expecting a boy named Grant from Georgetown, Ohio, at West Point. A boy your size, your name, a boy just like you."

"Oh, no," I moaned as I realized the full extent of the deception he was proposing. "That's just crazy—"

He would have none of it. "Just say your name is Ulysses S. Grant— you can say the *S* is for *Simpson*, your mother's maiden name. The old Ulysses S. Grant is running through the woods out there. You can be Ulysses S. Grant now. If we go quickly, we can get you to Cincinnati in time for the steamer."

"But we would never get away with it," I pleaded. "It would never work!"

He shut the lid of the chest and quickly positioned himself on the driver's bench of the cart. He backed the rig around and began heading south. "It's going to work, Hiram. I mean, Ulysses. Everything works in life when there's nothing to stop it from working. Nobody's going to know who you are and who you aren't. You've got no head for business; now you'll have the chance to make something of yourself. You'll have money, a wardrobe, papers, and all the other things you'd never get from me." He whipped the horse into a faster pace. "Fate's sent them to you."

"But it's wrong," I pleaded.

"It's not wrong," he spat. "You've been listening to the nonsense your mother gets from church. All that business about God. Don't you think gods make mistakes? People don't deserve everything they get in life. Do you think Judge Mayor Grant deserved everything he had? Or Useful was going to deserve everything he might get?" I shook my head in passive agreement and overwhelmed disbelief.

He gave the reins a snap. "You've been given a chance very few men have, Hi—I mean, *Ulysses*. What would you rather do—work in my tannery? Now you get to pick your destiny. You decide. Whose fate do you want? Yours? Or Useful's?"

I looked ahead as we sped along and, while I might not have said anything aloud, I realized that to pose the question was to answer it. I could change the trajectory of my life—escape the tannery, see the world—just by deciding to. I looked again at my father and at the life he represented, and when my gaze fixed once again on the road before us, I was reborn as Ulysses S. Grant.

CHAPTER II

ARRIVAL AT WEST POINT—MEETING SHERMAN— TALES OF BOBBY LEE—CLASS WITH HALLECK— JACKSON AND McCLELLAN—A LAST JUMP AT GRADUATION

THE LAST THING I remember about life as Hiram Grant—or perhaps the first thing I remember about life as Ulysses Grant—was the sight of my father standing on the dock as the steamboat for which Useful had a ticket left Cincinnati. My father didn't wave.

In retrospect, it is easy to see that the deception my father devised was fraught with risk. But one often heard stories of settlers kicked in the head by a horse or mule and whose personalities were irrevocably altered as a result. Perhaps Useful would prove such a case, I thought. More to the point, the opportunity to see the world, escape the tannery, and have some measure of revenge on Useful, the despoiler of my first love, was too alluring. And so I entered into my father's conspiracy, fully aware of the risk but prepared to take it in exchange for what might lie ahead. The boat took me to Harrisburg and a train that sped along at the then-stupefying rate of eighteen miles an hour, belching a cloud of black smoke over the windows of our carriage or, when the windows were open, us. I coughed and wiped and brushed my way to Philadelphia, then took a train from Philadelphia to New York, and a ferry to West Point. The next day, I was to appear before the registrar and enroll.

I rose early and dragged my inherited trunk to the campus. I was immediately struck by the beauty of the place. West Point is just that— a point jutting into the Hudson, where sailboats dotted the water with silvery white gossamers and steady winds gracefully rustled the sycamores and maples.

The Military Academy itself was well organized in a way that would have pleased my mother's utilitarianism and my father's parsimony. Its square-cut, stuccoed structures gave a feeling of order and solidity. I wandered among them until I came upon the main administrative building. The registrar—a squat fellow with glasses and a stock collar—sat at a table there with a small gaggle of older cadets resting on the steps behind him. A line of boys such as myself—or, perhaps, such as Useful—led up to his table and he regarded each severely when it was that lad's turn to come to the front.

The fellows ahead of me announced themselves. They were from every state of the young nation. The Eastern boys were generally better dressed and of a higher station. The Southerners' education lagged the Northerners', but their military tradition was strong, and while certainly more mannerly, they were also more odd. Last among all were we Westerners, the very few boys from west of the Appalachians. We were dismissed by both the Yankees and the Southerners as coarse, ignorant plowboys, and the fact I was coarse, largely ignorant, and spent my best days behind or atop a horse didn't make the categorization any less unfair. I was smaller then, only about sixty-one inches, with a fair complexion and a peach of a young face, and I walked with the kind of amble you acquire on top of horses. I looked at the other lads and worried about being out of place. But, of course, I *was* out of place, having taken somebody else's place for my own.

Three older boys loitered on the steps behind the registrar, making remarks and howling with laughter as each of the incoming lads came forward. I regarded them warily as I reached the front of the line.

The registrar addressed me with an icy, "And you are?"

"Grant," I said softly, hesitant to assert myself fraudulently as Ulysses S. of the same.

"I see," the registrar said, leafing through his papers. "Well, I have a Mr. Grant of Ohio and a Mr. Grant of New York. Which manner of Grant are you?"

"I am Grant of Ohio," I answered, not yet deceiving him.

The three older boys behind the registrar began to catcall. "Why, it's Grant of Ohio!" one of them cut in, a ruddy-faced boy with a hawklike nose and a protruding brow. "I have a dollar that says I know his first name!"

"I'll have that dollar, Rosey," said a rangy redhead with piercing eyes. "What is it?"

"It's Land! Land Grant of Ohio," the ruddy-faced boy named Rosey said, and the two of them shook with laughter. The third fellow—large, squarely built, and older, with a prominent nose and an uncanny resemblance to George Washington—nodded along and smiled decorously, much as Washington himself would have. "Why, Land Grant," he announced. "You're an institution in your own time!"

The registrar looked over his shoulder. "Set a good example for these younger fellows, Thomas."

"Yes, no having sport with Land Grant of Ohio," the boy called Rosey said, stirring the pot once again. "Besides, if he's from Ohio, his name is probably not Land, but Hezekiah, or perhaps Amos. After all, Westerners are named for the prophets, Southerners for the apostles, and Yankees for their ancestors!" Rosey exclaimed. "Why, Farmer Grant's pigs are probably named for the Sons of Jacob and his chickens for the Kings of Israel!" The fellow who looked like George Washington chuckled and the rangy red-haired lad smirked. I looked down at my shoes, embarrassed.

"Mr. Rosecrans!" the registrar barked, and the hawk-nosed boy quieted himself. He looked again at his records. "First name Ulysses?" he asked me.

That produced another predictable round of catcalls before I could respond. "Ulysses!" said the rangy redheaded boy. "Perhaps instead of a room in the barracks he will sleep in a bed built in an olive tree!"

The boy who looked like George Washington and the ruddy-faced boy named Rosey looked at him in confusion. "What the devil are you talking about, Cump?" George Washington asked.

"About the fucking *Odyssey*, Old Tom, you bonehead," the red-headed boy said to George Washington, the older one. "About Odysseus or, as he's called, Ulysses."

It was bad enough being Useless—now would I have to suffer as Ulysses? And such language! I needed a way out. "Ulysses Grant?" I asked with a screwed-up look. "There must be some mistake."

"Now, Mr. Grant of Ohio, what mistake would that be?" the registrar said with a heard-it-all expression.

"My name is Hiram U. Grant, sir."

"Hiram U. Grant?" the registrar asked. He peered down at his records. "You are Mr. Grant of Georgetown, Ohio, aren't you?"

I carefully considered all the possible answers. "Yes, I'm from Georgetown, Ohio."

"Then you must be Ulysses S. Grant," the registrar said triumphantly, "because that is the only Grant from Georgetown, Ohio, we have on this list." He lifted the list of enrollees to prove his point.

"It's some kind of mistake," I insisted.

"Mr. Grant, either you are Ulysses S. Grant or you are headed home on the next ferry," the registrar said with finality. "Now, you may pick from those two alternatives and none other."

"Then Ulysses S. Grant it is," I mumbled, wondering if the registrar's insistence absolved me of my wrongdoing.

"Very well, then," the registrar said triumphantly. "Welcome to West Point, Cadet U. S. Grant!"

"It's U. S. Grant!" said the rangy redheaded boy. "Why, he's been named for his uncle!"

"Which uncle is that, Cump?" Old Tom, the fellow who looked like George Washington, asked.

"His Uncle Sam!" the redheaded boy named Cump said with delight.

There was a chorus of mocking laughter. "That's quite enough," the registrar snapped. "Sherman, since you've named him, you will escort Uncle Sam here to his accommodations."

"Yes, sir," the redheaded boy said, jumping forward and ripping off a smart salute.

I picked up Useful's trunk and tried to hoist it onto my shoulder as this fellow Sherman watched me with amusement. "Would you please help me with this trunk?" I asked him.

The registrar looked up at us. "Help him with the trunk, Sherman, or you'll get yourself a week's worth of conduct marks, and it's only Monday!"

Sherman shrugged and bent over the trunk. "Very well then, Uncle Sam. Let's go."

We started toward the barracks. Sherman was taller than I was, so his end of the trunk was higher, leaving me with most of its weight. I regarded him for a moment before I spoke up. "Did the fellow say your name was Sherman?"

"Yup," he said, looking straight ahead. "Tecumseh Sherman."

"Like the Indian chief?" I asked. "Is that your real name?"

"Yes, it's my real fucking name," he said, and startled me again with his choice of language, as he would every time I spoke with him for the next forty-odd years. How he could cuss! There were times, I confess, when I thought his vocabulary not wholly inappropriate, like the morning I arrived at Shiloh and found Sherman spewing out a torrid purple streak, his finger squirming through the bullet hole in his hat, or the time I relieved McClernand of command at Vicksburg and permitted Sherman the last word. But then and there I simply kept walking, secretly aghast and hoping that my mother would never meet this foulmouthed lad. Sherman, meanwhile, had proceeded to expand on his answer. "Well, it sort of is. My father named me Tecumseh, on account of his admiration for the great chief. But he died very shortly after I was born, as did my mother. I was raised by a neighbor family, who added the name William. So I'm William Tecumseh Sherman now," he said.

"Should I call you Cump?" I asked, repeating the name the fellow named Old Tom had used.

"Suit yourself," he said, and shrugged. There was a moment's pause. "And what do you want to be called?" he asked.

He had asked a deeper question than he imagined. I suddenly hit upon a solution. "Why don't you call me Sam?" I said. But of course! Sam! It was perfect! Neither Hiram nor Ulysses, but a new name for a fellow caught between names!

I smiled at him in a way he could not understand. He stopped and looked down at me—he must have been close to seventy-two inches— and shifted his grip on the trunk so he could extend his right hand toward me. "I like a fellow who can take a fucking joke," Sherman said. "Put 'er there, Sam." I saw the first traces of his mad smile.

And so I met William Rosecrans and George Henry Thomas, both of whom would be illustrious Civil War generals in their own rights. In fact, before my four years at West Point were over, I had met most of the military leadership of our nation and its Confederate enemy: My West Point contemporaries and I went through life together—in Mexico, California, and then the Civil War.

But, most importantly, I had just met Sherman, who would be my lifelong best friend. Together we would fight the greatest war the world had ever seen. We would beat back Johnston at Shiloh, lay siege to Pemberton at Vicksburg, and push Bragg off Missionary Ridge. Sherman's capture of Atlanta at my direction in 1864 would allow Lincoln to win reelection over that gutless twit McClellan, cement my strategy of annihilation, and save the Union. There would be times when we wouldn't agree—when I announced my intention to run my ships down the Mississippi River under the guns on the bluffs at Vicksburg, I thought that Sherman would have to make up new words more potent than the ones he already knew. When I was President, he talked me out of using Federal troops to smash the Klan. And if there's one thing I truly regret, aside from that grisly hour of death at Cold Harbor, it is letting Sherman talk me into sending that strutting buffoon George Armstrong Custer into the Black Hills. At least Custer made up for it by getting killed.

But at that moment, I knew none of that. All I wanted to do was to put down Useful's trunk.

I shared a dormitory room with a fellow named Ingalls. It was small, spartan, and drafty, lit by candles and heated by a coal fireplace that had it roasting in the evening and freezing by midnight. We were wakened each morning at five-thirty to the beat of drums and made to study and march all day until dinner, whereupon we had some free time to talk and visit or do some other reading until about nine, when more drums signified "lights out."

One evening I was lying in bed and heard the drums. Ingalls was already asleep and I was engrossed in the novella I was reading, so I turned my lamp down, but not out, to continue. It must have been thirty minutes later when my door swung open and in walked a gravely offended cadet sergeant.

"Cadet Grant! Did you not hear the drumming for 'lights out'?" he demanded.

"Well, yes, I did," I said, turning agreeably to face him. "But I had only a few more pages to finish, and—"

"Two conduct marks!" he said, pointing a damning finger at me. "Now put out that lamp!"

I capped the lamp quietly as he walked out, resolving to find out the next morning how bad two conduct marks were.

"Just two conduct marks?" asked Sherman when I recounted my punishment at breakfast the next day.

"Yes, that's what the cadet sergeant said," I answered. Sherman, Rosecrans, and I, together with a few other lads, sat along a long, narrow table. The dining room was a cavernous stone affair filled by the echoing clatter of pewter utensils and plates.

A brutish boy across the table looked up while shoveling potatoes into his mouth. "Two's nothing," he said, smiling. "Sherman got five once for missing chapel." He smiled and extended a hand to me once he had wiped it on his coat. "Longstreet," he said.

"Shit, Street," Sherman interrupted. "You got eight for farting in chapel. That's why I didn't go," Sherman said, laughing at his own joke.

There was another boy sitting with us, a scrawny fellow with a wisp of thin hair who projected a stiff, touchy air. He poked at his food as disdainfully as Longstreet plowed eagerly through his. Sherman introduced him as Don Buell.

"Pleased to meet you, Donald," I said politely.

"It's not Donald. It's Don, Don Carlos, as in Sir Charles," he said with a sneer.

Sherman ignored Buell's self-righteous attitude, and I followed his lead. "But what do these conduct marks mean?" I repeated, trying to bring the conversation back to my problem.

"Means you're not a virgin anymore," Longstreet said with a laugh.

"Oh, it doesn't mean shit, Sam," Sherman said. "You'll get hundreds of them before you're through. You get 'em for everything," Sherman sneered.

"Or at least *you* do," Longstreet said, suppressing a belch.

"Says a man who prays out his asshole," Sherman said, reminding his friend of his transgression. "Besides, what did I ever do that was so bad? Visiting a buddy after hours for a smoke? Missing a sermon or two? It's a load, Sam," he said. "Ask Buell, here. He ought to know. He got a full year's worth in one day."

Buell testily put down his cutlery. "Do we have to go into this?" he snapped.

"He was confined to his room for six months," Longstreet added, gleefully dredging up the issue.

"What did you do?" I asked.

"I hit a waiter here in the mess hall," Buell said quietly, sighing and resuming his dissection of breakfast.

Longstreet and Sherman both burst into laughter. "Hit him?" Longstreet exclaimed. "He beat the living Jesus out of him, he did. Laid him out with his fists and started kicking him on the floor once he fell—"

"Let it rest, Street," Buell said peevishly.

"Come on, Don," Sherman jumped in. "The lad had it coming, didn't he? Spilling soup on your pantaloons?"

"They were *new* pantaloons," Buell said. "And aside from that, my record's pretty good," he added, busying himself once again in his meal.

"Well, Sam, you can knock yourself out learning your mathematics and your engineering and your natural philosophy, but if your shirt isn't buttoned the way some little asshole likes it, or if you let fly with a little choice language—and who doesn't, now and then?—you get these bad conduct marks and your class standing drops like a stone. I'm number six in my class," Sherman testified, "but I'd be number three, Sam, if I could get a hundred of these fucking conduct marks off my sheet."

"But if everybody gets these marks—"

"Yeah, but everybody doesn't get 'em the same, Sam," Sherman spat. "If you keep your corners square you can get through with hardly a scratch. Those are the ones who move to the top," he said, nodding along with Longstreet and Buell at the sad fact of this matter.

"I don't have as many as Cump or Buell," Longstreet said, grinning as he hovered over his plate. "Neither does Thomas or Rosecrans."

"Lee never got one," Buell said, as if to chastise the others.

"Who?" I asked.

Sherman put down the coffee he was drinking and traded looks with Longstreet and Rosecrans.

"He means Bobby Fucking Lee," Sherman said, annoyed. "Hell, you ask some of these old fools around here about him and they just about wet themselves." A look of resentment overtook him.

I shrugged.

"Son of Light-Horse Harry Lee," Sherman said. "Ever hear of *him*?"

"George Washington's friend, right?"

Sherman and Longstreet laughed. "The fellow who said that shit about 'first in war' when old George died, yes," Sherman continued. "And as I've heard it told elsewhere, the greatest cockmaster ever to fuck his way through the state of Virginia."

"You're speaking of a patriot." Buell glared.

"Had a dick of iron." Longstreet nodded, agreeing.

I must have dropped my fork along with my chin. "Light-Horse Harry Lee? George Washington's friend?"

"What d'you think, Sam? That ol' George himself never got any poontang? That he only did it with the Negress of the house? Hell yes, Light-Horse Harry Lee. He drank and whored and wagered away every fucking penny he had"—Sherman leered—"and then he ran through his wife's money, too. She was one of the Custises, the Martha Custises. George set him up with a rich girl, thought it would slow him down, but it was just more coal on the fire. And when Harry was done spending his wife's fortune, he ran off to the Bahamas, leaving her to raise the children, little Bobby among them. Married some other wench down there, too. When they brought his body back for burial, they couldn't find a penny in his pockets. So Bobby's mama wrote to her husband's old friends and, guilty as they felt, they set him up to come here."

"Were you here then?" I asked.

"No," Sherman said. "I came in '36. He was already gone a few years then."

"He's in the Corps of Engineers now," Longstreet said. "You get out of here head of your class and you'll be an engineer, too."

"Fat lot of that happening," Sherman spat. "Keep getting those demerits and your ass will be in the infantry before you can say Bobby Lee."

"Lee's the chief engineer for improvements on the Mississippi River," Buell added respectfully.

"Yeah," Sherman spat. "God didn't get it right, so Bobby's going to fix it for Him."

If Bobby Lee, or any other cadet, was a great military thinker, he didn't learn it at West Point. The curriculum was largely mathematics and engineering, with some physics and a bit of French thrown in. Military strategy was conspicuously absent—it was dispensed as if it were a secret to be shared by a small elite of the corps, rather than a necessary part of every cadet's military education. It was taught by a young assistant named Henry Wager Halleck, himself a recent West Point graduate. There he proved himself both smart enough and not smart enough to earn the nickname "Old Brains" and was asked to stay on to teach military science.

Halleck was a chore—a vain and petulant little man even then, just as he would prove to be when I first reported to him, and later he to me, twenty years later. And if there was a moment in our relationship that foretold this future, it was the day we took up the Battle of York-town, where Cornwallis surrendered to Washington.

I was sitting in the back of the room in Halleck's class when he surprised me by asking me to come to the board and recite the story of the battle, which every cadet was to have memorized. I dutifully marched to the front of the room and began. "Cornwallis and his commander, General Clinton, departed New York for Savannah in the spring of 1780 to open a second front and promptly took Charleston," I recited, hoping that Halleck would soon let someone else continue.

He didn't. I pressed on. "Cornwallis then moved against Lafayette, who retreated to the northwest in order to stretch Cornwallis's supply lines, while himself waiting to be reinforced by Wayne for a counterattack."

"Yes, supply lines!" Halleck burst out emphatically. "Defending one's supply lines is critical!"

I nodded tentatively and resumed. "Sensing a trap, Cornwallis returned to Yorktown, on the Virginia shore of the Chesapeake Bay," I said as I sketched the Eastern Seaboard on the chalkboard and highlighted the points of interest. "Clinton told Cornwallis he would reinforce him by sea, so Cornwallis dug in and waited. But by waiting, he gave his opponent time to act. Washington brought down both his armies from New York and was joined by the French navy. When the British boats arrived at Yorktown, they found the French boats in disarray—unloading their cargo, their working parties ashore. But rather than attacking swiftly, the British spent precious time getting into formation and allowed the French to prepare. As a result they were repulsed, leaving Cornwallis isolated and trapped. Washington arrived, laid siege, bombarded, and Cornwallis surrendered."

Halleck regarded me from a spot at the rear of the room. "Very good," he said. I nodded and set out for my seat when I heard Halleck speak up. "Just a moment, Cadet Grant," he commanded. "What lessons do we learn from Yorktown?"

I had no prospect of giving the correct answer, because Old Brains was so convinced of his singular understanding of military history that the answers were known only to him. But I proceeded to repeat as much as I recalled his having ever said on the subject. "Communication, sir," I began. "Washington, Lafayette, and the Revolutionary generals worked in concert, while Cornwallis and Clinton never worked from a common plan."

"Very good, Grant," Halleck said from his perch in the back.

"And swift action," I continued, gazing at the floor as I struggled to come up with an answer, but when I looked up again, Halleck was standing in the aisle, stupefied I had chosen to continue.

He folded his arms over his chest. "Swift action? I don't recall having discussed swift action, Cadet Grant. Please go on."

I had no choice but to continue. "Well, yes, sir. Washington moved his armies from north of New York to Yorktown in less than a month. He seized the initiative. And the British would have destroyed the French had they gone right at them."

Halleck sat on the edge of a cadet's desk and laughed sarcastically for the benefit of the class. "Well, Cadet Grant. Your regard for the manual of procedures leaves something to be desired. Swift action, if it undermines communication or compromises supply lines, can be an invitation to disaster."

"You should have told him to fuck himself," said Sherman, hacking through yet another installment of boiled mutton in the mess hall that evening. "How long did he make you stay up there?"

"An hour and a half," I mumbled.

"And what did you say?" Rosecrans asked, excitedly soaking up news of the confrontation.

"I gave wrong answers," I said. "Well, they seemed right when they occurred to me, but they were all wrong once I said them."

"Like what?" Sherman prodded.

I pushed a piece of sheep across my plate as I talked. "Like Cornwallis, for example. Why did he dig himself in? He was digging his own grave."

"Well, thank you, General Grant," said Thomas, whose resemblance to George Washington took on new meaning. "What would you have done instead?" he asked with sarcasm.

"I wouldn't have retreated in the first place. I'd have stayed in Carolina and gone after Lafayette. If Wayne got there first, I'd have taken on the both of them."

"They'd have pounded you," Buell muttered disdainfully from across the table.

"Cornwallis got pounded anyway, didn't he?" I pointed out. "And if I'd been at Yorktown, I'd have gone right after the Americans as soon as they arrived. They'd have marched hundreds of miles and would have been dog-tired. Digging in was stupid!"

That remark was greeted with a moment of silence. It was Sherman who broke it. "You know that Halleck's an engineer, don't you?"

"Yes," I said quietly.

"So you know all these fucking engineers know how to do is dig, don't you?"

"They can tell you the number of tons of dirt in a grave," Rosecrans snickered. "Often their own."

"Yes, I know." I sighed.

"You let it go at that, didn't you?" Sherman prodded.

"Well, there was also the part about what if Cornwallis had won," I said sheepishly.

Longstreet was so taken aback by the idea he put down his fork. "I can't see any good coming of that," he volunteered.

"You have your own theories on that, too?" Thomas asked.

"You're a regular Julius Caesar, Grant." Sherman chuckled.

I sighed again. "Cornwallis didn't understand the nature of the war he was fighting," I said. I was now so engrossed in my theory I scarcely noticed that all of them—Sherman, Rosecrans, Thomas, Buell, Longstreet—were staring at me. "Cornwallis thought his job was to capture cities and strategic points. But his real job was to defeat Washington's army, to suppress a revolution. The British occupied New York, but what good came of it? Or, for that matter, what if they occupied Baltimore and Boston and Philadelphia and Charleston and Richmond and Norfolk and Trenton as well? They had to crush the colonists' will, and that meant finding Washington and his army and killing or capturing it. Who cares about New York? If the British occupied New York for four years while Washington was camped just outside of it with the army that beat Cornwallis anyway, then it wasn't much of a victory, was it? The British had to destroy the colonists' will to resist, but they hadn't the inclination. When you get right down to it, the British didn't lose the war—they were unwilling to win it."

When I was done, there was much glancing about the table and a silence ensued that was broken only when Sherman peered across the table at me and spoke. "And what did Halleck say?"

"He told me to sit down," I said.

Sherman nodded. "I bet he did," he said. The rest of them looked down and continued their dinners. I had just had my first lesson in how the military, and Henry Halleck, dealt with new thinking.

Sherman and Thomas graduated that spring. Sherman had his heart set on entering the Corps of Engineers, as Lee had done. And had it not been for his demerits, he would have been able to do so. But his foul language, casual attitude, and volatile moods so lowered his standing his wish was denied. He ended up in the artillery corps.

Sherman's experience opened my eyes. You could work hard and get good grades, but it all came down to whether your coat was buttoned and your shoes shined, not to mention keeping your ideas to yourself. I resolved as my second year began to get by as best I could, without expending effort in a pointless pursuit of the top. I was no Bobby Lee, I thought. Whoever he was.

The letters between my father and me over those first two years were circumspect regarding Useful Grant, so I had to trust my father's handling of the situation—explaining my absence, Useful's disappearance, and so forth. But at the end of my second year, I was furloughed home and had the opportunity to discuss the matter with him.

The old man had bought a bigger tannery in the nearby town of Bethel and was prospering mightily, but nothing else had changed. He was still preoccupied with business and my mother with God. I unloaded my trunk at our family's new front door and my mother came out to greet me. She wiped her hands on her apron and looked me up and down.

"Hiram, you've grown much straighter," she said. Another mother might have hugged her son, but her arms were no doubt tired from prayer.

"My name is Ulysses now, Mother," I told her.

"Father told me all about that, Hiram," she said. "Never you mind."

"Hiram—I mean, *Ulysses!*" my father said as he stepped through the door. "Let me have a look at you!" He clasped me by both shoulders and scrutinized me as if he were appraising my hide. We went inside and I was struck by the opulence of our new surroundings. There was a parlor and sitting room, a dining room with table service for a dozen guests, and a pantry almost the size of our house in Georgetown. There was also a new baby, my third sister, Mary Frances, to go along with Clara and Jennie. Simpson was now sixteen, and Orvil six—still too young to steal anything, although he would later make up for lost time.

My father led me into the parlor and Simpson followed us. The two years had changed him: He was becoming a man and a corpse at the same time. He was pale, cold, and gaunt, and his cough was already taking root in his chest.

"Well, son, school seems to agree with you, if I can judge from your letters. You are to be congratulated for building up a good record."

"But what about our scheme?" I asked.

"Our scheme? Our scheme seems to be working perfectly well, don't you think?"

I could not contain my anxiety. "But what do people think? How could Useful and I both disappear, Judge Mayor Grant and his wife die, and nobody think it suspicious?"

"You can't be concerned with what people think," Simpson said matter-of-factly.

"It's all under control," my father said, holding out his palms to quell my nervousness. "There's nothing to worry about, Hir—" He stopped himself and chuckled. "Well, I suppose I'm not sure what to call you, am I?"

"My friends at West Point call me Sam."

"Sam? Why the devil do they call you that?" Simpson asked with an annoyed expression.

"Because the initials U. S. suggest Uncle Sam. A fellow named Sherman picked up on it. Everybody calls me Sam Grant."

My father shrugged. "Sam sounds good enough. Solves a problem, doesn't it?"

"That's what I thought," I agreed. "But what about what happened?"

My father reached across the table next to his chair, poured himself a whiskey, and downed it. "The day you left," he began, "nobody noticed. They were all at sixes and sevens about Judge Mayor and his wife. If you don't mind my saying so, it took them a while to miss you. Some folks said it was a kidnapping and Useful was abducted, which was why the trunk was missing. Some said whoever stole the trunk also killed Useful and his parents, but why would they take his body and not the others? Then there were some who said Useful killed his parents, although it was pretty hard for anybody to suggest why. So it remains something of a mystery to this day, actually."

"What about the congressman who appointed him to West Point?"

"Quit. The Judge Mayor's bribe bought you a career and him a comfortable retirement. What does he care?"

"And nobody has seen Useful since?"

"Oh, every so often somebody says he was seen one place or another, but nobody gives it much credence."

"There was that time in Galena," Simpson volunteered.

"That's right," my father agreed, as if talking with a business partner, which Simpson seemed to be becoming, rather than a son. "A fellow from around here thought he saw Useful up in Galena, Illinois." The old man rubbed his jaw. "I went up there myself to check it out, but I didn't run into anybody who looked like him."

"It's a pretty good town, though," Simpson continued for him. "It's a lead-mining town, and everybody's going to need lead. It's a fast-growing market. We're thinking about putting a store up there."

The old man nodded in agreement. Simpson was acquiring the knack, that was certain. "But what about me?" I pressed. "Did anybody notice I was missing?"

"Oh, sure, sure," the old man said. "After a while, they noticed you were gone, and they began to ask, 'Say, Jesse, where's that blamed boy of yours?' And I'd say, 'He's gone off to Kentucky, to learn the trade from my half-brother and see if we can build up our business there,' and they'd say, 'My, my,' and that would be it."

"And nobody put the two together?"

The old man snorted. "Why the hell should they?" He winced as he caught himself blaspheming and turned quickly to see if my mother was near.

"What about Julia?" I asked.

"Who?" my father asked, then remembered. "Oh, sure, the little fat one. Actually, she disappeared. Her folks said she'd gone to live with family somewhere."

"Where?"

"Didn't say. Doesn't matter, really, does it?"

There was a silent moment. "Well, what are we going to do?" I prompted.

"About what?" the old man asked.

"About me!" I exclaimed, wondering why he didn't get the point.

"About you?" he parroted. "Well, we're going to do what we've done, which has been to get by just fine."

"But in two more years I graduate, and then what?"

"And then we'll see," my father said casually. "Things take care of themselves, Hir—Sam," he corrected himself with a smile. "Like I told you, everything works in life when there's nothing to stop it from working."

"That's what he always says," Simpson said.

"And it's the truth," the old man said in return. "By then, who knows what people will think? They might forget the whole thing. People move from place to place. Nobody from Georgetown would ever believe you'd become a successful military man."

He had raised the next sensitive subject. "Well, I wanted to talk to you about that as well. I don't think I'm going to stay in the military," I confessed. "I want to teach one day, perhaps mathematics. I seem to have a good head for it."

He looked up, suddenly furious. "Teach? Teach mathematics?" he sputtered, agape. "You might as well have stayed here and driven a team and hauled hides!"

"Well," I persisted, "I might be able to teach mathematics in the military. Perhaps even at West Point."

"So the men can count the number of Black Hawk arrows in their backs? Oh, preserve me from this nonsense!" he cried, throwing up his hands in disbelief. "Did you hear this?" he exclaimed to Simpson, then turned back to me. "Mathematics! You know what mathematics is good for, Hiram?" he shouted. "For adding up the money in your pocket!"

"My name is Ulysses now," I said. "Or Sam."

"You call yourself whatever you want, boy," he said, "but you'll never be other than Useless as far as I can see!"

• • •

By the time my furlough ended, the outline of a plan began to emerge to me. I had no real interest in being a soldier. If there was no future in soldiering for Sherman, who had the temperament to be a great soldier, what future was there for a quiet and reserved lad who slouched, dressed messily, and, when asked, said what he thought? I would have to muddle through and keep my nose clean. As for Useful Grant, I came to see the matter as my father did—my deception would work because there was nothing to stop it from working.

And so I returned to West Point, where I made one friend among the incoming plebes that year, a fellow who reminded me of me—quiet and reserved, even-tempered, hesitant to call attention to himself. His name was Simon Bolivar Buckner, after Bolívar, the liberator of South America. People immediately paired us up—Uncle Sam and Simon Bolivar. We became friends as only two shy people can.

My third year was a good one, because horseback riding was added to the curriculum. I was a better rider than the other cadets, better than our instructor as well. I could do the tricks I used to do as a boy in Georgetown—riding while standing, jumping, spinning to the side of the horse and hiding behind his flanks. West Point had a large sorrel named York, a powerful, long-legged animal two hands taller than every other horse in the stable. No cadet was allowed to ride him, but after a few sessions I mastered the beast. I became known throughout the corps of cadets as the little fellow who rode York, and won the admiration of many of those who otherwise would not have noticed me.

By the time my last year at West Point came around, I was focused on the prospect of graduating and securing an appointment teaching mathematics. My roommate that year was a fellow named Fred Dent, who spent his time working (in vain, as it turned out) to avoid becoming the class "goat"—the fellow last in the rankings. This required a full-time effort on his part, as Fred had little in the way of academic aptitude. On the other hand, his poor performance liberated him from worrying about where he would be assigned to duty, since only the infantry would be open to him.

In my fourth and final year I also had the chance to look over two of the more interesting new plebes—Thomas "Stonewall" Jackson and George McClellan.

Jackson arrived as if he were dumped off the back of a cart. He was a perfect rube, dressed in homemade overalls that smelled of the mules he drove over the rocky hillsides of his backwoods Virginia home. "I have no interest in friends," he said to us. This was fortunate, as he had none. When you said hello to him he would regard you with an evil eye before mumbling inaudibly and turning away. He was also good at sweating: When called upon in class, he would exude moisture until his clothing made a smacking sound against his skin. Years later, when he was whipping McClellan or Hooker with his daring and composure in battle, I sometimes wondered if it could possibly be the same lad.

I remember seeing Jackson standing in line for the registrar—just as I had, three years before—together with McClellan. McClellan, later to be the terrified commander of the Union army whom Lincoln would dismiss, was as polished as Jackson was raw and as phony as Jackson was authentic, even if Jackson was only authentically crazy. McClellan was just sixteen and had already attended the University of Pennsylvania for two years. He was said to be a prodigy, and his family was well connected. Whether he was a prodigy, I wasn't sure. But he was self-infatuated, posturing, presumptuous, and condescending. That much I knew with certainty.

I was watching the new plebes as I sat with Ingalls, Buckner, and Dent on the same steps on which Sherman, Rosecrans, and Thomas sat the day I arrived. McClellan fidgeted while he waited in line: He seemed unused to waiting for anything or anybody and unwilling to learn how to do so. Jackson stood in front of him, not happy, of course—Jackson never was happy—but contented to stand in place as long as nobody accosted him with conversation. His contentment was short-lived. If his backwoods appearance and odor didn't attract enough notice, he was inexplicably holding his left arm straight up. It was the same arm, of course, that would be amputated at Chancellorsville and given its own burial, only to prowl the Union lines from beyond the grave, or so frightened Federal soldiers thought.

The sight of this smelly, dirty farm boy, his sweat-stained saddlebags holding his meager worldly goods, standing rigidly but not unhappily with his left arm in the air, wore McClellan down. "If you don't mind," he finally blurted out, drumming Jackson's shoulder from behind, "why are you holding your arm up in the air?"

Jackson turned to McClellan with startling quickness. "I'm trying to even out the humors in my body, sir. I suffer from dyspepsia, and as a result, the left side of my body is weak, at risk of death. But the right half of my body is fine. If I hold this arm up, it will redistribute the humors through the body, which aids both digestion and sleep." Then, with his right hand, Jackson produced a lemon from his overalls and bit into it with enthusiasm, spitting the rind to the ground. "Lemons help, too," he said, and turned from McClellan as if they had been discussing the weather.

McClellan stood stupefied. He wondered, I'm sure, how a lad so backward, smelly, and stupid could have been admitted to West Point as his classmate and peer. But the fact is, if the Civil War had been fought between Jackson and McClellan, the South would have won in as little time as it would take McClellan to wet himself.

It became obvious to me in my last year that a mathematics teaching appointment at West Point was not going to be forthcoming, given my mediocre record, and I was going to have to pick a unit in which to serve. I was not going to find myself in the engineering corps, or even the artillery, where Sherman had landed. In fact, seven of the previous year's class—standouts such as Rosecrans, Earl Van Dorn, and A. P. Hill—were let into the Corps of Engineers, meaning there would be less room for my class when it graduated. All the clever fellows who ordinarily would have been made engineers would end up in topography or ordnance, and all the fellows who ordinarily would have gone into topography or ordnance would end up in artillery and the dragoons, and all the fellows in artillery or the dragoons would end up in cavalry, and so on, leaving little room for a fellow at the bottom of the pile such as myself. If I was to avoid the infantry, it would have to be by virtue of my horsemanship getting me into the cavalry.

Horsemanship! Exactly! An idea suddenly occurred to me. The graduation exercises, only weeks away, were to include a demonstration of horsemanship. With only the slightest cajoling I was able to get the riding master to give me a special place on the program.

The long wooden benches in the riding hall were crowded with spectators on that final day, as various cadets paraded around the ring, brandishing their swords, spurring their mounts to rear into the air, and then racing them down the center aisle of the tanbark floor and taking them over the jumping bar, usually set around three feet.

When they were done, the riding master, following our agreement, came out alone, walked down the center aisle to the jumping bar, and reset it so that it was higher than his head—six feet, three inches, it was, a full six inches higher than the world record at that time. A murmur of anticipation spread through the crowd as he turned and shouted, "Cadet Grant!"

It was all the setup I needed. I rode York out of the ranks of cadets and cantered him down to the far end of the riding hall, then wheeled and galloped him down the center. York was magnificent, looking up about thirty yards away to see the bar and understanding immediately its meaning. He thundered closer and when I almost began to worry he was getting too close, he threw his long, strong front legs into the air and sailed up as if weightless, his body stretched into a magnificent parabola, and I felt my own body become weightless for an instant as we went up and over the bar together.

There was a thunderous ovation when we landed on the other side. I wheeled and doffed my hat to the crowd and heard the riding master cry, "Class dismissed!" Hats went into the air and I was suddenly besieged with congratulating friends and admirers. The jump record I set stood for a quarter century. Let them try to keep me out of the cavalry now, I thought.

I was now a West Point graduate.

I packed my things the next day and got on the ferry for my long trip back to Bethel. My assignment came several weeks later. I was promoted to second lieutenant and ordered to report to the Jefferson Barracks at St. Louis, Missouri. True to form, the army had just assigned the world-record high-jumping horseman to the infantry.

CHAPTER III

ARRIVAL AT JEFFERSON BARRACKS—COURTSHIP OF MRS. GRANT—THE INVASION OF MEXICO— AN ENCOUNTER WITH LEE

Mrs. Grant came by a moment ago with her pet theologian, that Methodist Bible-thumper Dr. Newman. He's hoping to run in and sprinkle me with some kind of water to reclaim my heathen soul the moment I die, which won't be long now. In two shakes of a cat's tail, he'll be jabbering how I accepted the word of God in my final hours and died secure in the knowledge that Christ was my savior. At least Sitting Bull wanted to scalp Custer in the heat of battle, although Custer was shot in the head before the chief had the opportunity. Newman, in contrast, intends to scalp my eternal soul only after I'm dead and defenseless.

It's like that old story about the soldier who comes back to camp to present his general with the leg of an enemy soldier. "Why didn't you bring me the head?" the general asked.

"It was already taken," the soldier said.

Mrs. Grant first brought Newman around a few months ago, as I was trying to write. "Ulys, there's someone I'd like you to meet," she said with that combination of coy sweetness and petulant insistence she had from the day I met her.

Newman sat down at my bedside and smiled the most unctuous smile I'd ever seen—a quick look convinced me I had better things to do than find out who he was. "Go away," I told him.

"This is Dr. Newman, Ulys," Mrs. Grant corrected me. "He's here to give you ministration for the world to come," she said, patting my hand.

"I don't need Dr. Newman to give me ministration for the world to come," I told her. "I need Dr. Douglas to give me another shot of morphine to prepare me for the afternoon to come."

"But Ulys," Mrs. Grant insisted, "you need to commemorate the Lord's Supper if you want to go to heaven."

"Julia, I need to finish this book if you want to eat supper after I do!"

Mrs. Grant led her preacher out of the room. Since then, she's brought him back on several occasions to see if disease has yet robbed me of my sensibilities. Much to her disappointment, I have remained lucid and resisted his effort. Now they sneak about together, checking to see if I'm in the throes of my final crisis, or perhaps just passed. If you're still warm, you're fair game for the Lord.

The Lord! That magnificent figment of my mother's obsessed imagination! Where was the Lord when I let Meade send thousands to die in fifteen brutal minutes at Cold Harbor? Where was the Lord when my injured men prayed for His mercy as they were consumed by the brush fires at the Wilderness? Why did He choose to save those three Biblical pups, Shadrach, Meshach, and the other fellow, from *their* flames and let thousands of my men die in *theirs*? The Lord was too busy listening to the prayers of deadbeats like Newman. The Lord my rear end.

Besides, Mrs. Grant couldn't give a fig for the Lord. All she wants is a properly sanctified corpse when the time comes. Which won't be long now.

I arrived at the Jefferson Barracks in September 1843, the jumping-off point for most military endeavors out West, where white men negotiated with Indians and then killed them. The post was an enormous three square miles of whitewashed and red brick buildings, a city in its own right set against a rolling, forested wilderness. I led my mount through the main gates and stopped the first soldier I saw to ask for directions.

"I am Lieutenant Grant," I said officiously, "here to report to the Fourth Infantry."

The soldier turned quickly. "I know that voice! It's my little friend Grant!" he said.

My shoulders hunched. It was Longstreet, Sherman's loutish friend.

"Grant, my sweetie-pie," he said as he looked up at me. He was juicily working a plug of tobacco about his mouth. "How was your last year at the Point?"

"The same as yours was, Street. I didn't make the cavalry or dragoons, so I'm here."

"Oh, it ain't so bad," Longstreet drawled. "The food's pretty good, and young officers like us are the toast of St. Louis. There's some high-grade poontang out there for the taking"—he grinned—"and some lesser grades, too, if you want to part with a few bucks."

"I'll be fine, Street," I mumbled.

"Hell, yes, you will," Longstreet said, missing my point. "Say, did you hear about Buell? He's here, too. Already in trouble—hit an enlisted man with his saber a few months back. Pounded him good. They court-martialed him."

No surprise there. "Is he in the brig?"

"Hell, no. He was acquitted. You don't expect a bunch of officers to condemn a fellow just for whipping an enlisted man, do you?"

The leniency showed Buell exemplified the nature of military practice at Jefferson Barracks. Many of the senior officers were drunks or martinets. My own captain, a fellow named Buchanan, proved to be a good example of the latter, demanding compliance with a host of petty rules and procedures solely for his own amusement.

The barracks' primary activity was the most common one in the military—waiting. Soldiers waited there to fight Indians, and many men at the fort told tales of successful skirmishes against the red man, which upon reflection was unsurprising, since the men who fought unsuccessful skirmishes against them did not report back.

When the men at Jefferson Barracks weren't waiting, they were arguing, usually over Texas.

Texas had declared its independence from Mexico in 1836, and from the moment it did, the slave states saw it as fertile ground for their political expansion. Slavery's adherents, such as Longstreet and Fred Dent, who was also stationed there, argued in wild, elliptical terms for its incorporation into the Union.

"Andy Jackson says if we don't take Texas, Great Britain will," Fred held forth. "He says they'll use it as a base for stirring up a slave revolt in the South and then seize the Mississippi Valley in the resulting turmoil."

"That's ridiculous," I told him plainly. "Why would Great Britain start a war in the South when it depends on Southern cotton for its manufactures?"

"Well, that's what Andy Jackson says." Fred shrugged. His command of politics was as superficial as his command of his academic subjects at West Point. Fred was soon dispatched to the Great Plains, an assignment that disappointed him immensely. He was afraid that, if war over Texas ever came, he would be too busy killing Indians to kill Mexicans. Moreover, Fred's family lived only a few miles from the barracks. He insisted I visit them after he left, and after a few months of languishing around the barracks and practicing my sitting and pipe smoking, I headed out to the Dent family farm.

As I rode up the front path, I wondered if I had taken a wrong turn and ended up in the Deep South. A few slave children dressed in tatters played in the front yard along with a white girl in crinolines, aged about eight. A mammy was sweeping the porch, working around a disagreeable-looking, corpulent, balding man in a rocker. He was reading a newspaper while muttering under his breath. "Black Julia, you damned Auntie," he swore as he looked up, "can't you watch where you're sweeping? I'm trying to read about how Henry Clay and those nefarious Whig traitors are trying to take your happy home away. Thank the Lord Democrats like Andy Jackson are fighting for your right to be a slave!" He shuddered as he contemplated the Whig propensity for abolition.

I was taking in the scene when the youngsters took note of me. "It's a soldierman!" one of the slave children shouted.

In an instant there was a swarm of giggles and stares around me. "Look! He's as cute as a doll!" the little white girl chirped—back then, clean-shaven and fresh-faced, I suppose I was. The old man looked up from his newspaper and stared at me warily, when the front door swung open and a small, lovely woman with a graceful smile and bright gray eyes came out of the house. "Children! Go and play," she said.

I dismounted and took off my hat. "Mrs. Dent?" She nodded pleasantly. "My name is Sam Grant."

"Sam Grant! Fred said you would come to visit one day!" Mrs. Dent shook my hand and walked me up to the porch. "Colonel, this is Sam Grant, Fred's roommate from West Point."

The old man squinted and then suddenly burst into delighted comprehension. "Of course! Why, this is a pleasure, Lieutenant Grant! Sit yourself down here and make yourself right at home!" He looked about agitatedly for either a chair or a slave to bring him one. "Black Julia, damn your hide, where are you? Get this man a proper chair!" He smiled at me as the Auntie positioned a second rocker next to his, as if he was bestowing a privilege on me, and for the next two hours I barely said another word. Off he went, telling me about his plantation—farm was more like it, but he had eighteen slaves and fancied himself a true Southern plantationer, right down to assuming for himself the traditional Southern honorific of Colonel, even though the closest he ever came to an army was reading about one in the *St. Louis Republican*.

Dent—the Colonel—had a thousand acres, about a mile and a half square, which he named White Haven, after some place in England he imagined he was from. He devoted his time to supervising the plantation, which meant sitting, rocking, reading, smoking, drinking, suing his neighbors, harboring strong and unfounded opinions, hectoring his four sons (of whom my roommate, Fred, Jr., was the youngest), and worshiping his three daughters.

The two youngest Dent girls lived at home—Emmy, the eight-year-old, and Nellie, who was sixteen. The third daughter, Julia—the same name as my lost Ohio love—was eighteen, away at a boarding school in St. Louis because, little Emmy confided, "Papa wants to teach her to act more proper. But he gives her anything she wants anyway."

Both Emmy and Nellie resembled their mother, a handsome woman of such obvious breeding and discernment that her presence in the midst of the wilderness outside St. Louis was anomalous. She welcomed me to White Haven and urged me to take it as a second home while I was stationed at Jefferson.

I spent many an evening there on the Dents' veranda—the old man called it a *piazza*, tempering his Southern pretensions with Continental ones—sipping sweet tea and having supper, and discussing politics, which meant explaining the realities of the Mexican situation to Mrs. Dent while the Colonel spouted invective at the Whigs in general and Henry Clay in particular. But I was unperturbed by having a garrulous old man around me, having been raised by one, and enjoyed the comforts of a home and Mrs. Dent's sociability. Moreover, her two charming daughters led me to wonder about the third. If Julia was her father's favorite and the fairest of the three, think what I might expect! Perhaps this was Fred's plan all along—to fix me up with his beautiful sister. In fact, having been to boarding school, she no doubt had an extra helping of charm to go with her mother's breeding. I began to anticipate her return as eagerly as her own family did, but for wholly different reasons.

I was sitting with the Dents on the veranda—the *piazza*—one afternoon when I spied a trail of dust coming down the road. But rather than the carriage I expected, a large brown mare suddenly cantered briskly around the turn, atop her a short, broad-shouldered figure in a buckskin coat, full blue skirt, and a broad leather hat tucked tightly on her head. The mare stopped and with a single fluid motion the rider threw her right leg over the horse's rump and glided down to the ground. She brushed off her jacket with two gloved hands, laid her hat on the pommel of her saddle, and spat on the ground without missing a beat.

"Julia," Mrs. Dent admonished, "I thought we agreed expectorating isn't ladylike."

"I'm sure we did, Mother," she said. "I'll try to be better soon." Not a soul believed her.

Mrs. Dent sighed with resignation and the Colonel rushed forward. "How is Daddy's little girl!" he shouted, and he embraced her as they turned together in a circle.

"Oh, Daddy," she said, "I've missed you and White Haven ever so much!"

Ever so much! It was like meeting two girls at once—one who rode like a banshee and spat, another a Southern Belle. I took a good look at the old man's flower. She was round—not fat, but certainly plump—and short, with thinning hair in a small brown bun. Her complexion was a pleasing rosy blond, suggesting time spent outdoors. Her features were average at best, plain and straight. All told, she might have been presentable in an unexceptional way were it not for her right eye, which seemed to go wherever it wanted to, regardless of where the other eye was pointing, a condition called strabismus. Julia, far from being a lithe, enchanting reproduction of her mother or sisters, was a female, cross-eyed version of her old man.

She turned to Nellie and Emmy and hugged them with sisterly affection, when her mother stepped forward. "Julia, there is somebody

I'd like you to meet." She turned her toward me. "This," Mrs. Dent said, "is Sam Grant, Fred's—"

"His roommate from West Point. Lieutenant Grant, of course," she said, extending both the word *Lieutenant* and her hand. "Why, I am so very pleased to meet you!" She allowed me to hold her round little fingertips for an extra second. "Little Emmy has told me so much about you. She says you are the finest horseman in the entire army!"

I blushed at this sentiment. "Well, perhaps that's so—"

"And you jumped a six-foot bar at graduation!"

"Well, it was a bit over six feet—"

"A bit over!" Mrs. Dent exclaimed. "My, that is remarkable!" The Colonel mumbled some disinterested agreement.

"Then let's see if you and your nag can catch Missouri Belle and me," she said, one eye brightly blazing, the other pointed upward and to the side. With that she sprang atop her brown mare and was off into the woods like a hummingbird.

"I'll be goddamned, but she's the best daughter I've got *and* the best son, too," the Colonel said, brushing aside an affectionate tear. "You'd better saddle up and catch her, Sam, or we'll have to wait until nightfall for supper."

"Go get her, Sam!" little Emmy shouted, and I swung myself onto my mount in pursuit. I followed her trail of fluttering branches and dust through the woods. Soon I spotted her and watched as she dug her heels into her mount and headed straight toward Gravois Creek: She stood her portly rear up like a master and the horse cleared the creek bed in a single, graceful leap as her rider looked over her shoulder to see if I would do the same.

Well, I wasn't on York, but it was an easy jump nonetheless. I spurred my horse on, and when I landed on the far side, Julia wheeled and came back toward me with an appraising look. "Well done, Lieutenant," she said. She swung off her mare and tied her reins to a tree near the creek bed, regarding me coyly. "Aren't you going to walk with me?" she asked. "I love the wildflowers along this river," she said, and started along the creek, leaving me to dismount and catch up to her.

"There's nothing like riding a worthy horse to a worthy place, don't you think?" she asked. She decided on a spot beside the creek and sat down in a dainty, if definite, way, then patted the ground beside her.

I lowered myself next to her and she drew herself toward me. "My daddy's a blowhard, don't you think?" she asked.

"He does seem opinionated," I answered. "Mine's like that, too."

She suddenly drew back and began to defend him. "Yes, but he's a very important man, you know. Our plantation is one of the largest in the area, and our flower garden is the envy of the county, as are our darkies. All of the congressmen and the senators from this state are our friends." She looked down modestly and then leaned toward me, switching tones. "Have you a girlfriend, Lieutenant?"

"No," I said with a shrug.

"I have had many affairs of the heart," she said, as if I had asked. "But I have no beau right now." She leaned toward me again, this time more intimately. "Aren't you the least bit curious?"

"About what?"

"About love! About the birds and the bees, silly!" she said conspiratorially.

Well, of course I was. I'd seen Useful have a throw and heard tales at West Point, and I was wondering when I was going to get a turn—I was twenty-two now, and the itch was pretty strong. Was this where we were going? Were the Gates of Paradise about to be thrown open to me? "I suppose every young person wonders," I said shyly, "but I have no girlfriends to speak of—"

"Are there any not to speak of?" she said, and giggled. "You're every bit the handsome little doll Emmy told me you were! And she told me you were shy, but I can fix that," she said. And with that she planted her lips against mine in a surprising and entirely pleasing way. She pushed me over, gently but resolutely, and we lay side by side in the grass, her kiss unabating and her hands smoothing my chest and shoulders. We went on like this for a moment when she pulled back and looked at me with an excited smile. "That was pretty good!" she said, and, as I nodded agreement, she pulled her skirt up toward her waist and threw her bloomered leg over me. She began to writhe slightly as we kissed again and I found myself in a growing state of agitation. My hands timidly felt her form: She was stout, to be sure, but strong, not soft—she certainly could have handled Useful Grant, I thought.

In a moment she came up for air again and regarded me with heavy-lidded eyes. She drew a hand across my nether region and, to my embarrassment, felt my excitement. "Why, Lieutenant!" she whispered. "You are standing at attention!"

This was it! I concluded—it was time for some horizontal refreshment, as the men used to call it. No flanking maneuvers, I reckoned, only a direct assault, and I recalled the most—and only—successful direct assault I'd ever seen, the night before I left for West Point six years before. I promptly rolled Julia over on her back and threw myself atop her, hands searching through the mystery of her foundation garments, and began to recite: *You have everything to offer, Julia. The beauty of a woman that can only be the product of a radiant soul that glows with all the colors of the heavens.*

I was so taken with knowing this all-powerful incantation that I did not notice Julia reaching back and letting fly a solid punch to my temple that knocked me off her with such stunning force I might have rolled into the creek had she not sprang up and straddled me. "Whoa, there, soldier," she said, looking down. "We're galloping before we trot, don't you think?"

"I—I'm sorry, please," I said, apologizing in hasty gulps. "I must have been very confused—"

She settled down on top of me and sighed. "Yes, but love is a confusing thing, isn't it? And my little man does have his needs, doesn't he? Are we going to behave now?"

"Of course. Please," I said, hoping she'd get off my rib cage.

"Please? Well, as long as the lieutenant is nice enough to say please." And with that she slid down alongside me as I cleared my head, and she began to work the buttons on the front-opening fly recently approved by the infantry. In a moment she had liberated me to the Missouri air. I had sagged a bit after her cuffing, but as she wrapped her nimble fingers around me I began to engorge in earnest. I closed my eyes for the absence of knowing where to look, and when I managed the courage to peek, I saw Julia leering excitedly as she manipulated my staff expertly.

"Now, Lieutenant, our artillery is ready to fire, if I am right," she said, and she was as right as rain. In an instant I was forced to surrender and shuddered as my whole body was caught up in the event, as if I were a pitcher and she had grabbed me by the handle and poured. I lay at rest after my crisis and my thoughts drifted to Bible reading in my mother's home.

"*But why can't we read about this fellow Onan tonight?*" my brother Simpson had complained. "*My friends in Sunday school say that Onan is the good part. We're up to that part, aren't we, Mother?*"

"*Mind yourself, Simpson,*" my mother had snapped. "*Hiram, go on with the next chapter, the story of Joseph and Potiphar.*"

Julia now tucked my dead soldier into my trousers as delicately as if she were doing needlework. She sighed and smiled at me. "I've always wondered how that worked on a man," she said dreamily.

"On a man?" I blurted out.

"Well, yes. After all, it's easy to do to horses," she replied, and as I began to fathom her remark, she was already swinging herself into the saddle. "You'd best hurry up if you want to catch me going back!" she said with a broad smile, and was off, heading back to the house and leaving me to realize I was in love.

This first encounter left me breathless for more, and in the following weeks I became a more regular visitor to White Haven, enjoying Mrs. Dent's table and tolerating the old man's ongoing political discourse as the price for time with Julia, including amorous horseback rides and walks in the woods.

Old man Dent probably would have disapproved if he had taken the time to notice, but he was too preoccupied with the *St. Louis Republican's* reporting of the most recent evidence of Whig perfidy: the Congress' recent vote to spurn Texan annexation and statehood, which denied the South a new source of senators in the slavery debate. He read the newspaper with greater attentiveness than he read the situation at home.

In fact, the person most disapproving of my newfound love interest was my commanding officer, Captain Buchanan. He was obsessed with punctuality, and tarrying at White Haven often left me late for dinner at Jefferson Barracks. Buchanan responded by announcing an arbitrary rule: Officers who arrived after soup was on the table owed the mess a bottle of wine. Thereafter he would bolt through his first course, eyes glued to the mess hall door in the hope some wayward lieutenant— me—would arrive after a waiter put Buchanan's hastily poured soup before him.

The issue boiled over one Sunday afternoon. I was at White Haven, sitting with Julia on the *piazza* when my eagerness to win her so overwhelmed me I decided it was time to advance upon the target. "These weeks have flown by for me, Julia," I blurted out, surprising myself as much as her.

"Why, Lieutenant," she cooed. "I value your friendship ever so highly as well."

I swallowed hard and charged. "I'm not talking about friendship, Julia. I am talking about the love between a man and a woman. Julia, marry me, and let us be husband and wife forever!"

No sooner did I say it than my every nightmare came to life. A voice bellowed out behind me. "Well, what have we here? Damned if it's not my two favorite little people in these parts!"

It was Longstreet! "For land's sakes, Street," I blurted. "What the devil are you doing here?"

"Why, Ulys!" Julia chirped excitedly as she went to Longstreet and embraced him. "Do you know my cousin Peter?"

Her cousin Peter! Fred never mentioned any such thing! Was I about to marry into Longstreet's family? "Why, yes, Julia, yes, I do!" I said, feigning cordiality for Julia's benefit. "How are you, Longstreet, old man?"

"I'm just as fine as when you saw me this morning, Grant." The big ape laughed, punching me painfully on the shoulder.

"Mother and Daddy are in the house, Peter. They'll be happy to see you."

"Well, I was just passing through, but if you insist, maybe I'll go in and say hello. Is there any supper out?"

Julia started to tell him about a chicken in the pantry, but Street was already through the door, working up a good head of saliva. I rubbed my arm and returned to my proposition. "My dearest Julia, what do you say to my proposal?"

"Oh, Ulys, don't be silly! I am too young to marry, and my father would never let me marry a military man!"

"But I won't be long in the military, Julia. I'll get a job teaching mathematics in a college, as I've promised. We'll have a secure and quiet life together."

"Ulys, please. I like things as they are." She smiled at me coquettishly. "Don't you, Lieutenant? After all, you are my little stallion, aren't you?"

I was not to be distracted.

"Julia, please. Let me speak to your father—" But at that moment the door swung open and Longstreet came bounding out, a chicken leg in his clumsy paw.

"Better saddle up, Sam, unless you want to give Captain Buch a third bottle this week," he said as he strode to his horse. He hoisted his large self into the saddle. "You coming?"

"I'll follow," I said curtly.

"Suit yourself." Longstreet turned and took off up the road. With relief, I watched him go away and turned to Julia.

"I must have your answer!"

"Then my answer is no!" she said firmly. "I am very fond of you, Ulys, but I am not ready to wed."

That ended that. We sat quietly for a while, not knowing what else to say, before I started back for the barracks. Needless to say, by the time I arrived, dinner was served and my seat was conspicuously empty.

"Here's Cousin Ulys now!" I heard Longstreet shout as I entered the officers' mess. "He's trying to endear himself to Fred Dent's cross-eyed sister. Any luck, sweet-ums?"

There was a chorus of catcalling as I sat down, blushing. Buchanan looked at me from his seat at the head table and gestured down to the soup at his place with condescending pleasure. "Well, Grant, my respect for Lieutenant Dent forbids me from asking as to whether you have had any success with this girl, but your lateness requires me to dun you for yet another bottle of wine, which I trust will accompany you to mess tomorrow."

Between Julia's rejection, Longstreet's derision, and Buchanan's petty authoritarianism, my frustration erupted. "If I am fined again, I shall repudiate!" I found myself shouting.

There was stunned silence in the mess and all eyes turned to Buchanan, who was turning a deep shade of red. "Lieutenant Grant," he said, and here no doubt referring to my small stature and fair face, "young people should be seen and not heard."

There was another round of groans and shouts led by Longstreet and I buried my face, eyes down, in my plate. I was mad at everybody and Buchanan was mad at me. What on earth was I doing in St. Louis, at a military barracks on the edge of the endless forever of the frontier, with nothing to do except wait for a chance to kill an Indian or a Mexican who had done nothing to deserve my enmity, all the while chasing a short, plump, cross-eyed girl who did not want me and whose horses enjoyed her as much as I did? My commanding officer despised me, I had no foreseeable prospect of success, and I was living the life of another man, a man I last saw running from a crime he did not commit.

It was time to stop going nowhere, I decided. If I could get a job teaching college mathematics, I would do it. I was considering going back to Ohio to open a livery business, or perhaps farm, when the Congress changed its mind about Texas, and the direction of my life. My regiment was ordered there as part of a so-called Army of Observation being assembled under General Zachary Taylor. The prospect of war with Mexico now loomed, and I would be a part of it.

But if I was to go to war I still had one matter to resolve, and I headed directly to White Haven. A hard rain left the roads almost unpassable, and when I reached Gravois Creek, instead of the usual trickle of water—hardly enough to drive a coffee mill, most days—the creek was surging, overflowing its banks. Most men would find some other place to ford, but I drove the horse into the swift current and grabbed the pommel of the saddle for dear life. I emerged on the other side and proceeded to White Haven, drenched.

I tethered my mount in front of the house and knocked forcefully on the door until it opened to reveal Julia. Her eyes widened with affection as she beheld me. "Ulys!" she exclaimed, and leapt forward to embrace me. "Ugh!" She recoiled, realizing I was soaked. She brushed the front of her dress and looked up at me, and her face was once again transformed into a beacon of adoration. "Ulys," she said, this time softly, and she fell into my arms again. "Don't you want to dry off? My brother John has some clothes—"

"Julia," I said, gazing intently into her eyes, "I have been ordered to Texas."

She burst into tears. "I know, I know," she sobbed, clutching me once again, this time ignoring the dampness.

"You know? How do you know?"

"Cousin Peter told me. He said you were going with Taylor's Army of Observation." She sniffled and sighed in my arms. "I was wrong to turn you away when you proposed. I couldn't let you leave without telling you I love you."

She looked up at me adoringly, her left eye gazing deeply into my soul while her right one twitched hither and yon. My moment was at hand.

"Marry me, Julia," I whispered.

"Yes, I will, Ulys," she whispered back, and our lips met. When she came up for air, she was suddenly concerned. "But Daddy must not know."

"Why not?" I asked, preparing to take offense.

"You know how he is. He'll find something wrong with the idea—either I'm too young or you're a soldier or an abolitionist. I love Daddy, but at times he can be a pain in the arse."

I looked down at her, more in love than ever. For all of the coquettish fawning she did, she had the old man dead to rights. I was flushed with admiration: She would make a great partner, a soul mate.

The thought then occurred to me: *Confide!* Tell her about Useful, about the whole affair. After all, what if Useful someday walked out of the woods to reclaim his destiny? She would be as profoundly affected as I.

I began to frame the words when my tongue suddenly froze. Telling her meant risking everything. What if she were to tell her brother Fred, or her loutish cousin Longstreet? Could they be trusted as well? Or her father—what if he were to know? It couldn't be risked. "Very well, my love," I said, returning to the matter at hand. "I know how to keep a secret. But you must swear you will keep your promise to me when I return."

"I swear, Ulys," she said, and we kissed once again. "And until then, it will be our secret. I will tell no one save my pillow and my horse."

Her horse! A moment's jealousy overcame me before I fell back into the warm mist of her affection.

I soon found myself, along with my unit, the Fourth Infantry, dispatched to a hot, humid, mosquito-infested site outside Natchitoches, Louisiana, on the banks of the Sabine River, the boundary between the United States and Texas. With no comforts and nothing to do, the place was oppressive beyond description, and my thoughts strayed constantly to Julia. She had accepted my proposal, but our relationship was still a secret. In the sweltering tedium of our encampment, with the prospect of war before me, I could think of nothing save the importance of cementing her promise. In the spring of 1845, therefore, I secured a leave and traveled to St. Louis to confront old man Dent and have the matter out.

I had unusually good luck. At the moment I led my mount up the path to White Haven, Colonel Dent was about to embark on a trip to Washington, D.C. The Colonel was always deeply in debt and entangled in lawsuits. Thus, he used what little money he had to bribe a steady stream of judges, legislators, and other officials in order to convince them he was still a man of means as he maneuvered the rapids of bankruptcy. He was in the saddle when I arrived.

"Sam! It is an indubitable pleasure to see you, as ever. Have you been brought back to Jefferson?" he asked, concerned my presence was a signal that the war with Mexico was no longer a prospect.

"No, Colonel. I've come back because I wish to speak with you, sir. Man to man."

He looked at me warily. "Well, Sam, I'd be happy to spend some time with you, but I am heading to the nation's capital on matters of importance to the financial prospects of this estate." He smiled and nervously tipped his hat. "Perhaps we will be able to visit on some other occasion."

"No, Colonel," I said softly as I took the reins of his mount and pulled its head down, stopping it. "Now."

Dent saw I was not to be moved and he lowered his eyes in thought. "Very well, then," he mumbled, dismounting. "We can spend a moment on the *piazza,* if you insist."

Which is what we did. I told him I intended to marry Julia and wanted his blessing to do so.

"Sam, Sam," he said. "Young people think that marriage is easy. But it's not. A military life is not for Julia. She's too pampered, unready for the deprivations that can arise."

"If army life is too demanding for her, I will quit the army as soon as my duty to them ends and pursue a career teaching mathematics."

The old man looked at his pocket watch and then at me. "Sam, I have to go."

"Then give me your hand on it," I said, offering him mine.

He looked at it warily and sighed deeply. "I'll tell you what," he said. "You go back to Mexico and write to your belle, and if you both want to marry after a year of separation, I'll accede."

Fair enough, I thought. "We have an agreement, then?" The old man nodded and we shook. In a moment he was off to the docks, leaving me to celebrate my good fortune with Julia, now unreservedly my intended. Years later, I learned that Julia had already confronted her father.

"You are young and the boy is too poor. He hasn't anything to give you," the Colonel had told her.

"I am poor, too, and haven't anything to give him," she responded, stating the truth more plainly than he liked.

Colonel Dent was still unconvinced, though, until Mrs. Dent told the old man he was either going to approve the plan or find his food poisoned. Thus, the two ladies had prepared him for his encounter with me.

Armed with this success on the battlefield of love, I was prepared to go to war and rejoined Taylor's Army of Observation.

Taylor was not the nation's leading general: Winfield Scott was. But Scott had pretensions to a political career while Taylor lacked interest in one, so President Polk saw Taylor as the superior choice for leading our troops into Mexico, a potentially heroic accomplishment of which political careers are made. Polk sent General Taylor and our army to the southern banks of the Nueces River—north of the Rio Grande, but in Mexico proper according to the boundary the Mexicans claimed— hoping it would provoke an attack, in the aftermath of which he hoped to claim Texas. All it provoked was a message from General Arista, the Mexican commander:

> *Unless your army crosses back over the Nueces River, Mexico shall regard it as a hostile act, and a state of war shall exist.*

Taylor, a weathered-looking man who conserved his energy by not shaving, washing, or changing clothes, received the message with great enthusiasm, since it promised the result he sought. But after a long winter of provocative activities that stopped just short of shooting— marching, drilling, drinking, and horseback riding—we remained unmolested. Accordingly, in February of 1846, Taylor marched farther south, into the vast zone of contention between the Nueces and the Rio Grande. General Arista sent another message:

If your army does not return to the Nueces River, Mexico shall regard it as a hostile act, and a state of war shall exist.

Taylor, who was known to spit rather than speak when pressed to express himself, received the message with guarded optimism and immediately marched farther south to build fortifications on the Rio Grande itself, opposite the Mexican town of Matamoros. A new message arrived:

If your army does not depart the Rio Grande River, Mexico shall regard it as a hostile act, and a state of war shall exist.

Taylor, who had a perpetual sun-baked squint, tried to maintain a positive attitude, but there was still no attack.

Finally he decided to press the issue by blockading the mouth of the Rio Grande, a vital supply route for the Mexicans. Arista sent yet another communication to Taylor:

If your army does not remove its blockade of the Rio Grande, then Mexico shall regard it as a hostile act, and a state of war shall exist.

Taylor spat, scratched, and squinted, and received the message with ill-disguised contempt. He had been made these promises before. He promptly increased the fortifications at the mouth of the river. This time the Mexicans responded. In April, a company of sixteen hundred Mexican soldiers came upon a posse of sixty-three American dragoons and ambushed them, killing eleven. Taylor reacted to these dead with great enthusiasm. He wrote to Polk, sharing with him the good news that he had been ambushed and that hostilities were under way, and moved his army deeper into Mexico.

On May 7, Taylor spotted the Mexican army ahead of us, near a town named Palo Alto. Despite being outnumbered in enemy territory, he sent them running.

Two days later Taylor located Arista once again, in the chaparral that extended north from the Rio Grande. Taylor was still outnumbered, but he was determined to give them what for.

Buchanan, my commanding officer, was assigned to take skirmishers to the front of the line, so I was to have my first battlefield command. I led my men out front, searching for the enemy. Mexican shot and shell fell continually around us: A man standing near me had his jaw shelled off with such force a fellow standing nearby, by the name of Wallen, was knocked down by the debris.

We moved forward through the chaparral until the enemy fire became too heavy. I ordered my men to lie down, only to find they had anticipated my thinking and already done so. When the firing slackened, we started forward through the brush once more. A moment later we came upon a wounded Mexican colonel and two of his orderlies cowering in a small huddle.

My first prisoners! *"Brazos arriba!"* I exclaimed, hoping I'd told them to put their hands up. As they did so, I felt the stock of a rifle smack up against my head, sending me to the ground.

I rolled over, wondering if I was about to meet my maker at the hands of a Mexican bayonet, when I beheld a tall, sandy-haired soldier wearing a Tennessee volunteer's uniform.

"What the hell is your problem, brother?" he said.

"My problem?" I asked, wincing in discomfort as I rose to my feet. "Do you mind explaining yourself before I have you shot?"

"What the hell are you doing with my prisoners?" the soldier demanded.

"Your prisoners?" I responded, getting back to my feet. "These men were sitting here—"

"Waiting for me to take them back to the line, you jackass," the volunteer said, and with that he shouldered me aside, stood his quarry up, and started them marching ahead of him.

That was my introduction to hand-to-hand combat.

Hundreds of small skirmishes were taking place across the front until late afternoon, when, tiring of battle, the Mexicans took off for the Rio Grande. Scores of them drowned as they clambered to the other side.

Two battles, two victories: Taylor was making it look easy. He crossed the Rio Grande, forcing the Mexicans to abandon the town of Matamoros.

It was around this time I was made regimental quartermaster of the Fourth Infantry. Being quartermaster meant getting up before the men marched, packing the wagons and mules, poring over the Mexican countryside for supplies as we marched—foodstuffs, cloth, nails, livestock, bridles and horseshoes, medicines, and everything else an army needs—then getting to the next night's camp before the men, setting up their tents, inspecting the animals for sores and diseases as the men ate and went to sleep, and getting up the next morning to do the same thing all over again. It was a job I had no desire to do.

"Why me?" I pleaded with an impassive Buchanan. "I want to fight with my men. I came here to do battle, not manage mule teams."

"Oh, let it be, Grant," Buchanan said, enjoying my discomfort. "You're a well-organized fellow—you were always able to find a bottle of wine when you needed to," he said, and snickered. "And you'll be free of me. Besides, your chances of getting killed are a good sight lower as a quartermaster."

"With the captain's permission, I will appeal this decision," I said.

"Well, you can appeal all you want, but this was Taylor's idea. He wants somebody who can manage a mule train, and your reputation preceded you. Didn't you jump six feet on a horse back at West Point?"

"That was a horse, not a mule."

"There's a war on, Grant. The mule was promoted. You're the man for the job."

And so I became a quartermaster. Meanwhile, the Mexicans retreated two hundred miles to Monterrey, the largest city in the region. Taylor, reinforced substantially with volunteers after his first successes, gave chase.

Taylor now thought the Mexicans pushovers, even though they outnumbered him and were fighting from within a walled city. He attacked Monterrey, and after two days of vicious street-by-street fighting, he changed his mind. By the afternoon of the second day we were running out of ammunition, when a volunteer was sought to go back to the lines—through heavy Mexican fire—to give word of our situation and bring back bullets.

I was supposed to be behind the lines, managing the flow of matériel. But I promptly volunteered, earning the sympathy if not the admiration and respect of those around me. I grabbed a horse, and hung my left foot on the back of its saddle and my left arm around its neck as I used to do when trick-riding as a boy in Georgetown, putting his bulk between me and the Mexicans as I raced through their lines.

My heroism was admired by all. Only later did it occur to me all the Mexicans needed to do was shoot the horse and I would soon follow.

By the time I returned to our position, the Mexicans had fallen back to the city's central square, only one block away, and Arista sent a message to Taylor proposing to surrender the city if he would allow them to march out under a flag of truce.

Taylor, who was outnumbered, outgunned, losing men rapidly, and just as trapped as was Arista, promptly accepted. He had won yet again.

A last note on the Monterrey campaign. When I was made quartermaster at Matamoros, I encountered a crooked Mexican teamster who claimed to have something to sell me. It was a map of the entire nation, one so rich in topographical detail and up to date in terms of roads and conditions it could only have been purloined from the Mexican military command.

The map was a valuable asset: We had invaded Mexico with not much more than a compass and knew little of the place. Taylor told me to hold it for safekeeping and maintain some circumspection about its existence, lest something untoward happen to it.

And so I traveled with it, and was in my tent one evening when there was a knock on one of the tent posts. A man six feet in height in a captain's uniform entered, about forty years of age, with sad but intense dark eyes, dark wavy hair, and great bearing and dignity.

We exchanged salutes and I asked the gentleman his business.

"Lieutenant Grant," he said. "I understand you have a map."

I looked up from my cot. "A quartermaster has many things, Captain—excuse me, but I did not get your name."

He smiled modestly, took off his right glove, and extended his hand. "Lee," he said. "Robert E. Lee. Corps of Engineers."

It is hard to imagine our second and more famous handshake was less than twenty years away, not a long time in the course of a life. But at that moment I was taken with meeting the best student ever to attend West Point.

"Sam Grant," I said, rising from my blanket to shake his hand. "The map is in this trunk, Captain." I fetched it and placed it on a small table in my tent. He leaned over and concentrated on it with an efficiency and focus I had never seen in another, as if he were memorizing every feature. He spent several moments lost in this pose and then looked up at me.

"Thank you, Lieutenant. I will be back to survey it again, I am sure." He put his glove back on and saluted me, then strode out as quickly and purposely as he strode in.

CHAPTER IV

TAYLOR AND SCOTT—CHRISTMAS 1846—LEE AT CERRO GORDO—SCOTT'S DARING GAMBLE— CONQUEST OF MEXICO—AN ENCOUNTER WITH THE MASTER

AFTER MONTERREY FELL, I got my first real education in the ways of war's most brutal and uncivilized combatants—politicians.

President Polk had originally seen Taylor as the solution to his problem—now he saw him as the problem. The American public, meanwhile, now saw Taylor as Polk had originally tried to cast him: an unwilling warrior marching peacefully about Texas, minding his own business, when he was attacked—ambushed!—by the Mexicans, whom he promptly whipped at Palo Alto, Resaca, and now Monterrey.

Polk, who didn't care that Taylor was lucky to be sitting inside Monterrey, as opposed to buried outside it, was furious Taylor had allowed a truce. He demanded Taylor break it.

"I'll end the truce when I'm damned good and ready," Taylor announced to all of us when he received Polk's orders.

Polk directed Taylor to push forward to Saltillo, the next city to the south.

"I'm not going to Saltillo or any other damned place," Taylor crowed for our benefit when Polk's command was forwarded to him.

If Taylor was determined to stay at Monterrey, then Polk instructed him to cede several thousand of his men to reinforce a naval campaign against the port of Tampico.

"The last thing I'm going to do is give up men to take a worthless hellhole like Tampico," Taylor announced when he read Polk's letter. He was content with the way things were going. He was now being hailed as the next Andy Jackson at the expense of Polk, who thought *he* was supposed to be the next Andy Jackson. The newspapers began to promote Taylor as Presidential material scant weeks after Palo Alto and Resaca, and Taylor began to hear the siren's song of a political career as the champion of a war-weary nation. Taylor, in short, was getting too big for Polk's britches. So, having no other option, Polk turned to the only other man who could win the war for him: Winfield Scott.

Scott—"Old Fuss and Feathers," he was called, in contrast to Taylor, who was called "Old Rough and Ready"—was a hero of both the War of 1812 and the Seminole War. He was the nation's senior general when the war began, but he was a Whig, not a Democrat, and Polk was then in no mood to boost Scott's political career. But Polk had already boosted Taylor's political career, to the point where Polk's concerns about Scott's political career were no longer foremost. When asked, Scott proposed an outlandish strategy—to invade Mexico from the sea, as Cortés had centuries ago, landing on the Gulf Coast near Veracruz and proceeding through the mountainous jungle to Mexico City. All thought him mad, but with Scott prepared to take the blame if his campaign failed, Polk gave him the command.

Now an experienced quartermaster, I was ordered to join Scott. Before I left, I hired a valet, a common practice among young officers.

"Hey, *mira, soldado.*"

I turned to see a young Mexican fellow, about twenty, with a sharp look and a broad smile. "You need man, yes?"

"A man?" I asked, backing off a step.

The young man laughed. "No, no, *valet,*" he said. "Me help you good. Yes?"

At first I demurred, but the young fellow made his case. "*Yo te veo*—you *bueno hombre, no como los otros,*" he said. "*Los otros* bad to the *Mexicanos,* but no you. You pay Mexicans good. I work you."

I knew what he meant. It was true. Just as I was never among those who bullied the more visible members of the incoming class at West Point, I saw no point in taking advantage of the Mexicans, and always gave them a fairer shake than the other quartermasters did. But still, I regarded the boy warily. What did this fellow know about being a valet? "What do you know about horses?" I asked.

"The horses? *Yo sabe* the horses real good. An' I keep you uniform an' boots clean, okay?" He sidled up to me and said confidentially, "My cousin, he valet for Scott, *el jefe,*" he assured. "I know *todos,* you see, *verdad.*" He smiled and tapped his head with a knowing finger. "You stick *Gregorio,*" he said with a wink, "and *Gregorio,* he stick you!"

I was skeptical of both his services and his syntax, but he offered to work for a pittance, and my quartermaster's duties were enormously time-consuming, so I hired him. Meanwhile, while I was behind the lines making sure they ate well, my former West Point compatriots were acting heroically at the front. Thomas, he of the George Washington countenance, was awarded a medal and a promotion for aiming an artillery piece into a crowd of Mexicans during Monterrey. Don Buell actually liked war and did well at it. And after having wasted a few years hoping to kill Indians, Fred Dent showed up and shifted his hopes to the Mexicans. He brought with him news of other West Point colleagues. Sherman and Halleck had been dispatched to the San Francisco Bay area, where Halleck was growing more pompous and Sherman more erratic with each passing day, Fred said. My shy friend Buckner had been sent to the New Mexico territories. McClellan, the clever lad, was graduated to the engineering unit at Matamoros, where he would serve under Bobby Lee. McClellan's classmate Tom—soon to be "Stonewall"—Jackson was eventually heard from as well.

"Un hombre loco arriva!" Gregorio said quite excitedly as he ran into my tent one day. It was Jackson, who had survived his dyspepsia and been assigned to the artillery. To the amazement of all, he had dragged a siege gun behind him all the way to Monterrey from Matamoros, normally a two-man job—and neither of them would be officers. But he delivered his cargo and walked away, satisfied he had not wasted the trip.

We spent the Christmas of 1846 in Tampico, on the Gulf Coast, as Scott planned his invasion. Lee—whose reputation as the army's most promising young officer was by then well established—had arrived to help Scott organize his expedition and was the toast of the camp. He had stopped at Mount Vernon on his way to Mexico and took from there the cutlery used by his grandma's husband, George Washington, during the Revolutionary War. If Lee was not the object of universal admiration among the social circle at Tampico, his silverware certainly was. If George Washington were in my family, I might have stored his silverware somewhere for safekeeping. But Bobby Lee imagined that if it was good enough for George to carry into battle, then it was good enough for him, too.

I, of course, continued as quartermaster and ate from tin plates and cups, living a life apart from both officers and common soldiers. And for a quartermaster, Christmas was just another set of specifications to be met—instead of bullets and blankets, they wanted turkeys and brandy.

So I spent Christmas Day delivering them. Lee, Joe Johnston, and the other members of Scott's staff were having a private dinner for the senior officers and those *señoritas* whose charms merited them an invitation. By suppertime I had just about everything where it was supposed to go. My last item was a keg of port wine I was able to contrive for the senior officers' dinner, a suitable last stop for a long day. I knocked on the front door of the old hacienda that served as the officers' headquarters to deliver the keg in person.

The door opened and there was Lee, his wavy hair neatly brushed and his dark eyes shining majestically. "Yes?" he asked.

I juggled the keg to my other arm. "Lieutenant Grant, Captain," I announced, raising my right hand in salute. Lee gave no reaction. I leaned forward and whispered, "The fellow with the map?"

"Oh, yes, of course," Lee said indifferently, and returned my salute, allowing me to drop my arm. "Is there a problem?" he asked.

"As divisional quartermaster, sir, I have obtained this keg of port," I said, with a feeling of accomplishment. "I brought it by for your guests' enjoyment, sir." I smiled.

Lee looked at the keg and then at me and smiled broadly. "Why, so you have!" he exclaimed with newfound enthusiasm. "Everyone!" he said over his shoulder to the other dinner guests. "The quartermaster has produced a keg of port for our enjoyment!" A pleased murmur bubbled out of the dining room.

I smiled at this appreciative noise. "Very well, then," I said as I started through the doorway. "It'll be no trouble to bring this inside and uncork it—"

Lee quickly put a hand against my chest. "Excuse me," he said in a hushed tone, "but aren't we making a mistake?" Lee saw my confused look. "Lieutenant," he whispered confidingly, *"you're not in proper dress uniform!"*

I looked down and smiled sheepishly. "Oh, yes! Heavens! Well, I've been making deliveries, and it *is* Christmas and all, so I thought I might just—"

Lee looked at me as if I were a child who didn't get his meaning. "Lieutenant, there are senior officers in that room! Colonel Johnston! Major Beauregard!" he said sternly, referring to two of his future fellow Confederate traitors. "And women! *Women*," he exclaimed, pointing behind himself, "*in that very room!*" I nodded dumbly, not yet fully comprehending his point. "Surely you don't wish to deliver your wares to a party of *women* while your uniform is not properly creased and you're missing your tie, do you?"

"Of course not, Captain Lee," I fumbled. "But I thought, it being Christmas, it's not like we were back at West Point getting demerits—"

No sooner had I said it than I wished I could have sucked the words back and swallowed them. Lee's face turned into a stony mask of contempt. "There is nothing amusing," he intoned in a funereal cadence, "about getting bad conduct marks."

"Nothing, sir!" I repeated as I saluted.

"Nothing at all," Lee added testily, and took the keg from my arm. "The lieutenant is dismissed!" he said curtly, saluted, and slammed the door in my face. I stood there for a moment, listening to the cries of excitement the keg induced, before I walked away.

In February 1847, Scott packed our entire expedition onto boats and left Tampico. His plan was simple: Storm the coastal city of Veracruz and proceed up the National Road from the coastal plain into the mountains, through the cities of Jalapa and Puebla, into the central Mexican highlands, and take the capital, Mexico City. The fact we had but ten thousand men to seize the capital of a nation of fifteen million people did not dissuade Scott in the least.

Scott's confidence rested on two observations. The first was that he had the finest military mind of his day. He knew this because he had the finest military mind of his day and was therefore capable of perceiving it was so. The second and perhaps even more compelling reason was that Hernando Cortés conquered Mexico in 1519 using the same route, same road, and same strategy. Cortés landed in Veracruz, burned his boats to convince his men they would have to conquer or die, and then marched them to Mexico City—the Halls of Montezuma—where the ancient Aztec chieftain was commanded to fill his chamber with gold up to Cortés's mark on the wall. The great conquistador's triumph convinced Scott it could be done, if the commander was up to it. Fortunately, Scott had the finest military mind of his day and could see that he was.

Scott landed at Veracruz, offered the city the option of an immediate surrender, and then proceeded with his bombardment. Veracruz was pounded as few places have ever been, a shell every twenty seconds. The big guns would roar, their projectiles would go whistling through the air, the distant impact would shake the ground as far away as where we stood, and there would be a moment's pause followed by the distant sounds of grievous wailing, just in time for the next volley.

"Here's another, *amigos*," the artillery officer mumbled as he touched the fuse with a lit cigar. His name was Braxton Bragg, and he was the most argumentative man in the army. He listened to the sequence of sounds, culminating in more anguished cries, and shrugged. "Sounds good," he said to the rest of us, by way of small talk.

"We might shift the next gun about two degrees left and see what we hit," Lee suggested helpfully. "I think an imperfection in the barrel is imparting an uneven spin to the shells and they are veering off to the right."

Bragg gave him the coldest look I'd ever seen. "Leave the firing to the artillery," he snapped.

"It was merely a suggestion," Lee said, trying to soothe him.

"That's exactly how I took it," Bragg responded curtly, hoping he might be able to precipitate an argument and kill some time. He looked at his watch—twenty seconds had elapsed. "Fire," he said. There was a roar, a whistle, a mighty explosion, and after a second the sound of grievous wailing once again. Bragg smirked. "Sounds like we're still on target," he said, and admired the afternoon sky, then checked his watch again. "Ready number four," he said. He struck a match to relight his cigar, then handed it to his gunnery sergeant for the fuse.

The bombardment continued for the better part of a week. On the twenty-eighth of March, the Mexicans agreed to Scott's terms—leave the city, abandon its garrison and its artillery and matériel, and the four thousand soldiers there would be paroled with their sidearms and horses. This meant they promised to go home and depart the war: If they were ever caught breaking that promise, they could be summarily executed.

Scott did so because he had no time for prisoners—it was April and the *vomito* season, yellow fever. We had to get off the seacoast and onto the National Road to Mexico City, up into the highlands, quickly.

At the head of the column was one of Scott's commanders, General Twiggs. Twiggs was a popular showman—profane, likable, and not too smart. When his scouting parties came back and told him Santa Anna, the Mexican commander, had choked off the road ahead with artillery and a goodly number of men, he was up to the challenge. "Very well, then, we're going to attack the sons of bitches and run 'em off the goddamned road!" He would have tried, had Scott not arrived on the scene.

"Where is the Mexican artillery?" he asked of Twiggs.

"Up ahead a piece," Twiggs replied, all business.

Scott sighed. "Well, I don't suppose they're behind us, General. How *far* up ahead did your advance party find them?"

"Two miles, maybe three. At a place called Cerro Gordo."

"And how were they deployed?"

"The advance guard? I simply sent 'em up. A cavalry unit."

"I mean the Mexicans," Scott said.

"Ah, yes, the Mexicans! They were on a series of peaks through which the road runs."

"Firing down on us?"

"Exactly!" Twiggs confirmed, pleased he had conveyed his point.

Thus, Twiggs had proposed sending his division, numbering about twenty-five hundred, against an elevated, entrenched position occupied by twelve thousand enemy with artillery. Scott knew a bad situation when he heard it. He instantly prepared an alternative plan.

"Go find Captain Lee," he ordered.

I was resting in my tent that evening, listening to Gregorio recite these events, which he had learned from his cousin, when there was a polite knock on my tent post.

It was Lee.

"Lieutenant," he said, saluting perfunctorily as he entered. He avoided pleasantries. "Your map, if I may." I opened a chest and retrieved it for him. He spread out the map on top of a low table, took my lamp from its nail on a post, and set it next to it. He studied the map in the lamplight, nodding and, if I was not mistaken, smiling slightly. After a minute he folded the map and returned it to me. "Thank you, Lieutenant," he said, saluting once again and departing as quickly as he had entered.

His behavior was a mystery until I heard—again, from Gregorio— that Scott had sent Lee to scout the dense wilderness on our right, searching for a way past the Mexican chokehold. Lee left camp the next morning to a chorus of enthusiasm among the officers that dampened considerably as the hours went by and day turned into evening and he had not yet returned. I wandered over to the campfire by Scott's tent, where the officers had grown increasingly pessimistic as midnight approached.

"I fear," Twiggs finally said, "we may have lost him."

A hushed despair came over the group.

"He was the soul of gallantry," Scott said, breaking the morose silence.

"That he was," Johnston agreed.

"The soul of gallantry," Scott said, "and the epitome of the military character."

"The very same," echoed Beauregard, a slight fellow from Louisiana with a long mustache.

"The epitome of military character and the paragon of battlefield virtue," Scott added, nodding with solemn respect for his own words.

"An engineer's engineer," said Johnston.

I was moved to participate in this spontaneous eulogizing. "And not a single bad conduct mark in four years," I said. He would have liked that, I thought.

"An engineer's engineer and a man's man," Scott added to Johnston's appraisal, ignoring my contribution. There was another heavy silence as we gazed into the campfire, when there suddenly came a rustling from the brush: We looked up to see our fallen hero stumble out into the light of the campfire, bedraggled and slumped with fatigue, his uniform ripped to tatters, and scrapes and scratches all over him.

"Captain Lee, sir," Lee said, saluting Scott with a looping, limp, exhausted swing of the arm, whereupon he fell to the ground like a marionette whose strings have been cut, and lay there without movement, facedown in the dirt.

We all sprang from our places and rolled Lee over onto his back. We were appalled to see his face, a grotesque mass of red, hivelike swellings.

"My word, Lee," Beauregard said, wetting his handkerchief and cleaning Lee's swollen face. "What on earth happened to you?"

"Insects," Lee whispered as he began to revive.

"My land!" Scott gasped. "Were you attacked by an entire swarm?"

"No," Lee whispered after he had sipped from a canteen Johnston put to his lips. "There could have been no more than three or four."

"Three or four!" Scott drew back. "How could three or four insects do such harm?"

"I could not brush them away! I could not move so much as a muscle for fear of my life," Lee panted between sips.

A collective gasp came from all of us. "How did such a thing happen?" Scott asked.

Lee turned toward Scott, his strength returning. "I was scouting a trail at about midday when I came upon a glade with a small pond fed by a spring. I'd not had a drink all morning, so I went to the edge. No sooner had my lips touched the water than I heard footsteps and laughter coming up the path ahead of me.

"I dove behind a log on the north side of the glade—the soil was loose and deep, which allowed me to slither and burrow in a bit. No sooner had I ducked down than a Mexican patrol of four or five men came upon the scene, plunged their heads into the pool, and then sat down on the very log behind which I lay."

"And they did not see you?" Twiggs asked.

"Had they, they'd have run me in like so!" Lee said grimly as he drew a finger across his neck. "But instead, they proceeded to have their lunches, which were mostly beans, I surmised, because their flatulence was almost as lethal as their bayonets would have been."

The thought of lying pinned beneath a battery of farting Mexican soldiers made every man shudder.

"And how long were you compelled to so endure?" Scott inquired.

"How long did I lay there, or how long were they breaking wind?" Lee asked methodically.

"How long did you lay there?" Scott clarified.

"Six hours," Lee answered, his austere voice never changing tone. "Six hours during which the insects feasted on me, during which I could not drink, or scratch, or pass water, or so much as twitch, lest a Mexican dagger do me in as I lay there."

"My most noble captain!" Scott leaned forward. "Your undaunted courage and unqualified determination will forever be an inspiration to each man you see before you! But your mission, Captain—is there a passage around the enemy on our right?"

All eyes turned toward Lee, whereupon he looked up and smiled. "Yes, General, there is. And when we avail ourselves of it, victory shall surely be ours!"

Scott fell to a knee and bowed his head. "Praise God!" he exclaimed. "Who hath delivered our comrade, Captain Lee, safely back to us and provided us with the means to vanquish our foe through the goodness of Almighty Providence." The entire campfire assemblage joined our commander in kneeling before our Maker and Savior. "Let us offer, therefore, a prayer of thanksgiving and supplication," Scott said, whereupon each of us bowed his uncovered head and looked down, failing to notice that Scott had risen to his feet. "General Twiggs, lead the men in such a prayer," he said, saluting Twiggs and walking off to his tent before Twiggs could return the salute or begin his invocation.

Scott now knew all he needed to know. He ordered the artillery units to break down their twenty-four-pound guns and sent his best units to haul the pieces through the wilderness and to reassemble them behind the Mexican fortifications. It was an order so outlandish I am sure Scott would have questioned it had he not given it. Amazingly, it worked. Several thousand men crept through the wilderness the next day, bearing the parts of an artillery division, dragging the wheels and heavy barrels on ropes up hillsides and down ravines, only to reemerge five miles ahead and reassemble them, whereupon they caught the Mexicans in a crossfire so surprising and devastating it took only a day's fighting to send those who were not taken prisoner running for their lives. I watched the engagement from a hillside with George McClellan—as an engineer, he had a better pair of binoculars.

Santa Anna himself fled Cerro Gordo in such a hurry that he left behind his luggage, including his best artificial leg, his real leg having been long ago severed at the knee. Its replacement was captured by Illinois regulars and was on display in Chicago for years afterward.

The town in our path after Cerro Gordo was Jalapa. Scott left a garrison there to maintain our supply line to Veracruz and the sea, and then pressed on to Puebla, the last town of consequence before the final march into the Mexican Central Valley and Mexico City. We now had but seven thousand men and had to await a new crop of volunteers. These arrived in August, led by General Franklin Pierce, a tall fellow with a resolute expression and a yen for the grape, which the expression concealed smartly enough to allow him in 1852 to defeat Scott for the Presidency.

As these new troops marched into Puebla, there was a mighty shout. Our strength would be up to fourteen thousand, a number greater than the force that reduced Veracruz and beat Santa Anna back at Cerro Gordo. Our confidence grew as each new brigade marched into the town square. But at the end of the procession we saw something so shocking that the cries that greeted the new recruits stopped in our throats and gave way to the most stunned of silences.

The men from the Jalapa garrison were following the new men into Puebla.

Scott had abandoned the garrison and cut his supply line to our base at Veracruz.

He had decided to either capture Mexico City—or die!

"*Mira, Grant,*" Gregorio whispered to me nervously, "this ain't *muy bueno!*"

Scott had decided that maintaining a supply line was too slow and cost too many men. Apparently he had never heard Henry Halleck on the subject. Just as Cortés had burned his boats on the beaches of Veracruz in 1519, Scott would cut his ties to his base of operations and forage off the land. Every man would be put to good use, and if that was not enough, then we would perish in the attempt.

By the end of August, Scott came up under Mexico City, outnumbered and low on supplies, but prepared to see a resolution.

We struggled through a series of hostilities with the Mexicans until we arrived at the castle of Chapultepec, the last fortification before the city gates proper. It was a massive stone castle atop a hill, able to withstand shelling with admirable durability. Thus, before the day was out, the order was given to charge and storm the castle itself.

The men froze in their tracks, so fierce was the firing coming down from the castle's walls. Then, suddenly, alone among the officers, Tom "Stonewall" Jackson came to the center of the battlefield—the same mad farm boy who ate lemons with his arm in the air and had dragged a siege gun from Matamoros to Monterrey. He quickly sprinted out in front of the line of attack and turned to the men who were stalled in terror behind him, with his arms stretched wide, his rifle held high.

"See?" he shouted back to them. "I'm not hit! They can't hit beans!" he cried, and then waved his arms and ran forward so commandingly his line took up the charge and followed him—partly out of conviction and patriotism, and partly to see what the madman would do next. I've since concluded the only reason he wasn't hit was that the Mexican soldiers on the castle's parapet were too amused and astonished to kill him.

The second hero that day was Joe Hooker, later to be one of the seven generals-in-chief of the Union cause Lincoln dismissed before he appointed me and resolved the matter. Hooker led a squadron of men bearing the first of fifty ladders to the castle's walls, thrust the base against the fort himself, and scaled it, fighting his way onto the parapet and killing a good number of Mexicans before the second man arrived.

It now remained to enter the city.

The gates to the city proper, of course, were heavily defended, with field artillery pointed directly into the ranks of our oncoming infantry. No amount of maneuvering or frontal assault could reduce it.

I searched the flanks for a better avenue of attack and noticed a steeple rising above a church not far from the city's wall. I ordered a nearby sergeant and half a dozen of his men to help me. We broke a small field howitzer down into pieces and carried them to the door of the church.

"*Permitte entrar*," I shouted, pounding on the door.

"*No es possible*," said a voice from the inside.

"*Debemos entrar* or *debemos destruir su casa*," I responded. One learned *destruir*—"to destroy"—quickly in this engagement.

I had used the word for "house" instead of "church," but *destruir* carried a good deal of weight. The priest began to see his duty in the same light that I did and opened the door, although he did not look as if it gave him special pleasure to do so. The gun was carried to the belfry and put together. We were not more than two or three hundred yards from the San Cosme gate. The shots from our little gun dropped in among the enemy and caused great consternation. Why they did not send out a small party to capture us, I do not know.

The effect of this gun upon the troops about the gate was so marked that one of Scott's generals saw it and sent a staff officer—Lieutenant Pemberton—to bring me to him. The general expressed his gratification at the services the howitzer in the steeple was providing and ordered a captain to report to me with another howitzer to be placed along with the one already so engaged. I could not tell the general that there was not room enough in the steeple for another gun for fear of contradicting him, and returned to my installation atop the church, where we continued to fire down upon the gate until the enemy fled and it was undefended.

We camped inside the city gate that night, and the next morning raced into the center of the city to receive its capitulation. It was noon when Scott arrived, impeccably dressed in his most regal uniform, and entered the city's palace. He wrote out a declaration giving thanks to God and began the military administration of the city. His campaign was won. He had landed his men thousands of miles away from home, reduced the most fortified city in the hemisphere with hardly a casualty, marched 260 miles inland with an outmanned army, snuck thousands of men through the woods to rout an enemy many times their number, cut himself loose from the outside world, defeated an overwhelmingly stronger force fighting from defended structures, and took the capital city in the space of six months. Scott had won the greatest gamble in warfare since Cortés three hundred years before.

A full year intervened between the day we marched into Mexico City and the arrival of orders to depart for the Gulf coast. I spent that year in Jalapa, procuring supplies for the several thousand men who waited, as I did, to go home. Gregorio proved himself immensely useful. As many as a thousand Mexicans—most, like Gregorio, were Indians—were involved in my operations, baking bread, sewing uniforms, weaving blankets, making implements, and growing vegetables.

Some men determined to stay in Mexico and take brides from among the many beautiful girls, with their engaging smiles and disengaged breasts. Others were offered substantial sums of money by Mexico's aristocrats to stay and manage their holdings. But to my thinking, no amount of money would justify perpetuating a system so iniquitous and unfair as that forced upon the Mexican masses. And, of course, no number of raven-tressed beauties could keep me from my rendezvous with Julia and our eagerly awaited postnuptial conjugation.

I would miss these people, though—Gregorio and the other Indians with whom I did daily business. I hoped the industry I brought to them would give them some lasting betterment.

Our departure imminent, I broke the news to Gregorio. "*Nos returnaramos a los Estados Unidos esta semana. Debo a salir.*" I told him as best I could that I appreciated his friendship and his gracious treatment of a *conquistador*.

He nodded again and then addressed me solemnly. "*Mira, Grant.* You *bueno* to Indian people. We want make *una fiesta para usted*. Can you come *anoche*?"

A party for me? I was flattered to be asked and accepted with pleasure. Gregorio told me to meet him in the village square at eight that evening.

When I returned at the appointed hour, I was struck by how different it looked in the moonlight, serene and almost mythical, with shadows cast across the face of the empty plaza by austere, forbidding structures that had stood long before the coming of Cortés. I stood there alone for a moment before suddenly becoming aware I was being watched. I turned and saw Gregorio and three other men, one of them older and two, like me, in their twenties. I approached them and extended my hand, which they took in a friendly, if formal, manner. Gregorio himself looked different to me, larger and more filled out, with a more focused expression and a stronger and steadier aspect to his carriage.

"*Hola, Grant,*" he said. "*Grant*, these are *mis amigos, Nestor y Jorge. Y esto es Don Carlos*. He great man, Grant," he said to me in a confidential way, and then turned to his companions. "*Don Carlos, compañeros, esto es el Capitan Grant, un gringo bueno qui comprar las ropas y las comidas hacedo aqui. Que piensen?*" He looked back at me and smiled awkwardly as I tried to make out what he said.

Don Carlos—I noted he had the same name as my classmate Buell—and the other two regarded me, and it seemed they all came to a beneficent conclusion. "*Lo creo,*" the one called Don Carlos said, and turned to me. "Hello, Grant," he said, with a broad smile that revealed half the expected number of teeth.

I was smiling back when Gregorio spoke once again. "Grant, you ready walk?"

I nodded, and with that Don Carlos got the proceedings under way. "*Pues, vamos.*"

Gregorio led us down a cobblestone street out of the square, and after what seemed like only a few moments, we were on a dirt path leading up into the dense foliage of the mountains, the same kind of terrain through which Lee scouted the trail that undid Santa Anna at Cerro Gordo. With every turn, my eyes became more accustomed to the starry, moonlit light, and the scenery, all of it bathed in silver, more eerily beautiful.

We followed the path for two hours as it rose higher and higher into the mountains. I expected to get tired, but the beautiful and mysterious views kept refreshing me. The Indians moved along at a pretty good pace, walking with long, strong steps, particularly the old man, who kept up effortlessly.

We had gone six or seven miles by my estimation when Gregorio suddenly headed off the path and whispered to me, "*Estamos aqui.*" We are here, I repeated to myself. It was a small clearing in the jungle, a circle perhaps twenty or twenty-five feet in diameter, with some large stones set around an often-used campfire. A dry bonfire was already set up, wood stacked and latticed into a very competent-looking box structure. The young Mexicans waited for Don Carlos to sit down on one of the large stones and then beckoned me to sit next to him. "*Hace el fuego,*" Don Carlos said to either Jorge or Nestor—I now forgot which was which—who took out a parcel of matches and lit the kindling. It went off like a torch, a strong, steady fire that cast a golden glow upon all of us.

"*Debemos a comer,*" Don Carlos then said—we need to eat—and the young Mexicans all nodded. I was getting a little hungry myself, and I watched as Jorge opened up a folded bandanna to reveal strips of salted meat, perhaps goat. This was passed around and we all took a piece. It was surprisingly chewy and fresh. It was quickly followed by a wineskin containing spring water, still cool despite the length of our trip.

I looked about, filled with quiet satisfaction. Don Carlos nodded to Gregorio, who reached into Jorge's sack and extracted another folded pouch. Gregorio opened it slowly, almost reverently. When he laid it on the ground, I could see it contained pieces, or lumps, of something that might have been a vegetable, or bark, or something else plantlike. Gregorio turned on his heels to face me.

"*Escuchame, Grant,*" he said pointedly. "Now we go Mescalito, yes?"

I nodded. "Who is Mescalito?" I asked.

"*Mescalito es un gran brujo, el rey de los brujos—*"

I wasn't as quick as that: It sounded as if he had said something about the king of the *brujos*. "*Un brujo? Que es un brujo?*"

"*Que es el brujo?*" He looked over at his colleagues and they laughed as one. He sighed. "*El brujo es*—how you say?—*el brujo hace la magia.* The ma-*jeek. Es un conjerador.*"

The magic? A conjurer? I nodded but still did not get the whole picture. "Will we be going now to see him? *Vamos a Mescalito ahora?*"

They all laughed again, this time even more uproariously. "*No, Grant,*" Don Carlos spoke up from his seat next to me, his smile dotted by his few teeth. "*Mescalito va aqui,*" he explained pleasantly, and took up the sliced vegetable on the unfolded bandanna to offer me a piece.

"*Que es?*" I asked.

"*Es una seta,*" Gregorio replied. *Seta*—a mushroom, I remembered: I had bought these for our mess on special occasions. "Is called *el peyote.* Eat *el peyote,* and Mescalito, he comes."

Peyote—the word sounded like *coyote,* I thought. It didn't make sense, but the only way to find out was to proceed. The slice of *peyote* had a terrible, bitter taste. I gagged and was about to spit it out when the Mexicans all lurched forward, hands in front of them, as if I were making a terrible mistake. I recovered and managed to get it down in the interest of courtesy. They encouraged me to take another bite. I did so, and once I was well into chewing it, each of them reached for a piece. It struck me this *peyote* was an acquired taste.

In a moment, we were done eating our *peyote,* and I looked at the others, wondering when this Mescalito fellow would make an appearance. But the others now seemed as if they were not interested in me or, for that matter, each other. Each sat quietly, looking straight ahead. I looked ahead, too, as if taking their cue, and noticed the fire. I watched the branches and logs burning in the fire glow a vivid red until a gray patina of ash covered them. I felt as if I could see the entire process of burning in an entirely new way, instant by instant, as if the fire were somehow burning more slowly, allowing me to understand fire with a thoroughness I had never experienced before.

I turned to my Mexican hosts to comment on this. They were sitting just as quietly as before, but now I was taken aback to see that *they* were glowing as well. A deep, resonant, purple hue emanated from them—not like a log aflame, more like a piece of glowing charcoal. *The bush burned, but was not consumed*, my mother used to read from the Book of Exodus. They seemed to exist within the purple glow; in fact, their bodies were indistinguishable from the purple glow—they *were* the glow. I then realized what I was seeing: It was their life force, the very energy that made them human. They were glowing because they were alive: I suddenly understood that to live was to glow.

But if they had this glow—if being alive meant a resonant purple combustion went on within you—then I, being human, must have it as well. I looked down at my hands, and there it was—a deep purple luminescence from the very core of my body—hands, arms, torso, all of me! My flesh was not flesh, but a weaving of strands of light into a fabric of flesh, a sea of fibers of being, each alive in its own right, with the glowing purple force of life flowing through each of the strands.

I felt a newfound calm as I suddenly experienced myself as a fibrous, purple, glowing entity woven together out of strands of life. I was overcome with joy, laughing for having been so blind to this reality all my life. I glanced at the Mexicans, at the trees and foliage around me, and was now aware that everything glowed softly in the night and everything was seamlessly interwoven—myself, the Mexicans, the trees, the foliage, the very night itself.

As I marveled at the reality of nature, I suddenly became aware of the night sky above me. It was a stunning, ravishing shade of the darkest blue, and I could see through it to the very blackness of the universe behind it. The moon was past overhead and headed west. It was full and silver-white, as round as if it had been trimmed on a jeweler's wheel. Its bright shine bounced off the contours of the clouds in the night sky.

The clouds themselves were brilliant and stark: I watched them as they swirled in the air. Though I could feel no wind, they were churning with a rapid urgency, threading and rethreading themselves until they began to take shape, miles above us. I watched them evolve, grow, and descend with complete fascination, until I realized that what I was seeing was not clouds at all. The clouds had become a mighty white horse, made of clouds but a horse nonetheless, the most exciting horse I had ever seen. I looked up with rapture at this horse descending from the sky, wondering what it would be like to ride, wondering how it could be broken. As it descended, I realized the horse had a majestic and magnificent rider dressed in flowing white robes, over them a serape of vibrant, vivid colors: blue, sapphire, aquamarine, cyan, cerullian, purple, indigo, azure, dark turquoise, teal, emerald, forest green—all the colors of living things in their luminous state.

I could now see the rider clearly. He had an honorable, handsome, eternal face, like that of the noblest Aztec encountered by Cortés, and his flesh, like all flesh, was a sea of fibrous sinews, except his glowed not a blue like men, but a warm, brilliant crimson, the color of a god. His eyes were not eyes, but two golden, blazing suns, their presence felt by everything on which he gazed. He had long white hair and atop his head sat a silver crown made of moonlight itself. He continued to descend on his magnificent white horse until he was hovering above us. He was so close that if I wanted to I could have reached out and touched him, yet he was so high above us that one leap of the horse's mighty haunches would have propelled him to the deepest recesses of the universe.

This was Mescalito! The realization filled me with elation and comfort, as if something for which I was intended—the missing piece of a puzzle—had finally been delivered to me. I laughed when I realized how silly it had been to ask whether we would go to him or he come to us. He pulled back on his reins and the mighty white stallion reared up in the sky, the most beautiful thing I had ever seen or could ever hope to see. And then I realized *Mescalito was looking at me!*

My laughter stopped and my bliss was displaced by total attentiveness, my mind cleared of thought, *open* in a way it had never been before. And then I could hear the Master's voice.

"*Grantito,*" Mescalito said.

"Yes, Master," I replied, without hesitation.

"*I have come to deliver to you a prophecy.*"

I could not tell if he was speaking in English or Spanish, nor did it matter. I was suddenly overwhelmed by a feeling of smallness and vulnerability. I wanted to soil myself as I cowered before him. Who was I, a mere bundle of fibers, to hear the words of the Master, the mightiest presence of the universe?

His horse reared again and he spoke. *"Grantito, a magnificent destiny awaits. Ulysses Grant will lead great masses of men in the glorious cause of their human redemption. A great time of turmoil will come, and out of the suffering will come Ulysses Grant, who will become the champion of those who seek deliverance."*

His words filled me with awe. How could that be true? I was a simple quartermaster; it was men like Lee and Hooker and Thomas who were already being propelled forward by the events of war to lead great masses of men. Before I could protest, his horse reared again and raced off, galloping up into the sky with strides measured in miles. In only an instant Mescalito's cape became the night sky, his horse and robes the clouds, his silver crown the moonlight, and he was gone.

As I looked up into the sky, his voice lived within me. *I would lead great masses of men in the glorious cause of their human redemption. Ulysses Grant would become the champion of those who seek deliverance.* The enormity of his message left me thunderstruck. I was to lead great masses of men. I was to be the champion of human redemption. *Out of the suffering would come—*

But wait! *Out of the suffering would come Ulysses Grant.* But which one? Did Mescalito know who I was? Was he talking to me, the man once called Hiram, now known as Ulysses Grant? Or was it really Useful he was talking about?

I grew frantic as the question overwhelmed me. Who would lead the great masses of men? Me? Or Useful? And if the destiny Mescalito described was not mine but Useful's, then where was Useful and how would he achieve it? And what destiny was mine instead? How would I ever know?

I looked up, hoping I might summon Mescalito once again and beg him to make clear for whom it was this prophecy was intended. But there was now only a cloudless night sky above me.

I stared into the fire in the throes of panic and despair, when I realized I had not been alone. Gregorio! The Mexicans! They knew Mescalito, they had brought him to me! They must have witnessed his appearance, heard him speak.

I turned to regard Don Carlos, Gregorio, and the others. They were motionless, their dark eyes still staring straight ahead. How could they sit so passively in the face of this amazing spectacle? Had they missed the entire astonishing event? Was it intended by the great Master, Mescalito, for my eyes only? I was flummoxed, speechless, when Don Carlos slowly turned to me.

"*Lo veo*," he said softly. I saw it.

Then he shrugged his shoulders with serene indifference. "*Quien sabe?*"

Who knows?

And then I passed out.

CHAPTER V

MARRIED TO MRS. GRANT—CROSSING THE ISTHMUS—BUSINESS IN THE NORTHWEST—THE CALIFORNIA CAMELS—I RESIGN THE ARMY— DEPARTING SAN FRANCISCO

A YOUNG MAN writes his life in pencil, a middle-aged man in ink, an old man reads the pages, and a dying man rewrites them. I was a young man when I went off to war in Mexico and saw men killed in battle, when I first learned that war was a train of mules balking on a muddy road and men drinking and peeing before they fought for their lives. And I was still a young man when I returned, a lean and sinewy soldier with a reddish brown beard and a look of steely determination both for my woman and the life ahead, a young man who still wrote in pencil, who believed in his own immortality and did not yet realize every moment spent in life was purchased at the cost of the moment that might have been.

By the time the Civil War had begun, thirteen years later, I was the middle-aged man, writing in ink. But while I had aged, I had not ripened or mellowed. I had simply grown old, worn by each passing day in a way I had not imagined a man could be worn. And at every moment later in life when I was offered the cup of victory, I drank from it deeply to wash away the aftertaste of failure, of which I had drunk my share and more. And it was not until I sat in Vanderbilt's library, toward the end of my days, when I realized that all of my heroism could not wash away the failure underneath.

In 1848 I was twenty-six. It was nine years after I took Useful's life for my own, five years after I jumped York at West Point, and three years after I went back to White Haven to make Colonel Dent agree I could marry his daughter, so long as we would wait a year.

Well, he had his wish, three times over. Which is why, as soon as I could, I secured a leave and hastened back to White Haven.

"Well damn me! It's young Grant! The hero of the San Cosme gate!" the Colonel shouted from the porch. The doors to the house flew open and Mrs. Dent came running out, wiping her hands on her apron.

"Sam, God bless you! We're so glad to have you back, alive and well!"

I smiled modestly but heroically and was about to respond when Julia appeared at the door, and the look in her eyes allowed me to put aside my doubts as to how we would greet each other after a three-year absence. After a round of pleasantries, we saddled up our horses and headed off to the Gravois Creek, to the very spot where we first encountered each other.

"Ulys, there's something you need to know," she said quickly. "It's Daddy. He's—" And here she stopped, searching for the right word.

"Does he intend to renege on his pledge?" I demanded.

"Oh, no, Ulys!" she insisted. "And I would not let him, regardless. Had you been away any longer, I'd have come and shared your tent, and had the Mexicans taken you prisoner, I'd have come to share your cell!" She stopped and sighed unhappily. "Daddy is busted, Ulys. Broke. Some of his dealings have gone wrong."

"What manner of dealings do you mean?" I asked, confused. He had never seemed far from broke in the first place. How much could have changed?

"You know how Daddy likes to sue people. Particularly abolitionists, for attempting to foment slave revolts. Well, he's lost some of these suits and had to pay restitution," she said. "My brother Louis decided to shoot the fellow to whom Daddy owed the money, but when he showed up at the fellow's house, the fellow and his sons beat him senseless and the resulting doctor bills have been formidable. And then there's the cost of maintaining all of Daddy's slaves. He's good to them, Sam," she said defensively. "He feeds them herring and lets them have fruit—it all costs so very much, and they hardly do a lick of work."

If John Brown had only known.

Colonel Dent had fallen on hard times, all right, or perhaps hard times had risen to Colonel Dent. The arrogant untenability of his situation had finally come back to haunt him: his unprofitably transplanted

Southern style of life, without a plantation crop such as cotton to support it; his promiscuous litigiousness; and, most of all, his self-indulgent lethargy, as if his indifferent supervision of what wasn't going on around him was part of some plan to create and preserve wealth.

Julia fell into my arms. "I have nothing to offer, Ulys, in the way of a dowry. You would have every right to extricate yourself from your promise," she said, and began to sob.

"Now, now," I comforted. "I made my promise because I wanted to, and I still do."

She used the sleeve of her dress to dab her eye. "We can't have a big wedding at White Haven—Daddy can't afford it."

"I don't care," I said plainly. "Any place will do as long as we can be wed soon."

"Daddy has a small house in St. Louis where my sisters and I stayed when we were in boarding school. We could get married there," she said, brightening. "There couldn't be more than a handful of people. Just my family—brother Louis should be up and around by then—and one or two of Daddy's few remaining friends. And cousin Peter."

I winced when she mentioned Longstreet, but collected myself. "That will be fine," I assured her. "Let us set a date, and I will go back to Ohio and fetch my parents. They will be most happy to come."

"I'd sooner kiss a pig's ass!" my father spat, his face red with anger, when I presented him with my wedding plans several days later. Just as Colonel Dent was foundering, my father was prospering, expanding his business. My brother Simpson, second to me in age, was now the natural heir to his commercial empire. And Orvil, only thirteen, was now a third partner in the business, sitting with them now in the parlor, dressed just as they in a proper suit rather than the knickers he wore when I'd last seen him.

"But you must!" I insisted.

"Well! Ulysses—or is it Sam?—here thinks you ought to kiss a pig's ass, Father," Simpson said with a sarcastic laugh.

Orvil tittered.

"That's not what I meant!" I snapped, and turned back to my father. "I am in love with this girl and will marry her with or without you!"

"The daughter of a lazy, thieving, busted plantationer! From what I hear, the man is so stupid he can't point a nigger to cotton!" he shouted. "I'll never have him in my house!"

"Then I won't bring him here, but marry I will!" I said, standing my ground.

My father struggled to contain his anger and appeal to what he saw as reason. "But you could do much better, Ulysses. You could come back here to Ohio. We're doing well, son," he said. "We're opening new stores, setting up a distribution system that will cover this entire region! You're a grown man now, a war hero! You could do any number of things."

"Our business is worth almost a hundred thousand dollars," Simpson said matter-of-factly.

"Absolutely," Orvil echoed, his voice cracking under the strains of pubescence. "We could find a place for you."

Our business? _We_ could find a place for _you?_ A _hundred thousand dollars?_ I didn't know whether to be overwhelmed more by these facts or by the way my younger brothers were presenting them to me, as if _I_ were the child, in need of their help. I rose to my feet and spoke plainly. "I wish you well, but I do not want to be in your business, and I will marry regardless! If you do not choose to attend my wedding, at least you can welcome my bride when I bring her here to meet you!"

"Oh, there, there, don't get your knickers in a twist," the old man said, placating me once he saw I was resolute. "You go ahead and get married and bring your bride here and we'll be happy to meet her." His words would have had the proper soothing effect had Orvil not chosen to snicker and Simpson to cough violently at that very moment.

We were married on August 22, 1848, in St. Louis. The parlor was simple and spare, and a solitary fiddler played while Julia entered in a borrowed dress. We traded vows before a rented preacher who, unlike the Reverend Newman, whose clumping footsteps I can hear out in the hall even as I write, promptly took his fee and allowed me the pleasure of never seeing him again. Mrs. Grant's family was there, including cousin Longstreet, as well as Wilcox and Pratte, two other fellows from the barracks. Longstreet behaved himself, save for a whispered remark about the wedding having "two brides." The last time the four of us were together was at Appomattox, where I told them that since they saw me surrender back then in St. Louis it was only fair I see them surrender now. I was in a better humor than they were at that later date.

We spent our honeymoon at my parents' home in Ravenna, where my mother decided my wife was extravagant of habit and my wife decided my mother was miserly of spirit, even as they professed their newfound affection for each other. My father warmed to Mrs. Grant, won over by her well-honed ability to be demure and coquettish in front of a gabby, opinionated old man. After our visit, we proceeded to the Madison Barracks in Detroit, where the Fourth Infantry had been transferred.

Detroit was a frontier trading post back then. The commander of the Fourth Infantry, Colonel Whistler—the father of the painter of the same name—had just retired, leaving us with a new commander, a fellow named Bonneville. Mrs. Grant and I settled there in the fall of 1848, and our eldest son, Frederick Dent Grant, named for Mrs. Grant's father, the Colonel, was born there in the spring of 1850.

I soon discovered that the words "peacetime army" really mean "nothing to do." I had cursed the mules I had to drive up the National Road to Jalapa; now I reminisced on them tenderly. Requisitioning and acquiring food became a dreary chore, as opposed to a wartime adventure: Foraging for supplies with a company of armed men was replaced with filling out forms for the local sutlers, or, as they called them here, "merchants." The Fates had been unkind to me, choosing to deceive me by first sending me off to war, with all of its glorious commotion, before I learned the mundane and endlessly repetitive reality of peace.

Mrs. Grant immersed herself in the details of setting up our home and was soon carrying baby Fred about our post. But she tired of Great Lakes winters and came to spend more time visiting White Haven and my family in Bethel. I often found myself alone and lonely for the wife I had just acquired.

In 1851 the Congress closed down the Madison Barracks and I was sent to Sacket's Harbor, on the shores of Lake Ontario. Mrs. Grant returned to live at White Haven with young Fred, visiting me only occasionally while I leased out a room from a Captain Gore and his family, with whom I passed the time amiably.

Early in 1852, during another of those long, gray, Great Lakes winters, I learned two things of consequence. The first, conveyed in a letter, was that Mrs. Grant was once again with child, confirming the value of our occasional visits. The second, conveyed by Colonel Bonneville, was that the Fourth Infantry was being transferred again, this time to California.

California: Sherman and Halleck had been stationed there but both had left the army. Sherman was said to have abruptly begun a career in banking while Halleck went into lawyering, and both were rolling in dough. In fact, everybody in California was said to be rich. It had been almost four years since gold was discovered there and the place was teeming with prospectors and settlers, all taking the routes discovered by "The Pathfinder," John Frémont, the preening, sissified dandy who later feigned generalship along the Mississippi in the early days of the Civil War.

But another baby! Frontier birthing was an uncertain thing and it was impossible to imagine Mrs. Grant, large with child, making the trip west. The trip west was said to be a grueling one—a boat passage to Panama, a rail connection through the mountains and rain forest to the Pacific, and then another boat to the California coast. I would have to go alone, leaving Mrs. Grant behind at White Haven to bear one child while raising the other. It would be lonely, but I could send for them once I was established. Besides, I was close to being promoted to captain. Everybody else was being promoted, even if only by brevet (meaning their ranks were only temporary)—Buell, Hooker, McClellan, all of them. Even crazy Tom Jackson, who dragged a siege gun from Matamoros to Monterrey and daftly threw out his arms in the face of enemy fire at Chapultepec, was already a brevet major—it took him all of fourteen months! Why shouldn't I be a captain, too? So I made arrangements for my family and went to New York, where, as quartermaster, I had orders to put the Fourth Infantry onto a boat sailing for the Isthmus of Panama. It was July 4, 1852.

I went to the dock the next morning to find that the steamship *Ohio*, on which the 650 men and all the matériel of the division was to travel, had a capacity of 350 and was already filled with civilians. This was Colonel Bonneville's work, but having no alternative, I boarded our company. I used all my wits, and an occasional tumbler of resolve from the captain's decanter, to place my men on decks, in hallways, and wherever else we might find room. Good fortune provided calm seas and fair weather, and though cramped, we made the passage from New York to the Gulf port of Colón, Panama, in eight days.

The port made a business of the endless traffic of prospectors heading for the goldfields of California. It was also a railhead, and I loaded our party and its attendant baggage on the railcars waiting for us there, accompanied by the civilians we outnumbered, and settled back with my traveling companion, Dr. Tripler, the company physician, to enjoy the journey. We admired the jungle scenery as our railcars pressed up into the mountains.

The train stopped, however, not at our presumed destination—the town of Panama on the Pacific Coast—but at a river landing in the midst of the jungle, where the order to vacate was given by its conductors. This was as far, we were told, as the train went. Our entire party was transferred onto large flat-bottomed boats and poled down the Chagres River by local Indians, most of them buck-naked save for loincloths, much to the embarrassment of the women, and the amusement of the children, among us.

It was a slow trip. After a few hours it began to rain in quantities as only the tropics in the rainy season can produce. The deluge beat down on our exposed party. We traveled, pelted by the storm, until we reached the small town of Cruces—ten miles from the coast, I was told—where the lead boat in the procession went ashore at a clearing and Colonel Bonneville called me forward.

I got out off my boat and ran, hunched, through the torrent. "The boats can go no farther," Bonneville announced. Cruces, it turned out, may have only been ten miles as the crow flies from the Port of Panama, but only the crow could fly. The only way to reach the Pacific coast and our boat, Bonneville said, was either on foot or by mule, through the storm, over overgrown, meandering mountain passes. The men of the division could walk, but our supplies and many of the civilians could not, and the agents who were supposed to provide us with mules were suddenly besieged with better offers from the wealthier and more desperate civilians.

"But we have contracts," I said to Bonneville as the rain pummeled us. "I'll take the mules at gunpoint. It's pouring, Colonel, and we can't go forward without them."

"Nonsense. At whom will you aim your guns? The American civilians riding them?"

He was right, of course. "Then what are your instructions?" I asked.

Bonneville leaned toward me to be heard over the din of the storm. "If we do not arrive at the port of Panama in short order, we may find our boat missing as well. I will hasten ahead to hold it. You'll have to find some mules and bring the rest of the party up behind us. I will take the division and the able-bodied civilian men, save for one company to provide you a guard, and we will continue along this road. There's another town some miles ahead, and if we cannot find mules there, then we can walk the remaining distance. I leave the rest to you. You may catch up to us as best you can."

"The rest?" I asked, hunching my shoulders to stop the rain from running down my neck.

"Yes—the women and children, and the baggage. Oh, and Tripler, the sawbones—he is with you, isn't he?"

"Yes, sir."

"Good, for some of the men have taken ill—bellyaches, that sort of thing. I leave them to his care and yours. You will convey all of these people and our baggage to the port of Panama. Those are your orders," he said, looking out at the complete disarray into which he had led us. "I will see you at the port of Panama, and Godspeed." And with that he saluted, assembled his men, and marched them down the forest road, leaving me to salvage what he left behind.

I was walking down the riverbank amid the deluge, watching the promised company come off their boats and the baggage be unloaded, when Tripler ran up to me, quite agitated.

"Where is Colonel Bonneville? I must speak with him immediately!" He struggled to make himself heard over the unrelenting rain around us.

"He's already left," I shouted back.

"There are sick men among our number."

"I know. Bellyaches, hangovers. Bonneville says we're to care for them."

A rivulet of water ran from the tip of Tripler's nose as he shook his head. "These men have cholera, Grant," he yelled over the crash of the storm.

I leaned toward him. "What did you say?"

"Cholera!" he shouted. "Look about you, Grant, it's the rainy season in the tropics. It's a breeding ground for cholera, particularly for a party of North Americans who've never been near it before."

I then remembered Scott's determination to leave Veracruz before the rainy season—*el vomito*—when we both heard a shout from a soldier falling to the ground about a hundred feet away.

We hastened to the man and found him doubled over on the ground, one arm pressing against his stomach, another hand reaching across his legs, his coat splattered with his own detritus. Tripler knelt beside him for a moment, then rose and spoke to me with urgency. "You see, Grant? He's been throwing up and exploding with diarrhea, seizing up with cramps in the abdomen and legs, unbearable pain. In about an hour he'll be crying for water, gripped by the most torturous thirst a man can imagine. His skin will turn blue. In the end, he'll be painfully hoarse—the *vox cholera*, it is called—he will beg to die, and within hours at best God will grant this request. He was feeling as chipper as a man at Sunday supper only hours ago, and only hours from now he'll be dead, as surely as we are standing here. And if this man has it, Grant, then every one of us has been exposed to it, and every one of us," he shouted, his hand sweeping in every direction, "including you and me, is at risk. Don't you understand? Bonneville has left behind everything that might slow him down and is racing to the coast to get away from the disease, to save his own neck. He's left us here to die!"

I considered his words. "What do we have to do?"

"We must clear out of here right now. This disease is all around us—in the water, in the air, the insects, everywhere. Each moment we stay here, more of our party will be exposed. As for you and I, we must travel with a bar of soap and use it every time we touch any man, woman, or child among us, and we cannot drink any water, no matter how inviting."

"Then what can we drink?"

"Usually anything you boil first, but we can't even light a match in this torrent, so we'll have to drink wine, spirits, anything with alcohol, which will sanitize the beverage. There are adequate quantities of wine in our provisions for all of this party if we husband those stocks carefully. But most importantly, we must leave this spot *right now*."

Another man might have been horrified. But the presence of danger around me was like a reunion with an old friend, and the race we were invited to run with the plague set me in motion in a way I had not experienced since storming San Cosme. So much for the tedium of the peacetime army. I turned, huddled against the rain, and accosted the first local fellow with a donkey I could find.

"*Mira, hombre,*" I said, grabbing him by the arm with newfound decisiveness. "*Cuanto vale su burro?*"

He looked me over. "*Los otros pagan mas que vente dolares,*" he said. Twenty dollars.

I did some calculations in my head—the amount of money in the regimental fund, my need for pack animals—and I looked this toothless fellow in the eye. "*Yo doy vente-cuatro dolares a cualquier hombre que deme su burro para ir a la villa de Panama ahora mismo. Comprendeme?*" Twenty-four dollars for every donkey that could be produced to go the ten miles to the coast, right away.

The rain continued to beat down on us as the fellow ambled away atop his animal to spread word of my offer, and by the end of the day a number of sorrowful beasts had been assembled, led by the seediest drivers upon whom I have ever laid eyes. They were yet half of what I needed, but the urgency was absolute.

"The women and children will walk. The sick men will be placed on hammocks and suspended between pack animals. The baggage will be strung up on the mules," I told the men of the company. "Every man is to pair himself with a native driver and accompany him, making sure our possessions are safe. We will depart in an hour."

And so we set out, single file, the pack animals with the dying men hanging between them, each member of the company at the nose of an animal next to its driver, the women and children slogging through the mud behind them. The rain would pound us until we would suddenly come upon a patch of blue sky overhead, whereupon the entire jungle would light up in brilliant colors and the wild birds would cry their remarkable cries, only to give way a few moments later to another thunderhead bringing even more rain than the last one. The path was even narrower and more impassable than the trail Lee found behind Cerro Gordo, and the merciless rain now made it more a river than a path, with pools and waterfalls interrupting our way.

The animals would balk as they were driven through this mire, and if the men gathered to drag a reluctant beast at one end of the line, then a native driver at the other end, already paid and having no commitment to the effort, would lead his mule off into the jungle and steal whatever cargo was strapped to its back. We made a mile or two on a good day, slowed by the balky mules, the exhausted women, the bedraggled children, and the need to bury the endless stream of dead—soldiers, civilians, women, children, each vomiting, squatting, cramping, crazed by their need for water and throwing themselves into pools and streams already contaminated by the previous victim, only to make their agony worse when their infection compounded, and then, in the end, turning blue and *vox*-whispering silent supplications to the God who had dictated they come this far from home only to die in agony as the rain beat down on them and the mules tramped by, braying their own misery.

I had supervised burials before, but there were more every hour—each leaving a madly bereaved or numbly silent survivor behind. And there was not earth in which to bury them: There was not the scratchy pumice of Chapultepec, the leafy topsoil of the Wilderness, the black loam of Petersburg, or the red clay of Shiloh. There was only mud—loose, running mud so saturated by rain a shovelful produced more water than dirt. So we buried the dead in the thin stew through which we slogged, after which I would utter a few words and then hastily return to the line of mules, perhaps reaching for my canteen and the red wine I kept inside of it, desperately pickling my insides in the hope I might live, unlike those who had been buried in puddles of rain. We meandered through that drenched purgatory until we reached the port. One in three who set out with us three days before was now dead, remanded to the runny mud for their eternal rest. I had no doubt that among their number would have been Mrs. Grant and our newborn, had they made the journey.

And when we reached port, we found Bonneville had taken the entire party and put them all on the steamer waiting to take us to California—the sick and the well alike.

"We're all going to die," Tripler said, shaking his head as we beheld the sight. "Bonneville has spread the infection! He's doomed us all."

"No, we're not," I said firmly. "There are adequate supplies of food and clean water here. And, there," I said, noting a beached ship that sat unoccupied in the harbor, "we can turn that into a hospital ship! If nothing else, it will be a hospice for the doomed, but we can still try to isolate the infected there."

Tripler agreed. We made each of our party appear before us, and if they showed the slightest trace of the infirmity in Tripler's eyes, they were taken to the hospital ship, some gratefully, some screaming that they were perfectly well and being sent to die regardless. And some of them were right: Some of them were being sent to die, just as surely as Lee sent Pickett's men to die at Gettysburg, but there was no alternative to excising the disease, just as the disease that has spread across my throat was not excised and leaves me lying here today. Where was Saveshammer, that soul of medical competence, the man who ministered to Ulysses Grant that awful night at Shiloh? Alas, not even Saveshammer could have saved these poor creatures!

Tripler and I ministered to these men as Bonneville waited on our ship, *The Golden Gate*, impatient to sail as soon as the weather allowed him, for his conscience would keep him no longer. But Captain Gore, my old landlord from Sacket's Harbor, steadied Bonneville when he contemplated fleeing in his worst moments of cowardice. It was six weeks before Dr. Tripler and I finally concluded the epidemic had run its course and we would be able to push off the next day.

That next night we had a small party of sorts on *The Golden Gate*, inviting the few officers who had helped us and some selected friends to join us for a few hands of euchre and some of the spirits on which we had subsisted in the jungle. Just when we were beginning to relax, Captain Gore threw his cards to the table and clutched his stomach.

"My God!" he screamed. "I've got the cholera!"

I looked at Tripler and then back at Gore with the most artificially unmoved of expressions. "Nonsense," I said without a hint of excitement. "You have only eaten something that disagrees with you."

"I'm gone," Gore sobbed.

"Hush," I told him. "Dr. Tripler, tend to this poor ward," I said with a smile. "He is feigning illness, angling for a drink."

He was dead, of course, by daybreak.

We reached San Francisco and then set sail for the Columbia River in the Northwest, where we arrived a short eight days later, on September 22, 1852. The Fourth Infantry was stationed throughout the various territories taken from either the Mexicans—such as California—or the British—what is now Oregon and Washington—and my division was assigned to the latter.

Fort Vancouver, my new home, stood proudly near the banks of the

Columbia River, and nothing else. The town of Portland was nearby, with its twenty or thirty shacks inhabited by prospectors, trappers, woodsmen, and other hermits. It would have been possible to put them in the same room to be counted, had the population bathed. Absent that meritorious habit, putting them in the same room would have been an abomination. The region abounded in Nature's great goods, but none of man's—soap, razors, and dental appliances among them.

To my great pleasure, I discovered my old roommate Ingalls had been in the advance party that built the fort—a stockade of massive felled trees—and the buildings for its inhabitants. One of the buildings, a neat little frame house with the crisp smell of cedar all about it, was the "Quartermaster's Ranch." As I was the quartermaster, this was both my ranch and a stroke of good fortune.

"Yup, it's all yours," Ingalls said, slapping the portals as he helped carry my trunk—I rarely thought of it as Useful's trunk anymore—inside, just as Sherman helped with it at West Point some thirteen years before. "You'll enjoy it here. There's nothing to do. The Indians are peaceful if left alone, and belligerent if we're belligerent to them first, so we can take our pick. Probably the only thing you'll ever have to do is outfit the exploratory parties the government sends when it gets the idea of building a railroad here. But it's already October and winter is coming, so the exploratory parties won't be able to get through for the rest of this year. They're like migratory birds: They only arrive in the spring."

I looked about at the rough-hewn plank walls, the poorly milled windows, and the drafty plank floor, and reconciled myself to the place. At least the windows let in some sunlight. "What about mess?" I asked, running my hands over a table in the middle of the room. "Where do you get a cook out here?"

Ingalls started to laugh. "A cook? Sam, what's your lieutenant's pay?"

I shrugged. "Fifty-six dollars a month."

"Well, a cook gets twice that. Food's cheap, but help isn't. This is the West, Sam, there's a gold rush on. A cook and victuals will run about a hundred and fifty a month. I have a mess going with Wallen and his family and a few others." I remembered Wallen from Mexico, the fellow knocked down by the jaw of the man standing next to him. "You can join up with us, if you like."

Ingalls was right about two things—there wasn't anything to do and it cost an awful lot to do it. A soldier's pay didn't go very far at all. If I was ever to raise enough money to bring Mrs. Grant, young Fred—the Little Dog, I called him, for he was like a puppy—and the other child I presumed I had, but of whom I had no confirmation, I would have to make some money.

Of course, every young officer out West had the same idea I did, if only because their paychecks were as slim and families as distant as my own. It was a good thing that our division had no pressing responsibilities, as they would have distracted us from trying to supplement our meager army pay. San Francisco was caught in the mad cadence of the Gold Rush. It had been a small hamlet of eight hundred people, built around a monastery, before gold was found at Sutter's Mill in 1848. Four years later it was a city of thirty thousand, overrun with people, money, and aspirations. So it was when Wallen said he had the solution to all our problems in a single word.

"Ice!" he exclaimed triumphantly. "Sam, think about it. San Francisco is overrun with saloons, restaurants, boardinghouses, every manner of public facility. And there's hardly a chunk of ice to be found in the place! And what's just a few days north of here, Sam? I'll tell you what—Alaska! Alaska, Sam! Why, the place abounds in ice, it's a veritable citadel of ice, for as far as the eye can see!"

I thought I felt my father's mercantalist blood running within me for the first time. "What do you propose?" I asked.

He eagerly plotted the details. "We can charter a crew to cut block ice up there. We can borrow against our pay from Bonneville. I know a captain who can sail it down to San Francisco. Why, remember when we came up here? It was only eight days on the water from the bay! We'll clean up!"

I knew a good idea when I heard one. I suppose the problem was that I didn't know a bad idea when I heard one. The reason it was such quick work sailing up to the Columbia River from San Francisco was that headwinds often blew up the coast. And when they did, they only blew one way. A boat heading south along the coast might as well have been becalmed in the Horse Latitudes. It was six weeks before our ship reached San Francisco, whereupon our captain delivered a boatload of cold water, and the venture failed.

Wallen was not one to be dissuaded. He was looking down at his plate as we were having supper one evening when he suddenly had a revelation. "Why, Sam, I've had an inspiration! Look down at your plate. What do you see?"

I saw salmon, in fact, which the local rivers had in great abundance. "Precisely!" Wallen said. "Not a speck of meat! There are pioneers coming up the Oregon Trail with the cattle that hauled their wagons. We can snap them up when they arrive, fatten them up, and sell them in San Francisco. There's no other way to get cattle to there in large quantities, Sam. We'd have a franchise that couldn't be broken!"

I was a bit unsure of myself after our ice venture, but Wallen was insistent. "Sam, you don't even have to do anything. We gather up the livestock, pen 'em up and fatten 'em, and I'll take 'em down to Frisco to sell 'em myself. You put your share up and I'll stand up to the investment, Sam, that's how confident I feel. I'll guarantee your money, safe and sound!"

I still had my doubts, but then a letter came from Mrs. Grant. I opened it to find the footprint of our second child, a boy named Ulysses S. Grant, Jr., called Buck by all those at White Haven; no doubt the Colonel could not stand to have the boy referred to as Ulysses. He was born, as it turned out, on July 22 of that year, the day we set out on mules in the torrent for the Panamanian coast. He would have died along with his mother had they come with me.

I now had a second son, a son I had never seen. And if I did not raise some revenue, I would not get to see him, or Fred, the Little Dog, very soon. "Very well, then," I agreed, and Wallen proceeded to gather up a plentiful herd, fattened them on the abundant grass, and put them on a boat for San Francisco. In contrast to our ice venture, he had a timely trip, and in the space of a few weeks he returned.

Broke.

"San Francisco abounds in cattle," he explained. "Mexicans are running them into the city from the south like a plague of locusts! Their flop fills the streets, their infernal lowing is heard on every corner, and the butchers and tanners are having a field day."

"What about our funds?"

Wallen shook his head and grimaced. "Lost, Sam, the whole roll. But I made you a promise and I'll stand by it—I'll return each and every dime, and I've written to you a note attesting to my pledge." He extracted a piece of paper and gave it to me, leaving me with exactly that—a piece of paper. It looked less formidable than when I first imagined it.

I was considering the losses a few days later while sitting at my desk when I heard a buggy's wheels coming up the road and a strong voice rang out, "Quartermaster Grant!" I came to the front door, and there, much to my surprise, was Hooker, the hero of Chapultepec, wearing a new leather coat and driving a fine new carriage.

"Hello, Hooker," I said, extending my hand to him. "I haven't seen you since Mexico City."

"Those were the days, weren't they, Grant?" he responded, hopping down from the buggy with great athleticism. "You gave them the devil's own goddamned time from that steeple in San Cosme!"

"As did you, going over the wall at Chapultepec," I answered.

"Hell, I had to give them something to shoot other than Tom Jackson," Hooker said. "Say! Did you hear about Scott? We got a newspaper a few weeks ago, says Pierce beat him in the election!"

This was the Presidential election of 1852, which was now a few months past, but news traveled slowly back then. It was astonishing to think of Pierce, a latecomer to the war, as President. I used to play cards with him and watch him get stewed. The Democrats nominated him because they could not agree on anybody else and wanted to go home, the convention being held in the heat of Baltimore in the summer. Pierce promised to tolerate slavery, and so fit the bill. And Scott, whose military genius was so amply demonstrated in the same war in which Pierce played so minor a part, was portrayed by the Democrats as a vain and thin-skinned old man, a characterization with the unfortunate aspect of being true.

"Well, you look very prosperous!" I said, turning the subject from politics. "I trust army life has been good to you."

"Army life my ass." Hooker laughed. "The army was good to me when it signed my discharge papers." He leaned forward confidentially. "What are you pulling down out here, Grant? Sixty-something a month on the outside? Sixty-something don't buy a coat or a carriage like this one!" He reached into his coat and extracted a mother-of-pearl flask. "Don't have to worry about who sees you drinkin', either." He winked, then threw back a long taste, wiped his mouth, and smiled. "Now, let's talk a little business."

"How's that?" I asked.

"I'm in the wood business now, Sam, got a timber ranch near Sonoma." It took me a moment to realize a timber ranch was a forest. He reached into another pocket and emerged with a few folded papers. "This here's my agreement with the Fourth, all signed by the military command back in San Francisco, Frémont himself." He tipped back the flask a second time and ran his sleeve across his mouth, then, remembering his manners, extended the flask toward me.

I declined. "Agreement for what?" I asked as I took the papers from him.

"Firewood," he said. "Fort Vancouver gets a couple dozen cords a month alone. Two-fifty a cord."

My eyes might have popped out of my head. "Two dollars and fifty cents for a cord of wood?"

"Yes, sir," Hooker said matter-of-factly. "That's the going rate. Says right here," he said, pointing to one of the papers.

I was incredulous—how could wood be so expensive in a region covered with trees? Hooker chatted on until his flask was empty and he left, promising deliveries soon. And he gave me something to discuss at the dinner table that night.

"Joe Hooker was by today," I said, picking at my salmon.

"He was?" Wallen asked. "I thought he quit the army."

"Yes, he did," I explained. "He's got a timber ranch now—I mean, a forest—near Sonoma. He's supplying this division with firewood at two-fifty a cord."

Wallen was as amazed as I had been. "Two dollars and fifty cents for a cord of wood?"

"That's what I thought, but he's got a contract signed by that idiot Frémont," I said, and shrugged.

Wallen sat back for a second and rubbed his chin thoughtfully. "Sam, do you realize the situation we're in? There's nothing for miles around us but trees! Why, this region abounds in trees! At two-fifty a cord, we could be earning hundreds of dollars a month! We could cut wood and send it to San Francisco, everywhere! And the beauty of it is, wood doesn't melt!"

I looked up at him and nodded slowly. "Yes, we would be safe from that angle," I deduced. "But what about the price? What if the price of wood falls as readily as the price of cows did?" My father's son was only going to be fooled once.

Wallen smiled confidently. "Well, if it does, we sell the wood to the division, undercut Hooker, and walk away with our capital intact."

I was, of course, skeptical, after our last several experiences. But my need to bring Mrs. Grant and the children west was driving me to desperation. So we had a go at logging. We cut, sawed, and wedged the area's stands of the finest firs and cedars. Wood, of course, must be cured if it is to burn, and so our plan was to stack it and sell it, on contract, for the following autumn. We found a plain on the banks of the nearby Columbia River to store our product—it was flat and dry, easily accessible by raft to transport our wares. By the time the early spring arrived, we were looking at what seemed like an acre covered with wood stacked four feet high. Wallen had already secured advance payments, and our profits, amounting to thousands, were now assured. In fact, we now had the capital for an additional venture.

"Potatoes!" Wallen said one afternoon. "Look at this newspaper, Sam. It says the price of potatoes in San Francisco is now nine dollars a bushel. Nine dollars, Sam!"

I reached for his newspaper and pursed my lips. Nine dollars, indeed. "Sam," Wallen continued, "I was down by our woodpile this morning, and do you know what I saw? I saw the blackest, richest earth it's ever been my privilege to tread. Why, if we put in sixty acres of potatoes—just sixty acres—and came up with one-quarter of the yield you'd have a right to expect, and if we saw just a fraction of the price they're getting now—even as little as a dollar and a half—we'd be turning a substantial profit! How many bushels of potatoes do you think an acre of this magnificent black dirt could produce?"

"Heavens," I replied. "Fifty, if any."

Wallen nodded enthusiastically. "Exactly! Think of it! That would be . . . well, eh . . ."

"Four thousand, five hundred dollars," I said. "And thirty dollars for every penny in price thereafter."

"Exactly!" he repeated, and before you knew it, I was hitching up a team and plowing furrows in the dirt, passing time with the horses. With not too large an investment from our firewood revenues, we were able to acquire seed potatoes. By March, I had laid these into sixty fine acres of thick Columbia River valley soil, and by May the green shoots with their curly leaves were reaching for the sky at a fantastic rate. I had little else to do. There was only one exploratory party due in the area that spring, to be led by McClellan, but that was all. Each day I would visit our enterprise—the wood, the potatoes, even a few acres of oats and barley I threw in as long as I had the horses hitched, casting the seed from behind the plow with magnificent sweeps of the hand, each of which beckoned my family closer to me. And when I was done each day, I would reach into my vest for the letter with Buck's little inked footprint, unfold it, and regard it quietly. For the first time since I left New York City, I felt the day on which my life would change was close at hand.

That day arrived in June 1853. The wood was piled high, the potatoes blossoming abundantly, and the Columbia River, swollen from the spring rains, suddenly rose out of its banks and swept away everything within a mile of its winter boundary in a flood of biblical proportion. The houses, the camps, the topsoil, my wood, my potatoes, my money, my hopes, my future—all of it gone. I was fortunate in one regard. Every other settler in the Northwest had heard about the price of potatoes and planted them as well. Those with crops on higher ground had to take their product to market that summer, where they found the price of potatoes had fallen to twenty-five cents. They all went broke.

I went back to the Quartermaster's Ranch that afternoon and proceeded to get loaded. Wallen and I had taken money for future delivery, and now we would have to secure other wood at the market rate, compounding our loss. Mrs. Grant, Fred the Little Dog, and Buck were now farther away than ever, living at White Haven with my miserable father-in-law, and I had heard not a word from them in months. I had a right to drink—I'd have been a fool not to. So I shut the door and went on a spree.

They ran me down all my life for being a drunk, but it was a special occasion when I turned the bottle over. I was young, with a young wife, and she was far away. Who could blame me? And, sure, we lived on wine as we slogged through the Valley of Death in Panama, and I got plastered once we reached the Pacific—who'd deny me the right? I'd buried thirty-seven souls in a single day; it would have been thirty-nine if Mrs. Grant had come with me. Who wouldn't drink then? And what if I now decided to find a moment's respite from the constant drumming of failure and loneliness? I defy any man to do differently.

A drunken butcher, they later called me. I learned to ignore it, greeting the criticism with a look of grim resolve, answering with all the rectitude my mother's taciturn joylessness had taught me. Maybe I had a bit too much that day in New Orleans after Vicksburg fell. Would they rather have had a sober Burnside instead? Lincoln, as practical as he was ugly, knew exactly what it was worth when they came to him after Shiloh—bitter, smart-mouthed Halleck leading the pack of jackals—and said I was a drunk. Send a case of whatever I was having to the rest of my generals, he told them. I drank to his health that night, as I was sure he did to mine.

But if every drink I took made sense at the time, it was only because drink had robbed me of my senses. If only doing the wrong thing in the wrong place at the wrong time were a virtue—my place in my mother's Heaven would be assured. I planted potatoes and gathered wood just in time for them to be flooded. I shipped cattle into a glut. I bought ice and it melted. I went to Panama and there was a plague.

And I got drunk the day George McClellan arrived.

I was sitting at the table in my cabin, wrapped in the warm glow of drink, when a soldier came to the door and knocked.

My head swam in the direction of the sound. "What in blazes is it?"

"It's about Captain McClellan, sir," the soldier said.

"What about him?" I slurred. "Has he figured out why crazy Tom Jackson sucked a lemon yet?" I snickered and grabbed for the bottle on the table before me—I landed a few fingers on it and coaxed it toward me.

"He's in Colonel Bonneville's cabin," the soldier said.

"That can't be," I said, blinking. "He's not due here for a week. How could he make such good time?"

In good time, McClellan found me and provided an answer. "We had the good fortune of arriving at the headwaters of the Columbia just as the river was cresting from the end of the spring snowmelt. I've never seen a river so fast, Sam. We put our entire party on rafts and cut a week's time off our journey," McClellan said with self-satisfied efficiency. He had grown into a little man with an unduly large mustache planted on a boyish face. He now stood in the main room of my cabin, where he had barged in followed by a constantly changing entourage of officers, orderlies, and other soldiers, all of whom ran in and out, delivering messages or seeking his guidance, toadying all the while. "The river's force was astonishing. We saw entire farmlands washed away. A shame, but they were foolish enough to plant on the floodplain," he said with a snicker. "At least they teach you about that in engineering class at West Point."

I shut my drunken eyes, but the image of the river washing away my fortune and delivering McClellan instead would not go away. "Yes, well, welcome, George," I said, gathering myself as best I could. "It's been . . . how many years since we watched Santa Anna fall at Cerro Gordo?" My own prospect of doing the math was now limited.

"This being 1854, by my count, seven," McClellan answered officiously, as if his count, and not algebra, were the final arbiter. "And you're looking . . . actually, you're looking a little pallid today. Are you well?"

"Well? Entirely well, George," I insisted, shaking off my cloudiness.

"Good!" McClellan said enthusiastically. "Now, the list of the matériel I need—did you get it?"

The list! Yes, there was a list—it was now coming back to me. "Well, yes, George, but owing to your early arrival, much of it isn't here yet." I shrank from his icy stare. "The chain of supply's not that strong out here, George. Bridles, saddles, fresh mules, canvas, the whole lot of it—much of it is in Humboldt, and some of it simply isn't out West at all."

McClellan glared at me with disdain. "Sam, I must have it all immediately!" He looked about to ensure we were alone and lowered his voice in confidence. "Do you think I want to be here, Sam? I want to be back East, back with my family." Had he looked at me with any interest or courtesy he would have seen the tears forming in my eyes. "But this exploratory party is too important to pass up. Crossing the mountains made Frémont a hero," he said. "If I can find a path for a railroad into these parts, I'll have a leg up when the time comes."

His last remark was confusing enough to attract my attention. "When the time comes? What time?"

"When Scott retires," McClellan confided. "Joe Johnston is the old dog, but down the line, Bobby Lee looks like the fellow to replace him." Lee was now the commandant of West Point and his star waxing. In fact, McClellan was prescient: The outbreak of violence in Kansas and Nebraska the next year would lead the Congress to create two new cavalry units, one of which would have Lee as a second-in-command to Johnston. "But if this drags out a few more years, I can build a record and have that job myself. You've got to help me, Sam."

I nodded, but between McClellan's overblown self-esteem and the weight of my inebriation, I could stand no longer and I swooned, hitting the floor with a thud.

"Heavens!" McClellan exclaimed. He bent over and I could see him recoil above me, his face a mask of disgust against the backdrop of the ceiling. "This man is dead drunk!" he shouted.

Not true—I was drunk, but alive enough to be called to Colonel Bonneville's office the next day to discuss the matter.

"McClellan says you were drunk when he arrived yesterday," Bonneville said flatly.

I scratched my head in search of a comfortable spot. "Was it only yesterday? It feels like I was out for a while."

Bonneville leaned across his desk. "Grant, everybody makes mistakes. I made one in Panama and you bailed me out. You've made one now, and I'm returning the favor," he said, trading his abandonment of our corps to cholera for my afternoon's bender. "McClellan left early this morning. He says he's going to file a report, the sanctimonious little son of a bitch. But you've done a pretty good job for me, and I'll stand by you. It's no crime to drink, Grant. All the officers drink around here, you probably less than the rest. The crime is being unable to hold your liquor. You've got to remember that down the line, wherever you end up."

I blinked at him in confusion. "Am I going somewhere?"

"You are," he said, opening a drawer and reaching for a letter. "I've received word from the divisional command at Humboldt Bay that Captain Bliss has died. You're the senior-ranking lieutenant in this division, so you succeed him. You're to report to Fort Humboldt and assume command of Company F there."

I shook my head to clear it. "I'm being made a captain?"

"As of right now," he said. "You know, you're only the fifth man in your year at West Point to make it. You've not a bad career in the army, Grant. If you could just square off your edges a little, act a little less preoccupied."

I sighed deeply. "I'd like to, Colonel, but it's just that . . . I'm so sad," I blurted. "Look," I said, reaching into my vest. "This is my boy's footprint—I've never seen him! I waited three years to marry my wife, and now I can't be with her. I couldn't be more miserable!"

"You think so, do you? Have you forgotten who the commanding officer at Humboldt is?"

I stared at him until I remembered. "Oh, no!" I cried, and buried my face in my hands.

Fort Humboldt stood amid the redwood forest, a magnificent bay shining before it. It was as splendorous a setting as Nature ever ordained. I regarded it for a moment before I entered the divisional headquarters, where my new commanding officer regarded me with as hearty a smirk as a man can muster.

"Well, look who we have here," Colonel—no longer just Captain—Buchanan said. It was now ten years after he derided me for being late to mess at Jefferson Barracks when I was courting Mrs. Grant, but our antipathy toward each other was as fresh as if it were yesterday. Now we were stuck with each other at Humboldt Bay, about a hundred miles north of San Francisco, where there was little to do beyond watch the madness that was the gold rush.

"Captain Grant reporting," I said, trying to keep things polite.

"Sit down, Grant," Colonel Buchanan said tersely. "We know each other pretty well, so I'll be direct. I expect crisp execution of duties and attention to detail. In a remote settlement such as this one, morale and discipline can break down rapidly, and I'll have none of that. Do we understand each other?"

"We do, sir."

"I hope so, Grant. Being late to mess doesn't cut it around here. Nor, I might add, does drink."

"I understand, sir."

He regarded me with palpable skepticism. "Well, George McClellan has something to say to the contrary. And if he's right, it would be entirely consistent with my experience of you. I've seen your type come and go, Grant. Remember—I run a tight ship."

Buchanan ran a tight ship, all right. It was so tight the planks were buckling and it was taking on water. I was walking through the fort only a few days later when I passed one of the residences for the junior officers—as a captain and company commander I was now a senior officer—when a young second lieutenant emerged, saw me walking along, and put his finger alongside his nose with a sly smile.

I stared back, wondering about his odd expression. "Are you looking at me?" I called.

The officer rolled his eyes, took a deep breath, and touched the side of his nose once again, his smile never fading. A second officer then staggered out of the house and stood next to the first fellow in the doorway. "Oh, that's Grant," the second fellow said, "he's new. Doesn't know the sign yet." He straightened up for a moment and hollered to me. "Ain't you Grant? Come here!"

This was a blatant abuse of military protocol, but my curiosity was piqued and I walked over to them. They managed to bring a few limp fingers to their brows in salute and I could see they were pasted drunk.

"As you were," I said.

"Well, I'm not sure how I was," the first fellow responded, whereupon he burst forward with laughter.

The second fellow looked up at me. "Excuse me, Captain, but this is the signal," he said, giving me a wink, and putting his finger to the side of his nose.

"The signal to what?"

"The signal the dipper's in the barrel, sir. We heard you were a regular sort about this kind of thing, sir, if you know what I mean."

Well, I knew what they meant, and I was taken aback that my reputation had preceded me. But with nothing to do and no one who cared for me at hand, what was wrong with a moment's refreshment? "Very well, then," I said, and followed them into the house.

Inside was a room—low ceiling, dark, very rough—with a handful of men sitting about a plank table, each with a tall glass of whiskey in front of him. A barrel of the stuff stood on a crate alongside them. "This is Captain Grant," the second officer said, and there was a round of pleasant mumbling as I took a seat. "Well, then, Captain, you look like a fellow who could use a hand."

It was a kind offer. "Actually, I have my things stowed away and I'm all bunked in."

"No, no, no," the second officer said as the others began to laugh. "Who'll show Captain Grant how a fellow gets a hand?"

"I will," one shouted. He threw back his drink and drained it, then slammed it on the table with his four fingers lined up tightly alongside the glass. "Give me a hand," he commanded the fellow near the barrel.

"A hand coming up for the gentleman," his colleague said, and he lifted the dipper from the barrel and poured whiskey into the fellow's glass until the liquor was as high as his four fingers. The fellow then lifted his glass and held it up to the man with the dipper. "Thank you, sir, for giving me a hand," he said, and proceeded to drink.

"Now you, Captain?" the pourer invited, and I readily accepted. No harm taking one, I thought, Captain Buchanan notwithstanding. I was given a glass and I stood it on the table, four fingers to the side, and it was filled just as was the last fellow's. "Now, Captain," the pourer said as I was about to imbibe, "would you like some water in that?"

"No, thank you," I said, whereupon I was interrupted by jovial shouts from all around.

"No, no, no," the second officer said as the other men laughed. "One doesn't say *no*, Captain. One says, *Do you mistake me, sir, for a camel?*"

I nodded and looked down at my glass, which was poised for refreshment. Very well, I thought. "Well, then," I replied, "do you mistake me, sir, for a camel?"

There was a chorus of huzzahs and much back-slapping, none of which appealed to me, but I lifted my drink to my lips and tasted sweet relief. I drained my glass in short order and put it on the table, my hand alongside it. If the first didn't hurt, how could a second? "Who'll give a new fellow a hand?" I asked, and I recall little of the day after that.

With plenty of time and little to do—a company commander had even less to do than a quartermaster, so long as the Indians didn't go off and kill any loggers or miners, or loggers and miners kill some Indians—I would go off riding for days on end to look about the area. I roamed the miles of wilderness around Fort Humboldt, did some hunting and fishing, but my interest in all matters except my loneliness and isolation was nil. I would take out little Buck's footprint and stare at it until I passed the camels' cabin and saw someone who would touch his nose knowingly.

One particularly hot afternoon I received a brief letter from home that made my mood more morose, and as I walked past the camels' cabin I was happy to get the signal. In the space of a few minutes I had caught up to the rest of the group and we sailed away together, each of us taking turns doing our little ritual.

"Can you give a fellow a hand?" I asked, laughing crudely, my eyes flushed with tears, my brow sweating, and my nose running snot. I laid my hand on the side of my glass, snuggling it tightly against the base, and one of the camels began to pour until the whiskey was as high as my index finger.

"A helping hand for a helping man," he said, and we burst out again into a chorus of drunken laughter. "Say," he added, suddenly sitting up straight and speaking with a tone of mock refinement, "would you like some water with that?" he asked.

I reared up in my chair, a hand to my breast, with a tone of affront. "Do you mistake me, sir, for a camel?" And we burst into laughter once again.

"To the dromedary! A noble beast with no need for water!" another man said, and I touched the rim of my glass to the brim of my cap in salute and drained it in an ecstatic, frenzied gulp.

Oh, sweet juice of the angels! Oh, heavenly potion of the cherubim! Waves of inebriation came over me like zephyrs over the prairie, and I sat back and enjoyed them. It was a miracle I stayed in my chair as the sensation overwhelmed me. The images of Fred the Little Dog and baby Buck—my supposition as to what he resembled—came to my mind, but wrapped in the comforting arms of strong drink they did no damage. Rather, I rose to my feet in a series of lurches and bumps and raised my glass earnestly. "To Fred the Dog and Little Buck!" I said, holding the glass aloft like a torch, and then swung it to my lips, only to discover it was empty. "Confound it!" I blasphemed. "Big gun, no shell!"

My comrades fell over in laughter once again and one of them reached over for the dipper. "Well, we can't turn our backs on Fred and Buck, can we?" he asked. I placed my glass on the table and reiterated the magic spell that produced drink. In flowed the redemptive elixir, finger by finger, until it was four fingers high, and I threw it back to salute my two beautiful children.

I fell back in my chair again, when the door opened and my eyes were flooded with light. I threw my hand in front of my face and heard the voice of a young lieutenant, a fellow from Kansas City named Cicero Younger.

"Captain Grant!" he said. "You in here?"

"Present!" I responded. "Come sit with me, Younger! I'm celebrating a letter from home!" I said.

"You're in it deep, Grant," the fellow said. "It's payday, and you're not there! Colonel Buch, he's mucho mad!"

"Oh, the devil!" I spat, reaching into my pocket in search of my watch. "Buchanan's going to skin me," I muttered as I struggled to my feet.

Cicero Younger stepped in front of me. "Sam, you're in no condition to go back to the fort! Let me tell Buchanan you're ill," he coaxed.

"Absolutely not," I said, standing firm in speech if not in fact. "If I don't show up, Buchanan will think I've been drinking! We must proceed at once," whereupon I took a decisive step forward, tripped over a plank in the floor, and went tumbling outside to where my wagon was hitched. I dropped myself into the seat, snapped the reins as I spurred the horse, and off we went. It would have been a smooth departure had I not forgotten that two other wagons were hitched to the back of mine. And so I careened through the woods like a wayward cannonball cutting a path through the high grass at Palo Alto, dragging two tethered mounts and wagons in a train behind me.

I pulled up in front of the fort's headquarters and there was Buchanan, wearing the same testy expression he'd had on ten years before back at Jefferson Barracks. "Captain Grant reporting," I said as I fell out of the carriage and landed in a heap at his feet.

He did not move a muscle or make a sound.

"Ready to dispense pay to the company," I said, rising from the dust and brushing myself off with my left hand, saluting him with my right.

Buchanan nodded toward the desk set up in front of us. One of his orderlies was giving out pay to my men. "Step inside, Grant," Buchanan said, and turned to lead the way.

We entered his office and he sat down. I was glad to be out of the heat and sunlight, which were making my skull pound. "Drunk again, Grant?" he sneered.

I rubbed my scalp in search of comfort. "I did have a drink, yes, sir, one," I said softly.

"One only in the sense you've obviously not come up for air since."

"Begging the colonel's indulgence, sir," I said hastily, "I regret forgetting what day it was and will be fine in the future."

"I'll not be that forgiving," Buchanan said tersely. "You'll stand for court-martial for this. I'm done with you."

I was thunderstruck and quickly tried to assemble myself. "If I may,

Colonel, I admit there have been occasions where I have allowed myself to succumb unduly to the influence—"

"That's less than a startling confession, Grant, coming from a man who's too dizzy to sit up straight in the presence of his commanding officer. I will proceed with the order for the court-martial immediately, Captain, unless . . ."

My head sprang up. "Unless what?"

"Unless I have your resignation, right here and now."

Was I really about to start life over at the age of thirty-two? The injustice of it all! I looked at Buchanan, afraid to hate him as much as I truly did, and asked him straightforwardly, "Why me, sir? My habit has been less, rather than more, than that of the other men, sir, whose imbibing is commonplace."

"If you mean my men are drunk off their asses, yes, that's not a secret," Buchanan said.

"Then why me? Is this all over the episode back at the barracks ten years ago?"

Buchanan snorted. "No, Grant, you weren't the first or last pipsqueak to make some rude remark at supper," he said dismissively. "It's your attitude."

"My attitude?"

"I don't mind the officers getting loaded, Grant. We're a thousand miles from nowhere and it takes mail three months to get here. But the point of getting loaded is to get happy, Grant, to walk out of that cabin as do the rest of these camels, or whatever they call themselves, and get over it. You never get over it, Grant. You wallow in self-pity. And when you get blasted, you get worse, not better. I won't have the officers under my command walking around as if the world were coming to an end on a daily basis. A good commanding officer inspires his men. I need commanders who are chipper, who can bear the burden. You're not cut from that cloth, Grant. You're not made to command. So you can either leave or have me throw you out. It's all up to you," he said, and with that, he took a piece of paper out of his desk.

Colonel S. Cooper
Adjutant General
Washington

*COL. I very respectfully tender my resignation of my commission as
an officer of the Army, and request that it take effect from the 31st
of July next.*

> *I am, Col.*
> *Very Respectfully*
> *Yr. Obt. Svt.*
> *U. S. Grant, Capt., 4th Inf.*

He'd already written my resignation for me!
"Sign here," he said.

I took a month to tie up my affairs, putting my company's paperwork
in order. It was early May 1854, when a timber ship picked me up at
Humboldt Bay and took me to San Francisco. The camels watched me
board, and I turned to them as they waved and I said, "Whoever hears
of me in ten years will hear of a well-to-do Missouri farmer."

Maybe I believed it, but I doubt any of them did.

I had not a penny to my name, but debts aplenty. I was so broke I
had to borrow sixty dollars from Cicero Younger for boat fare from San
Francisco back to New York. I clutched my steamer ticket as if it were
all I had in the world. And it was.

I meandered the streets of San Francisco for a few days, peeking
into the restaurants and faro dens while I husbanded my meager borrowed resources, my ticket safe inside my vest next to little Buck's footprint. And when the day of departure came, I assembled my trunk and
lumbered with it up to the gangplank. *Whoever hears of me in ten
years will hear of a well-to-do Missouri farmer.* I turned and took one
last look at San Francisco. It veritably glowed with energy and possibility, swarming with every manner of person going every which way. I
looked at the people disembarking, coming down the same gangway I
was now ascending. Families from the East, Latins and Orientals, Eu-
ropeans, Freedmen, and the slaves accompanying second-born Southern gentlemen, all of them pouring out of the ship, all of them wearing
the same expression of ambition and optimism and determination I
once had, all of them writing their stories anew in pencil.

One of them caught my eye. He was about my size and age; his face seemed a little finer, his eyes a little wider, his expression a little more wary than most. When we had just about passed each other on the gangway, the reason he had attracted my attention suddenly became clear.

It was Useful Grant.

I turned and stopped and I put down my trunk, ignoring the various souls that muttered as they bustled past me. I could see only the back of his head now, his wiry carriage, his body almost as bent and slouched as my own. Was it really him? I could not be sure. I watched as he walked off the gangway, along the wharf, and out onto the wooden sidewalks that traversed the city's swampy ground. And as he walked away—if it was him—he blended into a crowd of Useful Grants and Useless Grants, each on his own journey but with a shared sense of urgency. I wanted to leave my trunk and follow him, and find out the truth, when my hand slipped absentmindedly into my pocket and my fingers encountered a child's inky footprint on a well-thumbed page. I looked at it and my heart ached. And so I lifted my trunk once again and proceeded to board the ship, fully aware that Useful—if it was Useful—and I were going in different directions, one of us leaving, one of us arriving, and only one of us could be heading toward Mescalito's great prophecy. Having drunk myself out of the army, heading back to a family I'd not seen in two years, bringing with me debts but no prospects, I wondered how my direction could possibly be the right one.

CHAPTER VI

THE GRANTS, THE DENTS, AND THE KANSAS-NEBRASKA ACT—HARDSCRABBLE—FIREWOOD IN ST. LOUIS—WILLIAM JONES—CLERKSHIP IN GALENA—A SURPRISING CUSTOMER

THE TRIP HOME was blessedly uneventful—no cholera, no death, nothing but long, boring days on a boat that was a human refuse bin, a collection of the other drunks and failures, the miners who found no gold, the sutlers who couldn't sell, the other men unable to find a place. But as the voyage dragged on, I found myself brimming with the most surprising hope. Another man might have felt shame at having drunk himself out of the army, but I decided it was an army that had no place for me. I would have to endure no more separation from my family. It was a good thing, I told myself, that had happened to me.

The remaining problem was reaching them. When I arrived in New York, I hadn't a dollar left for a hotel room or train fare back home. I needed a loan until I could wire my father to advance me funds. Possessed of a naive confidence it all would work out, I proceeded to the New York military command center at Governor's Island, looking for somebody I knew from Mexico, or Detroit, or West Point who could help me out.

How often is naive confidence rewarded! My shy friend from West Point, Simon Bolivar Buckner, was stationed there, and he greeted me with kindness as he asked after my well-being.

"Well, I've had a hard run," I told him matter-of-factly. "I'm out now."

Buckner nodded sympathetically. "I heard. I heard Colonel Buchanan was hard on you."

Meaning word had gotten out I drank myself out of Buchanan's good graces and, in turn, the service. Buckner helped me wire my father and guaranteed my hotel bill while I waited for money to arrive. And the money did arrive after a week, but what I had not counted on was it arrived in my brother Simpson's pocket.

"The old man sent me to fetch you," he announced as he entered my hotel room. I'd not seen Simpson in several years and they had obviously been hard ones for him. His already pallid complexion had grown even more colorless, his gaunt appearance more drawn, and the cough from which he once only occasionally suffered now liberally punctuated his speech. His consumption was as obvious to everybody else as it was to him: there was no reason to mention it.

"Did the old man figure I'd drink it away if he just wired me the money at a bank?" I asked, offended.

"No," Simpson said. I was relieved to hear I had my father's confidence. "Orvil did."

"Orvil! Is he in charge now?" At first I was outraged, but when I saw a pained look briefly cloud Simpson's face, it occurred to me that my father, realizing I was not going to be a merchant and that Simpson would one day die of his disease, was going to rely ever more on Orvil, who was just nineteen, but in conniving temperament the closest to my father of us three Grant boys.

"Father trusts Orvil's judgment," Simpson replied gamely, "just as I'm sure he doubts yours. He's rip-roaring mad about your having quit the army."

"The army wasn't for me," I replied, "or I for it."

Simpson shrugged. "You made captain awful quick," he said, "and drank it away just as fast. But, more importantly, you got away with that West Point business," he said, when a coughing fit seized him, and he spat up some blood. The conversation stopped there.

We rode the train home and I learned more about my father's situation. He was caught in the grip of unabating success. Having reached his sixtieth birthday, he decided to retire, meaning he decided to run the business from over Simpson's and Orvil's shoulders. He was now worth the $100,000 Simpson promised a few years before, which was fifty times a pleasant annual wage, or over fifteen times my salary when I was Lieutenant General, a considerable sum.

My father moved to Covington, Kentucky, just across the river from the largest city in the area, Cincinnati. He chose it because of the cultural opportunities it offered my sisters, or to put it more plainly, improved prospects for marriage. (It didn't work, of course. My sister Mary Frances married a minister, my sister Clara died during the war, and my sister Jenny's inability to find a more suitable husband than Abel Corbin would eventually lead to the Crash of 1873.)

The tannery opened a wholesaling operation in Galena, Illinois, a mining town on the Mississippi River. "There's room for you in the operation, Ulysses, if you're willing to join us," young Orvil offered.

"You can board with Simpson up in Galena while your family lives here, which would save us all a substantial sum of money," the old man added, considering the matter settled.

"She might prefer to stay with her own family," I replied.

"Her family!" my father responded, his voice dripping scorn. "The Dents are slave people, son."

"They're the kind of people behind the Kansas-Nebraska Act," Orvil said, spitting out the words as if they were obscene.

My father winced as he heard the words. "That infernal traitor Douglas," he swore, referring to Stephen Douglas, the "Little Giant" and author of the Kansas-Nebraska Act, which allowed for the possibility of slavery in the soon-to-be-formed territories of Kansas and Nebraska. "You watch these slave people"—my father wagged his finger for emphasis—"first they got the Fugitive Slave Law. Then they got the Kansas-Nebraska Act. Then, before you know it, you'll have slaves in every quarter of the country. This country doesn't need slavery. It needs homesteaders, new settlers, land grant colleges, new roads. It needs a transcontinental railroad through Chicago! That's what it needs," he growled. "The slavocracy must go. The Whig Party is this country's only salvation!"

"The Whig Party?" I exclaimed. "There hasn't been a Whig Party since Scott was beaten by Pierce in '52! There's nothing left to the Whig Party save for a bunch of vile, Paddy-hating Know-Nothings!"

"There's nothing wrong with the Know-Nothings," my father shot back. "They're just trying to protect the Anglo-Saxon. It's getting so that *our* people can't get a fair shake! Those Paddies are disgusting people—they drink like fish, and they hardly work a lick. They just get off the boat from Dublin and go straight to the saloon, where some Democrat paper pusher makes them citizens and registers them to vote. Rum and Romanism, that's what they stand for! And then there's the Dutch," he continued, meaning the Germans. "They're better organized than an anthill! They read Dutch newspapers, send their kids to Dutch schools, and talk Dutch to each other. They're like some secret society, just like the dagos and the Jewboys—heaven help us if that kind ever gets here! The Dutch machine runs St. Louis and they'll be running every other city west of the Appalachians before they're through!"

"Well, I saw the Paddies and the Dutch fight in Mexico, and they seem to die like Americans, as far as I could tell," I said, unwilling to let his tirade go unchallenged. "Besides, you seem to have a warm feeling for the rights of Negroes that doesn't quite extend to the Paddies and the Dutch."

"Niggers? The hell with the niggers! I don't care a fig for the niggers. All I want is an end to slavery. After slavery, let 'em rot in the hell that turned 'em black! You know the real problem with slavery? Slaves don't buy harnesses! They don't buy bridles and saddles, they don't buy belts and boots the way small farmers do. When a nigger comes to my store with a dollar for a bridle, that's when *I'll* shake his hand, and not till then! Settlers, farmers, they create new business, they grow the market. Do you think we'd ever have accumulated one dollar if we were surrounded by plantations? That's my interest. Build the local market—homesteading, roads, railroads, tariffs, schools. Get rid of the niggers and the slavers and the Paddies and all the other types who want to compete with the small farmer and small businessman!" Simpson and Orvil nodded and all but said amen! I considered the prospect of trading my life with Mrs. Grant and my children for an existence with these people and took the train out of Cincinnati for St. Louis the next morning.

When I came up the path to White Haven, it was as if the scene had never changed. The Colonel was sitting on his porch, reading his newspaper and muttering to himself, a dog at his feet and a clay pipe in his hand. His last remaining able-bodied male slave, a mulatto named William, was repairing a railing as Black Julia swept. Slave children played with little white tots in the dirt in front of the house. But this time, the little tots were mine.

"Praise de Lawd, it's Marse Grant!" one of the older slave children exclaimed, and I was suddenly the center of a beehive of activity even more frenetic than the one that greeted me when I returned from

Mexico six years before. Mrs. Grant rushed to me and presented me with my sons. Fred, the Little Dog, was now four: He hugged me dutifully but regarded me as an immense curiosity just the same. Buck, now almost two, was as handsome a little boy as could be imagined, even if he squawked and pulled back in fear at the prospect of being lifted off the ground by a strange, bearded man.

I recounted my father's proposal to Mrs. Grant and it did not take us a moment to decide to stay in St. Louis. Colonel Dent—I was now getting used to his self-bestowed brevecy—had given Julia something on the order of sixty acres of land next to White Haven when we were married and we decided to stay there and farm them. Louis Dent, Julia's brother, escaped his assailants to try his luck in California a few years back and allowed us to live in his house—"Wish-ton-wish" he called it, which he said was Indian for "whippoorwill"—until I built one on our land.

I did not relish the idea of extending my ties to Colonel Dent, but I had no other way to keep my family together. He, on the other hand, was overjoyed by our decision.

"Delightful!" he exclaimed. "Just delightful! We need new blood like yours, Grant, if the slave economy is going to survive!" He was just as eager as my father to share his opinions on events since I went west. "Why, if it weren't for good Democrats like Stephen Douglas, the nigger-loving Whigs and their hateful friends the Know-Nothings— how a white man turns against his own kind, even if he speaks with a touch of brogue, is beyond me—would have long ago allowed the avaricious mercantile capitalists to strip slave society of its property and its freedom. There'd be a railroad on one side of this property and a land grant college on the other, none of it any use to me," he said, spitting angry invective. "Why the hell would I want a nigger to read? I can *tell* him what's in the Bible just fine as is. Why, if it weren't for the Kansas-Nebraska Act, Missouri would be surrounded on three sides by slave-thieving states! Think of it! Kansas, Iowa, Illinois—a nigger could run in any direction! That's what they want, Grant—they want to set the niggers free and bring 'em up North to balance out the Democrat advantage amongst the hardworking Irish and Germans in our cities! They want him to bring down wages in the name of their merciless quest to accumulate wealth and expand their dominance!" He sneered at this perfidious Republican scheme. "I say this country needs states' rights, freedom of property, and a transcontinental rail-road through New Orleans! Move that cotton east! That's what we need!" He caught his breath and leaned toward me, his clay pipe set in his teeth and one of his hamlike hands resting on my shoulder. "You know the radical Republican three-point program, don't you?" He briefly looked about, to assure himself that only gentlemen of his caliber were present. "It's a nigger in the jury box, a nigger at the ballot box, and a nigger in your daughter's box!" And with that he fell back in laughter, shaking his head at his great wisdom.

But I was fully prepared to ignore the Colonel's boorishness and focus instead on building a new life on our family farm. Almost all of Julia's acreage was densely wooded and would require clearing. This would be hard labor, but it would produce firewood in ample quantities—I estimated I could clear ten acres a year, producing three hundred cords at the going rate of four dollars a cord—even more than it fetched in California. And the acreage cleared could immediately be devoted to wheat, the price of which had risen dramatically since the Crimean War closed down the port of Odessa and prohibited the Russian grain harvest from going to market. And there would be some corn, oats, and potatoes to go with the wheat and the wood, all of it just as it was supposed to be before the banks of the Columbia River overflowed and swept away my future.

In the winter of 1854–55, it all seemed as if it were about to work. I cleared the elms and oaks and hired local Freedmen to help me—paying them ten cents a cord over the going rate to make a statement to the Colonel, I suppose—and borrowed the mulatto, William (Mrs. Grant's half-brother, I sometimes suspected), to help. I had just paid the Freedmen their wages one afternoon and was getting into the driver's bench of my buckboard to return home when William looked up at me with the most quizzical of expressions.

"Cap'n?" he began. "May I ask you somethin'?"

I nodded and his face went through a series of contortions as he mentally formed his words. "You pays them Free'men a tad more than the goin' rate, ain't that right?"

I nodded once again.

"Well, why's that? The only thing you got lots of is nothin'," he noted. "Where you come off payin' them Free'men like that?"

"I suppose I'm trying to do the right thing, William," I responded.

"The right thing, Cap'n?" he repeated.

"Why, yes, William. The right thing—the thing a man has a duty to—"

"Oh, beggin' the cap'n's pardon," William interrupted, "I reckon I know what you mean by *the right thing*. I'm just tryin' to figure what *the right thing* is. I mean, if payin' them Free'men an extra ten cents is *the right thing*, then what do I get?"

I laughed at William's little discourse. "Why, William, you're a slave! What good on earth would ten cents do you?" I snapped the reins and the buckboard started rolling forward, and I spent the trip back home amused by William's odd perspective on the situation.

We sold wood to neighboring farms and in St. Louis, as well as pit props and beams to local miners. Mrs. Grant and I also reacquainted ourselves with the joys of each other's company, so much so that our third child, Nellie, was expected the coming July. By the spring of 1856, I had my house built. It was an ample, notched log home with a center hall, dormered second-story rooms, milled windows and doors, and a plastered interior. Mrs. Grant, who, I would later learn, hated it from the day we moved in (she'd have stayed at White Haven forever and let me suffer the crotchety Colonel), adorned the walls and shelves as best she could and tried to be game about it. She even squeezed out a smile when I told her I named the plain, unpretentious house "Hardscrabble," much as the Dents gave their houses such grandiose names as White Haven, or Wish-ton-wish, or whatever nonsense came to their heads.

My major preoccupation in the summer of 1856 was clearing our land for the planting season next year. When I was not busy cutting wood with William or my Freedman help, I was hauling wood into St. Louis, where I sold it on street corners in my old slouch hat and faded blue army coat. Slumped behind the tired horse tied to my buckboard, I must have seemed quite a dejected figure. But I was happy then, building a life for my little family, living in a house I had built, playing on the floor by the fireplace with Fred the Little Dog and Buck in the evenings.

I was rolling down a street in downtown St. Louis late that fall of 1856 when a military man, resplendent in a new uniform with gold trimmings, came riding toward me. I peered at him, as I did every man in a uniform, wondering if it would be an old friend. This time I was not disappointed, for it was Harney, a colonel I knew from the Mexican War, now wearing a general's uniform.

"Grant!" he shouted when he beheld my rueful countenance. "What in blazes are you doing?"

"I'm hauling wood, Colonel," I said, truthful as it was.

"So you are," he replied, falling back in his saddle in laughter. "But it's General now," he added, tugging at his coat to show me the star on his shoulder. "I'm at Jefferson—we're staging a mission against the Sioux," he said with relish, "but first there's a card game at the Planters House waiting, and we would welcome your joining us."

I scratched my untrimmed beard. The Planters House was St. Louis' best hotel, and I was not groomed for the occasion. "Unfortunately, General, I'm not dressed for company," I said.

"A uniform is dress enough, however old, so long as it's not been disgraced," Harney said.

"Well"—I shrugged—"my uniform's only disgrace is having me in it."

Harney laughed. "A uniform that's been to Cerro Gordo and San Cosme has suffered no disgrace," he said. "Hitch your team and come in with us."

There was quite a reunion waiting for me inside. Buell was there, and Longstreet and Beauregard as well, along with Wilcox and Pratte, the fellows who'd been groomsmen at my wedding, and a few others I'd met along the line. "Heavens, Bill!" Buell called out to Harney when I entered. "Where did you find this stray dog? It's amazing how civilian life wears on a man!" I smiled thinly. Buell, headstrong as ever, had spoken the evident truth about me.

"Still masquerading as one of us?" Longstreet asked, pinching my coat.

"Only to move my goods," I replied. "And if I were Donald, I'd beware the stray dog who bites."

"It's *Don*," Buell said over a chorus of groans. Harney came back to our table with a bottle of whiskey. "Well, here's a drop of what you seem to need, Sam," he said, reaching with the bottle's rim for a glass set before me. Longstreet began dealing out a game of brag.

"Water and nothing more," I said, flipping my glass over before Harney could poison me. "Old Gentleman Tipsy and I have said goodbye."

I could see an eyebrow or two flutter, but not a word was spoken. I quickly turned the talk to politics and the army's business. "So where does one go to make a name in the peacetime army?" I asked casually.

"Kansas," Harney said flatly. "The nigger thieves are crawling all over the place."

"As are the border ruffians," Buell said, glaring at him in response. The sides of the debate were not hard to perceive.

Longstreet sat up in his seat as he played a card and gave them all a reprimanding look. "They're busy killing each other aplenty in Kansas, gentlemen. No need for us to help them here."

Harney nodded. "True enough. Johnston and Lee were sent out there to keep order, but it was no use. After John Brown did his dirty business at Pottawamie Creek—"

I looked up when I heard the name. "John Brown, did you say? From Ohio?"

"The same," Harney said. "Know him?" He then smiled, laying down his cards. "This hand's mine." Longstreet began to gather the deck back up.

"My father did," I said as Longstreet shuffled and dealt. I held back the rest of the story lest the slavery issue divide us again.

"Well, he's the most wanted man in the territory," Beauregard said. "Seems he and his sons were on their way to Lawrence to join in a battle between the two sides, only to find the Free-Soilers had been massacred in large number by the border ruffians. So they snuck into the town and marched a bunch of pro-slavery settlers and their children down to the Pottawamie and cut their heads off with a broadsword in revenge." He threw two cards out on the table and Longstreet replaced them.

"Like so!" Harney glared, drawing a line across his neck.

"John Brown?" I repeated.

"The same," Harney said. "He won't be satisfied until the niggers rise up and murder God-fearing white people in their beds."

"That's all you slavocrats seem to think about, slave uprisings," Buell said. "Ever wonder why that is?"

"Slavery's the natural condition of humanity," Harney responded. He looked at his cards. "This one's mine, too."

"Yes, well," Longstreet said as he gathered the cards again, "the Pot-

tawamie incident—if we may call it that—predictably led to retalia-
tion."

"And that started the cycle all over again. They're pounding each
other out there," Buell reported. "Even Johnston and Lee couldn't
keep a rein on the proceedings. There's a bogus legislature—"

"That's radical talk." Harney glared.

"When Frémont is elected, it won't be," Buell retorted. The Republicans had nominated Frémont, the flamboyant Pathfinder, as their
first Presidential candidate in 1856. To his credit, he was young and
good-looking, in contrast to the Democratic candidate, Buchanan—
not my old commander, but a shriveled old bachelor with the virtue of
being tolerant of slavery while also being from Pennsylvania, a Northern state.

"Well, Buchanan's my man," Longstreet said. "What about you,
Sam?"

"I suppose I'll vote for Buchanan," I admitted.

Buell was aghast. "Why the devil would you do that?"

I shrugged. "Because I knew Frémont, in California." No one could
argue with that.

We spent the rest of the evening playing cards and navigating the
edge of argument until Buell and Harney tired of it and we said our
good-byes. Longstreet and I walked through the hotel lobby together,
and though he spoke not a word, I could see the pity in his eyes for my
raggedness—I suppose the absence of his usual taunts gave him away
the most. So I reached into my pocket and took out a five-dollar gold
piece, the sum of what I had earned that day.

"Here," I said, taking his hand and pressing the coin into it. "I owe
you this."

"Owe me?" he replied, drawing away. "How could you owe me?"

"Right after Julia and I were married and before we left for Detroit.
You loaned it to me when I needed steamer fare for us to get to
Bethel."

He looked at me, puzzled. "I might have, I suppose—"

"You did." I smiled, and folded his big hand around the coin. "You
told me to buy myself a new dress."

He looked at me uncertainly and smiled. "Well, that sounds right,"
and he put the gold piece in his pocket.

"Thanks," I said. "I can't let a debt go unpaid." And with that we parted. I'd teach him not to pity me!

It was probably no more than fifteen minutes before I wished I had that gold piece back.

That winter was a brutal one. Mrs. Dent died in January 1857, which upset not only Mrs. Grant, of course, but me as well, not just for the loss of the good woman's charm, but also for her moderating influence on her husband, the Colonel, who left White Haven and the mulatto slave, William, to us and moved to St. Louis. And I had to finish clearing our acreage, with only my ragged army coat and a pair of threadbare gloves to protect me from the brutal cold, before the coming planting season, and do the chopping that remained, which kept me and the local Freedmen I hired busy, as well as the mulatto, William.

But planting required capital for seed and implements, and I had none. Nor did the Colonel, whose fortunes were waning faster than ever. It pained me to do it, but I was forced to appeal to my father for aid. I wrote to him explaining that, while I might have now been in my thirty-fifth year, I was really just starting out and a parent had a responsibility of sorts, didn't he? Besides, I was coming to like farming, I told both him and myself, and had no doubt I could muster three hundred bushels of potatoes or more, along with oats and barley, and the firewood I chopped. It was the perfect business plan, and I appealed to his senses of reason and obligation. He turned me down outright. No use pumping more money into a failed venture and those crazy Dents, he said.

And so he left me to fail. As I look back at it now, it was remarkable not that I had failed so often, but that I never seemed to tire of failing, that I endured each blow and struggled to my feet to prepare for the next one with a grim, stoic sense of purpose and resolve. I should have gone to Kentucky and grabbed the old man by the throat and shook the money out of him. But, instead, I blamed myself for his parsimony and, with an unrelenting determination, pressed on.

I scraped together what I could to begin planting wheat and potatoes, but my yields were low, and I was vexed by the end of the Crimean War, which lowered agricultural prices as Russian crops were once again on the world market. By the summer of 1857, everyone went broke. Banks failed, stock markets crashed, debtors went bank-rupt, and mobs swarmed city streets in search of bread—the nation had not seen such hardship in a generation. So by the end of the sum-mer I had no product to sell, no market to sell to, and was back to sell-ing wood on street corners.

I recall doing my regular turn in my faded army overcoat, standing by the Jefferson Barracks on a November afternoon, the kind of day that first foretells the coming winter. The air's autumnal bite led the occasional passerby to buy a few pieces of wood for his stove, and my good feeling about this venture was for a moment buoyed. I was cer-tainly no carnival barker, but a little boosting couldn't hurt, I reasoned, so I began to mumble to the people walking past.

"Wood, sir? Firewood, sir?" Some of them nodded and a few of them stopped, so I kept at it. "Wood, sir? Firewood, sir?" I continued, when a rangy fellow in a coat almost as worn as mine—a fellow who looked more like a wood seller than a wood buyer—turned toward me and snapped a peevish retort.

"Wood? Do I look like I need any fucking wood?"

I drew back at the fellow's vitriol when something—perhaps the man's gaunt look, perhaps his choice of language—made me realize who was addressing me. "Cump!" I exclaimed to my delight. "Cump, it's me, Sam!"

It had been seventeen years since we last saw each other at West Point, and I could not blame Sherman for wondering who was ad-dressing him. "What the . . ." He squinted at me, when a look of recog-nition came over him and his drawn face broke out into a smile. "Well, I'll be fucked and then goddamned! Sam Grant!" he drawled, rubbing his unshaven chin with his hand. "I heard you were out of the army! How's it going for you?"

I shrugged and nodded toward my pile of wood. "Well, I'm busy fighting poverty, Cump," I said, smiling as I stated the fact plainly. "How about you?"

He looked me and my buckboard of wood over, then bit his lip. "I'm a dead cock in the pit, Sam." He sighed, the joy quickly draining from him. "I'm flat bust."

I nodded in heartfelt agreement. "I had heard you were doing all right for a while in California."

Sherman shook his head. "California isn't a place, Sam. It's a madness. I was stationed at San Francisco in '48, before the whole thing hit." He shook his gaunt, twitchy head, his red hair amiss and his dark eyes burning as he spoke. "It was the damnedest thing you ever saw. I was the officer on duty at the telegraph station one night, and this fellow comes in, he's sweating, nervous, see?" Sherman grew more animated as he told his story. "He says, 'I've got to send a message east,' looking around like he was afraid someone might hear. So I says to him, 'Well, you've come to the right place. Why don't you just tell me what you want to say and I'll tap it out for you right here.' See, I had the telegraph key right there at my desk. So the man says, 'Well, how do I know I can trust you?' and I said, 'Well, because you can.' So the fellow looks me over and he writes a few words on a piece of paper, and I start tapping them out. It says: GOLD DISCOVERED AT SUTTER'S MILL."

He licked his lips as he paused and allowed me to reflect on this accident of fate. "Oh, I'd have been a rich man today, yessir," he said, a strained smile on his lips. "Another man might have bought up every fucking parcel of land he could, taken advantage of what he knew."

I nodded soberly. Sherman would have cut off his own hand before engaging in that kind of thing. "They were digging money out of the ground back then, Sam," he said.

"I know," I told him. "I was at Fort Vancouver and then Humboldt Bay."

Sherman looked down. "I heard. I heard they were going to throw your ass out for drinking."

"Well, I had a few nips once or twice." There was no sense in denying it. "I—I was lonely, Cump."

"You got a family now?" he asked.

"Yes," I said, "I got three kids, one more on the way." Mrs. Grant was due to have our fourth in February.

Sherman looked down for a moment. "Yeah, I'm married, too—I got married and went into the banking business. Hell, everybody gave me their money to invest—Halleck, Buell, Thomas, Hooker, even Bragg." He sighed heavily. "Well, the crash wiped us out." He meant the Crash of 1857, of course. It had cleaned him out just as it had me. "But I paid 'em all back every fucking cent, out of my own pocket, too, because I'd given each of them my word."

I shook my head sympathetically as I watched Sherman standing there, dying before my very eyes, a victim of his own sense of duty and honor. I admired him and sympathized with him—there were times, I thought, when a man was simply cursed to do *the right thing*.

"Well, Cump," I said consolingly, "you did what you had to do."

"Did what I had to do?" he snorted, and a distant look overcame him. "Everyone in California did what they had to do, Sam. The miners mined because they had to, the politicians stole because they had to, the whores filled the bordellos because they had to. There's no glory and no reward for doing what you have to do anymore, Sam. The whole fucking country is busy doing what it has to do, whether it's John Brown cutting the heads off innocent people or bounty hunters bringing runaway niggers back to the plantation."

He looked past me as if overwhelmed by a vision and raised his voice as if possessed. "This country is bound for Armageddon, Sam. White against black, North against South, master against slave, rich against poor. Rivers of blood will flow in every corner of this land, all of it drawn by the swords of men who did what they had to do! Oh, I hear them! They say, 'That's fucking Sherman for you, he's nuts.' But there'll come a day when all scores will be settled, Sam, settled by men who did what they had to do!"

He had so raised his voice and taken on a madman's temperament in the course of his rambling that passersby on the street stopped to regard us: a red-haired, wild-eyed man yelling to a dirty, slouching streetside wood seller. I scratched my head and looked up at him. "Well, you may be right, Cump."

He suddenly twitched and focused on me as if emerging from a trance, then shuffled his feet, embarrassed by his outburst. We stood there for a moment, avoiding each other's gazes as only failures can, until Sherman spoke up. "Well, I guess a West Point education doesn't do much to prepare a man for business," he said with a meek chuckle.

"I guess not, Cump," I said. Had I anything else to say, I'd have said it. But instead we let another moment go by and he nodded at me one last time.

"Hope you sell some wood, Sam."

"I'll be seeing you, Cump," I answered, not believing I ever would. Both of us seemed destined to dry up and blow away, regardless of what mad vision Sherman might have had or what some Mexican apparition might have had in mind for me. He tipped his fingers toward me in the hint of a salute and started walking down the street as I turned away. Sixth in his class, a young man of such energy and drive, now as busted and as beaten as I was. When I looked his way again, he was gone.

In a few weeks it was Christmas: I pawned my watch for twenty-two dollars to buy presents for Mrs. Grant and the children. In February, Mrs. Grant had our fourth child, and I found myself clinging to hope again. I even named the boy Jesse Root Grant after my father, just to please the old man in case I had to go back to him yet again.

The spring of 1858, I planted with one hand as I staved off bankruptcy with the other. By June, I could see it was no use. A late frost decimated my crop. An epidemic of typhoid followed, to which almost all of us succumbed. I was laid up for months, worried the disease was really tuberculosis and I was doomed to die as Simpson was dying. I was taking healthy doses of capsicum to alleviate the pain, which had the effect of leaving me looking as unsteady as if I'd never stopped imbibing. Drunk again, the neighbors said, and my reputation lived on. By that fall, we had at best a meager crop coming in and no money or options left.

Whoever hears of me in ten years will hear of a well-to-do Missouri farmer.

Well, there was another option—selling the slave William, whom the Colonel had given me. An able-bodied male such as William was worth about fifteen hundred dollars on the open market, and this at a time when I could not cajole an additional thousand dollars from my father. I always had some sympathy for my father's Free-Soil views, even if I was taken aback by the radicalism of some of its members— my father's old acquaintance John Brown among them. But now the courage of my convictions was being put to the test, and I spent a long night alone before I reached a decision.

I summoned William and waited for him, sitting in a rocker on the *piazza* of White Haven, just as the Colonel once had. I regarded him as he approached, slight of build and youthful-looking, wearing a slough hat like my own.

"You call me, Cap'n?" he asked.

"Yes, William, I did," I said as I plunged into the topic. "William, I've come to an important decision."

He looked at me, perplexed. "You goin' to sell the farm, Marse

Grant? It's about time, I reckon," he said, shaking his head sadly. "Ain't goin' your way at all."

His appraisal took me aback. "No, no, I'm not selling the farm," I said peevishly.

His face screwed up anxiously. "Then is you goin' to sell me, now? I'd sure fetch a pretty dollar nowadays, and you got to be stone-cold broke, for sure."

"Oh, I thought about it, William," I confessed. "But I concluded that one man does not have the right to sell another, regardless of the gain to be made. And that is why I am speaking with you," I said, reaching into the pocket of my vest and producing a letter I had written only an hour before. "William, you can read a bit, isn't that right?"

"Just the slightest bit," he said. "The Colonel always say he'd whip any his niggers that learned to read, so I had to be careful."

"Can you read this?" I asked, and handed him the letter. He took it and peered into it wide-eyed, but after a few moments his eyes began to move more fluidly. "Go ahead," I prodded. "Read it aloud, if you can."

He nodded. "If you insist," he said, and he recited with a clear voice:

"'*Know all persons by these presents, that I Ulysses S. Grant of the city & county of St. Louis in the State of Missouri, for divers good and valuable considerations—*'" Here he stopped tentatively. "Marse Grant, you might have spelt *diverse* incorrectly, unless your intention's to use the French word *divers*, although I can't be seeing that, but"— he shrugged—"well, anyways, '*do hereby emancipate and set free from Slavery my Negro man, William, sometimes called William Jones, of mulatto complexion, aged about thirty-five years, and about five feet seven inches in height and being the same slave purchased by me of Frederick Dent. And I do hereby manumit, emancipate, and set free said William from slavery forever.*'"

"You read that well," I remarked.

"Yes, well, now that I'm goin' to be free and not whupped by the Colonel, ain't no reason to hold back," he said matter-of-factly.

I was surprised by this revelation but pressed forward, regardless. "Well, that is the case, William, I have decided to set you free."

He examined the paper again. "That's all there's to it?" he said. I nodded. "And I can keep this here paper?"

"Yes, you'll certainly need it. I'll take a copy to the court tomorrow,"

I replied. He stood there, dumbfounded I imagined, and after a moment I found myself amused by his reaction. "Well, you're as quiet as a Plains Indian," I prodded. "At the very least you might move the conversation along with an expression of thanks," I chided him gently.

His face was suddenly hard. "Thank you, Grant? For my freedom?" I nodded and smiled good-naturedly. "Frankly, Grant, I was wonderin' how you got my freedom in the first place. I don't remember giving it to you, and I'm hard-pressed to deliver thank you for what got took from me in the first place."

I was disoriented both at being called Grant without the use of the title *Marse*, or even *Cap'n*, though that was the logical consequence of my decision, and at what felt like a challenge to the integrity of my good deed. "I've never had a slave before, William, but I've searched my soul and I know I'm doing *the right thing*."

He nodded, paused a moment, then fixed me with a stare. "And that's it? Does I get a 'pology, perhaps? Do your soul got a 'pology in it to go with the rest of it? I believe a 'pology ought come before a thank you, if you ask me."

"An apology? For doing the right thing?" I rankled at the suggestion. "Frankly, William, while I regret any mistreatment you may have experienced at the Colonel's hand, or any I may have inadvertently visited upon you, an apology seems out of order. I'm simply trying to—"

"Well, your heart is as big as the great outdoors, ain't it, Grant? But I bet your intentions wouldn't be as noble if your farm weren't nothing but dirt and you wasn't tryin' to get cozy with them Free-Soilers in Saint Louee who give out those gummint jobs. I bet for sure my hind end would be out chopping more damn green wood or maybe goin' to auction if you was making a go of it planting wheat and taters," he said.

"That's uncalled for!" I protested. "I'm just trying to do the right thing—this is about slavery, nothing else! I cannot be a part of it," I said, unwilling to look too deeply into my conscience to test William's hypothesis.

"Oh, this is about slavery all right, Grant. But if you want no part in it maybe you wanna look at the way you dropped yourself on the mercy of the ole Colonel for your sustenance, while his niggers was busting they hind ends."

I offered no response to the obvious truth of this statement, and he continued.

"My point ain't that I don't appreciate your manumizin' me, 'cause I surely will rejoice when I walk off this here plantation. It's just that before you get overwhelmed with your piety at doin' *the right thing*, you'd do well to examine your own situation," he said, looking at me as directly as—well, as directly as a free man.

He certainly was a source of fresh perspective, I thought. I had succeeded at reuniting myself with my family, but at the cost of posing as a gentleman farmer, a facade I could maintain no better than could the Colonel. What a paradox! In liberating William, I had set him free to show me the way—the way off this failed farm and out into a world in which I had yet to find my place. I was considering this proposition when I realized William was already, in fact, walking away. "William," I shouted after him. "Where will you go now?"

He turned and shrugged, then took a step or two back toward me. "I don't know, Grant. I suspect I ain't goin' to live much longer. Now that Dred Scott be a slave no matter where they take him, bounty hunters are out to catch a nigger no matter where he go. But that's the chance I'm going to take."

I nodded. William's freedom was perhaps less of a favor than I had imagined. "And what will you do?"

He smiled broadly. "I once told myself, if I ever got free, I would write a book."

"A book?"

"I'm goin' write a book called *Uncle William's Cabin*," he said with a wistful look. "I heard about Uncle Tom's book and I thought, I can write as good as some ole slave named Tom. But I ain't going to die like Tom did in his book, no suh. When Simon Lagree whup my hind end in my book, I'm going turn around and . . ." He sighed and shrugged off his unlikely dream. "Well, maybe. But writin' books beats farming, don't it, Grant?"

I laughed with him. "Most everything does," I admitted, and with that he turned and walked away.

If I was to find my place in the world, I would have to call upon my father and beg him for mercy, plead with him for a job in the leather goods operation. But Mrs. Grant was deathly opposed to my doing so and devised an alternative. She had a cousin in St. Louis named Harry

Boggs, who ran a real estate and rent collection agency there and would give me a job renting out properties and collecting old rents.

Now, why I thought I would be able to collect rents is beyond me—not only was I a soft touch for every hard-luck story I'd ever heard, but the economy was still recovering from the Crash of 1857 and indigent tenants were commonplace. But I was determined to give it a try, and we traded our farm for a house in St. Louis.

Regarding my career in real estate, I shall be as brief as was my career. Inside a few months of the winter of 1858–59, it became obvious to Harry Boggs and me that I was a drag on the operation. Delinquent renters always had stories that sent me away empty-handed, and potential new renters were able to secure terms from me that made no business sense. By the fall of 1859 I was done with this work, and now nothing stood between me and my father's doorstep.

"I'm going to send you to Galena," the old man said. "Simpson's not healthy enough to travel out into the country anymore. Somebody's got to go out there and buy hides for the operation. You can do that while you're clerking in the store and doing the books." He regarded me sternly. "I suppose we could have done this twenty-odd years ago and avoided all of the nonsense in between," he said.

"Yes," I answered. "I suppose so."

And so Mrs. Grant and the children and I moved to Galena in the spring of 1860. We found ourselves a modest house with a view of the cemetery and each day I walked to the store at 145 Main Street—J. R. Grant and Sons—where I donned my clerk's apron and began receiving the steady stream of customers our prospering business entertained. Orvil and Simpson spent most of their time in the back room of the place, by the big, potbellied stove around which they did their business, receiving a regular group of visitors whose relationships to them I did not at first understand.

No jail cell could have been more oppressive to me than the front room of that store, as I looked at its teeming shelves and piles of leather goods and contemplated my destiny. Had I really usurped my way to West Point, faced death in Mexico, led my charges through Panama, and endured my disgraceful disengagement from the army in California, only to find myself the junior partner of my avaricious younger brothers? This was not a job. This was internment.

I fought to deny it. I had a loving wife, four beautiful children, and a way to provide them with sustenance. I had seen men die of enemy fire and a plague's wrath. If my circumstances were uninspiringly common, that should not overcome my joy at being alive. And so each morning I rose and walked to 145 Main Street determined to find contentment in my surroundings.

I was in my second or third week in Galena, in the spring of 1860, a man of thirty-seven, my hope struggling against my despair, when the bell attached to the front door of our establishment rang to herald a young family entering the store.

I looked at the father of this ensemble, and this time there was no doubt in my mind, no uncertainty, as there had been when he passed me—if it was he who had passed me—on the gangway in San Francisco six years before.

Useful Grant stood before me.

He was dressed in a fine woolen suit and vest the color of dark chocolate, an ivory silk shirt, and a cravat of yellow and orange with a diamond pin stuck into it. He had on a gentleman's hat of dark brown beaver fur with a rich tan satin ribbon around its base. His wife was a handsome woman, perhaps ten years younger, wearing a blue satin dress with flared, brocaded skirts corseted around a slender waist. Four children trailed behind them, three boys and a girl, in the same sequence, and apparently the same ages, as Fred, Buck, Nellie, and Jessie. Each was dressed in a sailor suit or crinolines, their manner was calm, and their deportments perfect. The six of them were the picture of contented, domestic peace.

I could not help but gape, my eyes darting between Useful and his family, looking at him each time to confirm anew it was really he. He surveyed the inside of the store and then looked at me expectantly, as one regards a clerk. I struggled to hide my astonishment.

"How may I be of service?" I said hesitantly.

"My family and I are about to visit my wife's people," he said pleasantly, "and it occurred to me that a fine leather wallet might be an appropriate gift to present to my father-in-law upon our arrival. Have you such an item?"

"Why, yes, I think we do," I responded, and turned from him to inspect the various shelves. In reality, my pretense of search was only to give me time to probe. "From where have you come?" I asked in as casual a manner as I could muster.

"We have just arrived from San Francisco, where we resided these past several years," Useful said airily. It *was* him! We *had* crossed paths in San Francisco! "And a strenuous trip it was, across Central America, then to New Orleans, then upriver to here. We are headed for Chicago."

"I see," I said, nodding as I rummaged through various drawers, playing for time. "Cross at Panama, did you?"

"Nicaragua," he corrected. "Panama has the cholera. There was an epidemic in '52, in fact. Any poor fool would be daft to attempt it."

I clenched my teeth to dispel the ghastly remembrances of soldiers grabbing their bellies and dropping to the ground in the pelting rain, of the race to inter them in the runny mud and be off again. "Were you a prospector in San Francisco?" I asked.

He laughed. "Only for the briefest of moments, I can assure you," he replied. "It soon occurred to me there was more and surer money to be made around the goldfields than in them. I sold provisions—cattle, timber, potatoes, you name it, so long as it could be promptly delivered at an advantageous price," he crowed, absorbed in the retelling of his conquests. "Ice! Now, there was a pretty business! It's hard to imagine here in the North, but you could sail a boat up to Alaska, cut ice from the glaciers, and sail it back down to San Francisco—avoiding, of course, the northerlies that often blow up the coast—and sell it by the pound as if it were the very gold the miners strained to find!"

I could feel my insides curdle as he continued his story. "Once I amassed my capital, I began investing in real estate—lots, parcels, acreage, then whole tracts, claims, developments. The '57 crash slowed things down, to be sure, but fundamental value will always be preserved, that's my rule for investing." He smiled with great self-satisfaction and drew an arm around his young wife, who listened to his narrative with dutiful attention.

"And you're here on a visit, you said?" I asked as I perused a stack of garments as part of my feigned search.

"No, we're moving back home. I've liquidated my western holdings and have decided to search for business opportunities in these parts."

I nodded. "Then you're from here originally?"

"Ohio," he said quietly.

"Born there?"

"Been from there as long as I can remember," he said, leaving me to wonder if his words were the product of a dappled memory. "And that's why I wish to return. Because Ohio is a place where a man can build a life not just for himself and his family, but for his community," he orated as his wife put a small, soft hand on his sleeve, conveying by her expression it was time to move on. "Well, I have talked quite enough, clerk. In a moment I'll be asking you about yourself." He laughed, amused at the idea of being interested in a store clerk. "Have you been able to find the item in question?"

"I'm afraid not." I sighed. "Mr.—why, I don't believe that I had the pleasure of learning your name," I said.

"Robinson," he responded enthusiastically, extending a hand upon which perched a sizable diamond ring. "Charles Robinson. And you, sir, might be . . ."

"Grant," I obliged, slowly and carefully. "Ulysses Grant is my name."

He didn't so much as blink. "A pleasure, Mr. Grant," he said. "And I thank you for your assistance. Good day to you." And with that he shepherded his handsome wife and beautiful children out the door.

The sound of the bell attached to the door summoned Orvil from the back room. "Sell anything to that fellow?" he asked, sticking his head through the doorway.

"No," I said softly. "He just wanted directions."

Orvil grunted and left me silently alone.

Only when I felt them a moment later did I realize tears were running down my cheeks. Even now, twenty years after my father and I had stripped him of his name and future, Useful was still besting me at every turn. Ice! *Ice!* The cruel ignominy of it overwhelmed me, and I dropped my head into my hands and allowed myself to succumb at last to my misery over what had become of me.

I was a failure. I had failed as a soldier, a farmer, a woodcutter, a bill collector, and a clerk. I had drunk myself into oblivion and could not work my way out of it. I had condemned my wife to shame and my children to destitution. My mind reeled as I thought of every villain and every happenstance on which I had placed blame over the years— Bonneville, Buchanan, the cholera, the Columbia River, the Crimean War, my father, Simpson, Orvil, Colonel Dent, my well-developed sense of right and wrong, deadbeat debtors, the northerly winds, the southern cattle route into 'Frisco, the Crash of '57. But the list now ended, at last, with me. Useful, a man stripped of everything, sent off into the woods to run for his life, had returned in possession of the success and prosperity that had eluded me. And I, who had stripped him of those things, had squandered them and failed absolutely.

My chest heaved as I sobbed, sobbed as I never had before in life and never would again, my head throbbing and my heart engulfed in self-pity. And then it occurred to me: *Mescalito had the wrong man.* After all I had been through, how could I have been so blind? How could I have missed the daily grinding evidence of the Master's meaning? It was Useful who was destined for greatness. If I had ever been so destined, I had bartered that destiny away, exchanging it as had the befuddled Esau for the thin porridge of military life. I had tricked Useful out of nothing—I merely had a distracting dalliance with hope, the hope that a greater me than the real me would emerge from within me. And while I was distracted by hope, Fate had conspired with my own essential nature to condemn me to stand behind this forsaken counter while my brothers prattled in the back room and another man realized the life to which I had aspired.

I fell to the floor, still sobbing, defying a God in whom I had no faith to reveal to me the role my ineptitude played in some greater plan. I wept the bitter tears a man weeps when the promise of his humanity is broken. And when the last iota of my rage was spent, when I abandoned myself completely to my despair and was too exhausted to produce another tear, a numbness enveloped upon me to which I gladly surrendered, for numbness was now my only solace.

Of course, in a year I would be a general.

In three years I would take Vicksburg.

In five years I would defeat Lee.

In nine years I would be President of the United States.

And in twenty-three years, I would finally understand what it all really meant.

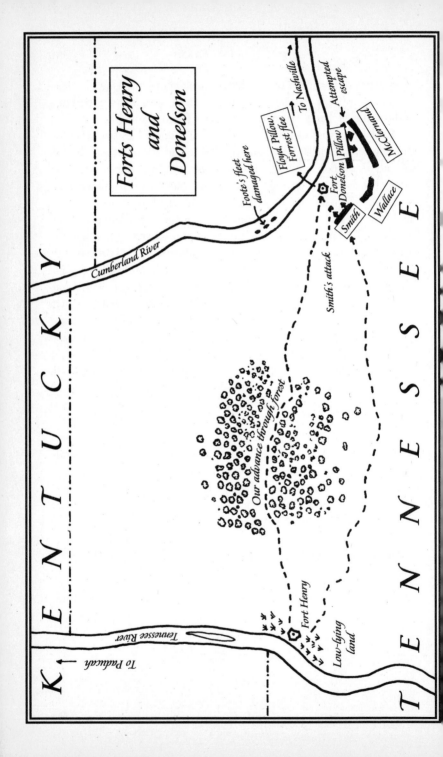

CHAPTER VII

WASHBURNE, RAWLINS, AND PARKER—THE WAR
BEGINS—PROMOTED TO GENERAL—FRÉMONT'S
COMMAND—THE BATTLE OF BELMONT—
HALLECK ARRIVES—THE CAPTURE OF
FORTS HENRY AND DONELSON

W E TEACH OUR CHILDREN that the Civil War began on April 11, 1861, the day the Confederates attacked Fort Sumter, as if the war would not have begun had Sumter not been attacked. But the reality is that war is madness, madness of the highest order and widest scale, and it begins not when some adventurer or divinely inspired zealot first fires a shot, but when the madness takes hold in a people's mind and they give their derangement free rein. The Civil War began not at Sumter, but in all the places where people were seized by the dementia that told them their cause was worthy of their sons' and brothers' lives. It began when they became convinced their righteousness made them invulnerable to bullets, when they concluded that one of *us* was the equal of five, or ten, or twenty of *them*.

And so the Civil War began, for some, the day the first six Confederate States of America convened in Montgomery and Jeff Davis vowed to cleanse with his own tongue each drop of blood spilled in defense of this new nation; for others, the day John Brown was hanged, or entered bloody Kansas to harvest the skulls of the border ruffians; for others, when the Missouri Compromise was set aside, or when Dred Scott was sent back to captivity. It began every time someone, somewhere, succumbed to the madness.

The madness first visited me as I was shucking oysters and pouring whiskey in front of J. R. Grant and Sons in November 1860, the night Lincoln was elected.

I spent much of that year traveling to La Crosse, Prairie du Chien, Cedar Rapids, or the railhead at Dubuque, buying hides or taking orders for the axes, augurs, stirrups, saddles, bridles, bits, and every other manner of tool and horse furniture we sold. When I wasn't traveling or tending to the walk-in trade, I was at a desk in the back room keeping the books, making sure invoices were issued and bills processed, growing ever more reconciled to the stultifying dullness of civilian quartermastering. From my seat, I watched a regular group of visitors gather in the evenings around the cast-iron stove in the center of the room.

The preeminent member of the J. R. Grant and Sons' backroom circle was Elihu B. Washburne, Galena's Republican congressman, a tall, hawkish, potbellied man with a decided limp and with whom Orvil and Simpson organized northern Illinois on behalf of Lincoln and the Republican governor, Yates. Congressman Washburne was a passionate believer in the Railsplitter's candidacy, knowing that were Lincoln and the Republicans to run the country, immense quantities of patronage would flow Congressman Washburne's way. And the Grant brothers were passionate believers in Congressman Washburne, knowing they would be in the flow, and so they financed his local political machine, kept him in sound investments, and generally took good care of him.

I was alone in the store one evening, a few weeks before the 1860 election, when one of the Grant and Sons' number, a six-footer with a massive chest, mountainous shoulders, and arms like pistons, swung the door open with a cabled hand: He was, despite a properly fitting suit worthy of the most respectable professional man, a pure-blooded Indian, with thick, straight, black hair in a braid, and a complexion like that of strong tea.

"Excuse me," I said, wondering where the Indian got the expensive suit. "We're closed now. Perhaps you would care to return—"

"Begging your indulgence, my esteemed shopkeeper," the Indian said, "I apologize for the breach of etiquette posed by my unanticipated arrival, but I was hoping to find my associates, Orvil and Simpson Grant."

Begging my indulgence? "They're not here now," I replied.

"Infinitely regrettable!" the Indian said. "I'm here to inspect a new earthwork fortification along the river and will have to leave tomorrow for the preparation of a rail connection between Davenport and Rock Island." He shrugged and sighed. "But, I suppose as the ancient Hebrews pronounced, *aizeh hoo ashir, hasameach bihelkoh*, or as the Romans said, *ars longa, vita brevis—*" And here he stopped abruptly. "Why, I apologize for my inexcusable mannerlessness, sir! My name is Parker, Eli Parker," he said, extending a massive brown hand toward me.

"Grant," I said awkwardly. "Ulysses Grant."

Parker's face lit up in recognition. "Grant? The hero of San Cosme?" he said excitedly.

"You've heard of me?"

"Simpson mentions you fairly regularly."

I blushed. "He spoke of me that way? As a hero?"

"He mentioned it in the context of your drinking your way out of the army," Parker replied matter-of-factly, "juxtaposing the august nature of your wartime accomplishments and your unanticipated resignation shortly thereafter, which he attributed to inebriation."

"I see," I murmured, wondering what else people in Galena imagined they knew of me. "Well, I am he, Mr. Parker—the hero of San Cosme, the drunkard of Fort Humboldt, the busted farmer of St. Louis, the sales clerk of Galena—all of them me and the pleasure is mine, sir."

The Indian told me his story. Parker had an engineering degree from Rensselaer Polytechnic Institute; he had previously graduated from law school, but was refused admission to the bar in New York State because of his race. He nonetheless chose the white world, becoming the chief engineer for the federal government in the Illinois region and rising to the highest chair in the Galena Freemasons, which is where Orvil, Simpson, and Congressman Washburne came across him. But not only was Parker as well educated as any white man, he was a leader among his own people as well. His father was a Seneca chieftain and his mother the daughter of an Iroquois chief, and he was raised on an Indian reservation in New York. He had been honored by the Senecas, despite his wanderings among the whites: They made him their sachem, which is something like a prime minister, and gave him an honorary new name to go with his title.

"*Do-no-ho-geh-weh*," Parker said, enunciating it clearly.

"And that means?" I asked.

"Keeper of the Western Door of the Long House of the Iroquois," he answered proudly.

"How does one get all of that into five syllables?" I asked.

"It's all how you say it," he replied, when the door opened again and Orvil and Simpson bustled in with the rest of their circle, eager to plot various marches, rallies, and broadsheet printings by the so-called Republican "Wide Awakes," while I returned to my desk for my nightly reading of newspaper accounts of recent political developments.

"The problem with our marches," Congressman Washburne said as they convened around the potbellied stove, "is that torches and banners are handsome but the marching itself, it's so, well . . ."

"Unorganized!" Orvil said.

"Yes! Precisely!" Congressman Washburne agreed. "Our men never seem to walk in rows or have the same foot going forward. They need something . . . they need . . ."

"Drill," Orvil concluded, and the lot of them nodded with enthusiastic unanimity.

"Well, if we need drill," Parker, the Seneca, cut in, "then why not ask Grant?"

Orvil shook his head. "I can't," he said with finality. "I've got a store to run."

"No," Parker corrected. "I meant Ulysses. That one," he said, pointing to me in the corner.

There was a sudden silence as they all turned to me. "He has everything one could ask," Parker went on. "He was a hero at San Cosme, and he was trained at West Point."

Congressman Washburne, a high-strung, fidgety man, leaned forward in his chair.

"You there!" Congressman Washburne called to me from across the room. "Is this true? Are you the hero of—the hero of what was it, Eli?"

"San Cosme. In the Mexican War," Parker repeated. "He is Captain Grant."

Congressman Washburne turned quickly to Orvil and Simpson. "Is this fellow your brother?" he asked, perplexed the news had not reached him before.

Simpson coughed as Orvil stroked his chin. "Yes, he is. I'm sure I must have mentioned him," he answered tentatively.

Congressman Washburne pursed his lips and shook his head. "No, I

don't think you ever did. I always presumed he was simply a clerk."
Congressman Washburne peered at me to confirm his impression.

"He *is* a clerk," Orvil responded.

"I see," Congressman Washburne said, now getting the whole picture. "Well, it's a capital idea!" he concluded.

Truth be told, I was still something of a Douglas Democrat, thinking them the party best suited to keep the Union together. Nonetheless, I was hectored into overseeing the Republican drills once or twice, instructing the men how to march until they could do so without embarrassment. And no doubt the quality of their marching made a difference in the final result, since Lincoln won eighteen states to Douglas's two, with ten others going to Southern candidates, which led the Wide Awakes to march again that night, this time to the top of the bluffs overlooking the Mississippi, where they fired a cannon and then marched back to J. R. Grant and Sons at 145 Main Street for what Orvil called a "jollification," meaning an excuse to get loaded on the Grant brothers' dime. So I found myself shucking oysters for the crowd in front of the store, together with the only other fellow in the backroom circle who did not drink, and with whom I had struck up a bit of friendship, John Rawlins.

Rawlins merited membership at the Grant stove by being the leading lawyer in Galena and, therefore, the lawyer for J. R. Grant and Sons, since Orvil's business practices often required leading lawyering. Rawlins was younger than the others—probably not yet thirty—a small, dark, intense fellow with glowing black eyes and a propensity for rough language exceeded in my experience only by Sherman's. He was fanatical about everything and everybody.

As a boy of sixteen he was abandoned by an alcoholic father and became a charcoal hauler for the lead mines near Galena. He was hauling a load of charcoal at the pits to the smelter when the oxen decided they had worked enough for that day and stalled. Rawlins was said to have beaten them as harshly as a man his size could, and after tiring of doing so hit upon the idea of selling the entire affair—wagon, load, and oxen—to somebody for $250, whereupon he ventured into Galena and asked the then-leading lawyer in town if he could read law under his tutelage. The fellow agreed and Rawlins soon drove his mentor into an early retirement.

Rawlins was fascinated by the Mexican War. He could recount my various adventures—my dash through Monterrey, the assault on Chapultepec, how I played brag with President Pierce, and, of course, my field gunnery from the steeple at San Cosme—to the point where I sometimes wondered which of us had actually done these things. But his greatest fanaticism regarded alcohol, which destroyed his family as a youth and which he vowed never to touch in adult life, a pledge he renewed daily. He abstained, perhaps, to excess.

"I admire the way you have forsworn the demon, Ulysses," he said—few in Galena knew me as Sam by this point—as Lincoln's supporters filled the air around us with a chorus of huzzahs. "I would sooner give my friend a glass of poison than a glass of whiskey."

"I drank to cure loneliness when separated from my family and now have no need of it," I answered as I poured full glasses for those who did.

He nodded toward the revelers around us as we shucked. "I can only hope these drunken Wide Awake sons of bitches are right and the strength of Lincoln's victory will prove the North's resolve and prevent Southern secession and war."

I shook my head. "No, John," I said resolutely. "The South will fight."

I was right. We were headed for war, and events propelled us forward more rapidly than anyone had expected. South Carolina seceded; Mississippi, Florida, Alabama, Georgia, and Louisiana all followed into the treacherous void. Texas joined them soon after. By February 1861, the Confederate States of America met in Montgomery and elected Jefferson Davis president, all while President Buchanan sat and watched. It was only a matter of time before the thirst for war reached Fort Sumter, a mere month after Lincoln was inaugurated. The madness was now in control, and I could hear it calling me using Congressman Washburne's voice.

"The governor is going to need trained officers," he said, taking me aside. "Come with me to Springfield," Congressman Washburne said, "and let me introduce you to him."

Now, I was never one for politics, but I did feel strongly that no state or group of states had the right to tear the Union asunder. The nation created in 1776 had to be preserved, I thought, and if war was required, then so be it. And so we went to Springfield—I eager to find a command, Congressman Washburne eager to offer the governor his newfound prize. As we traveled, my appetite for the effort grew by leaps and bounds. War, my old friend, was coming back, the only enterprise at which I had ever succeeded. No more clerking or selling wood, no more farming or bill collecting. Only war, the real thing, the thrill of combat, the exquisite tension of battle—it was coming back to rescue me from the dullness and failure in which I was entrapped. Congressman Washburne would make sure the governor learned of my training and experience—West Point, Jefferson Barracks, Mexico—and rewarded them. No more desk in the corner in the back. No more ruling lines in the account books and processing invoices.

And so my training and experience were rewarded—the governor gave me a job in Springfield ruling lines and processing invoices, and a desk in the corner in the back, a three-legged one at that.

A fellow named John Pope was designated by Governor Yates to coordinate the mustering of troops from Camp Yates, which the governor had humbly named after himself. Pope graduated a year before me at West Point and served with Taylor in Mexico. I am told Pope remembered me when Governor Yates mentioned my name.

"Washburne thinks very highly of him," Governor Yates was said to have said to Pope. "I think he brought him in a few days ago."

"Seedy-looking fellow," Pope said with a nod.

"Humble-looking," Governor Yates prompted.

"Shifty, vacant look," Pope described.

"Modest."

"Sullen."

"Earnest."

"Desperate."

"Quiet."

"Drinks."

"Loyal?"

"Democrat. Can't tell."

Governor Yates sighed. "What do we do with him?"

"Stick him somewhere."

"Fine," Governor Yates said, which was how I found myself ruling forms for the adjutant general. The only person with whom I had any conversation was the state auditor, who had to walk through my room to get to his offices.

But it was a strange coincidence involving the state auditor and

Pope that finally rescued me. Pope fully expected to be made brigadier general of volunteers for the state of Illinois once the job of mustering troops was done. But Yates wanted somebody with a more swashbuckling style—a swashbuckling style was considered an asset back then, before the actual killing started. He picked a fellow named Benjamin Prentiss, who had been a lieutenant in the regular army and also fought with Taylor.

Prentiss had already achieved notoriety back in Illinois over the expulsion of the Mormons, who had arrived there after being booted out of Missouri in 1839. They were hated for their odd beliefs and economic success, and conflict erupted when their leader, Joseph Smith, was murdered while in Prentiss's custody, which put Prentiss in good standing with the local population. Prentiss also built his legend by raiding contraband civilian gunboats heading south on the Mississippi in the first days of the war, so he exuded the heady air of confident accomplishment, as opposed to Pope, who exuded the stale gas of a career in the army.

Pope departed Camp Yates in a huff, leaving his division, the Illinois 12th Regiment, to be transported to Cairo, on the Missouri border, by rail. But the day after Pope left, the local railroad announced they lacked cars to take the men. Governor Yates turned to the state auditor to fashion a way to deliver them. He, in turn, came upon me as he was walking through my little room, the dilemma preoccupying him.

"Have them walk," I suggested.

"Walk?" he asked incredulously. "Why, it's a hundred miles from Springfield to Cairo," he said. "The men can't walk a hundred miles."

"Of course they can. They're soldiers. It will take them no longer than a week, and they'll be better soldiers for it."

The state auditor was taken with this advice and reported it to the governor, who recalled the conflicting evaluations given of me by Congressman Washburne, whom Governor Yates still valued, and Pope, whose opinions now had no currency. I suddenly found myself replacing Pope as the mustering officer at Camp Yates, a position that held the title of colonel and paid the handsome wage of $4.20 a day, more steady money than I had ever made by the age of thirty-nine.

A mustering officer actually was in charge of no more than creating a roll of volunteers and making sure that their paperwork was in order so they could be sworn into the army. The commanding officer of this regiment was a fellow named Goode, a bounder who drank to excess daily and whose regiment of twelve hundred men was a shambles. His men regularly left camp to drink or steal chickens. They had already rioted once over bad bread and, when jailed, burned down the guardhouse. There were no uniforms and few provisions. Desertions were a daily affair. Goode, however, disregarded any and all counsel I offered him, and after a few days I returned to Springfield. I spent the month after that shuttling from one office to another searching for a command of my own when a telegram arrived from Governor Yates. A mutiny had occurred at Camp Yates: Goode had disappeared. And when the junior officers were canvassed as to who could restore order, their recommendation was unanimous.

Me.

So on June 16, 1861, Governor Yates appointed me colonel of the Seventh District Regiment of Illinois.

I returned to camp and found indolence, drunkenness, and insubordination. But this was my camp now. I ordered the men to fall in so I could review them. It was a good fifteen minutes before a crowd gathered. In my scuffed hat and worn civilian coat, I did not cut an impressive figure. When I began to speak, I was met with catcalls and jeers.

I dismissed the men, turned away quickly, and summoned the junior officers to my tent. "How long has it been since the men had a roll call?" I asked.

"Weeks," one of them responded. "Goode gave up on them."

I assessed the situation for the briefest of moments. "Have the men a ringleader?"

"Yes, a private named Richmond."

"Take me to him," I ordered, and we marched across the campgrounds to a circle of men who were playing cards and sipping with suspicious enthusiasm from their canteens. "Which of you is Richmond?" I demanded.

A large fellow with a *bandillero* mustache staggered to his feet. "I am, little man. What of it?"

I raised my hand in salute and announced, "I am Colonel Grant, your commanding officer."

He watched me put my hand to my brow and began to laugh. "Look here, boys," he said as he turned away from me, "it's a new little toy colonel!"

"I am Colonel Grant, your commanding officer," I repeated. "Return my salute."

Richmond whirled around and thrust his middle finger at me. "Here's your fucking salute," he spat.

I imagined something along these lines would be his response, so I dropped my salute, breathed deeply, and proceeded to drive my fist into his face with as much force as I could muster. It was a blow that had been schooled on the heads of mules and was sufficient to send him sprawling into the dirt, where he remained. I then turned to my junior officers and issued my first command at the reborn Camp Yates.

"Take this man away, gag him, and tether him to a post in the middle of the camp," I said, and the junior officers set upon him and carried him away, to the astonishment of all those around us. I returned to my tent for a few hours and addressed the regiment's mishandled paperwork—we would now be able to make proper requisitions for buying foodstuffs and other supplies—and then led my officers back to where they had left Richmond. A crowd of enlisted men gathered as we approached.

Richmond was slumped against the post, glaring at me. "Stand up," I barked, and he slowly got to his feet.

"Take off his gag," I instructed. I once again raised my hand in salute. "I am Colonel Grant, your commanding officer," I said.

He watched me insolently and I repeated myself. "I am Colonel Grant, your commanding officer. Return my salute."

"No one does that to me," he snarled, and, to the limit of the tethers, he lurched toward me, whereupon I grabbed his head and yanked it sharply toward my upraised knee. He did not have far to fall to the ground and did so, with a healthy show of blood.

"Gag this man again and leave him tethered to the post," I commanded, and I returned to my tent to develop a schedule for roll calls and drills. It was almost evening when I reemerged and, followed by my junior officers, approached the impudent soldier again. His gag was removed a second time.

A crowd of men surrounded us—noticeably more than had fallen in for review that morning. There was hushed silence as I slowly raised my hand to my brow in as precise a salute as I could muster. "I am Colonel Grant, your commanding officer," I said.

Richmond looked at me for a long moment and, to my great pleasure, his immense, blood-crusted hand slowly rose to his forehead and acknowledged my salute. I snapped my hand back to my side and nodded to two of my officers, who untied the fellow and led him away.

A roar of approval came from the men and I turned to face them. When there was quiet once again, I spoke.

"I am Colonel Grant, your commanding officer. From now on, all camp guards will report to their companies and drill with the rest of the men. There will be three hours of drill daily. The remaining time will be spent attending to the sanitation and amenities of the camp. There will be five roll calls each day, from reveille to taps. All men must be present at each. The punishment for failing to do so is imprisonment. Once we enter the war, such an absence will be construed as desertion, and the punishment will be death. If a man is present at each of these roll calls and performs his other responsibilities faithfully, he may proceed as he wishes, so long as he obeys the laws of the land. Men who swear or are insubordinate will be tethered to this post until they see the error of their ways."

I paused for a second and assured myself their expressions were those of comprehension. "Men, go to your quarters," I concluded, and drew my hand up quickly in salute.

Six hundred men returned my salute and headed back to their tents, cheering me.

So ended my first day of command.

The first orders I received were to cross into Missouri and pursue a Confederate guerrilla named Harris, who was gainfully employed destroying bridges and ripping up railroad tracks. I was being sent to put an end to it. I had not been in battle in thirteen years. As we approached the brow of the hill from which we expected to see the enemy's camp, my heart kept getting higher and higher, until it felt to me as if it were in my throat. I would have given anything then to have been back in Illinois, but I had not the moral courage to halt and determine what to do. We kept right on. When we could see the valley below, I halted: Harris's camp was still there, but his troops were gone. It occurred to me at once that he had been as much afraid of me as I was of him. It was a lesson that I never forgot, even at the worst moments at Shiloh—the enemy has as much to fear as I do. War is fear, I learned, and the trick is to inspire more of it in the enemy than he does in you.

With the army growing by leaps and bounds, President Lincoln sent the Congress a bill to appoint thirty-four new generals. Those closest to the President politically were at the front of the line for nominating candidates, and Congressman Washburne was second to none in this regard. Asked to suggest a candidate, he lost no time in putting one forward—Galena's favorite son, the man who brought order to Camp Yates, the hero of San Cosme, the brother of his keepers—me. On August 7, 1861, I was sitting in my tent when my field chaplain came running in with a copy of a St. Louis newspaper bearing the names of thirty-four new generals of volunteers. On the list was John McClernand, a prominent Democratic congressman from Illinois at a time when Lincoln needed to keep his coalition together; Lew Wallace, a would-be writer and full-time politician; and Prentiss, whose nomination had already been announced by the governor. The eighteenth name on the list was that of General Ulysses S. Grant.

"Well, if it's in the paper"—I smiled at the chaplain—"it must be true."

The first thing I did upon hearing I had been made a general was to summon Rawlins from Galena and make him my chief of staff. Rawlins's strong approbation of drink would assure my patron, Congressman Washburne, that everything under my command was in order. And if I was to be Washburne's man, he would need to know what I was doing so he could take credit for it, which was what he wanted in the first place. Having watched the relationships between politicians and generals carefully in Mexico, I vowed not to let myself be blindsided by their war while fighting my own. All I wanted was a ticket to the field, and now I had one.

I was told to report to Jefferson Barracks, where my new commanding officer was John C. Frémont. I'd known him out West. He was a strutting, posturing, half-witted glory seeker whose primary source of information about the world around him was a mirror. He had commandeered the office of the mayor of Springfield, Illinois, and covered its walls with maps, complete with pins and ribbons in the finest Napoleonic tradition. He was waiting for me there with a surprise guest.

"General Grant, welcome! I'm sure you already know General Prentiss. I was just sharing with him a history of the frontier," Frémont said.

I dutifully shook Prentiss's hand. "Yes, of course," I said, meaning I knew of Prentiss's unsullied record of victory over the unarmed.

"Pleased, Grant," Prentiss replied, giving me the briefest of looks and then turning back to Frémont. "So once the California Republic was declared, you assumed leadership, you were saying?" He had wasted no time in toadying up.

"Yes. With our victory over the Mexicans finalized, I became military governor," Frémont said, omitting his being court-martialed for trying to get California to secede under his leadership. "Of course, none of that would have been possible had I not overcome overwhelming odds to blaze the Oregon Trail with Kit Carson in '43 and establish Fort Vancouver."

"I did some time there," I offered collegially.

Frémont looked at me, a curl in his lip. "So I've heard," he said, and proceeded to get on with business. "Gentlemen," he said, "our duty is to drive Confederate influences, both military and political, out of this area, preserving Missouri and Kentucky for the Union. Prentiss, as senior in rank of the two of you, will proceed to Cairo, Illinois—"

"Begging the general's pardon," I said, "but General Prentiss doesn't outrank me."

Frémont and Prentiss looked at each other with astonishment.

Prentiss jumped in as if I were a Mormon who was asking for it. "I most certainly do, Grant. You received your assignment as brigadier general of volunteers on the list issued in August, made retroactive to May seventeenth by an act of Congress," he recited. "I was made brigadier general of volunteers on May fourth by Governor Yates on behalf of President Lincoln. I therefore have enjoyed our common rank a full thirteen days longer than you, making me the senior officer," he pronounced with evident satisfaction.

I sighed gently and continued. "General Frémont, paragraph five of the *Handbook of Military Regulations* says—"

"Paragraph what?" Prentiss cut in. "Of what possible relevance is the *Handbook of Military Regulations* here, Grant?"

"Given that we're in the military, General Prentiss, I would consider it to be of the greatest relevance," I responded. "Paragraph five of the *Handbook of Military Regulations* states that if two officers are of the same rank in the volunteer army, regardless of the date they received their commissions, their seniority is to be determined by their ranks or tenure at their ranks in the regular army prior to their commissions in the volunteers."

Frémont and Prentiss looked at each other in confusion. "*So?*" Prentiss asked, with obvious annoyance.

"Well, I was a captain in the regular army, and you were a lieutenant. So I outrank you according to paragraph five of the *Handbook of Military Regulations*."

"I've never heard of this paragraph five," Prentiss said dismissively. "Have you, General Frémont?"

Frémont shook his head. "No, it's never come to my attention," he said, and squinted at me. "What exactly does it say?"

"It says that our seniority is determined by our ranks in the regular army," I repeated.

"But then you would outrank Prentiss, which you don't," Frémont argued.

Prentiss shook his head. "It doesn't sound like a very good regulation to me," he said.

"I have to operate on my authority as district commander," Frémont declared, puffing out his ribboned chest. "General Prentiss outranks you."

"Begging your pardon, General, but *I* outrank *him*," I insisted.

"I strongly doubt the *Handbook of Military Regulations* would turn over command to a fellow with a record such as your own," Prentiss snapped.

"General, as commanding officer for this district, you must have a copy of the *Handbook of Military Regulations!*" I said to Frémont. "Why don't we end this now by retrieving it?"

"General Grant, I cannot be hamstrung by some manual written by somebody at a desk in Washington, blithely unaware of the reality of our circumstances here in—"

"Then wire back to Washington and ask for guidance from the War Department! Because if you don't, I will!" I said curtly, and with that Frémont sat back, eyebrows raised, and raised his gloved hands into the air for silence.

"Very well," he said petulantly. "I will do exactly that, and we will find out about your paragraph five once and for all."

He summoned an orderly and gave him a hastily written note. "Wire this to Washington," he said. We sat there awkwardly for some time, regarding Frémont's maps and various souvenirs of his California campaign, when a messenger brought Frémont a slip of paper. He read it dutifully and looked up.

"Washington says Grant outranks you," he said to Prentiss.

"Let me see that!" Prentiss demanded. Frémont handed him the wire. Prentiss stared at it and leapt to his feet.

"Permission to take a leave of absence, sir!" he shouted.

"Denied," Frémont said, rubbing his temples.

"I hereby resign my commission, sir!"

"Refused," Frémont snapped back, never looking up.

"Then I'll place myself under arrest for insubordination."

"No you won't, unless Grant gives you the authority."

Prentiss turned to me and saluted. "Permission to put myself in irons, sir!"

"Sit down, Prentiss," Frémont said, and with the matter resolved, he dispatched me instead of Prentiss to Cairo, Illinois, across the Mississippi River from Kentucky.

Kentucky remained in the Union, and Lincoln feared the Confederates would invade it. South of Kentucky, in Tennessee, Confederate troops were gathering under General Leonidas Polk, a West Point graduate who had been an Episcopalian bishop before becoming a Confederate general—trading the purple for the gray, so to speak. This combination of professions allowed Polk to invoke the Deity's intercession before a battle and minister to those men whom he dispatched in His name to their demises after it.

Frémont was hesitant to enter Kentucky and appear as an invader himself, but he was favored by luck in the form of Polk, who took our massing on the border in anticipation of his invasion as a sign our invasion of Kentucky was imminent and decided he could wait no more. Polk invaded Kentucky to preempt the invasion we did not intend, coming up from the Tennessee border to seize Columbus, a strategic town atop a bluff overlooking the Mississippi, across the river from Missouri.

I quickly assembled my staff—which now included, among others,

Rawlins, a fellow named Hillyer whom I met in my St. Louis bill-collecting days, and the fellow assigned by Frémont to be my second-in-command, General C. F. Smith. Smith had been the commandant of cadets when I was at West Point, but his inability to toady limited a career otherwise characterized by distinction at such places as Monterrey and Chapultepec. Frémont, mistrustful of Smith's intelligence and experience, assigned him to me in the hopes of remanding him to oblivion.

We needed to respond to Polk somehow, lest he control the river at Columbus and maintain a base for insurrectionists in both Kentucky and Missouri, home to thousands of Southern sympathizers such as old man Dent. Both states could slip into rebel hands, giving them a base for threatening Illinois and Indiana.

I took Rawlins, Hillyer, and Smith to Frémont and Prentiss to discuss the matter. Smith presented one option—an assault on Columbus, winner take all, using the town of Paducah on the Ohio River as a base. Frémont flatly rejected it.

"Our numbers are simply insufficient," he said.

"Hell, we can always get more damn numbers," Smith argued, but Frémont considered the matter closed.

I outlined a second option. "We could ignore Polk and move down the Tennessee River to attack Fort Henry on the Tennessee-Kentucky border. If Fort Henry fell, Polk would be cut off from the rest of his army: He'd have to abandon Columbus and engage us, and we could create an opening into the Deep South."

The long stunned silence in the room recalled the moment at West Point when I described my ideas about Cornwallis's situation at Yorktown. Finally Smith whistled slowly, then spoke.

"Hell, that's good!" he said. "That's real good! I withdraw my suggestion and support General Grant's proposal. Let's do it right quick!"

Frémont scowled with disapproval as he rose and strode over to his wall-size map. "As I see it," he said, sweeping his white-gloved hand across its face, "Polk is here, on the Kentucky side of the Mississippi. That means he has a problem," Frémont continued, rubbing his hands together. "Polk doesn't know the direction from which we'll come at him—will we attack him from behind, from Paducah, or will we come down the Mississippi from Cairo? No, Polk has a problem, to be sure—at this very moment he is probably tied in a mental knot anticipating the direction from which the attack will come." Frémont snickered at Polk's plight for a moment, until Prentiss got the cue and joined in.

Polk had a problem, to be sure. It was picking the spot where he would attack us next. And if his problem wasn't picking the spot where he would attack us, it was how best to deploy the thousands of soldiers who would soon be reinforcing his position. If only we had his problems, I thought.

"So our strategy," Frémont concluded, "will be to feint and make demonstrations, both behind Polk on the Kentucky side of the river and in front of him on the Missouri side, with an eye," he said, nodding wisely, "*to confusing him.*"

Then at least Polk and Frémont would be even, I thought.

"Brilliant, General, brilliant," Prentiss announced. He was alone in his assessment. Rawlins's glare looked to set Frémont's map on fire, and Smith appeared ready to fall over dead under the overwhelming burden of seething frustration.

Frémont ordered Smith to take a column from Paducah and march it toward Columbus while I took another column—about three thousand men—and crossed to the Missouri side of the river, all of which, Frémont said with a self-satisfied smirk, "will lead Polk to wonder what we are doing." I restrained myself from noting that Polk would be far from alone.

So Rawlins, Hillyer, and I led a column across the river to Missouri, where we were under orders to march back and forth across from Columbus to keep Polk from guessing our destination. My chafing at the idiocy of this instruction was in stark contrast to the exuberance and evident pride of the men as they boarded their ships: They waved hats and guns in the air and sang patriotic songs in anticipation of experiencing their first battle—"seeing the elephant," they called it.

Thus we were marching near the town of Belmont on the far side of the Mississippi—it was lovely country, as beautiful as our demonstration was pointless—when my advance pickets came riding back to the line of march with an obvious sense of urgency. "They're here, General!" one of them shouted as they pulled up before me. "Just where you must have figured they would be!"

I knocked my hat back on my head. "Who's here?" I asked.

"The Rebs!" the scout answered, and the party began to shout excitedly at the prospect of engaging them.

"They are?" I replied, trying to conceal my surprise. I looked at Rawlins, who shrugged. No enemy was supposed to be on this bank of the Mississippi—that was the whole point of marching about pointlessly. Polk had apparently decided to dispatch some of his men from Columbus to our side of the river, most likely because he saw us marching around and mistook us for an army with a purpose. "Did you get a feel for their number?" I asked.

"We sure did," said one, a young boy with freckles. "I'd say there was about as many of them as there are of us."

"And do we have any idea of who's in command?" I asked.

"Yup. Some general named Pillow."

Pillow! Pillow was a half-witted politician who had been sent by President Polk to keep an eye on Scott in Mexico, a fellow who didn't know which side of a trench the enemy was coming from. This good news sparked my eagerness for battle, and I turned to Rawlins and Hillyer forthwith.

"Pillow is encamped ahead of us—I suspect that Polk had him cross the river to call our bluff. And, of course, to get him out of the fort."

"Should we turn back?" Rawlins asked.

"Those are our orders," Hillyer noted.

"The devil with that," I muttered. "I'm going to attack."

"Attack?" Rawlins replied. "Your orders say exactly the opposite—all feint, no shooting."

"Yes, well, this is an unforeseen situation." I've got an idiot with an army in front of me, I thought, ripe for the picking. Just because my commander is also an idiot with an army doesn't mean I'm going to pass up this opportunity. "Besides, if we turn back now," I added, "Pillow might attack us while we're trying to retreat."

Rawlins was not fooled—my orders were to turn around if confronted with the enemy, but I finally had the enemy in front of me and I wasn't going to let him go. I organized my men into lines in a cornfield and they buzzed with nervous excitement, more like boys about to take a ride in a hay wagon than men going to war.

When I gave the signal to advance, there came a mighty roar from their ranks, the likes of which I had not heard since the day Hooker and Jackson charged Chapultepec.

But their shouting changed in nature when we ran into Confederate infantry fire after only a few hundred yards. Pillow had gotten word of our advance, but rather than entrench his troops in a good defensive position where he would have an advantage, he chose to come out and fight us in the open. He was making it as easy as I hoped he would. Before I knew it we were driving everything in sight: The Confederates broke and ran. We chased them over an earthworks and through their camp to the river, where they huddled behind a bluff for protection and wondered what to do next.

One more push would compel their surrender, but once my men reached the Confederate camp, they suddenly fell into a festival of patriotic jollification worthy of a J. R. Grant and Sons rally. They went from tent to tent and liberated souvenirs—a flag for the lucky ones, a hat or tin cup for those who followed. Various officers atop their horses went from group to group among the infantrymen and led them in patriotic song or congratulated them on their just-completed victory. They had seen the elephant and lived. The battle was over.

But from a hilltop above the river, I saw something different—Polk had put more Rebel regiments on steamboats to cross the river and cut off our route to our boats and trap us, even as my men were running wild. I collapsed my spyglass and turned to Rawlins.

"Set fire to the Confederate camp," I said.

Rawlins executed the order with dispatch. In a few moments the entire encampment was ablaze: tents, cabins, defensive structures—everything. My men gathered quickly, now panic-stricken rather than jubilant. The officers huddled around me as the scouts I'd sent out came racing back from reconnoitering our northern flank.

"Polk's established a line between us and our boats!" the freckle-faced boy exclaimed, his face now ashen.

The officers promptly fell into fearful disarray. "We're finished!" one of them said.

"We must abandon our wounded!" a second cried.

"We must surrender now," a third one urged, "before they kill us all!"

"Nonsense," I said, as plainly and calmly as I could. "We cut our way in, and we will cut our way out."

It was easily said, but not easily done. The Confederates opposing us were this time more organized and confident; our own men felt they had already done their day's work and were ready to go home. Even as they began to march, there was a dazed and confused feeling to the column. Some men wept openly as they heard Confederate bullets cut into the trees overhead. It was tough going, but after a few hours of fighting, we broke through to our boats.

I positioned a regiment near the landing to ensure we were not attacked as my men boarded, and turned my thought to the day's wounded. I decided to take a quick ride to see if any more could be evacuated with us.

As I cantered back to the landing through the browned and withered autumn cornfields, I suddenly heard bullets passing by me and turned to see a Confederate platoon no more than a hundred yards behind. They gave chase, and I spurred my mount to race back to our boats. When I had come close enough, I saw that the regiment I had assigned to the landing was already on board, leaving no more than four or five worried sentries standing guard ashore.

"Get aboard!" I shouted, hoping to be heard across the clearing. The men squinted in my direction—one or two took their weapons from their shoulders and aimed them at me, leading me instinctively to duck behind my horse's neck. "Get aboard and cut the ropes! The enemy is right behind me!" I bellowed, peering out from behind my mount and waving as I rode.

The men suddenly came alive with motion, racing across the gangplanks. One of the soldiers grabbed an axe and had at the ropes, and the boat began to drift from the shore. The bullets were now whizzing past me, and a prompt exit was in order. A small berm protruded at the top of the bluff overlooking the landing, and I knew what to do. I gathered my mount underneath me and gave her the summons. She thundered closer and when I thought she might be getting too close, she threw her front legs into the air and sailed up, and we became weightless for an instant together as we went over the berm and landed on the deck of the departing steamer with a sharp *clop*. She was no York, but she had done her job well.

I immediately went down to the captain's rooms and lay down for a moment to collect my thinking. Fire was still being exchanged between our boat and the Confederates ashore. I lay there and imagined Frémont's wrath at my giving battle in opposition to his specific orders, and with little to show for it. This at the price of, I estimated, about one hundred dead and four hundred wounded, many of whom were left behind.

I avoided the conclusion that I had erred terribly, deciding instead to congratulate myself for my good judgment at engaging the enemy. I arose from the daybed to go inspect the top deck when a Confederate bullet ripped through the bulkhead and tore through the pillow on which my head had lain only a moment before.

A trickle of feathers and dust floated from the bullet hole. A near miss, I thought to myself, and headed up to the deck, where a fellow might be shot in a manner more in keeping with military tradition.

We landed back in Paducah to find Smith waiting for us. "Hell, was that ruckus across the river you, Grant?" he asked.

"We had a bit of an adventure," I confessed. "Now I'll have to go find Frémont and take a second beating." Smith looked down and seemed to be suppressing a smile. "Is there something amusing about all of this?" I asked him.

He shook his head. "Well, General," he said, "you won't have to bother with Frémont."

"No? And why is that?"

Smith allowed himself a grin. "Because Lincoln's dumped him."

I could not hold back a grin of my own. "To what does our nation owe its gratitude?"

"Frémont issued a proclamation freein' the slaves in Kentucky and Missouri," Smith said, reveling in the "Pathfinder's" demise. "Lincoln's madder than a bag of bobcats—he's gettin' all sorts of heat from the loyalists there, sayin' we're going to turn this district into a hotbed of colored insurrection, burnin' their houses and rapin' their daughters."

Rawlins let out a laugh. "These slaveholder sons of bitches must have the most attractive daughters known to mankind, I sometimes think," he said, "given this voracious need of every potential marauder to have at them."

"You're alluding to Mrs. Grant, you know," I warned him.

"She excepted," Rawlins quickly allowed, then realized what he'd said. "Well," he fumbled, "not on the score of attraction—"

"Leave it," I said.

"Well, Frémont ain't the half of it," Smith said, bringing us back to the matter at hand. "Lincoln's dismissed Scott and McDowell after they got whipped at Bull Run and made McClellan the general-in-chief." He shook his head in contempt. "The little twit. I used to wish crazy Tom Jackson would beat the shit out of him back at West Point."

I nodded in commiseration. McClellan's plan to jump past Lee when Scott retired was now complete. The most important figure in the Union army was a young plutocrat who thought me a drunk. It seemed so unfair—one lonely, inebriated swoon long ago and a man's branded for life, I thought. I gazed down at the ground when I realized the most important piece of information was yet to be revealed. "Wait!" I blurted. "Who is McClellan sending to replace Frémont?"

Smith looked at me as if measuring me for the blow. "I was afraid you was goin' to ask," he said.

"Well, Grant," General Henry Wager Halleck harrumphed, standing haughtily behind his desk at his new headquarters in St. Louis, arms thrust behind the small of his back as if he were posing before his strategy class at West Point. "It has been a very long while."

"Yes, it has, General Halleck," I responded, thinking that perhaps word of my reputation had not reached him since our days in the classrooms of West Point.

"Well, see that you keep the bottle corked. One such episode and you'll find your uniform a memory," he said with contempt he made no effort to hide.

Old Brains had aged noticeably. He had become a squattish man with a fringe of graying hair, a jowly, bedraggled air, and a pair of large, bulging eyes that gave him the appearance of being constantly half strangled. "I've got enough trouble as it is without your adding to it," he went on, his eyes darting nervously from the window to Frémont's wall-size maps, to me, to anything else they could find. "Frémont has left this place a mess, writing these foolish proclamations, allowing Polk to build up a fortress at Columbus, writing contracts with crooked speculators and swindlers. Simply placing this district aright is going to be a superhuman task," he said, honoring the bureaucratic tradition of amplifying the last man's miscarriages.

"What, if I may ask, is the broad strategy under which we'll be operating?"

"Yet to be defined," Halleck snapped. "To be coordinated between myself, General McClellan, and Secretary of War Stanton. Communication and coordination, Grant. Just like we discussed back at the Academy."

I bit my lip. "Begging General Halleck's indulgence," I responded, "and fully in support of his objectives, may I make a proposal?"

He looked up, eyebrows arched. "A proposal?" He chuckled. "From my student, the hero of Yorktown? Very well, have at it, Grant."

I laid it all out for him as precisely as I could, just as I had for Frémont. Our base at Paducah gave us access to the Tennessee and Cumberland Rivers. Admiral Foote promised his fleet of gunships and transports, including the *Tyler* and the *Lexington*, in support. We could move south on the Tennessee River, take Fort Henry on the Tennessee border, and force Polk to abandon Columbus or fight us on the open ground. And if we succeeded, there would be nothing between us and a series of prizes—the railhead at Corinth, Tupelo, Nashville, Memphis, Vicksburg, New Orleans, and Mobile. How could Southern surrender not follow?

Halleck gaped at me for a moment before he responded. "I can see the map just as well as the next man, Grant. But I can't go off adventuring in any direction my officers imagine. I have commands besides yours that pose their own problems, let me assure you."

"Your other major command is Sherman's in eastern Kentucky," I said. Sherman had found a place teaching at a military academy in Louisiana in 1859 but came north and back to the army as soon as the conflict started. I had not heard a word from him since our encounter on the street in St. Louis. "I will coordinate with Sherman," I said, eager to work with someone, crazy or not, whose judgment I could trust.

Halleck made no attempt to hide his annoyance. "Forget Sherman!" he ordered abruptly. "That crazy bastard!" He paused to calm himself. "There will be no expedition down the Tennessee, or any other place, until I so order. In the interim, you will manage your affairs in an appropriate fashion and await further instructions from me. Dismissed!" he barked, and I rose, saluted, and left, wondering where my good friend Frémont had gone.

When I returned to Paducah a few days later, I found Rawlins sitting in front of my tent with a young officer I did not recognize. They rose from two tree stumps as I dismounted, and Rawlins approached. "I need to speak to you," he said with a look of concern.

"Yes?" I said as I started toward the tent, expecting Rawlins to follow.

"There's someone in there," he said quickly, reaching for my arm.

"Who is that?" I muttered, and threw back the tent flap. A tall, thin man sat stooped over on a cot in the darkness inside. His head rose slowly until I could look into his vacant eyes.

"Cump!" I said happily. Halleck be blamed, it was Sherman! "Cump, how in the blazes are you? What are you doing here? Have you had a cup of coffee, or a bath?" I slapped my hands together merrily. "And to think it was only four years ago—" And it was only then I stopped and realized something was terribly wrong.

Sherman stared up at me, his expression never brightening and his gaze never abating. He looked as if he were dead.

"Cump! It's me, Sam," I said, kneeling in front of him and looking at him intently. "Cump, don't you recognize me? Come on, Sherman, it's me, Sam," I encouraged, but there was no response, and I became aware of Rawlins and the other officer now standing behind me.

"What is the matter with him?" I demanded.

"This is Captain Herold, General," Rawlins said quietly. I turned and rose to greet him. "He's here to escort General Sherman home."

"General Sherman has had an episode of some sort, General," Captain Herold explained. "He was under immense pressure in his command, and when a reporter interviewed him he became a little free with his words—made some public remarks about how it would take two hundred thousand troops and tens of thousands dead before the South surrendered. The press picked it up and he was bombarded from all sides—the loyalists called him a traitor and the Rebels called him a butcher. And they all hanged him out—Scott, Frémont, Halleck, Stanton, all of them walked away from him. The strain was too great. He snapped. His mind's gone." There was pity in his eyes as he turned toward Sherman.

I tried again, hoping to make contact. "Sherman, it's me, Sam."

He suddenly spoke up. "Is that you, Grant?"

"Yes, Cump, it's me," I said, hoping he would speak to me.

"Woe, Grant. Woe to all of us," he whispered.

"What do you mean? What is it?"

"Woe, Grant!" he suddenly exclaimed. "Thousands will die, Grant, thousands will die! The Mississippi will run red with blood before our Union is preserved!"

"They're expecting him back in St. Louis, General," Captain Herold broke in. "We only stopped here for a brief rest before we pushed on. General Sherman always spoke well of you. I thought it might help him if he saw you."

"Rivers of blood!" Sherman shouted, his eyes now blazing with rage. "They didn't want to believe me, Grant!" He grabbed two big handfuls of my uniform coat and pulled me down toward him. "I saw Bull Run, Grant! I was there! I saw McDowell and his men slaughtered by Beauregard! I saw the picnickers who came from Washington—they raced home in their buggies, afraid for their lives!"

He looked up at me furiously and spoke in a rapid whisper. "The South wants to kill us all, Grant! I was outnumbered back in Kentucky! I begged Scott for more reinforcements, begged him! The enemy was coalescing! Buckner fortifying Bowling Green, Zollicoffer coming north to reinforce him! I had four thousand men—volunteers, untrained, outnumbered—'*Make up your minds to die here*,' I told them!

"There is imminent danger, Grant!" He released my coat, rose from the cot, and began to pace about the tent with great agitation, speaking quickly, as if to himself. "Upon consideration, a larger picture of the war emerges! Cincinnati, St. Louis, Louisville—a coordinated attack by Pope, Longstreet, Johnston—both Johnstons, Albert *and* Joe— Beauregard, all of them! The Confederacy overrunning Kentucky from the South and attacking Indiana and Illinois, a massive simultaneous movement at all points along the Ohio River, up that channel to Pittsburgh, then the Allegheny to the Susquehanna and the seizure of Harrisburg, then Philadelphia and Baltimore, down the Potomac to Harpers Ferry and Washington! Total domination by overwhelming Southern forces using these waterways as their vehicles of conquest while our generals refuse to fight! McClellan! McDowell! All of them—afraid to engage the marauders! They think war can be won without death, but thousands will die! Thousands of men will face equal thousands of the enemy, and all will perish in an Armageddon the likes of which has never been seen before!" he shouted, and turned to me with a furious expression. "Because war is death, Grant! War is hell!" he screamed, and then his eyes rolled up into his head and he crumpled backward onto the cot.

I turned to Captain Herold as Sherman lay there. "What do people know about this?"

"His men know he's been extremely agitated. He didn't sleep for days on end. But not many have seen him this far gone. The story is that he's been ordered to report to Halleck's headquarters in St. Louis—his family's there; and his brother"—his brother, John Sherman, was a U.S. senator and a formidable political power—"is seeing to his circumstances."

I nodded. "Is there something I can do?"

Captain Herold shook his head. "No, we probably ought to be going," he said, and led his patient from the cot to a waiting carriage.

Rawlins stood next to me and watched them depart. "I thought you said Sherman cussed a blue streak," he said after a long moment.

"Only when he's in his right mind, I suppose." I shrugged and entered my tent, alone.

Halleck replaced my friend and ally, Sherman, with our old schoolmate Don Carlos Buell. The Union's enemy went unmolested, but Halleck now had *me* surrounded, with Buell to the east, and Halleck's other selection, John Pope, commanding in Missouri. Both John McClernand, Lincoln's political bride, and Lew Wallace, the unconsummated author, reported to Halleck as well. Buell promptly replaced Sherman's stream of telegrams to Halleck begging for reinforcements with his own, stressing the need for greater coordination and communication between himself, Halleck, McClellan, and, ultimately, Secretary of War Stanton, before Buell would be able to carry out his avowed determination to confront the enemy. If the outcome of wars were determined by volume of telegrams, the Union would have been preserved without the further effusion of blood.

The only two people who seemed to be frustrated by this cacophony of prefatory throat-clearings were myself and Lincoln, who took it upon himself to write to Halleck and ask if more could not be done.

"Look at this," Halleck said with exquisite exasperation as he waved the President's letter at us one winter's afternoon. A snowy downtown St. Louis sat beneath his window. "The Great Railsplitter wants us to give the Confederates battle and hang the cost! A coordinated attack on Washington's birthday! What was his great military preparation? I ask you. Marching through Springfield during the Black Hawk War? Does he have any idea of the sheer weight of numbers we face here?"

"Speaking as a friend of the President," McClernand said, "I can only attribute his misplaced entreaties to his overwhelming zeal to uphold the Union cause, which burns within him incessantly. Were he to know the true facts of the matter, I am sure he would fathom fully the brave efforts you, as commander, have made on his behalf."

"Were he to be here," my man Smith interrupted, "he'd be fed up with all this talkin' and fussin', and he'd tell us to commence to fightin' the enemy right damn quick!"

McClernand, a spindly man with a pointy nose and scrawny beard, ever the politician, ignored him. "Perhaps I could send the President a message, alerting him to our true circumstances—"

At this point, Wallace jumped in. "I might lend a hand in the drafting, if General McClernand doesn't mind."

"Oh, shut your traps, all of you!" Halleck exclaimed, pounding his desk with frustrated rage. And we would have sat on our hands in this fashion for the rest of the war, were it not for the good fortune of being matched against Confederates whose ineptitude rivaled our own. Zollicoffer, the Confederate general, was marching against Buell in eastern Kentucky and, for some reason known only to him and his Maker, chose to encamp on the far side of a river from the body of his Confederate corps. This mistake caught the attention of one of Buell's supporting generals—George Henry Thomas, our old classmate. Thomas, acting with the decisiveness of his forefather lookalike, ran Zollicoffer's troops into the Cumberland, killing quite a few, including Zollicoffer.

The news was received in Washington with elation, but not in St. Louis. "Now it's this!" Halleck moaned a few days later. "Thomas has gone off and defeated Zollicoffer, as if that made any difference whatsoever. But Lincoln thinks it's some kind of victory, and there's the prospect of promotions for Thomas and Buell!"

"For killin' a bunch of fellows with a river at their back? Hell, that's easy!" Smith sneered, allowing Halleck to nod vigorously.

"I think," McClernand interrupted, "we should read into the President's actions his very strong desire for a pretext to reward heroism wherever he may find it. And I must conclude our response needs be one of action," he said emphatically, "so we may provide for the President more evidence our cause is just and Providence commends it."

Smith looked up, confused. "Does this mean you're in favor of killin' the damn enemy?"

"Under these circumstances," McClernand said, nodding, "yes."

"Of course, we all feel that way," Halleck said, "but what can we do about it?"

I spoke up. "Let me attack Fort Henry," I said.

"Not that nonsense again!" Halleck snapped. "Fort Henry, Fort Henry—honestly Grant, sometimes I wouldn't mind your trying to do my job if you'd come up with a second idea!"

"But if we take Fort Henry, the Tennessee River would be—"

"Open! Open! I know! As open as a goose's entrails!" Halleck roared. "Yes, I've heard this all before, Grant! If we take Fort Henry, the Tennessee River would be—"

"Your conquest to offer the President, General," I interrupted, "in which Buell and Thomas played no part."

Halleck stopped ranting and stared at me, his bulging, owlish eyes wide. Having finally seen some advantage to my plan, he began to soften. "Do you actually think it can be done?"

"Yes, I do."

Halleck bit his lip as he savored the prospect of outshining his former student pets, Buell and Thomas, but his natural inclination toward inaction wrestled for control of his spirit. "But Polk is so strong at Columbus and Albert Johnston is building a force at Bowling Green. What if you have to confront them? It's not without risk."

"I'll sail down the Tennessee, safely in between them," I offered. "Besides, it's war. There are always risks."

Halleck looked down for a minute and then sighed. "Fine. Grant, you will take Smith, McClernand, and Wallace here and reduce Fort Henry with all due speed, after which you will await my orders."

"Yes," I said confidently, rising in salute.

The Civil War was finally under way.

On February 2, 1862, I put fifteen thousand men on Admiral Foote's steamers and headed south, up the Tennessee River. The river was high and swollen and had overflowed its banks. Unfortunately for the Confederates, Fort Henry was built on the floodplain, and was under two feet or more of standing water, water so high it made many of their artillery pieces useless. On the morning of February 6, I disembarked the first three thousand men at a landing three miles upriver from Fort Henry and then sent Foote's fleet forward with the rest.

Foote's gunboats—metal-clad, the latest innovation—began firing early that afternoon. They took out several Confederate cannons, and since the others were already underwater, the fort was defenseless. I ordered McClernand's division to shore and told him to proceed with haste, but by the time he organized his infantry and stumbled upon the fort, it had already surrendered. The fort's commanding Confederate colonel sent as many men and as much matériel as he could out the back to a second Rebel fort, Fort Donelson, twelve miles east on the Cumberland River, and then capitulated to Foote.

"Well, I'm sorry, old man," Foote offered when I joined him and McClernand aboard the admiral's command boat, now only a few hundred yards from the fort's walls, "but the colonel here surrendered right away."

"That's right, General," the Confederate colonel said as he extended his hand in greeting, one gentleman to another. "My officers held a counsel of war and decided we had no chance of surviving your attack." He shrugged. "I mean, we surely wanted the honor of surrendering to you—meaning no disrespect for Admiral Foote, of course—but there was nothing else we could do."

I regarded him for a long moment before I spoke. "Your men escaped to Donelson?"

McClernand interrupted. "They ran like dogs," he said with a sneer.

I wanted to wring McClernand's slothful neck. "For Heaven's sake," I said. "Each escapee is a man we'll have to fight again!" I looked at him angrily. "Have you learned who is in command at Donelson?" I asked.

"Floyd, supported by Pillow and Buckner."

I swallowed my wrath—Floyd and Pillow! An easier pair of targets could not be imagined! My experience at Belmont taught me that Pillow was the same imbecile I knew from Mexico. And Floyd was Buchanan's Secretary of War, a politician who received his generalship from Jeff Davis in exchange for the four years he spent stealing armaments for the South.

Sure, Buckner, my shy friend at West Point and New York, was a good fellow. But Floyd and Pillow outranked him and they were ripe for the taking. Besides, I had already reduced a fort! How I wished I could see Old Brains's strangled face when he heard! I had won! I was right all along! Why not reduce another? Reducing forts was downright *easy*, it struck me, all the more so when you had the navy's gunboats coming up the river and pounding the daylight out of your target even before you got there! I could reduce forts for a *livelihood*, I thought— it was easier than clerking or farming and infinitely more rewarding.

And so, like a fellow winning at brag, I saw no sense in getting up from the table while I was still being dealt the good cards. I quickly took out a tablet and wrote a message to Halleck:

> *Fort Henry is ours. The gunboats silenced the batteries before the investment was completed. I shall take and destroy Fort Donelson on the 8th.*

The die was cast—Donelson was my next move. Let Halleck and Buell and the rest of them write each other endlessly about the need for communication. I said I would communicate with him after I took Fort Henry, and I did. Besides, I was now out in the field, with fifteen thousand men under my command. When news of my victory and subsequent thrust against Fort Donelson got out, even more would be arriving. You can hire an architect, you know, but the man with the hammer builds the house, and now the architect was back in St. Louis and I alone held the hammer. I was most assuredly going to drive the nails wherever I chose. I had both Halleck and the enemy where I wanted them, at last.

It rained torrentially the next four days, turning the twelve miles of hills and gorges between Forts Henry and Donelson into a wallow of mud.

On February 12, we finally moved out—a warm, glorious afternoon that promised an early spring. My men tossed off their overcoats and blankets in the brilliant Tennessee sun, thankful for the end of rain. I rode at the head of our column and outlined my plans to Rawlins, Hillyer, Smith, Wallace, and McClernand. We would encircle the fort within shooting distance, with Smith on the left, Wallace in the center, and McClernand on the right, north to south. We would then wait for Foote's armada to arrive and begin shelling from behind, advancing against the place once its big guns were silenced. With Pillow and Floyd in charge, even with my old friend Buckner in support, it would not take long.

On the morning of the thirteenth we came up to inspect the fort, and the reality of it was sobering.

"Lordy, will you look at that god-awful thing!" Smith exclaimed. "It's set up on a damn hill! I thought all Confederate forts were built underwater!"

"The walls must be thirty feet high!" McClernand said, dismayed.

"The guns are enormous!" Wallace said with a schoolboy's awe.

"It appears impenetrable," Smith concluded.

I smiled at him. "I agree."

"When do we attack?" he asked.

He was reading my mind. "As soon as Foote arrives," I said confidently. And with that I ordered some light skirmishing to focus the fort's attention on our position rather than the river, and waited for Foote to arrive, which he did the next day. Our plan, of course, was for him to knock out the fort's guns and then continue south, passing the fort and blocking off any conceivable escape to Nashville, the nearest concentration of Confederate troops.

But Donelson was not the pushover that Fort Henry was. Its guns pounded Foote's fleet, and Foote himself was injured when a shell hit the boiler room of his command boat. The Confederates repulsed our first attack and I retreated to a farmhouse behind Smith's lines for the night.

And what a brutal night it was. Two days before it had been sunny and springlike, but that night was as cold as any I can now recall. The temperature fell and a furious blizzard came in from the northwest, blowing sleet horizontally and piling snow on our camp in a fierce wind. It was impossible to see more than a few yards ahead, nor hear more than the incessant howling of the fierce winter wind; there was no hope of discerning the sound of any enemy movement. My men had discarded their blankets and coats during the march from Fort Henry and were now unable to light matches or make campfires. They could do little more that night than march sleeplessly in circles to fight the cold, or lay down upon the ground and freeze to death.

It was imperative I confer with Foote. He was on his boat, a few miles north, but he was wounded and could not be moved. So I proceeded at daybreak to the landing where he was moored.

"My ships have been banged up pretty badly," Foote told me, lying in his captain's quarters, his wounded leg propped up and bandaged. "I need two weeks to repair them. You'll have to invest a siege."

"I can't invest a siege!" I responded. "There are as many of the enemy in there as we have out here, and they can be reenforced by Johnston out of Nashville. Buell would have to reenforce me, and the chances of Buell coming here to bail me out are minimal at best. And if he does, Halleck will show up to stop Buell from getting all the credit and then who knows what will happen? I need naval power so I can finish this job before it finishes us!"

"Grant," Foote insisted, reaching to adjust his bandaged leg, his face worn and pale, "my boats *are* finished—some are hit so badly along the waterline that they'll sink if they suffer another exchange." We eventually agreed to deploy a few gunboats on the river, if only to convince the Confederates they had not scored a decisive victory. As I left, Foote gave me a cigar from his collection—it was a good one, I noticed, and I stuck it between my teeth and got into a rowboat back to shore, where Hillyer was waiting for me in a state of great agitation.

"The Confederates have attacked!" he cried as soon as I was within earshot. "They've left the fort and attacked McClernand on our right—he's fallen back. If this keeps up, the Rebels will break our line and repel us!"

I instantly swung up into the saddle of a waiting horse and, chomping on Foote's cigar, took off through the frozen woods. I found our men congregated in tiny knots of confusion and fear, without any idea how to defend themselves or what to do next. Their demoralization was palpable. I rode toward the sound of battle and with good fortune found McClernand and Wallace together in a clearing, poring over those few maps we had. I dismounted, whereupon McClernand glared at me.

"This army wants a head," he said, his tone accusatory.

"It seems so," I replied tersely, and with that they repeated the same story Hillyer had told me—Pillow had moved against our right and had torn McClernand's division to pieces.

"Well," McClernand prodded, as if the whipping he took were my doing, "what are your orders?"

I confessed I had none ready and was struggling to find an answer when a moment of clarity suddenly came upon me. "Bring me one of our prisoners," I ordered. The Rebel private they found quivered as he saluted me, no doubt wondering why he was picked to be shot.

"Empty your knapsack," I instructed him.

The poor, confused Confederate silently poured his knapsack on the ground. There was what I was looking for! "Look!" I said, sure of myself now. I pointed with my chewed cigar. "Do you see that?"

"It's bacon and bread, Grant. What of it?" Wallace asked.

"These men have been given three days' rations. They aren't trying to repel us. They're trying to cut their way out."

"Very well, then," McClernand said. "But of what importance is it if they are trying to escape instead of merely trying to repel us? They are cutting us down just the same."

"Because," I explained patiently, "if they are trying to escape, then they have massed their power on our right, against you, which means they are weak on our left, where we will strike immediately."

"Grant, have you considered the condition of our men?" McClernand asked. "They have been repulsed by the enemy and they are cold, weak, and tired! How will they manage a counterattack?"

"Yes, some of our men are badly demoralized," I conceded, "but the enemy must be more so, for he is trying to force his way out and has not yet done so. The one who attacks first now will be victorious and the enemy will have to be in a hurry if he gets ahead of me." I rode off to find Smith, rallying the units I encountered along the way, telling them the Confederates were retreating and we must prepare to advance at once.

I encountered Smith sitting under a tree. "Do you want a light for that thing?" he said, looking up.

"What thing?" I said, and then realized Foote's cigar was still clenched in my teeth. I shook my head and then told him plainly, "McClernand has failed on our right. You must take Fort Donelson—an immediate, all-points attack against the Confederate right."

Smith rose to his feet, brushed off his mustache, and calmly told me, "I will do it," just as he must have told Scott he would push back Santa Anna's men outside Mexico City. He mounted his horse, rallied his men, and led them toward the fort.

With Smith assaulting the predictably undermanned and unprepared Rebel right, the Confederates retreated. By the end of the day, we had retaken all the lost ground and forced the Confederates back into the fort with heavy losses, wresting victory from the grasp of defeat. I fell asleep that night on the kitchen floor of a farmhouse, still wondering what to do next but confident the Confederates would either have to come out and fight again or quit.

It was Smith who awakened me early the next morning, his toe digging insubordinately into my side. "Quit your sleepin', General! I got somethin' here for you to read," he said lightheartedly.

I reached up sleepily for the letter he offered and to my amazement read:

In consideration of all the circumstances governing the present situation of affairs at this station, I propose to the Commanding Officer of the Federal forces the appointment of Commissioners to agree upon terms of capitulation of the forces and fort under my command, and in that view suggest an armistice until 12 o'clock to-day.

　I am, sir, very respectfully,

> **S. B. BUCKNER**
> **Brig. Gen. C.S.A.**

"Buckner wrote this!" I exclaimed. "Where are Floyd and Pillow? Did they lose the battle and let Buckner do the surrendering?"

"A bunch of sissies, if you ask me!" Smith railed. "You ain't goin' to give them Rebels any goddamned deals, are you?"

I rose from the floor and sat down at the pantry table, taking pen in hand. "No, Smith, I'm not," I said, and began to write, the words falling immediately into place.

Yours of this date proposing Armistice and appointment of Commissioners is just received. No terms other than unconditional and immediate surrender can be accepted.

　I propose to move immediately upon your works.

> **U. S. Grant**

"There," I said, handing the note to Smith. "Is this satisfactory?"

"Oh, it's prettified enough," Smith said, amused. "Halleck didn't teach you how to write battlefield correspondence notes like this back at West Point, did he?"

"No." I smiled. "The only battlefield correspondence we studied was Napoleon's." Smith laughed, saluted, and went off to deliver my response.

I soon had Buckner's answer:

SIR:

The distribution of forces under my command incident to an unexpected change of commanders and the overwhelming force under your command compel me, notwithstanding the brilliant success of the Confederate arms yesterday, to accept the ungenerous and unchivalrous terms which you propose.

I looked up at Smith and Rawlins. "It's over," I told them, and went to meet Buckner at an inn near Donelson to arrange for the surrender of the fort. His was the first of three armies I would capture whole during the course of the war, each larger than the one Washington captured at Yorktown or Scott did at Veracruz.

Buckner was having breakfast and waiting for me, nervously picking at his plate.

"Hello, Simon," I said as I sat down.

"Hello, Sam," he said. "You look a damn sight better than you did when I last saw you in New York in '54."

I nodded in return. "Well, I'm having a pretty good day," I said.

He nodded as I sat across from him. "Well, then," he sighed, "am I a prisoner of war or a traitor?"

It was a good question: A prisoner of war went to a camp. A traitor was shot. "Oh, you're our prisoner, Simon," I said. "If we shoot you for treason, the next general you send my way might be less inclined to surrender."

"Thank you," he said quietly.

I made nothing of it. I'd have shot him if I had to.

"Now would you tell me what happened in there? Where are Floyd and Pillow?"

Buckner took a deep breath. "Well . . ." He shrugged and continued. "When Smith pushed us back in, we held a council of war. Floyd announced he couldn't be taken prisoner, since he would be tried as a traitor, having moved Federal munitions to the South when he was War Secretary. So he turned over his command to Pillow and promptly rode off. Then Pillow said he was a political general and he'd be tried for treason as well, and he resigned *his* commission and turned the fort over to me. Then Bedford Forrest and the cavalry got on their horses and took off, leaving fifteen thousand men behind with no recourse but to capitulate. 'You surrender, Simon,' Forrest told me. 'You're a regular army man. You understand these things.' So I did. After all, our men deserve better than leaders who cut and run on them." Buckner sipped his tea and regarded me sadly. "You could have given me better terms," he said.

"I appreciated what you once did for me, Simon," I said, rising from the table, "but now there are only the victors and the vanquished." I nodded to a group of officers waiting to escort Buckner into captivity. "Here," I said, reaching for my purse and flipping it to him. "You'll need this, and if you need more, write to me. Our account is settled." He rose and saluted me and then shook my hand, and they led him away.

Rawlins looked at me. "Don't you think you ought to wire Halleck now?"

A laugh escaped me. "Of course," I replied. "I wouldn't want to be accused of not communicating." I sat down at the breakfast table and composed a short note.

We have taken Fort Donelson and from 12,000 to 15,000 prisoners, including General Buckner, 20,000 stands of guns, 48 pieces of artillery, 17 heavy guns, from 2,000 to 4,000 horses, and large quantities of commissary stores.

I was now the most successful commander in the Union army.

But at the end of the day, the only note of congratulations I received was not from Halleck, or from McClellan, or Stanton, or the President, for that matter, although these were all to come, but from a lone fellow back in St. Louis.

GRANT:

After several months of treatment here since our last meeting, to the extent I remember it, I have been given permission to return to my profession. Your impressive victory gives me the confidence to do so. You have proved our side can be victorious if it has the will to take the fight to the enemy. I have raised a volunteer regiment here and have wired the Secretary of War, asking I be returned to the Western District, and hope I may be placed under your command when I re-enter the war.

> *Yr. Obd. Svt.*
> *W. T. Sherman*

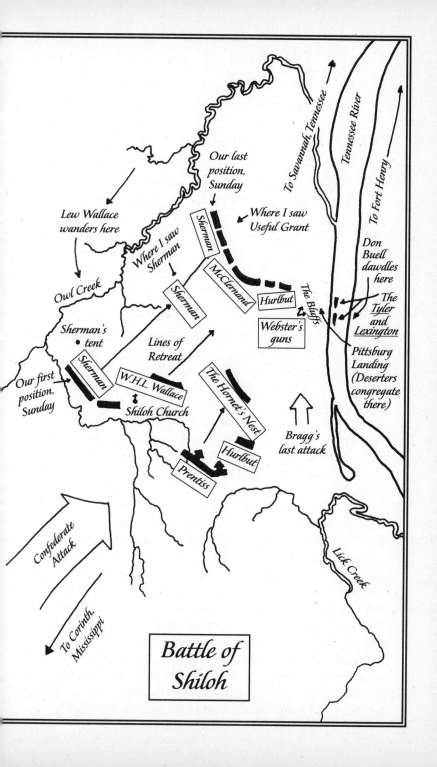

Lew Wallace
wanders here

Owl Creek

Sherman's
• tent

Our first
position,
Sunday

Where I saw
Sherman

Sherman

Sherman

Lines of
Retreat

W.H.L. Wallace

Shiloh Church

Our last
position,
Sunday

Sherman

McClernand

Hurlbut

Where I saw
Useful Grant

Webster's
guns

The Hornet's
Nest

Hurlbut

Prentiss

Bragg's
last attack

The Bluffs

To Savannah, Tennessee

Tennessee River

To Fort Henry

Don
Buell
dawdles
here

The
Tyler
and
Lexington

Pittsburg
Landing
(Deserters
congregate
there)

Lick Creek

Confederate
Attack

To Corinth,
Mississippi

Battle of
Shiloh

CHAPTER VIII

THE ASSAULT ON SHILOH—I TAKE COMMAND AT THE SCENE—END OF THE FIRST DAY—A SURPRISE AMONG THE INJURED—VICTORY ON DAY TWO—A FINAL NOTE ON SHERMAN

O N THE MORNING of Sunday, April 6, 1862, the Army of the Tennessee was encamped at Pittsburg Landing, on the shores of the Tennessee River. Two days later, it was encamped on the same spot. But in the interim, thirty thousand Confederates came storming out of the woods to attack it, twenty-five thousand men died, and the first battle of modern warfare was fought.

It all happened because I was careless, oblivious, and disinterested. We survived because I was methodical, calculating, and unruffled. When it was all over, I was a hero, a butcher, and I had introduced the word *annihilation* into modern warfare.

I was done being a clerk.

It would be an understatement to say my background had not prepared me for fame. But the news of Fort Donelson's surrender—the first Union victory of the war—made me famous. Politicians embraced, atheists thanked the divinity, bankers put down their ledgers and sang patriotic songs—every man, woman, and child in America knew that out West there was a fellow named Grant who did what nobody else could do—whip the Rebels. Oh, I was modest about it, presenting nothing more than clench-jawed rectitude and no-nonsense common sense, but the madness was boiling within me.

I got my first taste of newspapermen, too, watching writers I never met and who knew nothing about me make up stories about who I was and where I came from, elaborate personal histories with no basis in fact. And when a reporter mentioned I assaulted Donelson with a cigar clamped into my bite, the good people of our nation responded by sending me boxes and crates and barrels of cigars of every shape and size—good ones, too, perfect for smoking twenty a day, twenty years, as a prelude to dying of something epithelial in character. It seemed like a shameful waste not to smoke them, at least those I could not give away. Which reminds me—I hope Dr. Douglas comes by today with a dose of morphine before Newman gets here.

One man's ministrations cure the other's.

Celebrity found me and stuck to me. I had a name the nation could reckon with—U. S. Grant, Unconditional Surrender Grant, the man who made no deals with traitors and whose name plainly said so. They must have thought my mother named me in anticipation of the conflagration to come. In contrast to the pomp of a Scott or a McClellan, my plain, understated, matter-of-fact air, with a cigar firmly set in my square, determined jaw, could not have been more to the people's liking if Barnum himself had invented me.

And why not? I was right and I was winning. Yes, I was lucky—lucky that Fort Henry was under two feet of water, lucky that Pillow didn't push McClernand harder and escape Donelson. But you can't be lucky unless you're ready for luck. My strategy was ruthless and it worked. I told Halleck if we took Fort Henry, then Columbus would be isolated and we would force Polk out into the open. The day after Donelson fell, Polk beat a retreat down to Memphis, which made the upper Mississippi navigable for Union traffic and isolated the Rebel guerrillas across the river in Missouri, allowing them to be cleared out. Albert Sidney Johnston, the ranking Confederate general in the region and the mastermind who had chosen not to reinforce Donelson when he had the chance, panicked and prepared to disembark Nashville, though a long seventy miles lay between us. The Rebels thus packed in all of Kentucky and Tennessee. With one bold attack, I had saved two states for the Union.

I hoped my father was reading the papers.

Everybody else was, and everybody cheered me—everybody, that is, except Halleck.

That fatuous, double-dealing, conniving louse! He reacted as if my victories presented him with such problems that he would have preferred I'd lost: how to keep supplies moving to our new forward position; how to protect our flanks from attack by Confederates (who were clearing out faster than the proverbial rats); and, above all else, how to communicate and coordinate over a new, larger area with myself and an increasingly petulant Don Carlos Buell, who, like Halleck, resented the war for the nation's survival being won by the drunken, mangy likes of me. With Johnston reeling and his Confederate armies falling back in piecemeal disarray, Halleck's orders were to sit tight.

Not that Halleck hesitated in claiming credit for the victory. In exchange for the magnificent triumph he had delivered, he wrote to Lincoln asking for consolidation of the entire western theater of war under his command and promotions to major general for not only me, but Buell and Pope as well. He also managed to insinuate that I was up to "my old habits." Lincoln, of course, saw through the whole thing and asked the Senate to skip the others and promote me to major general. And so they did. I was still less than a year from clerkhood in the back room of J. R. Grant and Sons.

Halleck was enraged, but good fortune was about to shine on him. A frustrated Lincoln soon relieved McClellan as general-in-chief and gave Halleck command over the entire western district he sought, including me and Buell. Having won his prize, it would be bad form for Halleck to get into a fracas with his most—*only*—successful general, so he let his vendetta against me go, for the moment.

Halleck divided the western command: I was given command of the Army of the Tennessee and Buell the Army of the Ohio. I now had six division commanders: McClernand, who was Lincoln's favorite Democrat; Lew Wallace; old man Smith, but he was laid up with an injured and infected leg, so a fellow named W. H. L. Wallace—no relation to Lew—assumed his command; a fellow named Hurlbut; and Prentiss, the airy jackass who thought he outranked me. All five reported to me now.

The sixth was Sherman. He had either recuperated from his episode or had learned how to give the impression he was sane.

"I've purged my demons, Grant," he told me, availing himself of one of the countless cigars that sat on the table outside my tent.

"I'm glad to hear it, Cump," I said. "And I'm glad Halleck has put us together."

Sherman saluted, grinning. "You're the fucking head man, Sam," he said. "The way you put it to them at Donelson, you can call the shots. My men stand ready to take off after them tomorrow."

I sighed. "Our orders are to wait here for Buell to join us, at which point Halleck will direct an assault against Johnston, Polk, Beauregard, and Bragg at Corinth."

He looked at me, aghast. "But why put it off? The longer we wait, the longer they'll have to prepare."

"I know," I grumbled, "but those are our orders. In the meantime, find a place where we can drill the men."

Sherman selected a place called Pittsburg Landing, a few miles below the town of Savannah, Tennessee. It was a long plain leading away from a river landing with a high bluff separating them, with streams and swamps on both sides. His recommendation appeared acceptable, and on March 18 I moved my headquarters from Fort Henry to Savannah, a few miles north of the encampment, and told Sherman's men to be the first to set up camp there.

I considered giving the men shovels and having them entrench, in the event of a surprise attack, but both Smith and Sherman convinced me my instinct against it was the right one.

"Just teaches 'em shovelin' instead of fightin'," Smith growled from his sickbed, his leg bandaged and immobilized. "Hell, that ain't nothin' but a waste of time."

"I agree with the old man," Sherman said, reaching over the sickbed to slap Smith on the shoulder. "All that digging gives them the wrong idea. We should be training them to fight in case Buell and Halleck ever get here."

I smiled to see Sherman was well once again, or at least as well as a man of his volatile makeup would ever be. He had not lost his energy. We spent the time drilling, in the hope we could move against Corinth soon.

Sunday, April 6, I woke at my headquarters in Savannah and was down to breakfast at about six. Rawlins was, of course, already awake, agitated as usual—he probably stayed alert even when he went to sleep. Hillyer was there, too. They had already been into the coffee when I arrived. "Good morning, General," they chirped and popped up from their seats. I commenced to look for a cup of whatever they were having in the hope it would have the same result.

"We'll be out of here and up to Pittsburg Landing after breakfast," Rawlins said.

"Fine," I said. "We've got to get there today."

The problem was the chain of command. After his reorganization, Halleck made another request for promotions. Buell was made major general, my rank, so I now had the right to order him and he had the right to demur, more a model of marriage than of the military chain of command. This made things difficult for me, which made Halleck happy, given his overpowering fear I would attack the enemy and win battles: Like a mother checking her child for lice, he scoured my reports for evidence we might take the initiative.

Halleck then promoted those political half-wits McClernand and Lew Wallace to major general as well. Their qualifications, of course, were that both of them flattered Halleck unceasingly and didn't like me, which, in Halleck's eyes, made them almost as qualified as Buell.

The feeling of dislike was mutual. Both of them bellyached their way through the capture of Fort Donelson—particularly that smart-mouth jackass McClernand, telling me my army "wanted a head." Well, it certainly doesn't need a hind end as long as you're around, I thought at the time. But I kept the remark to myself, as I then still felt the need to appear the most stoic, sober soul ever to don a uniform. Today, I'd have him switch-whipped.

These promotions were an immediate problem, as McClernand was already down at the Pittsburg Landing staging area with Sherman, and Lew Wallace was on his way. Both of them outranked Sherman and relished ordering him about. The very point of being a general is to outrank everybody around you, particularly your fellow generals. The thought of Cump trying to train twenty thousand raw volunteers with McClernand and Lew Wallace interrupting him was a recipe for disaster. I would have to get myself there and establish my command over the lot of them, if not to save McClernand and Wallace from Sherman, then to save Sherman from Sherman. We would then wait for Buell to arrive with his twenty thousand men—he was only a day away, he said—and move on Corinth.

"Any more reports of skirmishers?" I asked as a breakfast was put before me. There were daily exchanges with Confederates on the edges of our camp, but with two large armies in close proximity, these were to be expected.

"None," Rawlins replied.

"There'll be more," I said. "Johnston knows we're getting ready to come down and lick him, and he'll keep an eye on us." And, of course, he would know where to find us, since we had to sit and wait for Buell, Wallace, and the like to join us before we could march on Corinth and get on with it.

I was pouring myself a cup of coffee when there suddenly came the loudest noise I had ever heard. It was a chorus of cannon blasts, obviously some miles away, followed by a welling of sound. And, just like the first time Mrs. Grant gave me the pleasure, the instant it happened I realized everything had suddenly changed.

Rawlins and Hillyer looked up with concern. "What the hell is that?" Rawlins asked, wide-eyed.

"Johnston's attacking us," I said, gazing into my coffee cup and making all the necessary deductions in an instant. I had underestimated Johnston completely, as had Halleck and everybody else. I grabbed my hat and started toward the door.

"Attacking us?" Rawlins repeated angrily as he followed me out. "But how can that be? The son of a bitch is in Corinth."

"No," I answered, "he *was* in Corinth. Now he's waging a full frontal assault against our position at Pittsburg Landing," I said, with anger directed only at myself. Johnston's change of strategy was so obvious, I wanted to have myself lashed for not seeing it earlier. "Johnston has decided his chances out in the field are better than his chances in Corinth," I explained. "He's decided to try to kill us before Buell arrives and we kill him. If he can push us back, the loss of Henry and Donelson will be undone," I said as we reached the dock. "Gentlemen, the ball is in motion."

We boarded the *Tyler* and headed south from Savannah, upstream on the Tennessee River, toward Pittsburg Landing. On the way we passed Lew Wallace's command boat, which was moored by the riverbank. Wallace had heard the noise and displayed both admirable inquisitiveness and stunning ignorance as to what it was.

"We're under attack!" I shouted to him as my boat pulled up alongside his.

"Who is attacking us?" he shouted over the gunwales.

"The enemy, Wallace! Johnston has obviously come up from Corinth to surprise us!"

He nodded grimly. "So the plot unfolds," he said, biting his lip. "What do you want me to do?"

"Send out a patrol to make sure there are no other Confederate attacks running parallel to the one at Pittsburg Landing. Then, on my order, I want you to march directly south, along the river, to join the battle." He nodded, saluted me, and we moved on.

The first thing I saw when I arrived at Pittsburg Landing was the throng of stragglers, deserters, and fugitives who had already fled the battle—a bluff separated them from the fields where, a mile or so away, a battle raged. Only a few hours before, the Confederates had swept out of the woods as our men were cooking breakfast. They poured in from the west. With creeks and swamps north and south of the encampment Sherman had chosen, the only place for our men to run was east, toward the river. Moreover, the divisions with the rawest men—new volunteers who camped at Pittsburg Landing to be trained for the capture of Corinth—were nearest to the Confederate attack. Outnumbered and unprepared, many turned and fled. I did not know whether to shoot them for desertion or congratulate them for common sense.

There must have been more than five thousand men milling about in terror, an awful spectacle. While I would have preferred these men were busy engaging the enemy, they were boxed in and weren't going anywhere. They would keep for a while, until I could determine what to do next.

As I rode up over the bluff atop the landing, the sound of the battle was overwhelming. Shots were going off at all times in every direction. Fearing our men might run out of bullets—most men had no more than a few rounds in their tents, a problem that had plagued us at Donelson—I immediately organized an ammunition delivery system, matching the supplies on our ammunition boat to the rifle types carried by the different divisions and brigades. I then took two regiments, boys from Iowa, and placed them at the top of the bluff shielding the landing and told them to stop all fugitives, of which we already had plenty. I then wrote a fast note to Lew Wallace, telling him to join us promptly. Only then did I ride toward the fighting to see how badly my army was being mauled.

The reserve division, camped at the rear, away from the battle, was W. H. L. Wallace's, so he was the first person in command I found. He confirmed the conclusion I had reached when I first heard the shots. Johnston had come out of the woods with thirty thousand men organized in three lines and went straight into our right, where Prentiss's and Sherman's untrained recruits were camped with only a third that number. Their divisions fell back to a line alongside McClernand and Hurlbut, but the onslaught continued and it was a struggle merely to hold this ground.

I told Wallace to move his men up. The enemy would be coming to him in a moment, and we'd do better taking the battle to them.

I then set out to find Sherman and found him where I thought he'd be, standing at the front line, deploying his men. His dark eyes were open wide and he looked every bit the loon the newspapermen had made him out to be, waving his arms in all directions at once as he shouted instructions. He'd already had one horse shot out from under him (the first of two that day, I'd learn), and his hand, now bandaged, had been hit with a minié ball. He was covered in dirt, his hair disheveled and his clothing in disarray. I hollered for him, and when he heard me, he turned where he stood and grabbed his head with both hands, as if it were crammed with demons.

"Damn it, Sam, this is all my fucking fault!" Sherman shouted against the whine of thousands of bullets in the air. He closed his eyes and puffed his chest out at me. "Just shoot me now, Sam, right fucking now," he said, his arms spread wide like Jesus. "Write a report later. No one will blame you for shooting a crazy bastard like me. I am the dumbest jackass—"

"What the devil are you talking about, Cump?" I asked, trying to keep my tone moderate and still be heard over the din.

He sighed and dropped his arms. "Sam, I should have told you," he said in the singsong of a child's confession as he pawed at the dirt with his boot. "Friday night, I lost seven pickets. And then yesterday the commander of one of my regiments, the Fifty-third Ohio, saw enemy in the woods out there and ran to my tent, shrieking like an old fucking woman. *'Enemy!'* he's hollering. *'There's enemy in the woods!'* I just about bit the idiot's head off. I told him there wasn't any enemy nearer than Corinth." He hung his head sheepishly and peered up at me. "As you can see," he mumbled, "I was mistaken."

"You owe that man an apology," I said as I looked out at the battle that raged behind him all the way to the horizon.

"Well, he's dead now, Sam, shot five fucking minutes into it." He grimaced and shook his head. "Sam, they were right under my nose, all hundred thousand of them—there had to be at least that many," he advised, "and I couldn't smell 'em." He sighed, closed his eyes, and spread his arms out again. "Go ahead, shoot me. Nobody will blame you. That crazy bastard Sherman. I fucking deserve it."

"Cump," I said evenly, "my mistakes today put yours to shame. But if you truly feel the weight of this responsibility, get your rear end out there and give some of these Rebels a chance to kill you."

"Well, that's what I've been *doing*, Sam," he groaned, as if the world were simply not going to cooperate with him. "Already had a horse shot out from under me. Got hit in the goddamned hand," he said, holding up the bandaged evidence. "Here, take a look at this." He took off his hat, stuck his good hand inside it, and ran a finger like a pink worm through a hole in its crown. "I took this ball about thirty minutes ago. Missed my noggin by an inch! I was bending over when it happened."

"I've always said you looked best lucky-side up, Cump."

"Do we have any prospect of reinforcements, Sam? There are too goddamned many of these graycoats out there."

"I'm waiting for Lew Wallace and Buell," I said. "But you'll have to hold up until then. Now go draw some more fire."

"Well, I'll go see what else I can attract," he said, his mood assuaged by my conversation. "And—hey!—I'm going to need some more bullets pretty soon," he yelled to me as I mounted my horse. "Got to have fucking bullets if you want to kill the fucking enemy."

"I've got them coming, Cump," I said, and he saluted me and walked back toward the battle with a fresh, energized step, barking new orders as he did.

My next stop was Prentiss. His men were falling back in the center of our line, bending under the weight of intense enemy pressure. Prentiss was doing what his mentor, Frémont, would have done—looking for a place to hide. And of course, when he found it, he'd use the respite to rehearse what he'd tell the press about how he'd won the battle, if not the war.

I searched the terrain to find Prentiss's division a natural place to throw up a line. I was in luck. A hundred yards into the brush behind their position was a stretch of woods with a dirt road running through it. Anyone trying to attack him would have to cross a forbidding field of entangled brush to get to it. I directed Prentiss and his men to the spot.

They fell back quickly and assembled a firing line at the edge of the woods, using the dirt road to position men along their line. I turned to Prentiss as his men opened fire. "It is imperative you maintain this ground at any cost. My plans rely upon it."

"Are you completely sure, sir?" Prentiss asked, raising his hand in salute.

"Yes," I replied.

"From this position?" he asked, his hand still frozen in salute. "Might there be a position closer to the mass of our forces that would be more defensible?"

"No, this position will do fine," I replied.

"Of course, sir," he said, snapping his hand to his side. "Begging the general's pardon, though—"

"That's enough," I said, ending our exchange. "You'll draw your line here or have yourself shot."

"Then I shall," he said, businesslike, snapping off a salute. I returned his salute and rode away. If Prentiss would hold that spot, we would be able to withstand Johnston's attack and let the enemy wear themselves out, while we concentrated on holding our right and left flanks to avoid a rout.

Prentiss indeed did hold his ground, meaning his men fought so gallantly they made it impossible for him to satisfy his longing to retreat farther. Throughout the morning there were various attacks on his position, which came to be known as the Hornet's Nest for the stinging that went on there. The firing was so intense it made a steady buzzing sound in the air, as would a swarm of angry insects, and it stripped the nearby trees of their leaves. Sometime around noon and then again in midafternoon, Johnston ordered charges on Prentiss's position, but he was repeatedly repelled. I later learned a bullet from this position killed Johnston that day. He was hit in the leg and an artery opened. The blood filled his boot to overflowing, and he was dead in two minutes.

I spent the midday reinforcing our line, where it had weakened under enemy pounding or where gaps were created by casualties and deserters. There was a constant circulation of men to and from the landing. Some ran in the face of enemy fire, over the bluff to the river landing, where they were safe so long as somebody else did the dying for them. Once they reached the landing, we tried our best to form them into new divisions and send them forward. Some men regained their nerve and returned of their own accord—others cowered through the day there, listening indifferently to the exhortations of officers and clergy to steel themselves and return to the front.

"Men!" I heard a chaplain beseech fervently when I returned to the landing to gather more reinforcements. "You must rejoin your army. You can still lead the Union cause to a glorious victory."

"Shut up, you addled moron," one of the men shouted back. "We're trying to hide."

"But men," the chaplain implored, "what of your nation? How can you refuse to fight while your nation is cleaved in twain?"

"What of it, Padre?" a second shot back. "My ass is cleaved in twain and it works just fine!"

"You must fight, men, lest the Union suffer great defeat!"

"If I die, I'll suffer a greater defeat," a third one returned. "What good is saving the Union if we don't live to enjoy it? I say we stay right here like true patriots!"

And with that there was a chorus of hurrahs from the thousands of men congregated there, and they returned to the work of circulating rumors: A retreat had been ordered and we would be crossing the river soon; a convoy of rafts was to be built to float downriver, back to Paducah; the Confederates had burst through our line and taken most of our men prisoner; I was alternatively dead, captured, drunk, or surrendered.

It occurred to me that several of these might soon be true.

It was around three in the afternoon when Rawlins found me with news: Buell had reached the landing. I hurried there as he was coming off his boat.

Buell surveyed the panicky scene at the landing and did his best impression of Halleck. "Your army is running rather than fighting, Grant," he said testily, his eyebrows arched in disdain. "I don't see how you can pound the enemy with your army hiding like schoolgirls. You had best prepare yourself to escape this place and take your losses."

"*Don*," I told him as he sneered at me, "you've entered the battle from the wrong end. There's never anybody at the rear other than those too afraid to fight. If we went to the Confederate rear, we'd see the same thing, only in gray." I remembered Harris in Missouri—the enemy is just as scared as we are. "And frankly, Buell, the men huddled here are still closer to battle than your troops are."

Which was true, because Buell had forgotten to bring his men with him. He actually had them near Savannah the day before the battle but had somehow forgotten to send word he had arrived. Had he done so, his men would have been at Pittsburg Landing by noon this day. Instead, he was still ferrying his men down six miles of river and they hadn't arrived yet.

I gave Buell a studied look and took a pad from my pocket. I wrote a note to the captain of one of the riverboats transporting men up and down the river. In a moment, the captain got the message, stoked his boiler, and fired up the calliope on board. It started to play "John Brown's Body" and I could hear a roar come from our troops on the field as it did. I smiled at Buell. "So much for morale, Don. If you're worried about morale, get your corps down here," I told him, and rode back up the bluff to the fighting.

The afternoon dragged on. Prentiss's men fought valiantly at the center of our line, but there was sagging all around them as Sherman and McClernand fell back. I kept thinking we would be fine once Lew Wallace entered the battle from our right, which would be any minute now. After all, I had sent word for him to march six miles about six hours before.

But Wallace was nowhere in sight. I began to experience a touch of nervousness regarding his absence, and I sent Rawlins out to find him. When he finally did, Wallace was going in the wrong direction and had to order a countermarch, meaning Wallace had to get his seventy-five hundred men to stop and turn around at the same time. Try that sometime and see what happens.

Rawlins brought me this news when he returned.

"I found him," he said, breathing hard after a demanding ride.

"Well, where has he been?"

"He was on the wrong road, Sam. The little son of a bitch wasn't heading south toward us. He was heading west."

"Away from the river?" I asked. If I'd had Wallace there in front of me, he would have gone south and west at the same time. "I'll tell you what he's doing, Rawlins," I said, my bile rising. "He's trying to move along our right flank, out of harm's way, then come up alongside and behind Bragg. He wants no part of a frontal assault. He wants to come marching out of the woods, shoot Bragg's men in the back, and be known as the man who saved Grant at Pittsburg Landing." (It was some while before the battle came to be known as Shiloh, the name of a nearby church.)

"The man who saved that *drunkard* Grant at Pittsburg Landing," Rawlins added, correctly anticipating what my enemies would make of it. He shook his head at Wallace's vain enterprise as we surveyed the dead littering the field in every direction. "That drunken *butcher* Grant," he said after a moment, projecting more fully the response. I turned to him, my eyes narrowing, when he elaborated once more.

"That *cowardly* drunken butcher Grant," he said, seething at the sentiment, then paused and thought for just a moment before continuing. "The man who saved that *befuddled, unprepared, cowardly . . .*" At which point I cleared my throat and he stopped.

"Thank you," I said, and we were done discussing it.

There are still some people who claim that Wallace simply got lost, or that he didn't understand my orders. Well, some dogs don't understand "Come!" But most generals do. History will determine if Wallace was a dullard or an opportunistic coward. As for me, when I had the chance later in the war, I cashiered him.

As the afternoon wore on, both Sherman and McClernand on the right, and Hurlbut on the left, continued to fall back in the face of superior numbers. By four-thirty, they had retreated so far that Prentiss's position in the Hornet's Nest was exposed on both flanks. After his men had held their line for most of the day, Prentiss surrendered.

When I learned of Prentiss's capture, I became concerned. My strategy was based on the assumption that Prentiss's men had greater courage than Prentiss, and while the fact that they surrendered didn't disprove my original premise, neither did it improve the situation. Now, with the center of our line collapsed, the Confederates would be coming straight at us. I began to anticipate a final, massive attack. But, to my surprise, a lull ensued. I only then understood the extent of the exhaustion the other side was feeling. They wanted to rest rather than follow through on the gap created by Prentiss's surrender. *Some of our men are badly demoralized, but the enemy must be even more so.* In retrospect, this was the moment when the difference between Johnston, who began the day in command and ended it dead, and Beauregard, who assumed command when Johnston was done bleeding to death, was most felt: Johnston would not have allowed it.

Suddenly, the end of the day seemed in sight. I assembled men from Sherman's, McClernand's, and Hurlbut's divisions, some stragglers, and fresh troops that had been coming across the river, and formed a new defensive line atop the bluff by the landing. I then told my staff to find some siege guns, big artillery pieces. Five of them were promptly arrayed side by side about a quarter of a mile up from the landing.

Not many fools would decide to run into such an artillery line, but Bragg was an uncommon fool and he decided on one last attack before dusk. He sent two of his divisions at us. Watching the results of his decision, I gained infinite respect for the Confederate fighting man and lost as much for Bragg. The men had to race down a ravine and then up out of it, straight at us. As targets go, they were slow. A thousand Confederates died in an hour. After two such assaults, Bragg gave up and the fighting was at last over. This would be where we ended that terrible day.

The evening gloom was now covering the field. We had not been crushed, which was a victory in its own right. We had taken their worst—a full frontal assault into our mass—and had been badly hurt as a result. W. H. L. Wallace, who might have been the most competent soldier under my command outside of Sherman and Smith, was himself hit and dying while filling in for Smith, who would eventually die of the leg wound he received after Donelson. Prentiss was captured, with the last two thousand of his men. But we had not been broken.

And we had not been forced across the Tennessee River. Had we retreated, we would have had to form the remaining demoralized troops into a new army while the Confederates would be able to reclaim the Tennessee River, taking back Henry, Donelson, Columbus, Paducah, and threatening St. Louis. Moreover, if the past was any guide, Halleck would have blamed me, despite the fact that we were attacked while sitting and waiting in the place he ordered us to sit and wait. He would have used our retreat as an excuse to send more of his choice correspondence to Stanton and Lincoln regarding some new malfeasance on my part to go with the bout of inebriation he decided to invent for me after Donelson. My reputation, already strained under the weight of my distinguished tenure out West and the heady accomplishment of my civilian career, could soon be overtaxed. So I decided I would rather die on this side of the river than live on the other.

Buell was aghast. "You haven't the means to escape across this river with any more than ten thousand men!" he had told me when we met earlier that afternoon.

"Don't worry," I'd said. "If we do have to retreat across the river, there won't be any more than ten thousand of us left." Buell blanched. Fortunately, it did not come to that.

The dark overtook us and the day's fighting ended. Storms blew in quickly from the west. Lightning struck and thunder rolled across the open field. Our men were trying to make camp in the little area left to them near the bluff. They were exhausted, wet, uncomfortable, and hungry. Occasional Confederate shells came down on them—one such missile hit an orderly who was delivering a message to me, splattering most of his thinking parts over my uniform. Another near miss, I thought.

The rain was falling on the other side, too. But the Confederate fighting man, while just as wet, tired, and hungry, was warmed by the thought of having proven himself the fighting equal of the Federal man who abandoned the field to him that morning. But that didn't mean that he had won the battle.

I told our artillery line to fire all the pieces they could find: We'd keep the Rebels awake and pinned down all night. By nightfall, there were at least fifty big field guns set up, and when I gave the command, all of these pieces went off at once. A more deafening roar could not be imagined. It shook the field and drowned out the very thunder from the sky. Men standing near the guns were thrown back and began bleeding from their noses and ears. It was a thing of unholy beauty.

Things finally began looking up. Buell's twenty thousand troops were now arriving at the landing: They appeared once the danger was past. All they had to do was come up the river about six miles, but they had turned it into an expedition to equal Magellan's.

Lew Wallace's men also began to arrive, now that their chances of dying seemed remote. They had spent the day marching through the woods the wrong way, following Wallace's convoluted path to glory. Several hours earlier, Wallace's men, coming in behind Sherman and McClernand, would have made it impossible to push our right side back, which would have protected Prentiss in the Hornet's Nest from being flanked and exposed, which in turn would have allowed us to re-supply him and allow his men to continue to kill the enemy quite hand-ily. We would then have turned the enemy to our left and cornered them in the ravine in which we shot up Bragg's men. But, as my mother often said, "That obviously wasn't how the Lord meant it, Hiram." I awaited the day I would try that one on Halleck.

But they were all here, at last, and all the pieces in place. I sent a regiment out into the woods on our right to see where the Rebels were. They came back close to midnight and reported they'd ventured out over half a mile and had seen not a one.

And then a remarkable conclusion came to me.

Beauregard thinks I'm going to retreat!

Our spies told us that evening that Albert Johnston had died, leav-ing Beauregard in charge—and Beauregard apparently thought the guns were covering our movement across the river rather than keeping him in place. So he sent no Confederates up as skirmishers or to do re-connaissance, and he wasn't digging any trenches or breastworks in the event of a counterattack. He thought it was all over and his job was done.

If I had believed all those horse apples about the Lord, I'd have prayed for exactly that. If *my* men had come out of the woods and kicked the other side's behinds the way they had kicked ours, you can be assured we would be digging trenches and assembling forward lines, preparing to hold our gains if attacked and to move forward if not. I can promise you we'd have driven the enemy into the swamps and captured the lot of them before lunch the next day. But instead, Beauregard's men were sitting in our captured tents, eating what food we had left behind, waiting for whatever would happen next.

Well, I'd show them what would happen next. I made some mental notes as to the next morning—put Buell's and Wallace's fresh men up front, have Hurlbut organize a new division out of the stragglers on the bluff by the landing, reform Sherman and McClernand and get Sher-man pointed right at Braxton Bragg, that sort of thing. At dawn, we would have at them.

The night rain was heavy now, the mud oozing, the creeks that de-fined the north and south boundaries of our position swelling. I needed someplace to go: I'd arrived at Pittsburg Landing that morning and gone directly to the field, so my headquarters were on my horse's hindquarters, so to speak. A log house had been set up for me and I was directed to it, but it had been turned into a field hospital. The sights awaiting me there were worse than those awaiting the sinner who arrived in the purgatory of my mother's imagination. Outside, men were lying in the rain and mud, wounded, dying, calling for aid that would never arrive. Orderlies were bringing them water, but most needed more than water. Most needed Heaven's intercession.

Inside, doctors were set up at tables with saws, removing the maimed limbs of those lucky enough to be shorn of their extremities. The smell of whiskey abounded, served in liberal amounts to the suffering. Severed arms and legs were stacked like the cordwood I sold in downtown St. Louis, piles growing in each corner of the cabin. Blood covered everything. The doctors looked as fatigued as the men who laid before them. There was hardly room to turn around, let alone walk.

Between the smell of the liquor, the stench of the blood and gore, and the sight of the maimed, I wanted to vomit, and I turned quickly and started to walk away. A few of the many men lying outside waiting for treatment recognized me and called for me as I walked past. "It's Grant!" one cried. "Don't worry, General, we'll whip 'em right back," said another. "They'll cut my arm off and I'll fight 'em with the other," I heard a third yell as he lay splayed out on the ground. I found myself hoping that if he did, the Confederates wouldn't shoot the poor fellow's other arm off as well.

But most were either silent—the silence of the doomed—or moaning unintelligibly. I stepped carefully among them and by the light of orderlies' lanterns saw the faces of boys whose deaths would be my doing. A boy of no more than sixteen lay gut-shot, hit between his waist and his groin, and would probably die. He scribbled a letter on a piece of paper and put it in his coat, hoping some mother or sweetheart would one day learn they had been in his thoughts at the end. Two older lads lay near him, expired in place, one of them head-shot.

A tall man with a salt-and-pepper beard and a hole in his stomach grimaced. A boy knelt and prayed with a bloody head. A man with a stoic expression lay completely still with a bullet hole in his chest—

I dropped to a knee beside him as I checked my senses. He was about forty, my own age, and of modest build. His wound was in his upper chest and off to a side—it might have pierced his lung. He breathed only lightly. I took his face in my hands and turned it slightly toward me.

It took all the steel I'd earned in war to suppress a cry of shock. As outlandish as it seemed, as much as I both dreaded and welcomed the realization, the more I looked, the less doubt I had.

It was Useful Grant.

He was lying wounded in the rain and mud before me, wearing the uniform of a common foot soldier, a wholly different picture than when I last saw him in Galena only two years before. He was covered with blood and mud, and by the shadow of the Angel of Death, and I knew I would just as soon die myself as see him die. I sprang to my feet and summoned a nearby orderly. "I want a tent set up over by those trees and I want this man put in it. And I want a doctor dispatched immediately," I snapped.

"Yes, General," he said, saluting before hurrying off.

I turned back to Useful. "Hold on, man. We're going to take care of you," I said, but he did not respond.

In a moment, a tent had been erected; I could only hope it was McClernand or one of his officers who had been evicted into the rain. Two men put Useful on a stretcher and ran him into the tent. I followed, tired and sore, limping along through the hard rain as it poured down, as if it would drown us all.

Useful was placed on a cot. His breathing was even weaker. The rain mixed with his blood to form small channels that dripped off him into the dirt. I lit a lamp and the tent filled with a ghostly yellow light. Useful lay there silently, and as I watched, he seemed to take on a glow, a golden richness, as if he were a painting by an Old Master, or perhaps made of light as I had seen everyone to be the night I encountered the Master himself.

The image of Mescalito suddenly came to me, resplendent in his cape of the colors of living things, riding a horse made of clouds. Was he looking down at us now, just as my mother believed her God did? Was he infusing Useful with a glow, just as he had me on that night long ago? I recalled the suns he had for eyes and wondered how anything could escape their unblinking gaze, when from over my left shoulder the briefest flicker of a shadow darted into my peripheral vision.

"You wanted a doc?" the man said.

He was disheveled and drenched, and smelled of the whiskey intended for his patients. He carried a saw with small shards of bone still in its teeth. His eyes were swollen and red, and he wiped them forcefully with the back of his bloody, dirt-caked hand.

"Who are you?" I asked.

"Who are you?" he shot back.

"I'm General Grant. This is my army." He grunted indifferently and folded his arms, and I regarded him warily. "What about this man?" I asked.

The doctor ambled over to Useful and bent over him, looking at him as a tanner would a carcass. "Bad hole," he muttered. "Hot poker ought to stop the bleeding. Then we can see what happens."

"He must live," I asserted.

"If he does, he will." The doctor shrugged, wiping his brow with his upper arm.

This would never do. I shouted for the orderly and he returned in an instant. "Get this butcher out of this tent. I want the doctor who would be sent to treat *me*."

The orderly nodded and ran out, the doctor muttering in exasperation as he followed him. A few minutes later, another doctor arrived. He was wearing a medical smock, covered with blood to be sure, but he had a clear look about him and an intelligent expression. "General," he said as he saluted.

I nodded. "Who are you?" I asked.

"Saveshammer, General," the doctor replied crisply. "Dr. Frederick Saveshammer."

This was more like it. "This man must not die," I repeated, pointing at Useful. "You must do everything in your power to save him."

"Of course," Dr. Saveshammer replied, then knelt beside Useful and went to work. The light that suffused Useful in its glow now seemed more meager and stark. The doctor checked Useful's air passageway and washed his wound with a wet rag. He turned away as he doused a rag with chloroform, then placed the rag over Useful's mouth and nose. He took out a scalpel and quickly made an incision through the bullet hole in the upper part of Useful's left breast. With some probing, he found and extracted the ball. He stitched Useful's chest adroitly and painted some iodine over the incision, carefully checking Useful's breathing and pulse at each step along the way. With the last stitch in place, Dr. Saveshammer stepped up from the cot and regarded his work.

"His lung is functioning and the bleeding is under control. He needs to rest quietly, although this isn't the place for quiet rest. Still, he's a lucky man." I nodded, considering the appraisal in all its aspects. Dr. Saveshammer shook his head as we listened to the thunder and the artillery pieces booming across the night. "I can send a nurse to attend to him, if you so desire," Dr. Saveshammer said.

"Leave him with me," I told the doctor. He began to put his equipment into a satchel. "And leave the chloroform with me," I added. "In case I need to administer it to him."

"Go easy with that, General. It's good that the man sleep, but at some point these ministrations can prove damaging."

"I understand," I told him. "Good night." And with that, Dr. Saveshammer was gone.

I sat down next to Useful, who was returning to the hazy border of consciousness, and regarded him for a long, quiet moment. At last, his secrets would be revealed.

"Who are you?" I asked him, waiting to hear the name that might emerge through Useful's fog. Would it be Grant? Or McKenna? Or Robinson?

His eyes did not open. "Who are you?" I said again.

I put my ear closer to his face. Useful's lips moved slowly as they began to whisper. "Let me die," he said softly.

"Who are you?" I repeated.

"Let me die, please," he whispered, this time more urgently. "Tend to the others."

His response puzzled me. "Why? Why do you want to die?"

His tongue emerged to wet his lips. I readied the rag and chloroform in case he began to rouse too quickly. I did not want him to see me, even if there was no reason to suspect he would recognize me. "Long ago. I killed two people," he began to speak. "A man and a woman. In Ohio."

After all these years, the incident lived on! The moral decrepitude of my father's scheme was matched only by its enduring brilliance. He had stolen Useful's life as craftily as he traded skins and hides, and here lay Useful now, two decades later and more, a living—or perhaps dying—testimonial to my father's flimflammery.

"They were running from me. I stole," he said softly. "Let me die, make my peace with God." Useful's eyes blinked open and I put the chloroform over his mouth and nose again, as I had seen the doctor do, until he returned to a hazier state. "Tell me your name," I repeated.

"Phipps," he whispered. "Fifty-third Ohio."

Phipps! Not Grant, or McKenna, or Robinson, but Phipps! The man had more aliases than the desk register in a bordello. "Is that your real name?"

"No," he whispered again.

I looked down at him, chloroform at the ready. "What about Robinson? Weren't you once Robinson?"

"They were going to hang me," he whispered.

His words both shocked and fascinated me. "Who was going to hang you?"

"I was a swindler," he said in a dreamy mumble that could barely be heard over the rain drumming on the roof of the tent. "Bought land, up by Sacramento. Sold it to the men coming off the boats." He stopped speaking and his chest sagged.

"Were you caught?" I prompted.

He wet his lips again and inexplicably began to sing deliriously. "*John Brown's body lies a-mouldering in the grave—*"

"Who were the people you killed?" I interrupted.

"A man and a woman," he said, suddenly focused on my question. "Almost caught."

"Who almost caught you?" I asked.

"Came out of nowhere," he said, in a whisper. "I escaped. Became Robinson. Ran off to California."

I pressed on. "So before you were Phipps, you were Robinson?"
"Yes."

"And before you were Robinson?"
"McKenna."

"And who were you before you were McKenna?"

Another bolt of lightning illuminated the tent as I waited for his answer. "*But his soul goes marching on,*" he sang again, dreamily.

I regarded him quietly. "What about Grant?" I asked.

"Grant," he mumbled. "Brought us here to die."

I held my breath for a long moment as the wind batted at the tent flaps. "And who is *Useful*?"

He began to weep. "I'm not useful. I'm useless. Not who they think I am. Let me die. Let me have peace."

Peace. No, I thought to myself, there would be no peace: Peace was the last thing in store for either of us. "You're not going to die," I told him with conviction. "You're going to go on living, for better or worse." I rose and summoned the orderly. "Take this man away. Make sure that he's given all necessary treatment."

I stepped out into the chaos of the dying, the din of the guns, and the torrent of rain, and surveyed the scene. While it was all wearying only a few moments before, now I took no notice of it. I felt draining from me every last doubt I had carried, through Belmont, through Henry and Donelson, to this drenched killing field around me. The memory of Mescalito, atop a white horse made of clouds, was now brilliant in my mind. There was no longer any question: Mescalito's prophecy was meant for me. My destiny was to be at this place, to be in command of these men encamped in the storm-soaked mud that stretched out for miles around me, and to overwhelm the men on the other side so utterly they could see no other outcome but defeat.

As I looked out over the bodies cast in every direction, both blue and gray, I suddenly saw the war clearly. Like everyone around me, I had believed the rebellion would collapse swiftly and suddenly if only a decisive victory could be won. Donelson and Henry were such victories—I stormed Donelson, killed or took away fifteen thousand men, and shut down the rebellion in large parts of Kentucky and Tennessee in a matter of days. But the war didn't end. Instead, the reality of the war came running out of the woods along with the Confederates. The reality of the war was spelled out in the thousands of dead lying among us. The Union could be saved by nothing less than complete conquest—total war, *total annihilation*.

The objective was no longer Corinth, Memphis, Mobile, or Richmond. The objective was not a city or a rail junction or a depot, or anything else on the maps that so mesmerized Halleck and McClellan and the other chess players. The objective was not to play chess at all, but to smash the enemy's pieces, to destroy the board itself. The objective was to crush so utterly the enemy that his home was gone and his way of life destroyed—everything he fought to defend. Our enemy was not the Southerner, but the South itself. All would have to be obliterated, leveled, utterly smashed. It would be my job—my destiny—to crush it.

Whether I was Ulysses S. Grant or Hiram U. Grant, Useless or Useful, made no difference. *I would lead great masses of men in the glorious cause of their human redemption.* The understanding of war that now filled me, and the victory that would surely follow from it, were all the proof needed of the Great Master's intent.

A war of total annihilation. The weight of this realization pressed down on me even as it gave me strength. *He has loosed the fateful lightning of his terrible swift sword.* Those unwilling to wage such a war only prolonged it. Those unprepared for waging such a war only diminished our prospects for winning it. Those unable to pursue such a war only stood in the way of those who were. Halleck and his maps. McClellan, now sitting outside of Yorktown, facing a vastly outnumbered enemy, contemplating the algebra of forces. Buell and his daylate communication and coordination. It was all dithering, all distractions from the one purpose we had—to kill the enemy in such prodigious numbers that the ones left alive lost all will to continue any further.

No terms other than unconditional and immediate surrender can be accepted. I propose to move immediately upon your works.

I took up a lantern and went out and into the rain. Some soldiers spread hay on a spot under a tree to spare me the mud, but there was no way to stay dry. I was sitting there, regarding the scene around me—the storm, the fury of the guns, the quiet murmuring of the wounded, the pitiful silence of the dying—when I suddenly became aware that Sherman had joined me while I was lost in thought. He sat down next to me, looking even more fatigued than I must have looked to him. He sighed deeply and turned to me.

"Well, Grant, we've had the devil's own day, haven't we?"

"Yes," I said, and I looked out at the scene that so readily confirmed his judgment. "Lick 'em tomorrow, though." He looked at me with his eyes glaring inside a drawn face. He seemed to feel my confidence, the first traces of his edgy smile returning. We managed to light two cigars in the rain and sat there together, saying as little as we did that day on the street in St. Louis, until the first outline of dawn could be perceived.

When the rain ended later in the morning, we went out and had at them. On my left I now put Buell's men and a division, led by General McCook, that had marched thirty miles the day before—when neither

Lew Wallace nor Buell could manage six—to join us. These reinforcements were fresh, confident, wholly organized, and would be able to protect the landing and access to the river. At my center, I placed Hurlbut's reorganized division of stragglers, scatterers, and survivors, and McClernand's and Sherman's divisions. On my far right, I placed Lew Wallace's recent arrivals, to protect our flank there. When the first light appeared, we were off.

The Confederates didn't fall back at first, but the big guns had softened them up and they now faced our thousands of reinforcements. Beauregard must have been stunned to realize that, rather than flee across the river, we were going to start all over from where we had left off only a few dark hours before.

As the day ground on, our advantage became overwhelming. Sherman sent a message at about three in the afternoon noting that, from his position on the right, he could see the Confederates assembling a rear-guard and flanking operation to protect themselves as they fell back. By late afternoon they were retreating, the wave of gray receding from the field as surely as it had overwhelmed it the day before. I organized two nearby regiments into an offensive line and had them charge, just to make sure the Confederates were broken. I am not sure if this is what finally led them to cut and run—the straw that broke their backs, so to speak—but it did serve to speed them up considerably.

I found Sherman at about four-thirty that afternoon. By then, the momentum had turned unquestionably. He was up front with his men, trying to keep their lines organized as they drove the enemy from the field, as frantic as he had been when they were getting whipped the day before. He was back at his old camp, the spot where he woke the previous morning to the sounds of the first onslaught, watching the battle with characteristic agitation.

"Cump!" I hollered as I rode up to him, Rawlins and Hillyer behind me.

"Grant, you son of a bitch! Will you look at this?" Sherman yelled, waving a piece of paper in his hand. As I approached he shouted, "Do you see that tent, Sam?" and pointed to one nearby that was ventilated with minié balls. "That was my fucking tent yesterday morning!" he growled. "Do you know who slept in that tent last night, Sam? Fucking

Braxton and Pete, Sam, that's who. Those damned traitorous clowns!"
He stomped the ground in rage.

I laughed out loud—he meant Bragg and Pierre Beauregard. Sherman had been a few years behind Beauregard at West Point, and Bragg was one of the investors Sherman repaid when his bank folded in the Crash of 1857. In fact, when Sherman was looking for work just before the war, it was Beauregard and Bragg who recommended him for a job as superintendent of the military academy down in Louisiana, which he held when the war broke out.

They did not think it inappropriate, therefore, to tweak Sherman's nose and spend the night in his tent.

Sherman looked as if the world's greatest practical joke had been played on him, and perhaps it had. "Look at this, Sam," he sputtered, brandishing the paper in his hand. "It's a fucking letter from Pete," he said, meaning Beauregard. "He left it in the tent for me!"

He handed it over to me, and I read:

Dear Sherman,

Braxton and I thank you for taking leave of your tent and showing us your hospitality as we drove you yesterday. It was as comfortable as any with which our own young country has seen fit to provide us during this campaign.

Your people deserve credit. When we stopped last night, I was sure Sam was firing off those guns of his to give your boys a chance to cross the river and escape. Frankly, had I thought that we were going to go at it again today, I'd have done things differently.

We're headed back to Corinth, to prepare to whip you fellows when you get there, worse than we gave you yesterday. We should be pretty well reenforced by the time you arrive and we'll pick up where we left off. In the meantime, don't let those scurvy newspaper dogs treat you as badly as they have: Braxton and I don't think you're crazy at all. And give our regards to Sam, who is the talk of our camp, that is, when we're not talking about you.

> *See you in Corinth.*
> *With best regards,*
> *yr. Obd. Svt.,*
> *Pierre Gustave Toutant Beauregard, CSA*

"Can you believe this?" Sherman demanded, caught between laughter and tears.

"It's a lot of cheek," I said with a chuckle. Sherman spat out a stream of expletives as he considered it, but there was other business at hand. "Cump, we've got to go after them," I said. "Let's not make the same mistake again. They're in terrible shape, and we could finish them off."

Sherman shook his head. "My men are going to go face first into the fucking dirt with exhaustion, Sam. They've been at it for two days."

"Any forward motion we can muster would be immensely helpful, Cump," I said.

"Let Buell go chase 'em," he said with a snort. "His men had a nice boat ride up the river yesterday while our boys were being killed."

I nodded, but reality was what it was. "You know the problem, Cump. He's a major general with his own command, so I can't order him to do anything. All I can do is remind him he can pursue them if he has the capability."

"Yeah, sure." Sherman laughed bitterly. "He's as tentative as a man trying to fuck a porcupine." He spat on the ground, then looked up at me and said, in a different tone of voice, "They're going to fuck with you, Sam."

I nodded: I knew exactly what he meant. "There will be some stories in the newspapers about the carnage, yes."

"Hell yes, there will be stories about the fucking carnage, Grant!" Sherman said, now more agitatedly. "Those traitorous newspapermen are going to skewer you. When I said the war would take years and thousands would die, they all but put me away in the fucking asylum. And the stories they wrote: Sherman's mad! Sherman's lost his mind! Well, here we are, Sam, and fucking thousands have died in *two fucking days*, haven't they? The world's never seen anything like this—tens of thousands fighting tens of thousands—it's never happened before! They're going to blame somebody! *Grant let thousands of our boys die!* That's what they'll say! And those fucking people up North," he said heatedly, pointing a finger in that general direction, "not one of them is ready to believe this is what it will take. Not a one. They all want to fuck the girl without taking their cocks out."

I wouldn't have put it in those terms, but he was right.

We watched our line forge ahead with increasing ease. "What about our buddy Henry?" he asked, meaning Halleck.

"Oh, he'll have plenty to tell me about, I'm sure," I answered.

Sherman smiled. "He's going to throw you to the wolves, Sam. But I'll stand up for you. This was my fault if it was anybody's. I'll tell my story—"

"That won't be necessary, Cump. You're my best man on the field."

He shook his head, trying to fathom the entirety of what was going on around us. "All this fucking death and then all that bullshit on top of it," he muttered. "Jesus Christ."

I told Sherman it was bad luck to take the Lord's name in vain, and I turned my horse and started away. And so the Battle of Shiloh ended, with the Confederates slinking away on the same road that brought them, and our men sitting exhausted where they had sat two days before. In the interim, twenty-five thousand men were killed—more than in all American wars combined. A new way of war was born—brutal confrontation and violence delivered at close range by waves of men to waves of their counterparts—not just on the battlefield at Shiloh, but in my own mind. Mescalito's prophecy was clear. This was what it meant to be Ulysses Grant, I realized. I was sent here to wage and win this war.

A final note on Shiloh. I invited Buell to pursue Beauregard, and he predictably passed up the opportunity. Sherman could not. Only a few months before, he had been hounded out of the army as a lunatic. At Shiloh, he had been redeemed, and he didn't want the moment to end. He quickly organized a cavalry division and two brigades of infantry and took off after them.

About six miles out, he found them. But the commander of the rear guard of the Confederate retreat was their master cavalry leader, Nathan Bedford Forrest. Forrest turned himself and surprised Sherman with a lightning counterattack that sent many of Sherman's men running. It was all Cump could do to organize a line and get some shots off. At that point, even Cump had to agree that his men were too tired to be of any practical use, and he turned them back toward camp.

When he arrived, a remarkable thing happened. His division, their number now two thousand less, saw him heading back to the ground around the Shiloh church where they had awoken Sunday morning to the sound of death racing toward them. The men stood and started to holler for Sherman as I have never seen men shout for their commander.

Two days ago, these men had never seen battle, and now they had lived through more war than the veterans of any preceding generation. They had each somehow survived, lived to breathe the spring air and drink cool water once again, to see again the light and colors around them, to feel again someday the kiss of the ones they loved. They had defied the gods of battle: They were, for an instant, immortal. And every shred of this great joy now escaped them in their shouts for the man who had ushered them through the valley of the shadow of death.

Sherman stopped for a moment and then started to smile so broadly I thought his face would burst. He had been delivered, too, delivered from his past, from the shadow of his madness, delivered by these men just as he had delivered them. He doffed his hat and waved it in the air, and a noise even louder than our siege guns went up, but this a joyful one. He cantered down to one end of the line and turned his horse and reared, hat in the air. Down the line his horse pranced as the men shouted. "We're with you, Uncle Billy!" they exclaimed, using the name they ordinarily used when he wasn't in front of them. "We'll follow you to Richmond, Uncle Billy!" And as they shouted, Sherman's smile got wider and wider and his carriage ever more animated. He wiggled his finger through the hole in the crown of his hat for them and waved his bandaged hand at men who waved theirs back. And at the end of the line he waved his arms over his head and there was silence in response to his command.

"Men," he shouted. "You have won a great victory! The enemy has retreated to Corinth!" And with that there was again a great roar and Sherman and his men stood there and adored each other as the sounds of euphoric cheering washed over them. I watched from across the field as the ghosts lifted from Sherman—the insanity, the banking failures, the moody inability to find a place in the world—all dispelled by the adoration of the men he commanded. I understood completely.

Rectitude be damned. Is it any wonder that at that moment, for the first time in the war, I wept?

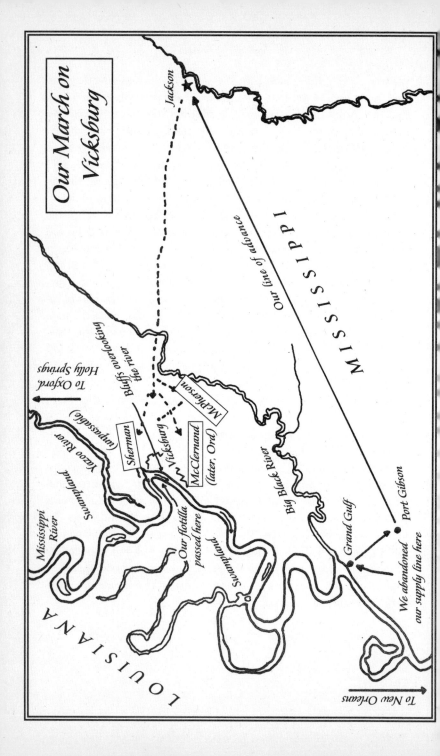

CHAPTER IX

HALLECK MOVES ON CORINTH—CONFERRING WITH SHERMAN—THE RINGLEADER OF THE COTTON SPECULATORS—THE VICKSBURG CAMPAIGN

OUR VICTORY AT SHILOH changed the war. Halleck sent the Confederacy reeling, abandoning his ideas about strategic positions and opting instead for the relentless pursuit and annihilation of the two remaining Confederate armies of significance—Lee's in Virginia and Joe Johnston's (the surviving Johnston, Albert having died in battle a few days before) in Georgia.

After taking a brief moment to commend me for repelling an attack neither he nor I foresaw, and with only a day's respite for organization, Halleck launched a three-pronged, lightning attack on Corinth, where Beauregard's demoralized forces cowered. Pope, having opened up the upper Mississippi after the Confederates abandoned Columbus, came down the western flank. Buell departed his headquarters in Nashville and prevented Beauregard's escape to Chattanooga to the east. My own Army of the Tennessee, with Sherman in advance, drove south from Pittsburg Landing and, with Pope and Buell guarding the flanks, crushed Beauregard at Corinth, compelling his surrender along with his second-in-command, Braxton Bragg, and his fiendish cavalry officer, Nathan Bedford Forrest.

With Beauregard's army taken whole, we outnumbered and outgunned the Rebels at every turn. Buell was dispatched to go after Joe Johnston, who had given McClellan a whipping the first time Little Mac tried to cross into Virginia. I sent Sherman to assist Buell and make sure that the enemy would be pressed. Meanwhile, Pope crossed the Mississippi again, raced south, and then met me at Vicksburg, the last remaining stronghold on the river, which we caught in a pincer movement and reduced in a week's time. After that, all that was left was Lee, who was caught between our combined force and the Army of the Potomac under a newly rejuvenated McClellan and Sherman, and who surrendered after a series of devastating open-field battles in the summer of 1863.

And I, of course, emerged the hero—prompt to respond to the challenge when Albert Johnston's men emerged from the forest, unruffled in the face of disaster, levelheaded and methodical while waiting for the arrival of Wallace and Buell, unflinching in meting out the punishment necessary to achieve victory, and the architect of the unceasing, remorseless attack that ground down the Confederates under the weight of our war-making capabilities.

And then I stopped dreaming.

Had Halleck learned from Shiloh and concentrated on waging war, history *might* have looked like that, but, as I learned in Mexico, once the fighting on the ground ends, the fighting among the generals and politicians begins. It wasn't a week before the newspapers explained how I led our boys to their doom, just as Sherman had said they would. They wrote that our soldiers were murdered in their bedrolls, bayoneted as they slept, entire divisions wiped out before they left their tents to relieve themselves that morning—the ones who lived did so because they fled in terror to the safety of the riverbank. They wrote I arrived late and wandered aimlessly when I finally did, that I was caught unawares and didn't know what to do, that Lew Wallace had his troops up and ready to march and wasn't summoned to the battle until after noon, that we would have been pushed to our deaths in the river had Buell not showed up to save us all. And they wrote what Rawlins said they were going to write—that I was drunk, stewed, tipsy, in my cups, a rummy, that ten thousand of our boys died as I cowered in inebriation.

The press howled, the public screamed. Each town whose regiment had been wiped out produced a new senator or congressman who wanted an explanation, or at least the appearance of an explanation, or to appear as if wanting the appearance of an explanation. But no matter what else they wanted, they wanted a head to roll, and only one was available. Mine.

As Congressman Washburne once told me, a lie can walk from Maine to Georgia before the truth has a chance to put on its boots.

Halleck showed up in the midst of all that commotion and his reaction was as I expected in its every dimension.

"What the devil went on here?" he said, his displeasure evident, as we assembled in the farmhouse he had commandeered for his headquarters. Sherman sat next to me, while Buell, Lew Wallace, and McClernand congregated across from us. The sides were clearly drawn.

"What do you think went on, Henry?" Sherman answered quickly. "Johnston came out of the fucking woods and attacked us."

"Spare me your colorful commentary, Sherman," Halleck replied. "Just tell me what to do with these!" His bulging eyes widened as he shook a handful of newspaper clippings in the air before us.

"Henry, do we really need to discuss those?" Sherman asked. "I say we find the lousy, traitorous newspaper bastards who wrote this stuff and shoot the fuckers!" He nodded as he looked at all of us, as if he expected every levelheaded man in the room to agree with this course of action, and looked disappointed when Halleck didn't.

"We're not going to shoot any newspapermen, Sherman!" Halleck shouted.

"I agree," McClernand spoke up. "Shooting newspapermen would be a terrible idea just now, a further embarrassment to my good friend the President—"

"And you shut up, too, damn it," Halleck barked, cutting him off. "Now, Grant, my prize student," he continued. "Is this all true? Were our men killed in their sleep? Did they cut and run until Buell here showed up?"

I took a breath to calm myself and tried to explain to Old Brains what seemed obvious to me. "With all due respect, Henry, if it were true, wouldn't all of us here be dead or captured? If our men were bayoneted in their sleep or turned tail and ran, then why was there one of the enemy's dead out there for each one of ours? Who shot them, Henry, the men hiding by the landing or the ones who were bayoneted in their sleep? And if I was scared or confused or drunk, then how did I manage to reform our lines and keep the enemy at bay until reinforcements arrived?"

"But these accounts!" Halleck exclaimed excitedly, shaking the newspaper clippings once again. "Men huddled in fear, refusing to fight! What does the mother of a casualty think when she reads about that?" He was a man desperate to have the blame moved elsewhere.

"Oh, Jesus," Sherman spat, irate. "Where do you think a yellow-tailed reporter is going to be during a damn battle other than hiding behind the lines? And while he's hiding back there, who's he going to find to talk to aside from the damned deserters? And what else would they tell him other than how their comrades were killed in their fucking beds? And while we're at it, what's this goddamned nonsense about Lew not getting an order until noon?" He turned and looked directly at Lew. "Who told these newspaper bastards that?"

Wallace shrugged. "I certainly didn't, Sherman," he said, lying outright. "But if I'd had clearer orders, perhaps we would have gotten an earlier start, or we wouldn't have taken the wrong road. You know, Grant, exposition is a much harder craft than many imagine, getting the sentences just right. I can't really be blamed—"

"Can't really be blamed!" I sputtered. "My orders were clear and specific, and if you failed to understand them, or"—and here I considered my words carefully, but was determined to make my allegation nonetheless—"you decided to improvise an entrance that would provide you a more dramatic scene for that novella you appear to believe you're living in, one in which you would emerge from the woods—"

"Here, now! Those are substantial accusations, Grant!" Buell interrupted, whereupon he began to make substantial accusations of his own. "General Halleck—Henry—with nothing in my heart but fairness to Grant, I must report that thousands of men cowering in panic barely begins to cover it. There was wholesale disorganization, and I feared for the entire enterprise when I beheld it."

Sherman could not contain himself. "Why you little whorehouse clerk! My men were dying in wholesale lots under enemy fire while you traipsed about, taking your merry fucking time! How much did you pay that newspaperman to write this shit about you, Buell?"

Buell's lips tightened. "I ought to pound you, Sherman!"

"You have a cordial fucking invitation to try, Buell," Sherman answered, calm and contemptuous. He looked as if he hoped Buell would.

Halleck called for silence on all parts and looked at me icily. "Why the devil didn't you dig in, Grant? Why were there no entrenchments?"

"Because I saw no use for them," I answered simply.

"Nor did I," Sherman spoke up quickly. "Or poor Smith," he added. Smith was now dying of his leg wound and would last only another two weeks.

"It was my decision, not Sherman's," I said. "We could dig trenches, or we could drill and train the fresh troops, which is what we were there to do. Besides, my feeling was that digging would be demoralizing."

"Demoralizing! Tell me about the morale of the ten thousand dead men out there, Grant!" Old Brains shouted. "Maybe if you had been able to plow a straight and sober furrow in civilian life, you'd have a little more respect for digging today!" That remark hung in the air until Halleck appeared to compose himself.

"What are your orders, Henry?" Buell asked.

Halleck nodded sagely and then shared his insight. "Well, first we're going to dig ourselves in, so we won't be surprised again."

Sherman's rage propelled him from his seat as he began to scream. "Who the fuck is going to surprise us this time, Henry? The Rebels just *tried* to surprise us, and Sam here drove them off the field and all the way back to Corinth! I don't suppose they're going to try to surprise us *again*! So who the hell is going to surprise us now, Henry? Are the *Prussians* going to surprise us? Are the *French*? Are the *Black Hawks* coming back, Henry? Are the fucking *deer* and *bunnies* going to run out of the woods and surprise us this time, Henry?" Sherman threw his hands up in the air, and I saw my chance.

"Cump's a little overwrought, Henry," I said, as Sherman dropped back into his seat, shaking his head. "But let me point out that right now Beauregard is outnumbered and outgunned, holed up in Corinth, his men beaten and demoralized. They gambled, Henry, and they lost, and whether you think I made mistakes, or Lew or Don made mistakes, we could go after Beauregard *right now* and finish him off. We could take the entire Mississippi region including Vicksburg, which means *complete control* of the Mississippi, from New Orleans to St. Louis. And we could take his army whole, just like Buckner's at Donelson, but this time, Henry," I said, offering him an incentive for doing his job that might actually move him to do it, "the credit would be all yours."

Unfortunately, it was not enough. "The enemy is no doubt massing in Corinth to renew the fighting," Halleck announced to all of us.

"Grant and Sherman were fooled once and are apparently prepared to be fooled again. We will dig in and wait for Pope."

Pope had finished driving Price out of Missouri, seizing on the opportunities created by my capture of Donelson, and secured the Mississippi as far south as Memphis.

"Pope!" Sherman exclaimed. "We have just about every white son of a bitch west of the goddamned Appalachians right here as it is! Why do we have to wait—"

Halleck didn't even look up. "Once he is here, we will number a hundred and twenty thousand, which to my thinking will be quite enough to advance on Corinth. We will dig in and wait for him. Those are your orders."

And that was what we did. It wasn't until the twenty-first of April, a full two weeks after Shiloh, that Pope arrived, and we didn't start out for Corinth until the thirtieth. And even though it was only twenty miles south of us, Halleck couldn't manage to move more than a mile a day, because once the sun began to drop, our hundred and twenty thousand men picked up a hundred and twenty thousand shovels and began to dig, dig like an army of moles burrowing into a vegetable patch, and once the sun rose again, the hundred and twenty thousand men would leave the holes they dug the night before and start the process all over again.

You know all these fucking engineers know how to do is dig, don't you?

It took Halleck's mole-army a full month before it finally tunneled to the outskirts of Corinth. He gave field command to Buell, Pope, and my old classmate George Henry Thomas, all of whom agreed with his every decision. I was made second-in-command to Halleck, meaning I was ignored.

Once we got near Corinth, the strangest sights and sounds awaited us. Explosions went off within the town at odd hours of the day and night.

"Artillery practice," Halleck pronounced ponderously.

"Absolutely," echoed Thomas.

"They're preparing for our assault," Buell added.

Train whistles were heard around the clock, each blast followed by the sound of men cheering. "Reinforcements," Halleck said in grim assessment.

"Tens of thousands if one," Buell said.

"They're massing," Pope added.

From the distance, Halleck's telescope sighted guns at each parapet and earthwork, with companies of sentries standing guard at each. "My Lord," he whispered in dread. "Corinth has become the most unassailable fortress imaginable!"

Buell, Thomas, and Pope nodded, appearing to accept their imminent doom.

By the thirtieth of May, Halleck dispatched a fearful Buell to the edge of Corinth. There he discovered the truth I had suspected from the very start. The town had been abandoned. The cheering railroad noises were an act—the trains were taking soldiers out, not in. The cannon were "Quaker guns"—logs painted black, attended in macabre silence by straw dummies dressed in the bullet-riddled uniforms of the dead. The explosions were Beauregard torching his ammunition dump, destroying what could not be carried. He had taken his army, repaired it, nursed it, resupplied it, and skipped out of town south to Tupelo, using every hour of the seven weeks of waiting and digging and dreading Halleck had given him to good effect.

Halleck entered an undefended Corinth the next day. A painted message on a whitewashed wall greeted him: WELCOME YANKEES.

"Victory is ours!" Halleck exulted, and sent a message to that effect to Lincoln.

It would have been more than I could stand had help not appeared in the strangest form, that of the Little Napoleon himself, George McClellan. Under pressure from Lincoln to take some decisive action, Little Mac took a hundred thousand men up the Yorktown peninsula to attack Richmond from the southeast. But by the end of June, Lee and Tom Jackson had repelled him in the Battle of the Seven Days, despite their being outnumbered at every turn. McClellan turned tail and ran back to Washington rather than attack again. A despairing Lincoln decided to relieve McClellan as general-in-chief, and he sent for the only senior Union commander with any track record of success.

My success. Henry Halleck.

"I'm giving you your command back, Grant," Halleck said when I came in to see him the next day. The streets of occupied Corinth—an otherwise laconic small town—could be seen from the window of the bank building where he had moved his headquarters. His bulging eyes now had the shine of the happiest man alive, and he leaned forward as if to tell me what Santa Claus was bringing. "There is good news!"

Getting my command back was good news enough, I thought, and wondered what else was in the sack.

"Lincoln has made me general-in-chief. I am off to Washington to win the war!" he announced, patting his stomach with satisfaction. "Oh, I most decidedly don't really want to return to Washington, to be sure," Halleck said, practicing his humility on me, "but the President has made it clear my nation needs me, so my own preferences be hanged, I say!"

I trembled for my nation but could not deny the prospective pleasure of being back in the field and far away from Halleck. "What will the command structure be now that you're going east?"

Halleck nodded, as if anticipating the question. "You will have your Army of the Tennessee once again, with headquarters in Corinth. Sherman, McClernand, and Lew Wallace will be under your command."

"What about Pope?" I asked.

"Pope has been called east, to subdue Tom Jackson—*Stonewall*, he's called now—" Halleck said dismissingly. "And I have selected Rosecrans to replace him. He and his army will report to you."

Rosecrans! His major qualification for a senior opening in the command structure was his quarter century of sucking up to Halleck. "And Buell?" I asked.

"You and Buell will divide the west," Halleck said, looking down at his desk, "both reporting to me."

For a moment, it seemed unfair. As the only general in the Union ranks who had secured the surrender of an entire Confederate army, I was the logical successor to Halleck in the west, but instead he would command both Buell and I directly. Still, the more I thought about it, who cared? At least Halleck was leaving.

"Congratulations, sir!" I said, saluting smartly, and went back to my tent to send a wire to Mrs. Ulysses Grant, care of Jesse R. Grant, Covington, Kentucky.

Have assumed command of the Army of the Tennessee, headquartered in Corinth, Mississippi. Bring the children and meet me here at once.

My orders were classic Halleck—to hold the territory. It was now summer, and what a long summer it was! Halleck, unconcerned with maintaining any forward momentum, had all of our troops repairing railroad track in order to maintain our supply lines in the months when the rivers ran low. Meanwhile, Bragg, sensing Halleck's lethargic strategy, brazenly organized an attack in eastern Kentucky against Buell and succeeded in driving him north.

I deployed Rosecrans and General E. O. C. Ord, a competent fellow in whom my trust was strong, to prevent the Confederate generals in Mississippi, Price and Van Dorn, from moving east and reinforcing Bragg. They stopped them from doing so at a town called Iuka, although Rosecrans allowed the Confederates to retreat without pursuit. Ord, however, acquitted himself well, as did the commander of Rosecrans's cavalry, a small, mustachioed fellow named Sheridan, who seemed to relish the destruction of his adversary in a way that commends itself in war but raises eyebrows in civilian life.

Mrs. Grant did not like Sheridan at first. I recall she met him one evening when he brought an intelligence report to our home in Corinth. We had received him and Rosecrans on our *piazza* one evening. They presented a report to me as Mrs. Grant sat next to me, and she did not hesitate to offer me her opinion when they were done. "He's small, don't you think?" she whispered.

I nodded, hoping that if Sheridan had heard, he would not take offense. "Many of the men are short, my dear."

"For a colonel, I mean. And his mustache is rather long," she added.

It was perhaps a bit, well, rakish in effect. But beyond being an exceptionally small fellow with an unduly long mustache, Sheridan gave off an air of intense confidence that transcended swagger. "I shall endeavor to trim it more appropriately in the presence of a lady as charming as yourself, Mrs. Grant," he said with a bow, having apparently overheard her last remark, and I knew right away this Sheridan fellow was all right.

But even without Price and Van Dorn, Bragg was having little trouble with Buell. He had raced Buell north through Kentucky to the Ohio River and beaten him at every turn. Buell fell back as far as Louisville without so much as a shot fired, as he desperately tried to find someplace to gather himself and stop Bragg before the Confederates crossed the river and threatened Cincinnati.

Sherman, meanwhile, set up headquarters in Memphis and went to work on the rail lines, just as my men were doing. And as the summer of 1862 turned into fall, we both wondered when we would be allowed to resume waging war.

"It strikes me that Henry has departed but left his thinking behind," I told Sherman, having gone to his headquarters in Memphis to confer. We sat, smoking my cigars, on the front lawn of the home he had commandeered, a fine structure with a commanding view of the autumn colors of the Mississippi Valley. "We're sitting here pinned, while Bragg makes a horse's ass out of Buell—"

"You can't make a horse's ass out of Buell," Sherman interrupted. "It's like making pig out of pork."

His humor was wasted on me. "We should propose to Halleck that we resume the offensive."

"And do you have a specific proposal in mind, Grant?"

I smiled and nodded. "Vicksburg," I said. Vicksburg was the last Rebel stronghold on the Mississippi. Taking it would open the Mississippi and cut the Rebels in half. "We form two columns," I continued, knowing Sherman was on the same track I was. "The first one crushes any possible support coming from Jackson"—the state capital, which lay forty miles east of Vicksburg—"and then we overwhelm the city. They surrender or starve."

"It would work," Sherman said, his eyes bright with the prospect.

"Who's in charge in Vicksburg now? Is it still Van Dorn?"

"Pemberton, I am told," Sherman said, tapping the ash from his cigar. "Never heard of him."

"The name seems familiar."

"Don't worry, you'll get a chance to place him when he surrenders to you," Sherman said with a laugh.

"Yes, if Henry gives us permission."

"I could talk to him," Sherman said. "You know he listens to me."

I turned to him. "Why does Henry put up with you? I wouldn't countenance a tenth of what you say to him. If I was him, I'd have taken you out and whipped you after what you said to him after Pittsburg Landing."

"Hell, Grant, you aren't me and you almost got fucking whipped after Shiloh, regardless." Sherman grinned his wicked, crazy grin, then settled back in his chair. "Henry respects my opinion. And it's probably because I don't scare him, like you do."

His remark startled me. "I do?"

"Hell yes, you do," he said. "You spent all of the Mexican War hauling salt pork on mules, drank yourself out of the army, couldn't grow dirt in a field of cow shit, and then suddenly appeared out of nowhere and took charge. If you were career army, or some kind of exceptional student back at West Point, Henry would love you, because the world would have worked the way it was supposed to. If you were me, number six, all the right answers in class, reciting all that shit about Cornwallis and Napoleon, you'd be the fucking golden boy, a few 'goddamns' or no. But you're a lousy farmer who doesn't wear a full uniform, doesn't say much, and thought Cornwallis blew it. You scare the shit right out of him."

I pursed my lips and considered the matter. "Perhaps you're right."

"I know I'm right," Sherman said, gazing at the sun setting across the river. "You'll scare all of them before this is over," he said, as if it would be plain to anyone, and took a long drag of his cigar. We watched his smoke escape into the autumn air. "Why don't you go see Henry?"

I shook my head. "I've got other things on my mind," I said.

"Like what?" Sherman snorted. "Repairing railroads?"

"Cotton speculators," I said. I was referring to the riffraff—generally Northern merchants—who traveled a few days ahead of our army as it moved through the South, buying up cotton from plantationers afraid of our impending arrival. They offered gold in payment, which went right into Confederate coffers. Each of these profiteers was more dangerous, in my estimation, than a thousand Rebel troops.

Sherman shook his head, suffering his exquisite displeasure. "It's all about fucking money, Sam. Mexico was, California was. We'll look up one day and figure that this was all about money, too. When the war is all over, money is going to win."

"This war's not about money, Sherman. It's about preserving the Union. If this nation wasn't worth saving, I'd never have put my uniform on again," I told him plainly.

"Save it for the Fourth of July picnic, Grant. You'll wake up and see it for what it is before it's all over," Sherman said gruffly.

"You're ill served by your cynicism, Cump," I said.

"You're ill served by your innocence, Sam," Sherman responded.

I changed the subject. "I'm going to Oxford"—a nearby town in Mississippi—"tomorrow," I told Sherman. "I'm told there's a ring-leader holed up there."

"Shoot him. Shoot the whole fucking lot of them. Just like the news-papermen."

I was smiling at Sherman's enthusiasm when a runner approached, a young boy bringing me a telegram. I unfolded it and began to read. The news was good. "Buell has defeated Bragg outside Louisville," I said to Sherman. "Beat him soundly, it says here."

Sherman gaped at me. "He did?" I nodded silently as Sherman's mind raced ahead. "Grant, do you realize the magnitude of this news? If Braxton's army is captured—" And here he observed my frowning expression. "Why are you shaking your head?"

"Bragg has escaped," I told him. "Buell allowed them to march away, just as he let them march in."

"They escaped?" He leapt up and threw his cigar on the ground, wasting a good two inches of the thing. "For the love of God, all there is in that part of Kentucky is two armies and a lot of nothing else! If you beat him, you've got him!" Sherman had just begun his rant, but stopped abruptly when he saw me suppressing a smile. "Why are you smiling, Grant?"

"Buell's been relieved of command by Lincoln," I said.

"He has?"

"For failing to pursue the enemy," I said.

"Goddamn, yes!" Sherman cheered. "Maybe Lincoln can explain to Henry how to fight a war!" He shook his head in wonderment and then abruptly turned back to me. "Wait! Who gets Buell's command?"

I smiled even more broadly, holding up the telegram. "Rosecrans."

Sherman's eyes widened. "You mean Buell's gone *and* you get to send Rosey to east Kentucky?" I nodded, delighted. "Shit, Grant! Lincoln's improved two fucking armies with one move!"

"Absolutely!" I said, my mood rapidly improving. "Let Rosecrans deal with Bragg. I'll draw up a message to Halleck tomorrow, asking for the Vicksburg campaign. What do you say?"

He extended his hand. "Vicksburg it is," he said.

I shook his hand and cemented our partnership. We spent the rest of the evening smoking and watching the sun set over the river, as quiet as we had been on the street corner in St. Louis, or under the tree at

Shiloh, but different just the same. The war was changing and we were changing, and one could not be separated from the other. For Sherman, Buell's dismissal and Rosecrans's transfer were merely the removal of impediments that fed his endless feeling of frustration. But for me they were signs, omens, that the Great Master's prophecy was fast approaching.

I left camp the next day and headed to Oxford to find the head of the cotton ring, armed with my new sense of optimism. The events of that day were to result in my issuing one of the most famous—more truthfully, infamous—directives of the war, one for which I have been pilloried ever since, and regarding which my motivations remain completely misunderstood. The exact text of my regrettable order was as follows:

> **The Jews, as a class violating every regulation of trade established by the Treasury Department and also department orders, are hereby expelled from the department within twenty-four hours from the receipt of this order.**
>
> **Post commanders will see that all of this class of people be furnished passes and required to leave, and any one returning after notification will be arrested and held in confinement, until an opportunity occurs of sending them out as prisoners, unless furnished with permit from headquarters.**
>
> **No passes will be given these people to visit headquarters for the purpose of making personal application for trade permits.**

The idea that I was prejudiced against the practitioners of the Hebrew faith is without merit. I had my reasons, and that was not among them. This, instead, is what transpired.

When Rawlins and I arrived by military train at Oxford, we were met by a detail that escorted us to a large brick house in the center of town. "This is where they operate," one of the soldiers said.

I nodded to Rawlins and we marched up the front steps, knocked on the door soundly, and waited until an old colored butler opened it. The hall behind him had been stripped of all art and decoration. "If I wanted to sell cotton, would I have come to the right place?" I asked him.

"Oh, yessuh, rightly so," the old uncle said, shuffling and bowing as he opened the door. "Down the hall toward the back, in the receiv' room," he said. "I'll take you there."

"Thank you, but there's no need," I said, and strode forcefully into the house and down the dark, dusty hall, followed by Rawlins, and pushed open the doors to the library in the rear. There they were, three men at a long library table in front of a red-draped wall, the ring-leader in the middle, all intently concentrating on their invoices and accounts spread out before them, along with stacks of gold, Federal shin-plaster paper money, Federal gold certificates, and Confederate notes, like the money changers that so offended Christ. As the recognition sank in, I felt a deep, angry revulsion at my core.

"Father!"

"Hiram! Look at you in your general's uniform!" my father exclaimed happily when he looked up from his work. "I mean Ulysses, of course," he said, catching himself. "Sit down, my boy, do sit down." He gestured to a seat opposite him, a broad smile on his face.

"I'm not here to visit, Father," I said directly. "I'm here to shut you down."

"Shut me down? Why, you've just arrived!" He spoke as if what I said carried no more weight than when I was a boy. "I had the feeling I might have the pleasure of running into you if I came down here to do business." He gestured again toward the seat and I took it, stunned by his ability to ignore me.

I watched him put his hands on his hips and smile broadly. "Mighty pretty country you've conquered here, isn't it?" he asked. "And this dirt, why, it's as black as the niggers who work it! If the Northern farmer and entrepreneur were ever to get his hands on this country, why, there's no telling how much wealth it would generate!" He shook his head in awe. "I am astonished by it every day, and I'm only working my way through the cotton! Imagine what I could do if I got to the hides! My Lord, Ulysses," he said, "I travel these roads and there are dead animals lying all over, abandoned in the face of this war of yours, each with a hide still attached. Think of the *output*. Think of the *value*. Think of the *economic progress* to be generated. It is a business opportunity greater than any other I have confronted in my lifetime. Say!" he suddenly exclaimed, interrupting himself and smiling with chagrin. "I haven't told you a thing about your brothers!"

I shook my head no as I tried to remind myself I was a general confronting a war profiteer, and not a son catching up with his father.

"Well, they're fine," my father continued. "I'm sure they'd have sent their regards if they knew we were to meet. Can you imagine the kind of business they're doing? This war needs hides—tens of thousands of hides! Why Ulysses, hides are being bought in such quantities the military doesn't have the time or resources to count them upon delivery, and we are trading them by the hundredweight, son, by the *hundredweight*! Why, there's not even the need to make sure each one is thoroughly cleaned and cured—as Orvil says, the army's paying for the shreds as well as the skin!" He laughed triumphantly, along with the men on either side of him, whom I had until then largely ignored.

I regarded for the first time the two men flanking my father. Each was angular and thin, each wore a white cravat, a black broadcloth suit, a beaver hat, and gold spectacles, and each had dark brows that ran together over a prominent nose.

My father noticed when I scrutinized them. "My Lord, I've not introduced my associates, have I, son? This is Levi Mack," he said, extending an honoring hand toward the man on his right, "my business associate, and a shrewd one he is," he extolled. "Levi, this is my son, General Ulysses S. Grant."

The man nodded at me, his broad, toothy smile never waning as he offered me his hand.

"And this," my father continued, shifting to his left, "is Issachar Mack, Levi's brother, also my good friend, partner, and close advisor. Without these two distinguished Israelite gentlemen alongside me, I wouldn't be able to maintain this operation for a single day. They are businessmen of the highest caliber!"

The other man also extended his hand to me. "General Grant! This is a great pleasure for my brother and me. We are honored to have you come to visit us."

"I am not here to visit you," I said sternly to my father, who beamed like the ringmaster of a circus. "Father, what you're doing is traitorous. You're giving aid and comfort to an enemy who is killing the men I command!"

Levi Mack looked up, a reproving expression under his dark brow. "Is that any way to speak to your father?"

The other Mack, Issachar, nodded severely. "It's a sin!" he concurred.

"There, there, gentlemen," my father said, quieting them before
turning back to me. "You'll have to excuse my associates, Ulysses.
They're men of strong ethical and religious beliefs, educated in the
ways of the Mosaic school and the finest ancestral traditions of the San-
hedrin."

"The gold you bring to this region only aids an enemy who seeks to
destroy us," I said.

My father's two associates shook their heads, and he spoke for them
all. "Nonsense, utter nonsense. We're taking the cotton crop north, so
that the wheels of commerce may turn, just as Simpson and Orvil are
turning them back in Galena. It's the way of the world, Ulysses. Our
nation needs cheap cotton, and cheap cotton needs our nation." He
leaned toward me as if telling me the secret of the universe itself.
"*Eight dollars*, Ulysses," he whispered. "*Eight dollars* for a shipment of
cotton that will sell for *three hundred* when it arrives in New England!
If we were not here, this would all go to waste, a treasure left un-
claimed, and who better than us to do the claiming?" He stood back
and spread his arms wide. "Tell me what you need, son. Salt? Mules?
Gold? Trace chains? Bridles and bits? Harnesses? We can supply you,
supply you at a fraction of the cost you pay through your quartermasters! We would gladly contribute to the war effort."

"If not to you personally," Levi Mack added, fingering a stack of
coins.

"You shall leave this place immediately!" I told them.

My father's expression suddenly hardened. "Leave? Do you think
you can command me the way you commanded the farm boys, the
ones who died listening to you at Shiloh? Do you think that after you
crawled to me with nothing but lint in your pockets, unable to support
your family, you have the right to order me and my colleagues away
from the king's ransom that awaits us?"

"A boy should honor his father!" Levi Mack said.

"A boy *should* honor his father, that's goddamned right," my father
echoed. "Where were you and your enthusiasm for the nation when
the Whigs were trying to spread the gospel of family farming and honest entrepreneurship? Living off that old fool Dent and *his* niggers?
Don't you tell me what you think is traitorous and what isn't, *Ulysses*,

because I don't need your instruction any more than I asked for your thanks."

"What you're doing is wrong—"

"When you needed employment in your darkest hour, and I gave it to you, was that wrong? And when I gave you the chance to become the man you are today, was that wrong, too?" He glared at me, as if threatening to expose my closely guarded deception.

"This is a treason to your nation," I said, jaw clenched. "If you weren't my father, I'd have you shot."

Issachar Mack recoiled. "May the ears of the Lord, our God, shut themselves, so the injurious din of such words will not be visited upon them!"

"May the prayers of the just and righteous rise to Heaven and arrive before these sinful words at the throne of judgment!" his brother concurred.

My father acknowledged each with a pious nod. "Gentlemen, gentlemen, be lenient with a man's son, I pray you," he said, echoing their tone as if he were becoming an Israelite himself. "Ulysses," he said, his voice softening as quickly as it had hardened. "I'm not asking you to protect us, or to abuse your rank on our behalf. I just want to be free to go about my business with my associates." The three of them assumed innocent looks and waited expectantly.

I rose from my seat. "Father, I have no choice but to take any and all necessary actions to resolve this matter. I regret we had to meet again under these circumstances."

"As do I, Ulysses. I hope you will be circumspect in any action you take."

I had nothing else to say. I turned and left, Rawlins close behind. "What do you intend to do?" he asked as we rode away from the house.

I shook my head. "I don't know, but I've got to do something," I replied. "You know what Sherman says about the newspapermen. If one of them writes a story about General Grant's father being a profiteer, it will be the end of General Grant."

Rawlins nodded in grim agreement. "You mean the end of that *cowardly butcher*—"

"I know, I know," I said somewhat testily.

"Throw him out of your district!" Rawlins prompted.

"I can't do that," I said. "The newspapermen will get wind of that and it will be just as bad if not worse—'Derelict General Expels Profiteering Father'—that's what they'll write."

It was then that the idea of expelling the Jews came to me—if the Mack brothers had to leave, my father would have to go with them. "But isn't that a bit unfair to the Jews?" Rawlins asked.

"Everybody's unfair to the Jews," I snapped. "It's better than being unfair to *me*." And so I dictated the order to save myself any embarrassment.

"Very smartly done. *These people*—" Rawlins said, rereading the text. "That's good. Nobody much cares for the Israelite sons of bitches anyway, and I suppose you've left your father out of it." He looked me over. "You're not going to have a drink now, are you?"

I smiled weakly. "I'm fine. Send it out and let's get on with it," I ordered, and started toward our carriage, hoping to put my encounter with my father behind me as I put distance between us.

(When Stanton and Lincoln heard about the order some time later, it was rescinded. There was much hand-wringing, and I was publicly castigated, all to the anguished cries of the Hebrew community, but I meant them no harm, and I took my chastisement willingly. My father went back to Covington in the end, so it was well worth it.)

When Rawlins and I returned to Corinth, we were met with good news. Halleck, to my surprise, not only approved my Vicksburg campaign, but instructed me that Sherman and I were to proceed at once. I promptly summoned Ord, who had conducted himself admirably in the conflict to date, to give him the command Rosecrans had before he was promoted.

"Wire Sherman and fetch McClernand," I told him. "It is time to discuss the coming Vicksburg campaign."

"McClernand's not at his headquarters," Ord said. "He went to Washington, I'm told, and is now somewhere in Wisconsin or Indiana."

"Are there enemy in Wisconsin and Indiana?" I asked.

"I'm told he's been recruiting."

Rawlins and I exchanged sober looks. "Send for Sherman," I told Ord. "Tell him to get here at once."

Ord left Rawlins and me alone. "McClernand had no reason to go to Washington other than to see his old friend Lincoln," I said.

"And if he went off to raise new troops after meeting with Lincoln, it would stand to reason the President has given the son of a bitch permission to raise an army," Rawlins agreed, following my train of thought. "After all, isn't that what McClernand always thought—*this army wants a head*?"

I nodded.

"But if he is raising his own army, what does he intend to do with it?" Rawlins asked.

The answer, it struck me, was simple. McClernand's political base was the farmers of Illinois and the surrounding region. What those people wanted was the Mississippi open to commercial traffic, so they could ship grain downriver and out to the world market. When you put the pieces together, it added up to this: McClernand had received Lincoln's approval to mount his own expedition to open the Mississippi!

"That's got to be it," Sherman said when I met him at the train station in Corinth and shared my political conjectures. We lit cigars and walked briskly through the old stone structure, past lines of troops waiting to be reviewed, both of us alive with energy.

"Absolutely," I agreed. "It's why Henry's suddenly in such a hurry. With his own expedition, McClernand reports directly to Lincoln, and Henry has little to say in the matter." Lines of soldiers snapped to attention as we strode past, absorbed in our conversation. "But if McClernand shows up here with orders from the President to let him go after Vicksburg, and we've already left to do exactly that, all he can do is chase after us. He can't outrank us so long as we're not here!" I said.

We reached the carriage waiting for us outside the station, and we both climbed up onto the driver's bench. "We're not attacking Vicksburg," I said, taking the reins and spurring the team forward. "We're escaping from McClernand."

Sherman smiled at me as we lurched forward. "I told you war was hell, didn't I, Grant?"

We put our plan into action at once. I started south down the rail line through Holly Springs and Oxford, the town where my father and the Mack brothers had operated. A hundred miles south was Jackson, the state capital, where the line I was following crossed the Southern Railroad of Mississippi, which ran forty miles west to Vicksburg. Meanwhile, Sherman proceeded down the Mississippi toward the Yazoo River, which would lead him to Vicksburg from the north. We would meet at Vicksburg and crush it.

It was a great plan, an elegant one, the plan of a man clearly destined to lead great masses of men, right up to the moment it failed. I had progressed a good eighty miles into Mississippi when the Confederates figured out what I was up to and sent Nathan Bedford Forrest to cut my telegraph connection and supply line. His guerrillas, armed with turpentine and matches, turned my supply depot into a bonfire that could be seen and smelled for miles—our pork, our beans, our coffee, our medicines, our cotton, our wagons, everything was torched. I had no more than the provisions in my men's knapsacks, and with our telegraph lines cut, I had no way to tell Sherman that I had to withdraw without ever having engaged the enemy. It was Christmas Eve, 1862.

My supply lines cut, just as Halleck had warned! I imagine he got some grim satisfaction out of that.

What I did not know yet was that McClernand—now the commander of the newly formed Army of the Mississippi—had arrived at Memphis shortly after Sherman had left and turned the town upside down looking for him. The little man just about threw a fit when he found out Sherman was already on the river, heading south. McClernand got himself a small fleet and started after him.

I didn't know how it all turned out until I retreated back to Corinth and found Rawlins waiting for me with a handful of dispatches.

"This one's from Halleck," Rawlins said. "He says Sherman's been beaten north of Vicksburg, at a place called Chickasaw Bayou."

"It's as good a place to be beaten as any other." I shrugged. Once Forrest had forced me to withdraw, Sherman was doomed.

"It gets worse," he said. "McClernand caught up to Sherman and assumed command of Sherman's forces. He ordered them back up the Mississippi."

I remained unperturbed. "Well, it could be worse," I confessed. "The best thing to do is to withdraw smartly, get back here, and sort out who reports to whom."

"I didn't say the son of a bitch did *that*," Rawlins corrected. He read the rest of the dispatch. Having assumed command, McClernand decided to attack the Post of Arkansas, a Confederate fort on the Arkansas River, which dumps into the Mississippi below Memphis.

"He decided to take a little jaunt up the Arkansas River and attack an installation there, just because he happened to be in the vicinity?" I asked, dumbfounded.

"In essence, yes."

"Why would he waste the time, the men, and the supplies to take a fort that doesn't threaten our campaign? It's stupid," I said.

"It's so stupid it's indefensible," Rawlins replied.

"It's so indefensible it's perfect," I agreed.

"Perfect for what?" Rawlins asked, confused.

"For getting rid of him," I answered, and I did, wiring Washington that McClernand was off on a wild goose chase without military merit. It was all Halleck needed to take his case to Lincoln. Only a few days later, he replied to me:

> **You are hereby authorized to relieve Genl McClernand from command of the Expedition against Vicksburg, giving it to the next in rank, or taking it yourself.**

The response was precisely as I anticipated—Halleck may not have liked me, but McClernand threatened Halleck's position, and Halleck got rid of him at the first opportunity.

I went to share the news with Sherman when he got off his boat at the Memphis dock, back from his adventure down the river, but he had his own agenda.

"Where the fuck were you?" he demanded, his balding forehead red with anger. "I'm heading up the Yazoo and suddenly I'm getting the shit beaten out of me!"

"Van Dorn and Forrest cut my supply lines," I explained. "I had to retreat."

His anger drained and he broke into a smile. "Ha! Henry had one thing to teach you back at West Point besides digging, and you forgot it. You overextend your supply line and it becomes a better target than you," he commiserated as we walked along the pier. I nodded grimly. "What did Henry say when you told him?"

"He said if you overextend your supply line—"

Sherman laughed and held up a hand to stop me. "Well," he said with a sigh, stepping onto dry land, "that explains how I got my ass whipped. The Yazoo—jolly Jesus, Grant, I never saw a place like that one. The ground is too wet to walk on, the river too narrow to navigate—knee-deep muck, fallen logs, vines, you can't move. For the life of me, I can't see how we're going to get an army and its provisions through there."

"How many men did you lose?" I asked.

"About seventeen hundred," Sherman said. "Hell, I figured taking Vicksburg would cost me five thousand," he added, "we might as well start losing them there." I offered him a cigar and he declined. "So now what? Do we report to McClernand?"

"Halleck says I rank him. I wired him about the attack on the Post of Arkansas and he agreed it was the dumbest thing he ever heard of."

Sherman winced. "He did? Does he know I told McClernand to do it?"

My jaw dropped. "How could you have done such a thing?"

Sherman shrugged. "It seemed like a good idea at the time. We needed a victory. And besides, it accomplished a vital strategic objective, didn't it?" He grinned, referring to McClernand's demotion.

"I ought to cashier you," I told him, smiling.

"I'm an arrogant, volatile, foul-mouthed, insubordinate madman, Grant," Sherman responded. "You can't afford to lose me."

I assigned McClernand to command a corps, along with Sherman and a third commander, a talented fellow named McPherson. But I had not yet solved the Vicksburg problem. You couldn't travel south on the Mississippi to Vicksburg because there was no place to land safely. Sherman had learned that. You couldn't march in from behind the city, because it was two hundred miles south of the Tennessee border and your supply lines would be cut. *I* had learned that. And while you could march an army down the Louisiana side of the river, where the swamps, bayous, and backwaters were not quite as bad, to a point south of Vicksburg, you could never get a supply column of several thousand wagons, oxen, and mules over that terrain with food, stores, artillery, and ammunition.

Which left me, by March of 1863, without any reasonable options at my disposal.

"You'd better come up with something quick," Sherman told me.

"It's either that or Lincoln will turn this mess back over to McClernand," Rawlins agreed.

They were right: It was time to see the problem differently. "Okay then, how about this?" I offered. "We can always march our force down the far side of the Mississippi and cross over below Vicksburg, right?"

Sherman and Rawlins agreed.

"And if we had an army in place there," I said, "then it would be easy to establish a supply line to Banks in New Orleans, right?" Banks was the commander at New Orleans, but he did not have enough men and matériel to do more than support an attack.

They concurred once again.

"So the only problem is getting our supplies south of Vicksburg to meet an army there, so we don't run out of matériel before Banks re-supplies us."

They again agreed.

"But the only available route south is the river itself."

They nodded sadly.

"Then that's what we'll do—sail everything down the river!"

They looked at me incredulously. "And if it weren't for the fifteen miles of guns they have placed on top of the bluffs at Vicksburg, that would be a good idea," Sherman said, dismissing me angrily. "In fact, I seem to recall those fucking guns are why we need to capture Vicksburg in the first place."

I was suddenly overpowered by the beautiful simplicity of the whole thing. "We can run past the guns! We pile everything we need on a fleet of steamers, we pick a new moon, a dark night, float it all down the river, engines off, run the gauntlet, and if we lose a few boats, we're still fine! Once they get past—"

"*If* they get past," Sherman said.

"*Once* they get past," I insisted, "because *some* of them will, we meet our army on the Louisiana side of the river, below the city, and use the boats to ferry them over to the Vicksburg side. Then we use the boats to shuttle anything else we need up from New Orleans to stay supplied. Meanwhile, our troops merge with men brought up from New Orleans under Banks and we take Vicksburg using our numerical advantage."

Rawlins and Sherman looked at me as if I'd lost my mind. "You have to be the fucking craziest bastard who ever wore a uniform, Grant," Sherman said, shaking his head. "It will never work."

"Well then, who wants to go back to Memphis and turn this operation over to McClernand? Who wants Lincoln to relieve them of command?" They stared at me unhappily, neither volunteering. "Then it's decided," I said.

"Do me one favor, Sam," Sherman asked, throwing his hat on the ground as he rose to walk away. "Leave me your cigars in your fucking will."

Admiral Porter, to his credit, was enthusiastic about the idea, if only because he wanted no part of McClernand. Porter was brilliant in his preparations. He lashed coal scows to the far side of each of our steamers, keeping the near side clear for guns to fire if fired upon. He stacked water-soaked bails of cotton and hay everywhere, to prevent fires if we were hit. All lights were doused, and the boats were spaced at fifty-yard intervals, with each captain steering to the side of the boat ahead, so each could continue downstream if the one ahead were hit.

What a night it was! The sky was clear and the stars were bright, and we drifted in eerie, moonless silence. The river was wide and flat, and it moved well. We were halfway down our course when we spotted some activity on the Vicksburg bluffs. Suddenly their guns opened fire, and in a moment they were torching houses on the bluffs to shed some light on our tiny armada. I must confess I was transfixed by the scarlet arcs their shells traced across the sky and the way their glow illuminated the faces around me. Porter commanded the boats to start their engines once we were fired upon, and we hastened on our way. In the end, only one of our boats went down. I had moved our supplies past Vicksburg, and I immediately ordered McClernand and McPherson to start a march down the other side of the river to meet us as planned.

This was beginning to be fun: Running the Rebels' guns seemed almost as easy as reducing their forts. I ordered a cavalry patrol north of Vicksburg on a campaign that would have made Nathan Bedford Forrest proud, cutting telegraph wires, tearing up railroads, and misleading Pemberton—from where did I know this fellow?—as to our true intent, a landing south of the city. I then sent Sherman, who grudgingly acceded to the fact my plan was working, on a feint to the north side of town, as if he were going to repeat his last ill-fated attempt to land on the Yazoo.

Pemberton bought it and sent his troops north of the city at exactly the moment when McClernand and McPherson arrived on the Louisiana side of the river, thirty-five miles to the south of Vicksburg. Two weeks after the first flotilla ran the guns, I had my men and my supplies south of Vicksburg, looking for a place to cross the river.

There was a Confederate installation on the Mississippi side of the river called Grand Gulf.

"I say we pull our gunboats up and hammer them until they capitulate," McClernand advised.

"What if I suggested instead that we land south of there, move inland, and force them to come out and fight, which would make their big artillery pieces aimed out at the river meaningless?" I responded.

McClernand looked at me dumbfounded. "Yes, that would be better," he acceded.

So that was what I did. A scouting party found a spot called Port Gibson about eight miles below Grand Gulf, where we could land on solid ground. The Confederates at Grand Gulf predictably came out to meet us and attacked with confidence, until they realized I had somehow put over thirty thousand men in front of them, all of whom seemed to appear out of nowhere. They abandoned Grand Gulf and beat a hasty retreat back to Vicksburg.

After months of maneuvering, I was finally on dry land, on the same side of the river as the enemy. I had reached the point of no return. Once Banks came up from New Orleans with his army and a firm supply line, we would come up underneath Vicksburg and take it.

Sherman soon joined us, and it was all finally coming together. Or at least it was all finally coming together until we heard from Banks.

Sherman, McClernand, McPherson, Ord, and I were sitting in our command tent after the battle, awaiting word from him, when Rawlins entered, holding a telegram.

"Banks has gone up the Red River," he announced to us all.

Sherman laughed. "You ought to teach Rawlins some geography, Sam," Sherman said, then corrected Rawlins. "You mean the Mississippi River."

"No, Sherman, I mean the son of a bitch has gone up the Red River," Rawlins repeated.

I was stopped cold. "He's gone up the wrong river!" I said. "Why the devil has he—"

"Something about wanting to ensure a Confederate force doesn't come up behind us," Rawlins said, scrutinizing the message.

Sherman shot from his seat with such force I was surprised gravity pulled him back down again so soon. "That stupid ass! He's abandoned us! What does he think he's doing?"

I shook my head, completely flabbergasted. "I have no idea."

McClernand began to sweat. "We're trapped!" he shouted. "Without Banks, we're trapped, Grant! We're isolated behind the enemy, with no way to be resupplied."

I nodded calmly. "So it would seem."

McClernand rose, now even more agitated. "Do you realize what you've done, Grant? We're completely cut off from our base! We'll have to escape south, flee down the Mississippi! There's no other way!"

"No, we can't do that," Ord said definitively. "It would give the Rebels all of Tennessee and Kentucky. Rosecrans would be crushed." Sherman and I exchanged some sober nodding at Ord's perfect grasp of the situation.

"Then what do you expect to do, Grant?" McClernand screamed, gesticulating wildly. "You've brought us here to die!"

And then it occurred to me—this was exactly what the men in Mexico said when Scott abandoned the garrison at Jalapa. *Scott had abandoned the garrison and cut his ties with our base at Veracruz. He had decided either to capture Mexico City—or die!*

Van Dorn and Forrest had cut my supply line earlier, and now it was cut again. Why had I not until then understood what Scott understood back in Mexico? It had been obvious all along!

"We're going forward," I announced.

"What the devil do you mean, 'going forward'?" McClernand demanded. "Forward *where*? Forward with *what*?"

"We're going to go forward and engage the enemy. We're going to abandon our base and press into the country. Just like Scott did in Mexico."

"And what shall we do for a supply line?" McClernand asked.

"A supply line is a vulnerability," I said. "We'll bring our own bullets and abandon the rest."

"And what the devil do you expect us to eat?"

"Whatever the land provides," I said plainly. "We cannot retreat, we cannot go back, and we cannot wait here. We're in the same position Scott was when he reached Jalapa. We're going to take Vicksburg or die."

"Are you mad?" McClernand exclaimed. "Do you know what I shall have to wire back to Lincoln?"

Sherman laughed out loud and slapped McClernand on the back.

"Well, you can tell him Grant decided that we're all going to die some-time, and it might as fucking well be here."

McClernand blanched, but Sherman was right. The more I consid-ered the matter, the simpler it became. Joe Johnston was inland, prob-ably near Jackson. If we abandoned our supply line, we could find him, beat him, and then double back to take Vicksburg, all before our true strength was understood. It was springtime, and Mississippi would surely provide something to eat. I told Rawlins to send a message back to Halleck, asking his consent, and made sure we were on our way in-land before he could withhold it.

We covered the forty-odd miles to Jackson in a few quick days. Pem-berton, inside Vicksburg, now knew where we were, so he predictably moved south—to find and cut off our supply line. But, of course, there was no supply line to find. Pemberton led his men through Grand Gulf, Port Gibson, and all the other towns we had left behind, looking for our base of operations. He found nothing, for there was nothing to find. By the time he gave up and headed back in confusion to Vicks-burg, we were almost on top of Jackson. Moreover, my men were eat-ing better than they would have if Union mules were bringing them hardtack and beans from Banks's supply chain: They found beef, pork, mutton, ducks, chickens, turkey, and other wild game; they encoun-tered plantations, still undisturbed by the war, with immense stores of bacon and hams. They begged their quartermasters for a potato or a loaf of bread, so filled were they with meat—the smell of steaks on grills and in pans filled the air at our encampment every night as if it were Commodore Vanderbilt's table at Delmonico's.

On May 12, we encountered Johnston outside of Jackson. Like a fish who takes the bait, Johnston went after McPherson's lead corps, think-ing it was the bulk of our strength. Once he committed to battle, I had Sherman and McClernand ride around his flanks to attack him from three sides. He was stunned. By the time he fled Jackson, he had but five thousand men left. On May 14, we rode into Jackson: I let Sher-man raise the Stars and Stripes over the state capital building. I slept that night in the bed Johnston had slept in the night before, and I thought of the note Sherman received from Bragg and Beauregard at Shiloh.

The next day we turned west and went after Pemberton, who was now presented with his last chance to turn the battle. If he'd done the same thing a few days before, he and Johnston might have caught us between them, but his unwillingness to take the fight to us—coupled with his inability to comprehend what I'd done—doomed him. We beat him at a place called Champion's Hill, about ten miles east of Vicksburg, on May 16, and again the next day at the Big Black River, about five miles east of town. He had to blow up a bridge, abandoning five thousand of his men to us, just to slow down our advance. He got back to Vicksburg and locked himself in. Sherman, on the right wing of our assault, broke through to the Mississippi north of town, so we were now back in contact with, and receiving supplies from, Memphis and the north. I now had the place surrounded. In just eighteen days, I had landed below the city, marched inland, taken the state capital, defeated one army outright, captured five thousand men, and bottled up another army in their city, either to starve or surrender.

Reinforcements began to come down the Mississippi, and I decided to press an attack rather than wait out a siege. On May 22, I mounted an assault, a ferocious one. Pemberton had dug in, though, and this attack amounted to little, despite a heavy casualty count. I was prepared to call it off when a message came from McClernand stating that he had captured two forts outside the city and could make productive use of reinforcements. Sensing an opportunity for victory, I promptly sent messages to Sherman and McPherson, telling them to send troops to him, and then went to see how he was doing.

In fact, McClernand had made no progress. He had lied in the vainglorious hope that word of his imagined victories would spread and be taken as truth by his political constituents. I cut the attack off at suppertime, but only after an additional two thousand men had died because of his maneuvering. If I'd had the time, I would have court-martialed him then and there.

Still, it was necessary to get rid of this idiot, even if he was Lincoln's pet; fortunately, he made it easy for me the very next day.

"I cannot *believe* what I just read in this newspaper, Sam!" Sherman said, waving the offending journal as he walked into my tent. "I cannot *believe* a single fucking *word*—"

I extended a hand. "Give it here, Cump, and let's see what has you in such an uproar." As I began to read, I considered asking him to resume his oration. McClernand had released an order to his troops commending himself for single-handedly winning the Vicksburg campaign, stating that he alone was doing Lincoln's direct bidding—that he was *"born a Warrior,"* that's what he actually said. It was, in fact, a propaganda sheet written for his political supporters back in Illinois.

Sherman was disgusted. I was overjoyed. Army regulations banned the publication of such self-promoting orders on the penalty of dismissal on the spot—no court-martial required. So I sent an order to McClernand's tent, instructing him to depart the theater of battle and to turn his command over to Ord.

He was in front of me in seconds. "You can't do that!" he screamed.

Sherman and I had been waiting for him. I finished lighting my cigar. "I can and I have," I said.

"I'll take this to the President!"

"I wish you well on your way," I said, not looking up at him.

"You'll hear from me," he shouted over his shoulder to us as he climbed up on his horse and stormed away.

Sherman leapt to respond to the departing figure. "We'll be right here, fighting the fucking war, you fucking coward!" he called after him.

"You know, Sherman," I said calmly, "as commanding officer, it falls to me to respond to insubordination, unless I choose to delegate this duty."

Sherman looked at me and nodded. "Of course, Grant," he said, the picture of contrition. "My apologies."

"Accepted," I said. "Very well then, as your commanding officer, I direct you to respond to General McClernand."

Sherman turned and cupped his hands to ensure McClernand could hear him. "Fuck you, McClernand!" he shouted as McClernand rode away.

"Smartly done, Sherman," I said, and we returned to the work of war.

Since Vicksburg refused to fall, we would have to lay siege to it. By June, our entrenchments were so deep and well established that four men could march abreast without being seen. Meanwhile, the reports we got from the city—in a newspaper brought out by a spy, or from the conversations sometimes shouted between our soldiers and theirs, so close were the entrenchments—told of conditions growing progressively worse. Mules were being skinned and eaten. Rats were caught for food. On June 28, after six weeks of siege, a group of deserters told us that there were but six days' rations left inside the city. Predictably, on July 3, a letter came out from Pemberton under a white flag:

I have the honor to propose an armistice with a view to arranging terms for the capitulation of Vicksburg. I will appoint three commissioners, to meet a like number to be named by yourself, at such place and hour to-day as you find convenient. I make this proposition to save the further effusion of blood, which must otherwise be shed to a frightful extent, feeling myself capable to maintain my position for a yet indefinite period.

I sat down to write a response.

Your note of this date is just received, proposing an armistice. The useless effusion of blood you propose stopping by this course can be ended at any time you choose, by the unconditional surrender of the city and garrison. I do not favor the proposition of appointing commissioners to arrange for terms of capitulation, because I have no other terms than those indicated above.

"I'm getting good at these notes," I commented to Rawlins. *No other terms than those indicated above!* How plain! How unadorned! I was in my glory—the plain man who spoke plainly and fought plainly, who failed plainly and now triumphed plainly. No sash or saber, no fuss or feathers. Let them all regard this, my moment of conquest—Halleck, McClellan, Colonel Buchanan (wherever he now was), Bobby Lee, my father, my brothers, McClernand, Lincoln. I had written this note to all of them.

I handed it to Rawlins. "Send him that."

Pemberton came out to meet me that afternoon. When I saw him, I realized who he was—the officer who came to the steeple of the church outside San Cosme, the fellow who was sent to find out who was shelling the Mexican position at the gate. No wonder his name seemed vaguely familiar.

"You mean you didn't remember me?" he asked, a bit crestfallen.

"No," I confessed. "Although now that I've seen you, I can place you," I said, hoping that would be some consolation.

He still seemed disappointed, but nonetheless had more spunk than Buckner did under similar circumstances and actually tried to negotiate. "You'll bury a good many more men before you enter Vicksburg," he said, making the best case he could.

Good for him, I thought. "Tomorrow's July Fourth. If the conflict persists, I shall fire a national salute into the city at daylight," I told him.

That got him to thinking. By the end of the day, he capitulated. I did allow that I would not take his men as prisoners, but would instead parole them—take their names and allow them to go home, which was all most of them wanted, anyway. I would be criticized, I knew, for doing so, but Porter didn't have the boats to send thirty-one thousand prisoners north, and I didn't have the time to direct their removal. I sent a wire to Halleck telling him we had taken our objective and retired to my tent, taking a moment to dispatch Sherman to find Johnston and finish him off.

I sat there on my cot and took it all in. I had done what Scott had done, perhaps more. Risking everything, I had brought down the most impregnable fortress in the South, captured a second army whole, opened the Mississippi from one end to the other, and cut the Confederacy in half. I was Ulysses Grant now, the conqueror of Vicksburg. *I had led great masses of men in the glorious cause of their human redemption.*

I was preparing to sleep that night when Rawlins entered with a telegram he insisted I read immediately:

My Dear General:

I do not remember that you and I ever met personally. I write this now as a grateful acknowledgment for the most inestimable service you have done your country. I wish to say a word further. When you got below Vicksburg, and took Port Gibson, Grand Gulf, and the vicinity, I thought you should go down the river and join Gen. Banks; and when you turned Northward East of the Big Black, I feared it was a mistake. I now wish to make the personal acknowledgment that you were right, and I was wrong.

> *Very truly yours,*
> *A. Lincoln*

You were right, and I was wrong. Even I was impressed.

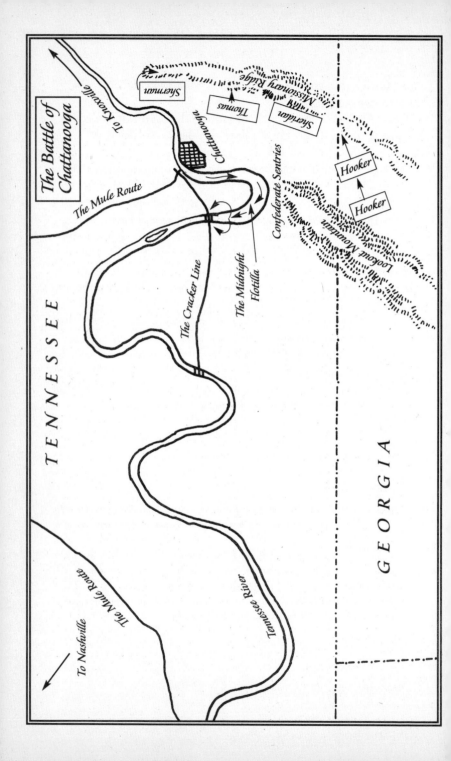

CHAPTER X

VICKSBURG'S AFTERMATH—A TRIP TO NEW ORLEANS—THE RELIEF OF CHATTANOOGA— VICTORY OVER BRAGG—MEETING WITH LINCOLN—VISITING THE WHITE HOUSE

PITY GENERAL GEORGE MEADE. On the very day he defeated Bobby Lee at Gettysburg, I captured Vicksburg, and he lost his chance for singular glory. Meade made mistakes, of course, like failing to pursue Lee—he was from the Henry Halleck school of meet, beat, and retreat. Still, he might have been a hero for the day, were it not for me.

Lee fought the entire Gettysburg campaign in that overly complex, clever-by-half way of his, just like when he split his men up in the face of Hooker's overpowering numbers at Chancellorsville. They're still talking about that one. Not that you had to be a genius to outmaneuver Hooker. He was so slow and frightened that he never noticed when Lee sent Tom—now "Stonewall"—Jackson around his right flank, and suddenly Hooker was getting it from both sides at once. The only good news for our side that day was that the Confederates shot and killed their own man: poor, crazy Tom.

I fought Lee, and I know that Lee was no better than the last hole he dug. And of course, he had a callous disregard for human life, a disregard so striking that Longstreet, the brute, could barely stomach relaying Lee's order to Pickett to charge Hancock's positions along Cemetery Ridge. Fifteen thousand of his own men, mowed down like wheat, a testament to Lee's genius.

What was Lee thinking at Gettysburg? Move north, take Harrisburg, then Philadelphia and sue for peace? We'd have trapped Lee's army inside Philadelphia and annihilated them. Either way, he'd have come up a loser.

When I heard about Gettysburg, I knew that when the time came, I could take him.

But it would be most of a year before I would get the chance.

First, there was the aftermath of Vicksburg to tend to, starting with Lincoln. His note was a gracious—and accurate—one, but I had run his friend McClernand out of both Vicksburg and the army in the most humiliating fashion, which was bound to upset him. Moreover, I was now the most successful military figure in the North, and Lincoln and I were going to have to come to terms, establish some mutual understanding. So I sent Rawlins to Washington with my report of the Vicksburg campaign, a list of the thirty-one thousand parolees taken there, and a clear message: I was a Lincoln man, loyal to the cause of preserving the Union, who only wanted to stay in the West and move on to the next target.

The second person I needed to tend to was Mrs. Grant, who made her way down to Vicksburg with Fred, Buck, Nellie, and Jesse as soon as she could. After commandeering the largest plantation home I'd ever seen in the South, complete with *piazza*, I sent for her.

"Have you been drinking?" she asked after a brief hello and perfunctory peck on the cheek. "The newspapers say you've been drinking."

"The newspapers always say I've been drinking," I protested. "McClernand's been saying that ever since I relieved him. Henry Halleck said it after Donelson. You didn't believe them then, did you?" Mrs. Grant shook her head tentatively. "Then why would you believe them now?"

She regarded me skeptically. "Well, all right. It's just that everyone else believes them," she finally said. "And you drank out West."

"I only drank out West when I was bored and lonely."

"Well, weren't you lonely when you were besieging Vicksburg?" she asked, warming up to me now and fingering my uniform buttons.

"Of course I was," I confessed, "but I wasn't bored."

"Aren't sieges boring?"

"Not when you're winning."

"Okay," she said finally, "but if Rawlins tells me you've been drinking, you'll hear from me." She then turned her attention to the house. "At least you picked a nice place for us. It makes me wish for White

Haven." She turned back to me when she remembered to say, "Speaking of which, Father sends his regards. He says he's very proud of you."

"Proud of me? He's a secessionist! He supports the enemy!"

"Don't make such a big to-do of it. He's glad you're finally making a living."

"Is that how he sees it? Well, it's more than that. I'm saving my country."

"Oh, Ulys, don't be such a drudge!" she chided. "Frankly, if you weren't a general, this war would be a total bore. It is taking up all your time, and the children need your attention."

Perhaps her view had merit, but I had tens of thousands of children, all in uniform, who needed my attention, and at the moment they were lying about with nothing to do: Vicksburg had been captured, Sherman was pushing Joe Johnston back into the deepest regions of Georgia, and it was time to move forward again.

The next target of opportunity was Mobile, the last open port on the gulf. It was ripe, and Banks, still in command at New Orleans (despite his lapse during Vicksburg), had the same idea. Major General Nathaniel Banks was a roly-poly fellow who had been the Speaker of the U.S. House of Representatives, a post not known for its military heroes. Fortunately, he knew when he was in over his head, and having seen me dispatch McClernand, he was ready to cooperate with me. I decided to visit New Orleans in short order, while Mrs. Grant set up our household in Vicksburg, to confer with Banks on how to proceed.

It was eighteen years since I had been there last, when embarking for the Mexican War under Taylor in '45. Then, of course, I was one of thousands of young faces staring up at Taylor. Now the thousands of young faces were staring up at me.

The morning I arrived, Banks was standing in front of my hotel with the most delightful surprise.

"If what I've heard about you is true, Grant," he said, a broad smile occupying his beefy, avuncular face, "this should be to your liking." He was holding the reins to a large and handsome Arabian that he termed the "fleetest and best" of all the horses he had in his command, a stallion who wanted to gallop. I held my breath as I approached it—I had not seen such an animal since before the war. "He is yours, sir," Banks said, offering the reins to me, and I promptly accepted his kindness and climbed on.

Banks had scheduled a review of the troops for us—they were positioned along a parade line that stretched for the better part of a mile, and we were supposed to ride past them. But who was I to deny the horse its nature? I spurred the mount, and it took off like one of Zeus's thunderbolts. Banks and the other commanders made a brave effort to keep up, but I was of no mind to let them. I bolted ahead, and the troops cheered wildly and their regimental colors dipped like wheat in the wind as I galloped past. I stopped at the end of the line under a large oak tree and let Banks and the others catch up, whereupon the troops marched past us in formation. At the end of the procession came Ord, with my old Army of the Tennessee: the men who floated into Fort Henry and shivered in the sleet at Fort Donelson; who faced death as it rushed out of the woods at Shiloh and forced it back from whence it had come; who marched down the Louisiana bayous; who raced with Sherman to Jackson; who won at Champion Hill and Big Black River; and who entered Vicksburg as conquerors. Their marching was the easy, gangling lope of the veteran soldiers they had become under my command—farm boys and town folk whom I had turned into a magnificent, monstrous engine of war, their flags riddled with bullet holes and the stains of battle. *I would lead great masses of men in the cause of their human redemption*—these were the masses I led. I lifted my hat in salute to them as they marched past, struggling not to reveal to them a tear in my eye, and then allowed Banks to lead me to a luncheon in my honor in the city. What a wonderful day, what a glorious moment!

Like the maiden whose heart and more are captured in the heat of the moment—like my first Julia, succumbing to Useful's flattery and charms in his father's barn back in Georgetown—I should have known better. Better to be drunk on liquor than inebriated by hubris. But there we sat in the dining room of the city's finest hotel, even finer than the Planters House in St. Louis, and the light played off the chandeliers, the music soothed, my honors were sung, and the applause washed over me, and before I knew it, Banks was pouring a bottle of French champagne into a graceful crystal glass with a smile that bespoke infinite hospitality. "I am sure that you will enjoy this," he said.

Ord, who was sitting on the other side of me, hesitantly reached toward me, fully aware of my reputation. "General, I know it may be presumptuous of me—" he said hesitantly.

I turned to him coldly and cut him off. "Well, it is."

"It's just that Rawlins always said—"

"Oh, *hang* Rawlins! *Rawlins* this, *Rawlins* that—you'd think I would fall apart along with my army were it not for *Rawlins*," I said, sneering. Ord ceased his protests, and I reached for the glass as Cleopatra reached for the asp. A roar came up from the other guests as I raised my glass, and they raised theirs with me. "To Grant!" they shouted, and drained their vessels as smartly as I did, whereupon Banks filled my glass once again. As he did so, Ord leaned over to me with a tone of great concern and tried again.

"My dear general," he whispered urgently. "Were Mrs. Grant here—"

"But she's not here, is she? She's back in Vicksburg, figuring out which side of this godforsaken war she and her father are on," I said. I raised my glass, and as I did, I heard from all the guests once again: "To Grant!" How could I not drink the bubbly nectar? How could I deny them that?

What sweet reward! How warm and pleasant the world could be made by simple drink! And I had gone so long without a taste, what harm could come from one brief trip to the well? I began to feel an internal glow as I drained the second glass, and it reminded me of the boilers glowing hot in the bellies of the boats Porter had floated past Vicksburg, and how the shells lit up the sky that night. I smiled out at the guests as I thought of my victory there and noticed, through the swirling cacophony, Banks leading them all in a chorus of some patriotic song (who knows which? I knew then and know now only two tunes—one of them is "Yankee Doodle" and the other isn't) before he filled my glass yet again.

"General!" Ord again whispered, now more frantically. "President Lincoln will hear of this! Your enemies—"

"Lincoln?" I asked, laughing. "Did I ever tell you how they went to Lincoln after Shiloh and said I'd been drinking—and I hadn't, you know, I'd not touched a drop, the lying little *bastards*—and he told them, 'Send a case of whatever he's drinking to my other generals.' Ha! That's what he said!" I told him. "Lincoln knows what's what and who's who!"

"General, please reconsider!" Ord beseeched me.

"Never mind about me," I said to Ord, my head swimming. "I can take it or leave it alone. Didn't you ever hear the story about how Halleck went to Lincoln to complain about me drinking too much? 'McClernand says Grant drinks too much,' Halleck says. 'McClernand is a fool,' Lincoln says. So Halleck went out to McClernand and told him what Lincoln said, and McClernand came roaring to Lincoln about it. 'Did you tell Halleck I was a fool?' he asks. 'No,' said Lincoln, 'I thought he knew it.'" I deftly brought a hand to my mouth to suppress a belch. "That's where I stand with Lincoln," I said, proudly, then I held my glass out to Banks. "To President Lincoln!"

I remember little more of the lunch except going outside to get atop the magnificent Arabian mount Banks had provided. For a moment I thought I sat astride York once again. Once I steadied myself in the saddle, off we flew back into town, with the others falling behind once again. I saw them over my shoulder and reeled gleefully, drunk on liquor, pride, and speed, when the highway took a turn toward the railroad tracks. Suddenly a locomotive was racing alongside us, its whistle piercing the air and scaring the horse.

The next thing I recall was that I was lying upon the ground, wracked with pain, and could hardly breathe. The sky overhead was dotted with a variety of faces, some of which spoke as if they belonged to doctors. I remember hearing "Nothing appears to be broken" before I passed out.

I was laid up in New Orleans for about two weeks, my left side swollen and painful, and was then sent upriver to Vicksburg to continue my recuperation under the supervision of Rawlins and Mrs. Grant.

"So? What was it this time? Bored or lonely?" Mrs. Grant inquired upon my arrival.

"Wait until I get my hands on that son of a bitch Banks," Rawlins groused when he saw me. "Ord told me how he plied you. If there's one thing I detest, it's a sycophant!" I raised my eyebrows at that, but Rawlins was too caught up in abstential fervor to notice. "All he wanted was to get on your good side," he nagged.

I winced and held my battered ribs. "Well, you won't have to worry about it happening again—I no longer have a good side."

While my sides would get better if I would just stay in bed and do nothing, it seemed that the longer I did so, the more my side in the war got worse. Rosecrans took his time pursuing Braxton Bragg through eastern Tennessee, but by the summer of 1863 he had Bragg holed up in Chattanooga and was pondering what to do with him. Bragg then suddenly departed the city for points south. Rosey sent his men after Bragg and realized too late that Bragg was not retreating at all.

Instead, Bragg was setting a trap. He had been reinforced by Longstreet and was preparing to fight Rosecrans on open ground. He did so at Chickamauga Creek in September and would have destroyed Rosecrans outright were it not for George Henry Thomas, who staged a robust, last-minute defense that earned him the appellation the "Rock of Chickamauga," which is probably as much heroism as you can milk from a battle in which you're being thrashed.

In a fit of panic, Rosecrans himself now retreated into Chattanooga, where he looked up to find himself as trapped as Bragg had been a few weeks before. Now Rosecrans got to observe what a real tactician— one capable of getting an opponent to step into the same trap from which he himself had just escaped—did in that situation. Bragg seized Lookout Mountain to the south, Missionary Ridge to the east, and the road and rail connections along the Tennessee River to the west. You could get no closer to Chattanooga from the west than thirty miles before you would most likely be shot. The sole remaining access to Chattanooga was a mule path through the mountains that came into town from the north, a rocky, muddy route impassable to all but the most stout-hearted, and an eight-day journey, even for them. Bragg had done to Rosecrans what Rosecrans couldn't do to Bragg—trap the enemy in Chattanooga and begin to starve him out.

Halleck and Stanton, Lincoln's War Secretary, followed these developments closely and decided to send Hooker from Virginia to Chattanooga to provide assistance. He only got as close as the predictable thirty miles away before he discovered the enemy was shooting at him and stopped.

Having followed all this myself, I was unsurprised when I received a telegram from Washington directing me to proceed to Louisville to meet with "an official of the War Department." I summoned Rawlins and we were joined by my Indian associate from Galena, Eli Parker, whom I had asked to join my staff. We set off to Louisville by way of Indianapolis, when the train I'd been instructed to take was stopped en route on a rainy night and the "official" appeared unexpectedly. It was Secretary of War Stanton.

Stanton—the god of war himself! The man who spoke with Lincoln's lips and whose power was greater than Henry Halleck's! He entered my parlor car wheezing and coughing—he was asthmatic and had a bad cold to boot—and confidently strode up to the doctor who traveled with me, a bearded man about my age, and extended an eager wet hand to him.

"Grant, my good fellow," Stanton said, hailing him vigorously. "I'd know you anywhere from your photographs! The prayers and thanks of a nation go with you, sir!" he exclaimed.

"I am a doctor, not Grant," Dr. Kittoe said calmly, "but it is gratifying to know that my services are so highly valued. You should stay out of the rain with that cough," he added.

Stanton turned away abruptly, dismissing him. "Which of you is Grant?" he asked the rest of us in the car.

I identified myself, whereupon Stanton provided me with my nation's prayers and thanks, then quickly proceeded to sit down and get to work.

"President Lincoln has sent me to announce a change in the command structure of our military forces," he said. "We are creating a Military Division of the Mississippi, combining the old Armies of the Tennessee and Cumberland with the Army of the Ohio," he said, not without some grandiosity, "and we have chosen you to head it." He took off his glasses and searched his pockets for a handkerchief with which to dry them.

I nodded briefly as I considered the honor. "Well, Mr. Secretary, I am flattered by the compliment you and the President have chosen to bestow upon me. But if I am not mistaken, the real point of the matter is that you wish me to go and bail Rosecrans out of Chattanooga."

Stanton blinked his reddened, squinty eyes at me as a puddle formed at his feet. "What do you mean?"

"Well," I said, "the effect of this new arrangement is to give me control over Rosecrans and the Army of the Cumberland, which you probably now wish Henry had done long before he divided his command between me and Buell, or before he got rid of Buell and replaced him with Rosecrans. Since Rosecrans has managed to bottle himself up in Chattanooga, you are giving me command over an army trapped and on the verge of extermination."

Stanton cleared his throat and peered at me over his spectacles.

"See here, Grant! I didn't drag myself all the way from Washington to Indianapolis to be subject to your impudence!"

"It's not impudence," I said, "it's the plain truth."

His coughing interrupted him long enough to consider what I'd said. "Yes," he finally croaked, "I suppose this is so."

"So you want me to rescue Rosecrans?" I asked.

Stanton paused before he spoke. "Actually, the President is willing to let you decide whom you wish to rescue," he said. "He wants to replace Rosecrans with Thomas, but only if you're comfortable with it."

"Why doesn't the President issue orders relieving Rosecrans himself?" I asked. "Or have you or Henry do it? Since when is a general in the field asked about this sort of a thing?"

Stanton wiped his forehead, obviously fatigued as well as ill. "Rosecrans is very popular in Ohio and wields great political influence. His chief of staff, James Abram Garfield, is an important Republican member of the House of Representatives. We can't afford to alienate anybody, particularly after the way you cut McClernand down to nothing."

"What if I want to replace Rosecrans with somebody else?" I asked. "Say, for example, Sherman."

"Sherman! I'll be damned before I let that lunatic take command!" He scowled at me. "Rosecrans or Thomas," he said. "Your choice."

I regarded him directly. "So it comes down to this: You'll promote me to the western command if I'll take responsibility for replacing Rosecrans with Thomas and then somehow break the siege, drive off Bragg, and save Chattanooga. Do I have this right?"

Stanton nodded, dabbing his nose. "I see we understand each other."

"We surely do," I told him, and by the end of the day news of the new chain of command was wired to Chattanooga along with my message: *Hold Chattanooga at all hazards. I will be there as soon as possible.*

As soon as Thomas, the new commander, had taken charge, he wired back: *I will hold the town until we starve.*

Frankly, I thought, that seemed to have been Rosecrans's strategy as well. And it hadn't gotten him very far.

I continued south, along with Rawlins and Parker, proceeding by way of Nashville, that gem of a city, until I reached the point thirty miles outside of Chattanooga, as far as any of our forces had gotten. My first visitor, predictably, was Rosecrans, along with his chief of staff, Garfield.

It had been almost a quarter of a century since West Point, but Rosecrans was little different, still a high-strung man with a ruddy complexion. Now he had been tested by the madness and found wanting, and I would end his career. I did not feel sorry for him as he came to my headquarters, but I did, for the slightest moment, marvel at the workings of Fate, which were apparent to me at that moment.

Introductions were made and Rosecrans, awkwardly but cordially, explained his circumstances. There were but a few days' rations left in the city. "I had an idea as to how to get us resupplied," he said uncomfortably. "Thomas can tell you about it—it involves a night flotilla, some pontoon bridges, that sort of thing," he mumbled.

"It's a brilliant goddamned plan," Garfield interrupted arrogantly.

We all turned at this outburst. "Please, James," Rosecrans demurred, in the tones of a man more broken than modest. "It might work. I was unsure as to whether to order it."

"We'll look it over," Rawlins said noncommittally.

"It's a brilliant plan," Garfield repeated, turning to Rawlins, obviously seeking a confrontation. "And I pity the poor sons of bitches who fail to see its merit."

Rawlins looked up, his posture stiffening. "Excuse me, Garfield, but are you calling either General Grant or, perhaps, *me* a son of a bitch?"

Garfield was as much the bantam as Rawlins. He was taller and more robust, to be sure, and possessed of a long, dramatically arched nose, but like Rawlins he had an intense and deep-set glare that never seemed to rest. He was equal to any gauntlet Rawlins threw at his feet. "If you had listened carefully to what I said," he responded slowly, "you'd have heard me say quite distinctly that the fellow who fails to take the time to understand General Rosecrans's brilliant plan for the relief of Chattanooga is a poor son of a bitch."

"Well, that's a goddamned good thing," Rawlins said, leaning forward, his face pointed up at Garfield's. "Because any son of a bitch who calls the commander of the Military Division of the Mississippi, let alone *me*, a son of a bitch would be one son of a bitch for sure."

Rawlins's stare got flintier as Garfield now inched yet closer, his large nose almost against Rawlins's face. "Yes, it is a fine thing we are in complete agreement," he said when Rawlins finished, "because were it the case some addlepated son of a bitch called me a son of a bitch, why I'd probably have to punch that son of a bitch right in his sallow, sunken face and knock his few remaining teeth out, by Jesus!"

"Gentlemen!" Rosecrans interrupted. "Let us allow no misunderstanding among us!"

"There are none, General Rosecrans," Garfield said. "I'm just in the process of informing Colonel Rawlins about the son of a bitch situation here at Chattanooga. You know, we've only got five days' rations left here in the city," he said, glaring at Rawlins, "but new sons of bitches seem to be getting past Bragg's siege line every day!"

"It strikes me, sir, that you are shifting from the hypothetical to the specific," Rawlins started, his fists coming up with what I perceived as malicious intent. I debated jumping in between them, but this was unbecoming an officer of my rank, and my left side was still profoundly sore from my fall in New Orleans. Besides, I wanted to see how the fight turned out. Rosecrans, however, had none of these concerns, and he stepped between them.

"Let there be no more of this," he said, his hands pressed against the chests of the belligerents. "Sam, let me take my leave." And in a gracious manner he extended a hand to me, which I shook respectfully. He nodded at Rawlins and Parker and walked out. When the door had closed behind him, Garfield turned and regarded Rawlins and me angrily.

"Well, I hope you're satisfied," he said curtly. "There goes a broken man!"

I maintained my reserve but answered him directly. "He may be a broken man, but he's left behind a broken army. Allowing Bragg to outmaneuver him so was inexcusable!"

"As if you've never made mistakes!" he fumed. "I'll tell you what it is—you just don't like politicians like me—men of my stature—being in the war!"

"You?" I blurted, astonished. "What do *you* have to do with this?"

"Why, I am a member of the House of Representatives!" Garfield crowed. "Do you know what I am called back in Ohio? Why, the newspapers there call me the 'Scourge of the Confederacy'!"

"Frankly," I replied, "they can call you what they wish. I am unaffected by it."

"Ha! Deny it!" Garfield said. "You have it in for McClernand, for

Wallace, for all the generals with political backgrounds—anybody who was successful before the war, for that matter."

"I have it in for any general unprepared to fight."

"Unprepared! You call a man of Rosecrans's stature unprepared? And what was your preparation? Drinking yourself into poverty?"

With that my patience wore out. "Now see here, you keep your big nose—"

No sooner had I said the words than I regretted them—he was sensitive about his nose, and with good reason—but he had provoked me, and all his talk of stature had set my mind running in one direction.

"My big nose, is it?" He nodded bitterly, arms akimbo. "You'll regret your words, Grant," he said, sneering. "The day will come when you'll wish you'd shown me the proper respect!" With that, he strode to the door and departed in a huff.

Rawlins looked at me and shook his head. "He's possessed of something," he said, and I nodded in agreement.

I had too many other problems to worry about Garfield's wounded pride, and I returned my attention to the job facing me—relieving Chattanooga. I had Rawlins help me onto a horse the next day and Parker guided us up the northern mule trail to reach the city. I had not anticipated the bedlam I'd be traveling through. It was continually rainy in the mountains, and the trail was nearly impassable. Nonetheless, the army had no recourse but to send its mule trains by that route, and as they got caught in the mud, either the provisions they carried were thrown overboard or the animals themselves were allowed to starve and the provisions saved. Carcasses littered the road, blocking the mule trains that followed, compounding the problem even further. I camped by the side of that trail and arrived at Thomas's headquarters the next night, in the midst of a hellish storm, dirty, drenched, and exhausted.

Thomas was waiting for me. He had acquired a house every bit the equal of my father's stately home in Ravenna. He saluted me smartly and beckoned me to a welcome seat by a fire in the well-appointed parlor. I dropped into it unceremoniously and extended my boots toward the hearth, and after some perfunctory small talk Thomas launched into a recitation of the circumstances he had inherited.

"Well, General—or Sam, if I may—now that you have traversed the northward mule path, you have a sense of our situation. It is our only means of supply, it is woefully inadequate, and it will be even more so as the winter sets in. I have taken every possible measure to stretch our resources—the men are on half rations, and armed sentries are guarding the horses' forage troughs so the men cannot steal their food. But my second-in-command, General Smith, and I have developed a plan for relieving the situation, which I will have him explain."

William "Baldy" Smith now stepped forward. (Though not even very bald, just thinning on top, he had acquired the name while serving alongside C. F. Smith, my colleague who died shortly after the capture of Fort Donelson, out of a need to distinguish the one from the other and the lack of any more appropriate physical characteristic between them.) "Here is our proposal, General: As the Tennessee River moves west, away from town, it takes a sharp southern turn down to a place called Moccasin Point, then a sharp northern turn." He went on to outline what had been Rosecrans's plan to seize a point along the river, erect pontoon bridges, capture a farther point, and so on, until we could hook up with the rail lines running west to Memphis. It would require around fifteen hundred men, and it seemed our one chance to open a supply road—a cracker line, he called it, since crackers were the staple of which they had the greatest need.

I lit a cigar and was about to reply when Rawlins suddenly interrupted. "Good Lord, General Thomas, don't you see that General Grant is wet and cold? He is recovering from injuries and he's in need of a meal and a dry change of clothes!"

Thomas stopped short and examined me with curiosity. "Why, so he is! My most earnest apologies, General—or Sam, if I may. See here!" he shouted to a staff officer standing at the door. "Fetch the general a dry change of clothes! Can't you see that he's—"

"I can get a change of clothes later," I said, interrupting him, as I was now eagerly engaged in examining the map Baldy Smith had used in his presentation. "There's only one question," I said, when I fully comprehended the situation. "How do you get fifteen hundred men to the point of attack on the river without Bragg noticing?"

Baldy Smith answered, to Thomas's approval. "We've thought of that. We sail a fleet of pontoon boats out of Chattanooga and down the river, going west, with the current, in the middle of the night. Not a sound, just drift past the sentries, and come ashore at daybreak."

An armada floating down the river, right under the enemy's nose!

Where had I heard that one before? How could I say no? Besides, of course, the only alternative was sitting in Chattanooga, starving, and surrendering, in that order.

So, two nights later, Baldy Smith led his pontoon boats down the Tennessee River. Luck was with him—it was a foggy, misty sort of night, and though his boats drifted within earshot of Confederate pickets on shore, none of them perceived him going by. At worst, he was mistaken for driftwood. He landed just as he predicted, sustained a minimum of casualties, and erected his pontoon bridges. Floating downriver past enemy installations now seemed as easy as taking forts! In the space of a day, the cracker line was reopened and supplies were once again entering the city.

So much for that. Now all I needed was Sherman.

It took a while for my messages to reach Sherman back in Memphis, but when they did, he taught these other fellows how to move in a hurry. He arrived outside of town on November 13, 1863, and proceeded up the cracker line into Chattanooga, where I was waiting for him at headquarters. "Where's Grant?" I heard his voice booming, his rapid, hard strides resounding through the building. "I want to see the head fucking man!"

"I'm in here, Sherman!" I shouted from a small study I used for an office, and in he bounded.

"Well, if it isn't the commander of the Military Division of the Mississippi himself!" he said with a laugh as he pumped my hand. "It's humbling as all hell just to be in your presence," he cracked.

"Your inestimable deference deserves a cigar," I said, producing two and extending one to him.

"My pleasure, if it's one of yours," he said, taking it from me and jamming it resolutely between his teeth. He saluted Thomas, Baldy Smith, and the other assembled senior staff, then bent at the waist and extended himself toward the match I offered. He peered about the room as he fired up his cigar. "Hello, Rawlins," he said out of the corner of his mouth. "How's the other Mrs. Grant? Keeping the head man out of trouble?"

Rawlins gave Sherman a dark stare. He always suspected a man as foulmouthed and headstrong as Sherman probably drank. Sherman investigated the tip of his smoke, found it satisfactory, and looked about the room some more. "See here," he suddenly said with amused surprise, "who's the chief?"

"This is Colonel Eli Parker, Sherman, whom I have invited onto my staff for the duration," I answered, motioning toward the erudite Seneca.

"Pleased, Chief," Sherman muttered, extending his hand.

"General Sherman! *Bos Williamos*, as the Greeks would have it!" Parker replied, taking Sherman's hand in his oversize bronzed grip. "It is a monumental pleasure to meet a namesake of the great chief Tecumseh, let alone the vanquisher of Joe Johnston and his wretched corps of Rebels!"

"How!" Sherman responded, palm out, then looked at me and smirked. "That's quite a fucking Indian you've got there, Grant." He patted Parker on the arm, then stepped over to Thomas. "Now, Old Tom, how's the war been while I've been gone?"

Before Thomas could answer, Sherman turned away and dropped himself into a large rocking chair in the center of the room. "This is the first fucking piece of furniture I've seen in two weeks, Grant. My men marched two hundred miles in fourteen days to get here," he crowed, rocking vigorously.

"How did you supply them?" I asked.

"Grant style! We stopped for a bite along the way!" He grinned at me. "If there's a pig or a cow left alive between here and Memphis, it's got a pair of fucking crutches and a Federal medal for service, believe me! We'd better find some Rebels for my men to fight, Grant, because they're gaining too much goddamned weight marching through this countryside!" He sent a cloud of smoke out into the center of the room. "Your fellows getting any exercise, Thomas?" he asked, laughing.

"Never mind that," I remarked, and proceeded to outline for Sherman my thinking. Bragg had sent Longstreet to Knoxville to prevent Burnside, who was encamped there, from reinforcing us. But I'd never intended to call on Burnside's men—it was a complete waste on Bragg's part. The loss of Longstreet's men meant Bragg's forces atop Lookout Mountain to the south and Missionary Ridge to the east were stretched thin, even if they did hold the high ground. If we moved aggressively now, we could stretch them further.

I determined that we would array Thomas at the foot of Missionary Ridge, in plain sight. Sherman's men would march around the north side of Chattanooga, out of sight of the enemy, and emerge at the north end of the ridge, where he would attack Bragg's right. Bragg would have to weaken his left—his force on Lookout Mountain—at which point we would send Hooker's men to assault the ridge from the southern end. With Hooker pressuring Bragg from the south and Thomas massed directly in front of him, Sherman would be able to drive down from the north and Bragg would have to surrender or flee.

It all happened exactly that way, except for the details. Hooker did assault Lookout Mountain, on the morning of November 23, 1863. Reminiscent of the brazen field commander who led his men, ladder in hand, against the walls of Chapultepec, Hooker gave the order to attack and marched up the mountain as if called to it by destiny.

From the plain before the ridge, Thomas, Rawlins, Parker, and I watched the entire affair as if it were theater. Hooker's men started up the mountain. But the cool morning autumn air left the slope shrouded in fog, and in a few moments his entire army had marched into the clouds and was completely hidden from view as the sounds of their battle raged for miles around.

By midday the fog had burned away and we beheld an amazing sight—Hooker's men were in complete control of the mountain! Their battle flags ran all the way up its side. The gray coats of the enemy could be seen running from the front lines, and Union blue covered the face of the slope!

"My stars, we're driving them!" Thomas said, slack-jawed.

"We certainly are," I agreed.

Meanwhile, Sherman set off for the north end of the ridge and reached the top with little resistance. When he got there, he found out why—Sherman had not assaulted Missionary Ridge. Instead, he had assaulted a hill just north of Missionary Ridge, one separated completely from the north end of the ridge by a steep valley and a well-situated Confederate force. I looked angrily at Thomas once Sherman's messenger reached me with this troubling news.

"I thought you gave Sherman a map of this theater!"

"Well, yes, I did," Thomas replied, "but the map must have been in error."

"I'll say it's in error! Sherman's stuck on a hill separated from the ridge!" I considered the situation for the briefest moment and decided to change the plan. "He's going to be ground to dust if he has to climb up the north face of the ridge without help," I told Thomas. "If you attack now, Bragg would have to draw troops away from him. It's our one chance to save him and turn the battle. Go do it!"

In one sense this had been my plan all along—force Bragg to decide where to mass and then push him from the other directions. What I did not imagine was how it would all play out. Thomas's twenty thousand men were placed in formation three lines deep and two miles long, and they all began to move forward as one. When Phil Sheridan rode in front of these men and gave the order to charge, the sight was so awesome and convincing—twenty thousand men surging forward, running, shouting, their rifles and bayonets glinting in the sunlight— the Rebels in the rifle pits either threw their guns down and their arms up or turned and took off up the mountain.

But rather than stopping at the rifle pits at the base of the ridge, Thomas's men began scaling the ridge!

"Who ordered this ascent?" I said as I watched the first waves of men climb up the ridge toward the enemy's stronghold and realized what was happening. "The Confederate position's unassailable!"

"It certainly wasn't me," Thomas volunteered in a defensive tone.

I chose not to tell him at the moment what I thought of a commanding officer who would order such a suicidal charge, or indeed one whose men were executing it without his knowledge. If it failed, someone would surely pay.

Seemingly unmindful of the danger, on Thomas's army went—stomachs to the rock wall, slithering up the ravines, a rising tide of blue moving up the mountain, each group in turn racing ahead of the one next to it. They hugged the escarpments and hunkered into depressions in the ground. A Confederate rifleman would have to arch himself into the line of fire to hit his target, thus taking away the advantage of high ground. It was a moment of great bravery. But it was also true that the Confederate soldiers atop the ridge had an easy shot at our men as long as they remained in the captured rifle pits at the base of the mountain. The only way to get out of the line of fire was to storm the ridge, and so they did. It was Sheridan, of course, who first realized it and who rode out into the open, making brazen sword loops in the air, crying, "Forward, boys, forward!" Once he started out, the divisions on the left and right of him had little choice but to follow, and soon he was at the top.

"We've taken the ridge!" Rawlins said when he realized it was done.

"So we have," I said. Thomas sighed with relief.

"I thought you said that position was unassailable," Rawlins said.

"I was mistaken," I responded.

"The Seneca have a saying," Parker offered, contemplating the scene with perfect serenity. "Fortune favors the warrior with a great heart, but it is better yet to be a lucky son of a bitch."

Our forces had done what nobody—least of all me—thought they could do. It was the last act of a month-long drama that started with our troops cornered in a besieged city and ended with the expulsion of the enemy from Tennessee. Since my arrival, I had broken the siege of Chattanooga, restored the army, driven the enemy from unassailable entrenchments, scattered Bragg's army in disarray, and liberated a key region of the country.

Back in Washington, Congressman Washburne introduced a bill to give me a third star—lieutenant general, the only one in the history of the Republic since George Washington. There was some token opposition, led by a vindictive Garfield, now back in Congress, who argued such an honor should be bestowed only after the war had been won. Besides, he whispered, the man drinks! Hang that, his colleagues replied as they drank to me, and the deed was done. My third star was on its way. Halleck wrote to say I was to come to Washington, meet with the President, and assume command of the Union's armies.

How many commanders had Lincoln now had? McDowell, McClellan, Burnside, Pope, Hooker, Halleck—each had had a throw. Each of them, in their own way, so full of themselves that there was no room left for a fighting heart. Well, I would show them, I thought. I would show them plain thinking and plain speaking, rectitude and indefatigable discipline, unrelenting determination and swift movement. My destiny was finally within reach—*I would lead great masses of men in the cause of their human redemption.* I had only to claim it.

And so I was off to Washington. I took young Fred with me. It was March 8, 1864, when we arrived at the Willard Hotel on Pennsylvania Avenue—he in a suit selected by his mother, I in a well-worn, wrinkled general's uniform—and I asked for a room.

The clerk behind the front desk looked at us indifferently. "You have no reservation and we're fairly full." He regarded his lists and suggested a small room in the back on the top floor.

"That will be fine," I said, and wrote in the register: *U. S. Grant and son, Galena, Ill.*

The clerk glanced at the register as he handed me a key. A few moments later, Fred and I were in the same suite Lincoln had occupied when he was inaugurated. Good hotel rooms, like promotions, seemed to come most easily when not asked for.

In short order, a delegation arrived to take me to the White House to meet the President.

The White House! What a magnificent place it was, as perfectly delightful as any mansion I had liberated for my own use in the South. We entered a vaulted, marbled front hall and walked into a red-carpeted main hall. I barely had time to look around when I was whisked into the East Room, a large salon with a formidable fireplace, ceiling-high windows, and an intricate inlaid wooden floor. A crowd awaited me there, the men in their finely tailored suits, the women in their elaborately detailed gowns. I could feel them gasp as I entered— the great man had arrived!—although they were probably gasping at the realization that U. S. Grant was a slight and plain fellow with a stooped walk, worn clothes, and a seedy look. Like it or not, though, I was their savior, and I had arrived.

I was busy shaking each hand thrust toward me when, from across the room, I saw a tall bearded man approaching. I recognized Lincoln instantly. My word, what a homely yokel he was! He had a sunken, craggy face, an immense nose, and massive, flappy ears. He reminded me more of the farm boys who went to battle than the man who led them. He was six-foot-four if an inch, with not a pick of extra meat on him—he was built like a Barnum sideshow attraction. He ambled toward me on the legs of a crane and extended the largest hand I'd ever seen.

"It is General Grant, is it not?" he asked.

"Yes," I replied, and shook the giant paw.

Suddenly the room closed in around us both. Seward, the Secretary of State, looking like Shakespeare's Polonius, came by to examine me. Chase, the Treasury Secretary, stood next to him, making small talk with me as if we were business associates. Stanton came by, looking a bit healthier now, though not much, and flaunted his familiarity with me for all the rest to see. We were all engaged in exchanging pleasantries for a moment when Seward took my arm and whispered, "There are people waiting to see you in the Green Room, among them Mrs. Lincoln." I found myself being guided by the arm down the main corridor, past statuary and portraits of past presidents, to a small, crowded receiving room.

A new throng burst into applause and raced toward me, parting even as it did to let me be taken to Mrs. Lincoln. She sat on a green-and-white-striped sofa, and wore a red dress that stood out against the room's green walls. A window behind her looked out over the moonlit South Lawn, and beyond it to the unfinished Washington Monument. She was a short, dark woman with a lined face, who looked as if she knew how to snarl even as she smiled.

"Why, General Grant, I am *ever* so pleased to meet you!" she exclaimed as I approached, her drawl exaggerated as if to emphasize her native Southernness. "You are the toast of the town!"

"Thank you, Mrs. Lincoln," I said politely.

"I will make it my personal mission to ensure you enjoy your stay here in Washington," she said, and gave me a look I would have thought provocative in a woman of lesser standing.

"I appreciate that, madam, but I must soon return to the field."

"I am no stranger to the field," she said, and with that she took out an ivory fan and held it in front of herself demurely, fluttering it to allow me glimpses of a smile that brought to mind the widespread gossip that she was, well . . . a little *off*.

I felt Seward's hand on my arm again, summoning me back to the main event. "It has been my honor to meet you," I said. "Now, if you'll excuse me . . ."

"Oh, we shall meet again," she said, peeking out from behind her fan. I then found myself led, again, back to the East Room and onto a sofa, on which I stood so that I might shake the hand of seemingly every person present. Each reached up to greet me with more frantic enthusiasm than the last, each told me their name, and most managed to cite some connection to me, no matter how distant: "I served in Congress with Washburne." "Joe Hooker and I were in business together once." "My father fought with Scott at Niagara in the 1812 War!"

I was shaking hands still, a frenzied hour later, when the attention of those around me was drawn to a hand waving high in the air at the other end of the room, attached to which was Lincoln. His somber mien calmed the crowd in short order.

"Now that all of you have had the opportunity to chat with General Grant," he said softly, standing in the doorway, "I would like to do the same." I recognized my cue and stepped down off the couch and through the East Room to Lincoln's side. "If I may ask the Cabinet to repair with me to the Blue Room, we can get on with the work ahead of us," he said, and walked out to the main corridor of the East Wing, I and the Cabinet hastily following him. He stopped at the door to the Blue Room and nodded to the assemblage that had followed us down the corridor. When he turned to open the door and enter, a voice from the back of the crowd said, "Speak to us, Mr. President!"

A murmur of approval filled the hall. Lincoln turned and nodded in the most imperceptible way, and the bustling crowd became instantly silent. His high-pitched, reedy voice didn't fit his lanky frame, but he used it to masterful effect. "My friends," he began, "we are grateful to have General Grant with us this evening, and we are grateful as well to Providence, who has allowed us to take the hilt of His swift sword and reunite the nation our Forefathers gave to us, to redeem the sacred vow we made to those who perished at Antietam, and Gettysburg, and Manassas," he intoned, taking pains not to mention, I noted, Shiloh or Missionary Ridge or anyplace else those who perished had done so in my care, "and to reclaim the destiny Our Maker provided to us, not one of conquest or vengeance, but one of mercy and justice."

The crowd was now completely hushed, awed, reverentially attentive, and I admit I was right there among them—I was completely absorbed by the man's words, his bearing, the saintliness that emanated from his gigantic gnarled body. "So let us now go forward," he continued, all eyes fixed on him, "with malice toward none, with charity for all, with firmness in the right as God gives us to see the right. Let us strive on to finish the work we are in, to bind up the nation's wounds, and to achieve a just and lasting peace among ourselves and among all nations, both in the name of those we have lost, and of the nation and the Holy God for whom so many have perished."

As he finished, I felt a tear roll down my cheek, so moving were his words, and I was not alone. Wet cheeks and shining eyes could be seen on every face, and these were not the faces of those easily moved by noble sentiment; they were speculators, profiteers, legislators, War Democrats, shin-plaster traders, substitute-hirers, and every other type of political lowlife our nation's capital could muster. Yet this gangly, apish, ugly yokel (and heaven help him, he was ugly—ugly enough to tax a mother's love) spewed out the most beautiful words I'd ever heard, all in that squeaky treble pitch that would have made dogs bark.

It was beyond beautiful. It was holy.

After a pristine moment of silence, I expected a deluge of applause, and I would have eagerly joined. But not one individual in the room felt worthy to break the silence. They just stared at their divine, ungainly monkey, tears trickling down their cheeks. He nodded to them and then stepped to the side and extended a graceful, mannerly arm, beckoning me to enter the Blue Room, which I did, followed quickly by the Cabinet. Once inside the room, I watched him bow ever so slightly to the crowd and then close the door.

As the door slammed, Lincoln turned and faced us with this same sacred gaze, whereupon the broadest of smiles suddenly came over him, and without warning, he was overcome with laughter, slapping his bony knee with his hand as he guffawed. *"Didja see that?"* he asked, his twangy, squeaky voice taking on an entirely different character. "Did you, Grant?" he howled, shaking with delight. "They just eat that stuff up!"

"Abe, please, quiet down, they're still out there," Seward said, his palms pushing down the air before him in a calming gesture.

"Oh, hell, Seward, you worrywart. They're probably beseeching the Lord for my health and well-being." Lincoln laughed, pointing at the door behind him. "Did you see me light 'em up, Grant?" he cackled, turning to me. "I can do that, you know. It's a gift! A *Providence* here and a couple of *Forefathers* there and pretty soon a crowd will forget they didn't like you to begin with." He laughed, then turned back to Seward, excited. "Hell, that was good! I can use that in my inauguration speech if *Providence* favors my bony rear end with reelection this fall!" He shook his head in amazement. "Sometimes I wonder where it comes from, Grant. You just *say this stuff* and everybody gets to glowing." And he suddenly stood erect, hand on lapel, orating in his public manner. *"Four score and seven years ago—"* Whereupon he fell back and clapped his hands with delight. "You see what I mean? You say *four score and seven years ago* and you're the second coming of Cicero! If I'd have said, 'It was eighty-seven years ago,' they'd have all said, 'Oh, that Lincoln's an idiot.'" He shook his head and laughed once again.

"Abe, Abe, it's past midnight, we've yet to get down to business with General Grant here," Seward interrupted the President again. I looked around the circular room at his Cabinet. They stood about, wearing identical expressions—put-upon but patient, as if waiting for a moment of inclement weather to pass.

"Stop spoiling my fun, Seward, or there won't be a penny for Alaska when this is all over." He shook his head and smiled at me. "Can you believe this nonsense? Seward wants me to buy *Alaska* from Czar Poopovich, or whatever his name is, when this is all over. A goddamned ice house good for nothing but catching herring! I declare!" He plopped himself down at one end of the fine oak table in the center of the Blue Room, and his Cabinet arrayed themselves around it. He took a deep breath—it was late and he seemed tired.

"Well, I suppose now that General Grant—*Yoo-lisses*, I suppose they called you back on the frontier, am I right?—is here with us, we ought to go over how we're going to whip these Confederates." He looked at me expectantly, waiting for me to respond.

"Well, Mr. President," I began, "I know how to pursue this conflict, but my plan requires the highest level of coordination among all aspects of the government's army and cannot go forward without your strong support."

Lincoln held out his large, gnarled hand to silence me. "I heard this part before, *Yoo-lisses*. Just tell me one thing: Are you going to whip some of these Rebels this time? I mean, are you ready to fight, or is there going to be some kind of problem, like there always was with that little mouse McClellan, or that befuddled Hooker fellow, or Burnside, or the rest of them?"

"Well, no, there won't be any problem," I said flatly. "I intend to pursue their armies until they are incapable of resistance and accede to our objectives."

Lincoln took on a grave expression for a moment as he appraised me and then suddenly broke into the broadest of smiles all over again. "Hell, yes!" he shouted, slapping his knee once more. "Stanton, you finally found me a goddamned soldier instead of the flea-bitten bums and pimple-assed Napoleons you kept digging up." As I had the opportunity to work with all my predecessors, I was impressed with the President's ability to judge character. "You know, Grant, those bums reminded me of Jocko, the monkey. Did you ever hear the story of the king of all monkeys?" Lincoln asked me, his expression suddenly serious.

"Come now, Abe," Stanton interrupted. "It's a little late for this sort of thing, isn't it?" The entire Cabinet seemed to shift in their seats uncomfortably.

Lincoln shot Stanton a murderous look. "Quit interruptin' me while I'm delivering a parable, Stanton." He turned toward me, shaking his head dismissively. "My word, if Jesus had the likes of these fellows around, we never would have heard the Sermon on the Mount. Now, where was I?" he asked himself. "Oh yeah. Now I recall. You see," Lincoln began, leaning back and putting his oversized feet upon the table, "there was this monkey named Jocko who was the king of all the monkeys, and he decided that he was going to be the greatest king of all the monkeys there ever was. And he decided that he needed to have the longest tail of all the monkeys to do that. So he had the monkey doctors cut off all the tails of all the other monkeys and sew them up onto his own. But when they were all sewed together, the tail was too heavy for him to drag, so he had the other monkeys wind it around his shoulder like a braid, until it got so heavy that it *snapped* his back, just like that," Lincoln said, and snapped his spiny, gnarled fingers. "End of story!" he declared with an emphatic nod, looking me right in the eye. "Do you see what I'm saying to you, Grant?"

I understood the gist of his remarks and nodded agreement with him, while from across the room the Cabinet fidgeted and rolled their eyes. Trusting any further nuances would come clear to me later, I then proceeded to outline my thinking as briefly as I could. Lincoln gave me his complete attention. Meade and Burnside would cross the James River—this time for good, whatever the cost, I said—and advance on Richmond from below. Sherman would be sent through Georgia, against Joe Johnston, to Atlanta. He would obliterate everything along his path, so as to impair the South's ability to support the conflict and keep Johnston from joining Lee. On a third front, Sigel, the Army of the Potomac's cavalry commander, would proceed through the Shenandoah Valley, destroying their capacity to grow food while bottling them up from above in case Lee got one of his periodic urges to invade the North. Meanwhile, Banks would come up the Mississippi from New Orleans, and from the sea, Farragut would enter the Carolinas, encircling the Confederacy and destroying their armies.

"Now, I know Banks, and Burnside, too," Lincoln interrupted. "And I have no reason to think better of Sigel. What makes you think they can whip anybody at all?"

"Frankly, I don't think they can," I said. "But simply by exerting offensive pressure, they can make it impossible for the forces they confront to take any other offensive action, thereby thinning the Confederacy's fighting power."

Lincoln nodded with a smile of recognition. "I get it!" he squealed. "Just like we used to say back home: If you don't know how to skin an animal, at least you can hold a leg!"

He grasped the essential point—that we must attack from everywhere at once so as to maximize our material and numerical advantages and wage a war of total annihilation, without mercy or remorse. There would be losses, I said flatly, sizable losses, and there would be political costs to them. But the alternative was an ongoing stalemate that would ultimately mean defeat and the loss of the overriding objective Lincoln and I shared—the preservation of the Union.

"It's as simple as that," I concluded. "If we fail to pursue the matter, we will lose the war. But victory will take fighting, which means blood and death, and there will be many more widows and orphans before we are done."

Lincoln realized we were speaking the same language. He nodded slowly and turned to the Cabinet with a glare. "Now isn't that *exactly* what I've been saying? Have everybody go after them at once?" He peered over at Stanton, who sat off to the side. "Where have you been hiding this little guy?

"Grant," Lincoln drawled as he regarded me once again, this time more somberly, "I heard a bunch about you. Everybody seems to have a complaint about you. When you captured Donelson, McClernand told me you were lucky that poor old Smith bailed you out. When you pushed back Johnston at Shiloh, that pea-brained Halleck told me you were a drunk who got caught with his drawers at half mast, if I may paraphrase his remarks. When you were abandoning your lines to reduce Jackson before you turned on Vicksburg, they all told me you were gone in the head. And when you paroled Pemberton's army after he gave up, they told me you were walking a fine line between victory and treason."

"I had my reasons," I said firmly. "Most of those men were from Texas. They wanted to go home, not fight. Besides, we couldn't afford the food, men, and railcars to transport—"

"Hell, Grant, I know that," Lincoln said. "That's what I told them myself! They didn't get it, so I told them the story about Sykes's dog. Did you ever hear the story of Sykes's dog?" I barely had time to shake my head before it was Chase, the Treasury Secretary, who cut in.

"As a matter of fact, Mr. President, we have all had the good fortune of having heard you discuss this homily, which concerns, as I recall, the predisposition of some villainous young fellows against poor Sykes's beloved canine friend—"

"Oh, hush up!" Lincoln snapped. "If somebody had told the lot of you a few stories back when you were all attending your colleges and seminaries, maybe you'd all know something today!" He glared at the Cabinet, all of whom looked down to avoid his angry stare, then turned back to me. "This is the crew that recommended McClellan and Burnside," he sneered, looking at me in full anticipation of my sympathy, which I was given to deliver. "Well, back to the matter of Sykes's dog, which is what I was getting to before Aristotle over there interrupted me. This fellow Sykes had a yeller dog he set great store by, but there were some small boys who didn't share Sykes's views, and they were not disposed to let the dog have a fair show. So the boys fixed up a cartridge with a long fuse, put the cartridge in a piece of meat, dropped the meat in front of Sykes's door, and then perched on a fence a good distance off. Then they whistled for the dog. When he came out and bolted the meat, the boys touched off the fuse with a cigar, and in about a second a report came from that dog that sounded like a clap of thunder."

Lincoln was now lost in his story, leaning forward in his chair to deliver it, oblivious to his Cabinet as they looked about the room indifferently, variously examining the walls, the ceiling, their pocket watches or fingernails. "So Sykes came bounding out of the house," he continued, "and saw the air filled with pieces of yellow dog. He picked up the biggest piece he could find, a portion of the back with the tail still hanging to it, and he said, 'Well, I guess he'll never be much account again—as a dog.' And that's what I figure about Pemberton. His men may account for something, but not much as an army."

Lincoln fell back in his seat and folded his hands across his chest, satisfied he had made his point. I looked away from the President to see most of the Cabinet giving me a collective, clandestine shrug.

"Well, Mr. President, I appreciate your support," I said, responding to the last thing he said I had understood.

"Well, that's just it. I'm done listening to what *they* say about you, since *they* haven't won anything and *you* have. My support is gratefully given," Lincoln said, and then suddenly he leapt from his seat, pulled his coat off his shoulders and tossed it at Seward, and crouched down with his arms in a circle in front of him, crablike. I gaped at the President as he lurched back and forth in this awkward position "Hey, Grant, my little friend! You ever do any rasslin'?"

Wrestling? In fact, it involved exactly the kind of close physical contact for which I had never much cared. "Actually, no, Mr. President—"

"No? Well, how about it? C'mon, Mr. Granty-panty! If you lack the gumption to rassle the chief executive, you're never going to whip the Rebels! Two out of three!" He took a few surprisingly quick steps to the side and back. "Didn't you ever hear about how I thumped that bully boy Jack Armstrong back in Illinois? Hell, if you believed my campaign, then when I wasn't splitting rails and returning pennies and reading law by the fire, I was beating Jack Armstrong! Hell, I beat him harder in that campaign than I did Stephen Douglas!" he said, whereupon he suddenly lunged at me with feline quickness, grabbing the back of my neck with the iron grip of his massive right hand.

"Let him go, Abe," Seward said soothingly, as Stanton shook his head. "It's late."

Lincoln's hands fell to his side. "I suppose so," he said with good-natured resignation. "I just wanted to see how much fight the little guy had in him." He looked me over. "Hooker was fool enough to give it a try," he said sotto voce, and winked at me.

Part of me wanted to pursue Lincoln's last remark, but I thought it best to bring our meeting to an end. "Give me your support and you will find out how much fight is in me, Mr. President," I responded.

Lincoln looked at me, a grin over his angular face, and slapped his knee. "Hell, *Yoo-lisses*, you're all right! Any man who can talk like that is bound for great things!" He rose to his feet and extended his hand to me. "This meeting is over!" he said. "Come by tomorrow and I'll toss a few *Providences* and *Forefathers* your way and you can get on with what you're here to do." He stuck his thumbs into his britches, gave them an upward hoist, and nodded.

And so ended my first day at the White House.

I returned to the hotel, told young Fred a slightly altered version of the evening's events, and went to bed. At the War Department the next day, I told Halleck that he was being promoted to Chief of Staff, which meant his job was now to get me what I needed in the way of matériel and men—he was through making strategy one shovelful at a time. I then returned to the White House, where with a brief ceremony, the President bestowed my new rank on me and I made some mercifully brief remarks.

The political sideshow was over—time to retrieve young Fred and head off to win the war. I had said my good-byes, and I was walking down the main corridor of the East Wing, heading for the door, when a singsong voice called out, "Oh, General Grant!" I stopped and peered into the Green Room, where Mrs. Lincoln sat on the green and white sofa, where she had been perched the night before. "Won't you join me for a moment?" she said coyly from behind the same ivory fan.

I took off my hat. "I would be pleased to, ma'am, but I must be off—"

"Doesn't the wife of the commander-in-chief have any rank in this war?" she asked demurely, her soft tone only emphasizing that her invitation was an order.

A table laid out with a silver tea service sat in front of her and she beckoned me to a chair. I dutifully entered and sat.

"May I pour?" she asked, reaching for the teapot and pouring a cup of tea for each of us. She lifted her cup, drained it in a long, single draw, rather than a sociable sip, then gave me an encouraging look.

I lifted my cup and sipped, and almost spit it out. Mrs. Lincoln's tea was laced with a healthy dose of bourbon—the tea, in fact, contributed more to the beverage's temperature than its color or taste. "Mrs. Lincoln," I gasped. "This is most improper. I am not a drinking man!"

"Oh, I am told differently," she cooed.

"Then you are misinformed," I said, standing up. "I'm afraid I must be going," I said, and reached down to gather my hat, when I felt her hand on my shoulder.

"General, I merely wanted you to know that a man of such power and command as yourself can be accommodated in all of his needs," she said, her free hand placing her cup and saucer on the table. "Let me show you something." She stood and walked to a window overlooking the southern lawn of the White House, guiding me alongside her with a firm grip. Illuminated by the midday sun, the half-built Washington Monument stood before us.

"Do you see it?" she asked. "It is yet unfinished, like the work of our great nation, the work you and my husband are engaged in. It is so tall, so *erect*, yet so incomplete, so desperately in need of consummation," she said, and sighed, as I stood uncomfortably beside her. "You are like that monument, General, firm and strong, bristling with power and energy." She placed a hand on her breast as emotion seemed to overwhelm her, and looked into my eyes. "And just as our nation has been tested, her leaders must be, too," she proclaimed, whereupon she reached into the sash at the top of my trousers, scouted the territory, raced forward, and firmly grasped my member.

"Ah!" she cried. "Richmond!"

I gulped and pulled back, but she had the tenacity of a bulldog, seizing the object of her campaign with the determination and resolve missing in all of the commanders at Chattanooga. "Mrs. Lincoln, please," I sputtered, but she only tightened her grip and pulled me closer as if she were holding my reins.

"General, your conquest awaits!"

"Madam!" I said in an urgent whisper, and, grabbing her arm with both hands, I forced her to withdraw.

"Please, General," she said, seizing upon the lapels of my coat. "My need for you is as great as our nation's!"

"Madam, you must let me go," I ordered, and shook her a bit roughly, reflecting my increasing alarm.

She gasped loudly and her hands fell away, and a longing expression suddenly spread over her face.

"Oh, Sam—they call you Sam, don't they?—" she said, as if from a dream. "I shall remember this moment always."

"There is nothing to remember," I said, backing out of the room.

"Oh, how happy I am to hear that my feelings are returned!"

"Madam, do not misunderstand me—"

"Oh, I do not, I swear!"

"Then excuse me," I said, and exited quickly out the door. As I raced down the corridor, I could hear her voice fading behind me.

"I will wait for you here!" she cried.

Such was my introduction to Washington.

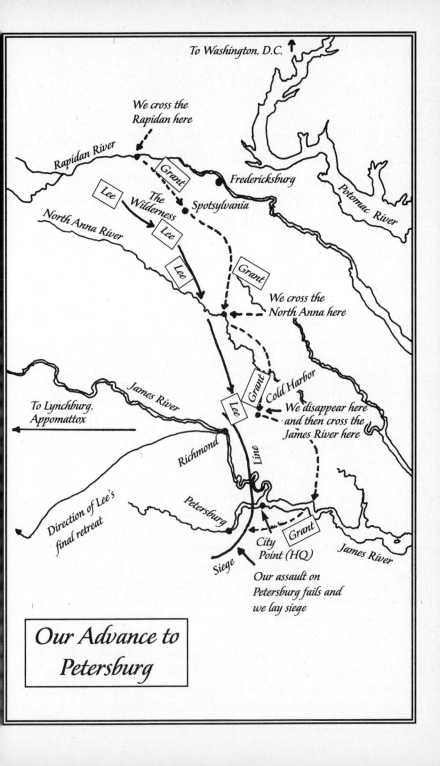

To Washington, D.C.

We cross the
Rapidan here

Rapidan River

Grant

Fredericksburg

Lee

The
Wilderness

Spotsylvania

North Anna River

Lee

Lee

Potomac River

Grant

We cross the
North Anna here

James River

To Lynchburg,
Appomattox

Lee

Grant

Cold Harbor

We disappear here
and then cross the
James River here

Richmond

Line

Direction of Lee's
final retreat

Petersburg

City
Point (HQ)

James River

Siege

Grant

Our assault on
Petersburg fails and
we lay siege

*Our Advance to
Petersburg*

CHAPTER XI

FROM THE RAPIDAN TO THE JAMES—THE SIEGE OF PETERSBURG—CONFERENCE WITH LINCOLN—LEE BREAKS OUT—SURRENDER AT APPOMATTOX—THE ASSASSINATION OF THE PRESIDENT

I STILL HEAR IT TODAY—Grant was a butcher, he was lucky, he had superior numbers, he was outsmarted by Lee every step of the way. A choir of know-it-alls will offer every explanation for Bobby Lee's surrender in McLean's parlor at Appomattox, except the obvious one.

I whipped him, and whipped him good.

I'm not bragging, I'm not boasting, and I'm not making any undue claims. I don't ask for credit beyond that one simple fact: Nobody beat him but me.

But they still talk behind my back, and I'll tell you why—it was because I was a tanner's boy who began the war commanding a regiment of unruly Illinois farm boys, while Lee was Martha Washington's grandson-in-law and began the war commanding Winfield Scott's admiration. The flower of chivalry, they called him.

But I didn't care what people thought about him any more than I cared what they thought about me. I simply did the job they asked me to do—and if somebody doesn't like the way I did it, he can count the number of stars on the flag waving over his head and thank me when he gets past thirty.

By the spring of 1864, when I was made lieutenant general, the Army of the Potomac had crossed the Rapidan River on its way to Richmond six times, and six times it was pushed back. My job was to ensure that it would not be pushed back a seventh time.

Now, if I had Sherman, McPherson, Ord, and the Army of the Tennessee, I'd have done what no one else had had the nerve to do. I'd have crossed the Rapidan and gone west, around Lee's left, with two weeks' rations in knapsacks. I would have beaten Lee to Lynchburg just like I took Jackson before I took Vicksburg. Then I would have pushed east, back into Richmond, and forced Lee to fight in the open, rolling farmland at the front of the Blue Ridge, where I would have used my artillery to blow him to bits, sweep around his left, take Richmond, and end the war.

But the Army of the Potomac was stiff, slow, and demoralized, its leadership ponderous and afraid of defeat—they were the kings of the monkeys with nothing to show for the last three years beyond Gettysburg, where Lee's own brilliance got the better of him; and Antietam, where McClellan discovered a purloined Confederate message outlining the enemy's plans. This army would not sweep swiftly and fearlessly around Lee's left, taking the fight to the enemy with no more provisions than what fit in their pockets. Instead, I would have to go east, around Lee's right—closer to Washington for my lines of communication, closer to roads to carry the wounded back to hospitals, closer to the Chesapeake Bay and the various rivers that would allow us to be resupplied—even if it meant a long, hard slog, face-to-face with the enemy. This army would somehow have to move around Lee and get between him and Richmond the hard way, which is exactly how they did it.

As I did after receiving my commission from Frémont in '61, I assembled a new staff to help with the campaign. Rawlins was always with me, of course, as was now Meade. I also brought in an engineer named Orville Babcock, a trustworthy and efficient sort I had met in earlier campaigns. Horace Porter was a young aide to General Thomas at Chattanooga—he had a good head on his shoulders. And, of course, I would have the brightest man I knew alongside me—Eli Parker.

The Army of the Potomac crossed the Rapidan River for the seventh and last time on May 4, 1864—sixty miles from Richmond. Time was of the essence. We were entering an extended area of thick forest and tangled brush aptly termed the Wilderness, where our greater numbers and firepower would be ineffective.

The Army of the Tennessee, of course, would have marched through this entanglement in a few hours, pushing out into the open

fields where we could get right down to work. But the Army of the Potomac was a different story. Its supply train got so bogged down the infantry had to stop and wait, which gave Lee time to send A. P. Hill and
Richard Ewell smashing into our right flank. Our first battle—the Battle of the Wilderness—had begun.

We were badly positioned, but if Lee was ready, so was I. I would
rather have had Sherman in command of the Army of the Potomac in
Meade's place, but politics dictated otherwise, and so Meade kept his
job. I turned Meade's men to face Lee's and they fought bravely, but
the terrain worked against them. Actually, it worked against everybody.
It was hardly a battle between two trained armies—it was more a gathering of two opposing swarms, set loose in the woods to kill each other.
Bodies, dead or wounded, fell to the leafy ground as shots came in all
directions.

That's what Lee—the flower of chivalry—wanted: carnage.

After the first day's fighting ended, I conferred with Meade.

"I propose we counterattack tomorrow, first thing," he said.

"Excellent," I agreed. "Four-thirty?"

Meade bit his lip, every inch an Army of the Potomac man. "I was
thinking more like six. The men need their rest," he countered apolo-
getically.

"If we attack at six, the Rebels will be ready and the men will get
some *eternal* rest. Why don't we say five?"

Agreed, we retired for the night, but what a terrible night it was!
Awake on my cot, I could hear the screams of the wounded in the distance. The forest floor on which they lay was a bed of dried leaves, and
the charges from their muskets had set off a series of small fires that
crept along the ground throughout the night. Those who could,
dragged themselves ahead of the flames, berserk with fear they would
be consumed. Those too badly wounded to move wailed for God's
mercy as the flames inched toward them and, when He did not answer,
called on their comrades to shoot them and end their ordeal as the
flames roasted them alive.

I managed to sleep for a short while amid the ghastly howling and
woke up at around three-thirty. I had, fortunately, already washed and
dressed and had a breakfast of sliced cucumbers when I heard a sudden chorus of artillery explosions—Lee was coming back for more.

I spent only a few seconds wondering if Meade had gotten enough rest.

Our fortunes were at first good. We repelled Lee's favorite commander, A. P. Hill, and were making steady progress when Hill was reinforced by Longstreet, whereupon they rolled us up like a blanket. We had retreated almost a mile when our fortunes again were reversed: Longstreet was shot by one of his own men, much as "Stonewall" Jackson was killed by some Confederate sharpshooter the year before in virtually the same spot. Longstreet didn't die, but his absence left the Confederates confused and leaderless in the field. By the end of the second day of fighting, we found ourselves just about where we'd been two days before.

"Grant's never been beaten," Rawlins said that night, and in a way he was correct. We were still south of the Rapidan, so in that sense we had won. Since all Lee wanted was to force men on both sides to die—to drag this thing out until Lincoln's defeat by a peace candidate in the November elections—he had won as well.

But with Longstreet shot, and so many men dead, Lee would need to reorganize. I decided to use the time marching to Spotsylvania, a small crossroads town ten miles to the southeast, on the road to Richmond. If we got there quickly, we could slip around Lee's right, get between him and Richmond, and force him to come fight us in the open.

It was a good idea—Lee had it, too. He managed to get his army to Spotsylvania before ours, whereupon his men dug trenches and built log barricades, creating a defended line several miles long. They were waiting for us when we arrived.

Grant was outsmarted by Lee! they said. To this day, they talk about what a genius Lee was, as if I'd surrendered to him. So what if Lee got to Spotsylvania before me? What else was he going to do? If I wasn't going to retreat—and everybody knew that would have been politically disastrous and therefore unlikely—I was going to move around his right flank, which meant going to Spotsylvania, simple as that. It didn't take a genius to think of getting there before me.

In fact, I would have beat him there, but Lee's advance division accidentally took a road directly downwind of the ongoing forest fires in the Wilderness. They were marching through an endless cloud of smoke, unable to find a place to rest, so they kept marching without stopping, while my divisions were moving at the speed of—well, at the

speed of the Army of the Potomac. By the time we arrived at Spotsylvania on May 10 and had prepared to attack his positions, Lee had dug
himself in and our assault met little success. On May 11 a heavy rain
set in, postponing the next assault, and I took the time to send a report
to Halleck back in Washington, so that he might communicate my intentions to Lincoln and Stanton:

I propose to fight it out on this line if it takes all summer.

If only Lee responded to my sword as readily as the public responded to my pen. People loved it. Newspapers printed it. It proved
even more popular than *No terms other than immediate and unconditional surrender can be accepted.* More plain speech from the plain-
speaking general. The carnage, apparently, was acceptable if
forthrightly explained. It was a good thing, too, for I was not yet finished delivering it.

On May 12, I ordered a new assault. Our men succeeded in racing
to the Confederate earthworks, only to find themselves pressed up,
twenty or thirty deep, against the Rebel barricades. What ensued was
as grotesque a spectacle as I have ever seen in war. Separated by only
the log structure, the battle broke down to hand-to-hand fighting. Men
stabbed each other through chinks in the logs with their bayonets. Others held their muskets over the works and shot down indiscriminately,
or shot each other through the cracks. Often, one gun's muzzle was directly up against an opponent's. Men caught up in the battle leapt over
the works to see how many of the enemy they could kill before they
themselves were killed. On either side of the works, the dead (one
prayed they *were* dead) were trodden into the ground by those who
came up behind them; entire sections of Confederate trench were
filled in with bodies and red mud. The fighting continued until almost
midnight, each side too wild with fear to back down, until those who
did not fall in battle were falling from exhaustion. Our men pulled back
and we prepared for an assault the next day, but the mercy of Providence intervened: It rained the next five days.

The incessant rain made further offensive operations impossible, so
I did again what I had set out to do—move south toward Richmond
and force Lee to come out and fight.

When I reached the North Anna River, only thirty miles from Richmond, I found that Lee had again anticipated me—he was again dug in, entrenched and well defended, before I'd even arrived.

Grant had been outsmarted again!

Meade expressed great concern. "Lee's beat us here!" he cried.

"Of course he did," I responded calmly. "It was obvious where we were going and he had a shorter route." Porter and Babcock nodded in agreement.

"What are we going to do now?" Meade moaned.

This answer was also obvious. "We're going to cross the river," I told him.

Meade looked at me, agog. "We're not going to attack him?"

"Not on his terms, no."

Meade wiped a line of sweat from his turtlelike brow. "But Lee's only a few miles away! If we cross the river here, he'll attack us while we do!"

"Really? Do you think he'll finally come out and fight?"

Meade's eyes widened, my strategy now dawning on him.

"Let's find out," I said. "We'll cross the river. If Lee decides to stay within his defenses, we'll cross unimpeded and find a place to attack his right flank. If he decides to come out to attack us, we'll fight him."

Eli Parker grinned as he contemplated our strategy. "It is as simple a matter as Newton's postulates, isn't it?"

We had no idea what the big Indian meant but were sure he was right nonetheless, and so on May 29 we crossed the North Anna River. Lee did not attack, choosing instead to fall back, and in a few days we were only ten miles east of Richmond. Sheridan went ahead with the cavalry and found a small crossroads on the way. He took the place, called for reinforcements, and on June 1 we found ourselves beyond Lee's entrenched right flank. Only ten miles of undefended road now stood between us and victory. By the next morning I planned to have twenty thousand men assembled, and Lee would be forced to leave the comfort of his trenches and race south to stop us from taking his capital. He would finally have to come out and fight at this strangely named place, Cold Harbor.

Had we attacked that next morning as I planned, things might well have gone that way. But our divisions got lost and arrived exhausted. They took the wrong road, as I was told, their artillery had wedged between trees—if you could beat the enemy with excuses, the Army of the Potomac could have won the war on its own. The troops I had expected by six that morning did not arrive until shortly before suppertime.

"I request permission for an assault tomorrow morning," Meade said upon his arrival.

"Well, if we're ever going to attack, we'd better do so tomorrow morning," I said. "Are you sure we've waited long enough to make it fair?"

"I will attack at all hazards at four-thirty," Meade replied. At least he was beginning to emphasize fighting over sleep. "I request your permission to supervise the assault directly."

Had I only known. When I agreed to let Meade lead the assault, I doomed thousands of my men. In truth, I have always regretted that the last assault at Cold Harbor was ever made under Meade. No advantage whatsoever was gained to compensate for the heavy losses he sustained. He did everything wrong one could imagine: He formed up his men in broad lines as opposed to dense columns, he did no reconnaissance before the battle, and he held no units in reserve. Instead, he threw everything he had in broad array against an entrenched enemy whose fortifications he had not studied. The enemy killed seven thousand of our men in fifteen minutes. They were harvested by a scythe of fire from the Confederate positions.

I was behind our lines, listening to the distant sounds of battle, whittling. They made a big thing out of that, my cold-bloodedness, whittling during the battle, but what else was I supposed to do? Meade was directing the attack—all I could do was wait, when a messenger burst upon our camp with a note from the front. Rawlins read it to us:

I should be very glad of your views as to the continuance of these efforts, if unsuccessful.

Rawlins looked up at me, his black eyes narrowed with suspicion. "What does Meade mean by this?" he asked.

I dropped my whittling, kicked through the pile of wood chips that had fallen about my feet, and grabbed the reins of my horse. "It means he's getting his brains beaten in," I said plainly, throwing my leg over the saddle. "Send Meade a message. Tell him that the moment it becomes certain an assault cannot succeed, he is to suspend the offensive. I'm going to the front."

Meade's camp was a few miles ahead. A quick survey of the scene and discussions with the field commanders made it clear we had been soundly beaten. I ordered the attack halted and promptly wrote a report to Halleck, telling him our losses were not severe. I lied. It was a slaughter. Even so, we had now fought a third battle without falling back. And Meade's losses, as great and as needless as they were, were not as great as those we sustained in Spotsylvania or the Wilderness.

The two armies now sat facing each other, exhausted, with hundreds of my wounded men lying between our trenches awaiting medical attention in the June heat, and even more bodies awaiting burial. Confederate sharpshooters prevented us from retrieving them.

I wrote to Lee, proposing we both suspend fire while our unarmed litter bearers collected these unfortunates. I did not get Lee's reply until the following morning, in which he agreed both sides would be allowed to collect their wounded under a flag of truce. But before I had a chance to send out stretcher bearers under a white flag that afternoon, I received another message from Lee. He demanded I first send him a message under a flag of truce requesting his permission to collect our wounded—growing fewer by the hour—*before* he would allow it: *I have directed any parties you may send out under white flags as mentioned in your letter to be turned back*, he said, meaning they would be shot.

The cur! This was Lee, the real Lee—the man who let the wounded die and the dead rot in the heat, who allowed Bedford Forrest to kill colored soldiers with their hands up, who dragged out the last days of the war, trading the lives of his men to maintain his reputation for a few more moments. To his limited military mind, my request for a truce would be an admission of defeat, and he was going to make me beg before he let me save a single man. And in the end, he knew I would, because he knew I valued human life more than he did. So I wrote back to him, straining to maintain the obsequious tone that pleased the patrician dog as much as it once did my mother, asking I be granted such a flag of truce, and waited for his reply.

He allowed that, having asked, we could retrieve our casualties that evening from eight to ten, but his note did not reach me until eleven, and so I had to ask him all over again for another grace period. He replied the next morning that we could send out parties between six and eight that next evening, June 7. Thus, after four days in the summer sun without food or water, our wounded, of which there had been hundreds, would receive aid.

Two of them were still alive—and it is me they called a butcher!

My plan to proceed against the Confederacy on simultaneous fronts was bogging down. Sherman was approaching Atlanta against Joe Johnston using the same flanking maneuvers I was employing against Lee, with little more in the way of success. Butler, who was supposed to come up the James River from the Chesapeake Bay to pressure Richmond from the rear, was so flummoxed when confronted with Beauregard's minimal opposition he stopped twenty miles from his objective. Sigel, who was supposed to clear Confederates out of the Shenandoah Valley, ended up being whipped at the town of New Market by a force headed by two hundred cadets from the Virginia Military Institute.

As these assaults failed, so Lee remained at Cold Harbor, between us and Richmond, with ample supply lines behind him. With his interior position, he was prepared to weather any and all assaults.

"The Senecas have a saying," Parker said as we considered strategy at a staff meeting. "The great spirits weep when warriors hide."

"Can you get the great spirits to drag the son of a bitch out into the open?" Rawlins asked.

"They're only so great," Parker said.

"There is no way to attack him," Meade offered, having come to this view the hard way. "We must flank him."

"There's no way to flank him," Orville Babcock said, staring at the map on the table around which we stood. "He can move faster than we can along his lines. He's proved that. He's done everything he can to keep you from Richmond."

At which point Parker looked up with a broad smile. "Which means, accepting the basic axioms of Euclid, as well as the theories of exchange found in the political economy of Ricardo, he must be giving inadequate attention to your going everywhere else!"

I stared at Parker's bronze grin for a moment before I got it. Lee was hunkered down in place to stop me from reaching Richmond—but what if I went somewhere else? "Petersburg!" I said.

"Petersburg? What about Petersburg?" asked Meade.

"Every rail connection to Richmond, with the exception of the Lynchburg line, runs through Petersburg, to the south," I said. "It's the back door to Richmond. Beauregard is defending it, but Lee has probably thinned out his force to keep us at bay here—that's exactly Parker's point! If we could get a jump on Lee, cross the Chickahominy and then the James, and come up under Petersburg from the east, it would be virtually undefended. If we take Petersburg, Lee has to come out and fight us for his rail connections or Richmond will starve!"

"But how do you break away from Lee here without his knowing it?" Horace Porter asked. "His men are no more than a few hundred yards from ours."

"We thin out our lines and roll them out under cover of night—starting at the right flank, taking them behind the line until we reach the left flank and they're all up and gone."

"And what will prevent Lee from noticing a force of a hundred and twenty thousand men moving south?"

"Sheridan and the cavalry will screen our movement with a feint around Lee's right," I said. "He'll think it's another strike at Richmond."

"But there are two rivers to cross!" Meade protested.

I smiled. "That's why they build pontoon bridges. The Chickahominy is narrow, it's no problem. How wide is the James?"

"About two thousand feet," Parker said.

"Have we ever built a pontoon bridge that long?"

"It's never been done. Maybe half that, at best," Babcock replied, this being his expertise.

"Then we'll be the first," I said, "and we'll also be the first to make an army disappear."

How I wish I could have seen Lee's face on the morning of June 13, when his patrols returned to tell him our entrenchments were empty and they had no idea where we had gone. By the time he figured it out, we had moved a hundred and twenty thousand men fifty miles in three days, built the longest pontoon bridge in the history of warfare—a two-mile road built out of rafts atop barrels, lashed together to form a span twelve feet wide—and marched a column twenty-five miles long across it. Making armies disappear and reappear was almost as easy as floating boats past the enemy and reducing forts! Our lead divisions would link up with Butler's for a full frontal assault on Petersburg. There could have been no more than ten thousand Confederate troops there, I reasoned, while we could have forty-five thousand men to face them. We would take Petersburg and, when Lee arrived to reclaim it, force him to have it out, at last. Donelson. Vicksburg. Chattanooga. Petersburg. Victory. I began to wonder if I ever actually was a clerk.

Of course, the plan failed. Baldy Smith lost his nerve in front of Petersburg while staring at miles of empty trenches. Shell-shocked from the experience of Cold Harbor, he decided to poke tentatively at the city's defenses, despite his overwhelming numerical superiority. Enough time passed to allow Lee and Beauregard to reenforce the place.

It was all Rawlins could do not to tear his hair out. "What the hell is wrong with these goddamned people? Doesn't anyone want to win this war?"

"It's possible Baldy has been a bit too tentative," Meade concluded.

"How melancholy is the spirit waning under the shadow of fear," Parker mused.

My last chance to catch Lee in the open—the most daring and imaginative maneuver of the war—ended in failure because my general was a bit too tentative. I would now have to take Petersburg *and* Richmond, together, by siege.

Reducing forts and floating flotillas and even making armies disappear may be easy, but as was Vicksburg, sieges are wearying affairs, hot in summer and cold in winter, stifling and frustrating. We would have to pour men into our trenches and extend them to the left and right, eventually reaching the railroad lines that ran into Petersburg on their way to Richmond.

But for all of this, the war was as good as over the moment the trenches around Petersburg were dug. So long as I held Lee within my trenches, Sherman would move through Georgia and Sheridan through the Shenandoah, where I had sent him to replace Sigel after the latter's defeat at the hands of VMI schoolboys. Lee was powerless to stop these movements. We would destroy the South's economic base, and sooner or later Lee would have to make the choice I had tried to force upon him from the day we crossed the Rapidan—either give up or come out and fight.

The transition to this final stage of the war was obvious to all concerned, and we were not there for more than a few days when an important ship arrived at my headquarters on the James, a spot aptly named City Point. An elaborate white, paddle-wheeled steamer, the *River Queen*, pulled up to the dock, and a surprise guest strode off.

"Mr. President!" I said, extending a hand.

Lincoln's gangly legs bounced down the ramp, his sleeves too short, his pale, hairy legs emerging from his trousers, and he pumped my hand eagerly. "*Yoo-lisses*, my friend! I see you have your mouse trapped here!"

I accompanied him back to the log house I used for my headquarters to discuss the war's progress. "I'd have rather taken Lee in the field," I said, "but he is trapped, and we will have him, sooner or later."

"Hell, I understand," Lincoln commiserated, as he sat at a table in the main room of the cabin. "I don't see how Lee is doing us any harm, from a war standpoint. Reminds me of the story of the Barber of Sangamon County. Did I ever tell you that one?"

I shook my head slightly and hoped I looked more interested than I was.

"Well, this fellow had four days' beard on his face, and he was going to take a girl to a ball, so that beard had to come off. The barber began by lathering his face, and then made a drive at the man's countenance as if he had practiced mowing in a stubble field. The man's cheeks were so hollow that the barber couldn't get down into the valleys with his razor. It occurred to him to stick his fingers in the man's mouth and press out the cheeks. It worked some, but then he cut through the cheek and into his own finger. He yanked his finger out of the man's mouth and yelled, 'You lantern-jawed cuss, you've made me cut my finger!' Now, I figure Lee's thinking he might be giving you the razor, but in the end he's going to cut his own finger!"

I nodded politely while considering the relationship between his story and the business at hand. It was most prudent simply to agree. "Well, yes, it is my intention that he do so," I said.

Lincoln's smile suddenly waned and was supplanted by a look of concern. "Yes, but the problem is it's almost July. Your buddy Sherman is stuck outside of Atlanta just the same as you are here, and those other apples, like Sigel and Banks, did no better. The people up North are getting uncomfortable. Might we actually win something before the people exercise their right to remove me this fall?"

I sighed. "I can't make you any promises, Mr. President."

Lincoln shook his sizable head. "Well, this isn't good business at all, Grant. The folks back home are thinking about how many boys we've lost and that this is all we have to show for it. You can imagine how I feel about having to go back and tell them there's going to be another draft. I might not have that many *Providences* and *Forefathers* left."

"I've done my best, Mr. President," I said, sharing his frustration. "As to whether we should have secured a more favorable result—"

Lincoln raised his hand to silence me. "Now now, Grant, all I'm telling you here is that unless we make some big progress by Election Day, I'm going to be out on my lanky rear end and you're going to be right behind my behind, if you catch my drift."

I did, but in the weeks ahead, the situation went from bad to worse. First, there was the crater incident. Burnside had some Pennsylvania coal miners under his command who convinced him to dig a tunnel under the Confederate fortifications, load it with powder, and blow it up. He would then dispatch a battalion of Negro troops he'd trained for this particular action, but Meade objected, worried we would appear to regard Negro troops as expendable, getting us into trouble with the abolitionists.

"But won't the abolitionists object if we *don't* use Negroes in battle?" I asked.

Meade shrugged. "They're abolitionists," he said. "They object to everything."

In the end I made the mistake of listening to Meade again. I gave him permission to change Burnside's plan and substitute a white division. When the first explosion occurred early one July morning, creating a two-hundred-foot crater, the replacements were so unprepared that they panicked and ran. Once they were reassembled and moved forward, they climbed into the crater, but they had neglected to bring ladders or any other means to assist them in climbing out. The Negro troops who had trained for the mission were now dispatched to bail their replacements out. By this time, though, the Confederates had advanced to the crater's rim, where they found shooting down at the men trapped inside easy work. Our men surrendered: The white men were taken prisoner, the Negroes were killed without a word of complaint from Lee, the flower of chivalry.

At least the incident gave me an excuse to get rid of Burnside. I gave his command to Ord.

Things were not looking up for Sherman, either, until good fortune in the form of Jeff Davis intervened. Davis had never liked Joe Johnston, and after watching Johnston back up toward Atlanta, he decided to replace him with a young hothead named John Bell Hood. Hood, eager to please his boss, decided to come out and fight Sherman. It was a colossal mistake. By September 1, Sherman had him beaten, and he entered Atlanta, letting loose the havoc that made him the great success he is today.

The one overpowering loss of the Atlanta campaign was McPherson, who had served both Sherman and me so ably. He was leading a charge against the enemy when he came up against a row of Confederate pickets. He stopped and reared his horse, tipped his hat to them, whirled, and sped away. He was shot in the back.

But Atlanta was now ours, and Sherman's conquest filled the North with euphoria. Lincoln was reelected with acclaim, losing only three states to his opponent, McClellan, the Little Napoleon, who ran on the Democratic platform of peace between the "two nations." But there weren't two nations: There was only one nation at war with itself, the war I was trying to win.

With Lincoln reelected, it was time to resolve the matter. Sheridan was told to put the torch to the Shenandoah Valley so there could be no new planting season. On November 15, Sherman burned Atlanta and began his march to the sea. I continued to pepper Lee with assaults along his lines as we extended them in both directions, knowing that sooner or later his ranks would get too thin. Thomas, who was now serving under Sherman, cleaned up John Bell Hood after Sherman departed for the coast, and Sherman himself showed up in Savannah just before Christmas, after taking his sixty-five thousand men four hundred miles through Georgia, destroying everything in their path. He could now proceed up through the Carolinas virtually unopposed and, if it came to that, join me in southern Virginia to finish Lee. In fact, the situation began to look so promising I sent for Mrs. Grant and the children to come and live in the small cabin I used for a residence at City Point.

"This?" Mrs. Grant asked when they arrived. "It's smaller than that awful shack you built for us back in Missouri!"

"I thought you liked Hardscrabble," I said, feeling the slight. "I built it with my own two hands."

"I was humoring you," she said, running a finger along a dusty windowsill. "Isn't there a plantation somewhere you could commandeer? Say what you will about slavery, Ulys, you've got to love the houses."

"I'm afraid I'm too busy leading the nation's armies to find you a new house right now."

"I suppose," she said, disappointed. "But could you make this quick?"

She and Lincoln were both due to be pleased. By March, we were in control of the railroad lines I had been after since the day we arrived at Petersburg. Sheridan, meanwhile, had epic success in terrorizing the western part of the state, and the end suddenly seemed in sight.

"You should invite the Lincolns down here," Mrs. Grant said one evening. "If the war's really about to end, he'd want to be here. And we should probably start thinking about finding you some work for after the war," she said fondly, one eye gazing at me lovingly and the other surveying our cabin. "Besides," she said playfully, "I'd like to meet Mrs. Lincoln."

That was not a meeting I was looking forward to, but there was no way out of inviting them both. They arrived on March 24, and Mrs. Grant and I led a delegation to welcome them. We found them aboard the *River Queen*, the steamer that had brought them and that would serve as their home while they were here.

"Grant!" the President shouted when we were escorted onto the boat. "I hear that, as the preacher said after reading Revelation, the end is nigh!"

"So I believe, Mr. President," I reported with satisfaction. "And good day to you, Mrs. Lincoln," I said, nodding at her politely as she broke into a wide smile.

"Why, General Grant!" she cooed. "I must think back to the last time we met to recall when I've had such a pleasure!"

I touched the rim of my hat and nodded in her direction, then quickly turned back to the President. "Allow me to present to you Mrs. Grant," I said.

"And such a charmer, too!" Lincoln said, bowing and smiling like a bearded satyr.

"Oh, the pleasure is mine," Mrs. Grant said, and turned to Mrs. Lincoln. "And I'm pleased to meet you, too, Mrs. Lincoln," she said, offering a gloved hand.

Mrs. Lincoln refused it. "Where I come from, a gentlewoman awaits a proper introduction," she said snippily.

"My apologies," Mrs. Grant sniffed. "Where I come from, a gentlewoman minds her tongue when being introduced."

"Now, now," Lincoln said. "Mary, I bet Mrs. Grant would love to hear about our trip down here! Don't you think so?"

"I was hoping General Grant would show me around his *headquarters*," she replied, her smile almost a leer.

"I'm sure he'd love to," Lincoln said, oblivious to her agenda, "but I need to confer with the general right now. Besides, I'm sure Mrs. Grant could discuss the war with you with a woman's perspective in mind, and a charming one at that."

"Where I come from," Mrs. Lincoln said, her narrowed eyes fixed intently on Mrs. Grant, "a woman doesn't mix in her husband's affairs."

"Where I come from," Mrs. Grant replied, "a husband doesn't have affairs."

Lincoln laughed and slapped his thigh. "I'll be damned if you're not two of a kind!" he exclaimed. "Now, go on along like the two little angels you are so I can talk to my general here," he said, and, with a broad smile, shooed the two women out the door.

The President and I proceeded to discuss the situation, and I shared with him my view that Lee was now stretched so thin that pressing him all along his line would bring a breakthrough. We agreed on this course of action and then Lincoln retired for a nap, so I returned to my headquarters, where Mrs. Grant awaited me.

"The little hussy!" she cried, dispensing with any other greeting, and launched into a recitation of the day's events. She and Mrs. Lincoln had been brought into a small stateroom on the steamer, where Mrs. Lincoln extended a welcoming hand into the room. Mrs. Grant proceeded to make herself comfortable on a small sofa in the center of the room, only to see Mrs. Lincoln glowering down at her—as wife of the President, she was used to being seated first in such situations, and she favored the same settee. Mrs. Grant reported she jumped up immediately and apologized, whereupon Mrs. Lincoln sat on the sofa and, with a satisfied smile, beckoned Mrs. Grant to sit down beside her.

"Well, I don't have to tell you, Ulys, that woman's rear end is even wider than mine," she snapped. "There we were, snuggled up against each other, each stone silent, too close to look at each other or to have a conversation, until I got up and took a chair."

The next day was no better.

"Babcock ordered a carriage so we could ride out to review Sheridan's troops," Mrs. Grant told me at the end of another harrowing day, "and all that fat little shrew could say was 'Can't we go any faster?' But when they spurred the team, the mud and bumps were so numerous we were thrown into the roof, and she spent the rest of the trip telling Babcock she had a mind to have him shot."

The two women soon refused to be in the same room. The President's visit would have degenerated into a disaster were it not for the arrival of Sherman, whom I had summoned to confer with us. I was therefore particularly glad to see him when he pulled into City Point the next day.

"Grant, you son of a bitch!" Sherman shouted, grasping my hand eagerly and grinning from ear to ear. "Sell any firewood lately?"

"Sherman, you dog." I laughed. "Have the doctors cured your lunacy yet?"

"Ha!" he brayed, and slapped me solidly on the back. He pulled up his britches and looked around. "You're the mayor of a city here, Grant! You always took the easy jobs!"

"Me? Come now, Sherman. You've had six months' vacation touring the countryside!"

"Let me tell you about those fucking swamps in Carolina, Grant. They're like the preacher's sermon—they're not very deep, but they go on without end!" He cackled as he scratched a few days' stubble on his chin.

"All of those swamps laid end to end wouldn't fill the trench I've dug around Bobby Lee, Sherman."

"You know your problem, Grant? Not only are you a drunk, you're a braggart, too."

I reached into my pocket for a pair of cigars. "Well, Sherman, you hateful deflowerer of Southern womanhood, I'd love to sit here and listen to you describe your exploits, but the President of the United States is waiting!" I responded.

Sherman took the cigar I offered him. "Thank you, Grant," he said.

"I was worried I'd have to smoke my own!" We lit up and went off to meet Lincoln on the *River Queen*.

I introduced Lincoln to Sherman—Admiral Porter, as commander of the navy, joined us as well—and we were getting down to business when a messenger arrived. Lee had attempted to break through our lines on my right but had been repulsed.

"This is what we've been waiting for," I told Lincoln. "If Lee has come out to attack, he is out of options. It means the end is at hand. We shall press them at all points along the line at once."

"Hallelujah!" Lincoln intoned. "What will happen now?"

"Lee will try to head south," I explained. "Jeff Davis has given Johnston his army back—or at least what Hood left of it—and Lee will try to link up with them."

"Shouldn't you be back with your men, Sherman?"

"My men will be fine, Mr. President," Sherman replied. "In fact, let Lee and Johnston link up—Grant will be right behind them and we'll crush the fucking life out of them," he hissed, whereupon his fingers raced to his lips and his dark eyes opened wide at his faux pas.

Lincoln turned to Sherman, his back arched and eyebrows raised—had Sherman finally gone too far? A long moment of silence ensued as Lincoln moved his hand to a dignified position on his lapel. He regarded the two of us sternly, cleared his throat, and finally spoke. "Well, just see that you fucking do!"

"Done," Sherman said, and the two of them broke out into laughter. When the cackling had subsided, I outlined the rest of my plan. I would keep Meade back at City Point—now that we were closing in, I wanted men who would crush the enemy without hesitation, and Meade was not one of them. Instead, Ord would take the Army of the Potomac out into the field and drive Lee west. Sheridan's cavalry would ride south of Lee and block his movement in that direction until Ord could catch up to him.

"Okay, then," Lincoln said, nodding eagerly. "Just let me tell you one last thing. Sherman, Grant here will tell you that I am awfully fond of rasslin'. And back when I was rasslin' in Springfield, we used to have a saying—*let 'em up easy*. Once you've whipped your man, you have to *let 'em up easy*. That's what we've got to do now. Once they say they're beat, it's over. Once they give up, we're all part of one country—no slavery for them, no recriminations for us. Like I said at the inauguration—*malice toward none, charity to all.* Or whatever it was. Does everybody hear me?"

Sherman and I endorsed Lincoln's view without reservation. This pleased Lincoln greatly and he called an end to our discussion. By the end of that day, both he and Sherman had left, leaving me to prosecute the end of the war.

Pressed along his lines, Lee's army was starving and plagued with desertions. On April 2, 1865, Lee predictably took off, abandoning Petersburg and then Richmond and swinging below the two cities to head south. Jeff Davis was summoned from church and told he had but hours to escape our advancing troops. He left town disguised in a dress.

Lee's southern path was blocked, so he went west, as I had imagined, dividing up his forces and having them converge about twenty miles west of Petersburg on April 5, still looking for a route south. Sheridan, however, came up below him and forced him to keep moving west. He reached the town of Farmville on April 7, hoping to find a supply train carrying fresh rations, but found Sheridan instead, with Ord right behind.

I arrived in Farmville that afternoon and wrote to Lee, pointing out the hopelessness of further resistance. Lee ignored me and pushed on to Appomattox on April 8. This time he not only found Sheridan, but Sheridan had reached Lee's supply train first. Ord's infantry came up behind him, and he was boxed in. He wrote to me, saying he did not intend to propose the surrender of the Army of Virginia but merely wanted to ask what terms might be available and how we might achieve the "restoration of peace."

The flower of chivalry, the knight of the South, was intent on dragging it out. I went to bed and awoke very early, the victim of a pounding headache. I poured a cup of coffee and wrote back to Lee, telling him surrender was the only topic I wished to discuss and I hoped we could discuss it soon. I then saddled up and led my staff—Rawlins, Babcock, and Eli Parker among them—toward Sheridan's position, when a messenger appeared, riding toward me with great enthusiasm and waving a note from Lee.

I now ask an interview in accordance with the offer contained in your letter of yesterday for the purpose of surrender.

I noticed my headache had disappeared and I dismounted. I wrote Lee a note telling him to meet me up ahead along this same road, and gave the note to Babcock, instructing him to find Lee and bring him there. He galloped off. I rode on for a while, toward the front line, when I saw a group of officers dismounted at the next crest and made out the figures of Sheridan and Ord among them. Rawlins, Parker, and I approached them.

"Lee's waiting for you at a farmhouse about half a mile up the road," Ord said. "Babcock's staying with him."

"He found him under an apple tree," Sheridan noted.

I nodded. Rawlins whispered a muted *"Son of a bitch."*

"The time has come to end this thing," I said, my horse whinnying beneath me. "We're all going to get some rest." The war was going to end! I looked down at Sheridan and Ord as I entertained the thought. It was a magnificent spring day, the kind that never materialized when I needed one: I thought of the torrents in Panama, the sleet at Donelson, the thunder and lightning after the first day at Shiloh, the blazing heat in which the wounded baked at Cold Harbor. Each time I supplicated Fate for fair weather I was denied it; now I realized the beautiful weather was being saved for peace. For an instant I wanted to dispense with ceremony—send Ord or Sheridan to meet Lee and simply go home to play with the children.

We all stood there for a moment, quiet, and then it was time for it to end. "Well, Bobby Lee's waiting for us, isn't he?" I said, to smiles and nods from all. "Let's be off," I added, but then stopped. "No, first I have to attend to one detail."

I had been in the saddle and without a change of clothes for two days, and was wearing my favorite garment—a private's standard undershirt. It was my habit to pin my three stars to the shoulder: I had hardly worn anything else since the day we crossed the Rapidan.

I was considering this attire and the likely sartorial splendor we would see from Lee when I noticed a puddle of mud along the side of the road. I dismounted and walked over to it and regarded it for a moment. *Excuse me, but aren't we making a mistake?* Lee had asked me that Christmas in 1846, and I'd spent Christmas alone because my uniform had not met his approval.

The mud was deep and wet and I smiled broadly as I bent my knees and leapt into the center of it with as much energy as I could muster.

The muck flew everywhere, over my boots, my pants, my shirt, in glorious blobs and spurts. I looked down and saw my splattered uniform, mottled everywhere with the thick brown slop, and smiled. "There," I said, turning to my colleagues and extending my arms to give them a view.

Sheridan laughed as he looked at me. "I thought we were done giving offense."

"I'm just settling an old account," I said. "I've been waiting for this longer than you know." With that, we mounted and started toward the farmhouse where Babcock had taken Lee to surrender.

I approached the place. It was a handsome two-story brick affair with a sizable porch. A big gray horse was tied up outside, as big as York—it was Traveller, Lee's favorite mount. He looked like a good one—I was considering asking Lee to let me ride him when I was distracted by a civilian fellow approaching us—a stout, balding man wearing glasses and an angry expression.

"Are you Grant? Are you General Grant?" he demanded. "I'm Wilmer McLean, sir, and this is my house!"

"I'm pleased, Mr. McLean," I replied, reaching down from the saddle and offering him my hand. "You're fortunate to have so dramatic a moment occur in your home."

"The hell with that, Grant!" McLean snapped. "I lived back in Manassas in '61 and that's what Beauregard said when he took my house there to be his headquarters. 'Oh, think of the glory when they learn your house was my headquarters when we whipped them Yankees,' he told me. Well, I ended up with a shell coming through my parlor and everybody took all my furniture for souvenirs! And a year later, at Second Manassas, they were all back. 'Say, why don't we go back to old man McLean's place?' they all said, like it was a family get-together! They stripped the place all over again! So I moved out here to get away from the war, and now look what's happened!"

"Nobody's going to fire a shell through your parlor this time," I assured him.

"Yes, but what about the furniture? I don't want you or any of your men taking any of it! And I've said the same to Lee!"

I looked about the ranks of my delegation. "Well, if Lee agrees not to take the furniture, we'd be unmannerly to do any different," I said. "Does everybody agree not to take this fellow's furniture?" There was some nodding and a suppressed smile from Sheridan. "There you have it, Mr. McLean. May we end the war now?"

He twisted his lips into a dubious frown. "I suppose so. But remember—nobody leaves with anything that's not theirs! Now be quick about it. And clean some of that damn mud off your boots before you enter my parlor!" he added, then stood aside as we passed.

I dismounted in front of McLean's home, walked up the seven steps to the porch, regarded with satisfaction the splotches of mud over my pants, and went inside. The front room was not deep, but wide. Babcock was standing by the door, and sitting on a sofa was Lee, with but one attendant in the room with him—his command was either destroyed or dispersed, and he sat there starkly alone. "General Lee," I said pleasantly, extending a hand.

"General Grant," he said, rising to reply.

I looked him over. I remembered him from Mexico, of course, but that was a younger man. He was still a good six feet or so, but age and defeat had given him a mournful bearing; his dark eyes, fierce and piercing then, were now only sad. He was wearing a uniform and sash so fresh and well pressed I wondered where they had been throughout the war. His hair was perfectly groomed and his beard trimmed. At his side hung a beautiful bejeweled sword. He wore new boots trimmed with red silk and had placed a pair of gray buckskin gloves on the table before him.

"I apologize for my appearance," I said, smiling as I sat down opposite him, "but I have been in the field and the amenities are often lacking, as I'm sure you well understand. Sometimes a fellow just can't find a regulation uniform, you know?" I took out a fresh cigar and lit it, tossing the spent match into the fireplace and putting the first puffs of smoke into the air. "Fortunately," I added, "there are no women present."

His nose wrinkled in the smoke. "I have been in the field as well," he said humorlessly, his hands folded in his lap.

"I'm sure," I replied, "but I have been able to leave my trunk behind these last several days, secure in the knowledge it would be there when I came to reclaim it." He said nothing, but watched distractedly as my muddy boot swung back and forth from a crossed leg. "That's a lovely sword," I commented.

"It was given to me by supporters in England," he said, then sighed. His hands went to its buckle. "Will you want it?" he asked resignedly.

"Oh, no, no," I answered, waving my hand through the smoke accumulating around me. "I have a sword, thanks."

There was another moment of silence. He looked down at the floor.

"Well, it is a pleasure to see you again," I said, unwilling to let the small talk die. "We met in Mexico, you know."

"Yes," he said, "I am told by Longstreet. Unfortunately, I do not seem to remember you."

"I'm not really that memorable," I said with a modest smile. "Besides, I was just a quartermaster. You sometimes came to me for maps."

"Maps?" Lee asked. "There were all manner of maps back then."

"I remember you consulted this one before going into the wilderness at Cerro Gordo."

Lee turned when he heard that, then paused and looked at me, his dark eyes wide. "No," he said slowly, "I don't recall." He averted his gaze from mine so as not to be caught in a lie.

"We were all very concerned for your safety that day."

"It was in the line of duty," he said. He looked delightfully uncomfortable.

"Of course, you were legendary when I was a student at West Point," I continued. "Not a single demerit!" Lee nodded, but began to show his frustration as I babbled on. "And it was my pleasure to deliver a keg of port to you on Christmas Day, back in '46." I smiled, then looked down at my pants and ceremoniously brushed some caked dirt off them.

Lee watched with revulsion as the dirt skittered on the floor, then finally spoke. "Yes, well, I regret that I can't place you—"

"Well, here I am!" I chirped.

"Yes, here we are," he said, sighing again. "Now perhaps we could discuss the business at hand."

"The business?" I asked.

"The *surrender*," he said testily.

"Oh, *the surrender*," I repeated. "Yes, I suppose we should. If you don't mind, I have a number of my officers outside who would desire to be present, if you've no objections."

"No, none." He sighed and rose from his chair. I nodded to Babcock, who opened the door and in they filed, like unwanted family for holiday dinner—Sheridan, Ord, Rawlins, Parker, and the rest. Each greeted Lee as he entered.

"My pleasure, General," Ord said, bowing slightly in response to Lee's gaze.

"Howdy, General," Sheridan said, ambling up to Lee and winking at him with a smirk.

"So you're Lee," Rawlins said, glowering at him despite my disapproving look.

"General Lee, my poor modern Hector, now cruelly dragged as Achilles did Priam's son thrice around Ilium, I commend you for your noble grace on this momentous day!" Parker said.

Lee turned to me. "Who's the nigger?" he asked.

"I am Eli Parker, sir," Parker told him, "or *Do-no-ho-geh-weh*, Keeper of the Western Door of the Long House of the Iroquois."

Lee arched his eyebrows. "Well, I suppose it's good that a real American be here today," he said.

Parker smiled at him broadly. "We're all real Americans now, aren't we?"

I smiled as Parker's point penetrated Lee, who nodded at the chief and then turned to me. "I suppose, General Grant, that the object of our present meeting is fully understood. I have asked to see you to ascertain under what terms you would receive the surrender of my army," he said, cold and brittle.

We all sat down and got down to business. "They are the terms I have stated in my letter," I said, leaning back and stretching out my splattered legs—the mud was falling off in satisfying clumps. "The officers and men surrendered to be paroled and disqualified from taking up arms until properly exchanged, and all arms, ammunitions, and supplies to be delivered up as captured property." My terms were generous ones, free of reprisals.

Lee nodded. "Those are the conditions I expected." A simple thank you might have been appropriate, I thought, as he continued. "I suggest that you commit to writing the terms you have proposed, so that they may be formally acted upon."

"Very well," I said, "I'll write them out." I billowed some cigar smoke into the air, contemplated it, and began to write as I thought of Lincoln—*let 'em up easy*, he had urged. So I wrote that Lee's men would be allowed to take their sidearms and horses back to their homes. After all, the best place for them to go was back to their farms, and as quickly as possible. And I then wrote the final line, the one that spared Lee's life: *Each officer and man will be allowed to return to his home, not to be disturbed by the United States authorities so long as they observe their paroles and the laws in force where they reside*. So long as Lee lived within the law and took up no further arms against his nation again, no one could hang him. After all, if I was now going to bask in the glory of having saved the nation, I needed a live trophy to parade around, didn't I? He'd do me no good as a corpse!

Lee read the draft and smiled as thankful a smile as his sense of superiority would allow. "This will have a very happy effect upon my army," he said.

"Could you make good use of rations?" I asked.

Lee would have begged for food for his men if he was man enough. "We've been on half rations for some while and have nothing now on hand," he confessed.

I nodded. "Would twenty-five thousand rations suffice for now?" Sheridan suppressed a laugh as he heard this—the rations I offered were the ones he had seized from Lee's supply train only the day before, and insofar as we had more than enough to eat, it seemed a waste not to turn them over.

"That will be a great relief, I assure you," he said, avoiding *thank you* once again.

At this point we seemed to be done, and the weight of the moment suddenly struck me—*it was over*. I had defeated Lee. *I would lead great masses of men in the cause of their human redemption*. I had won the war. Parker, who had been transcribing our agreements, gave each of us a copy of the surrender, and Lee put his in his breast pocket and rose. We shook hands, Lee nodded to the assembled officers, and he and his solitary aide walked out onto the porch, where he signaled for Traveller to be brought to him.

I watched him strike the palm of his left hand with his right fist a few times as he stared off into the distance, then he mounted and rode off slowly. For an instant, I had to fight the urge to call him back. I *needed* Lee—what was a life without adversaries? Who was I without Lee? Whom would I fight? What would I do now? *Come back!*

I was pulled from my reverie by the cheers that had begun to spread through the room, whereupon Mr. McLean flew up the porch steps and into the parlor, followed by the officers who had been peering through the windows outside to watch the momentous event.

McLean jumped onto a chair. "All right," he shouted to all assembled, his arms out in the air, "who wants what?"

There was an immediate stampede, a flurry of bodies and arms and fists full of cash and coin. The parlor where the world had changed only a few seconds before now looked like a trader's market, with furniture, fixtures, paintings, bric-a-brac, and every other possible object coming off the wall or the shelf or the floor. McLean whirled in every direction, quoting prices and haggling like an Arab in a bazaar. Ord coughed up forty bucks for the table at which Lee sat. Another general went ten bucks for the candlesticks on the mantel, another the same price for the inkstands. The chairs on which we sat went for a good piece of change, and a child's doll found in a corner of the room was bought by one of Sheridan's staff. Sheridan himself parted with twenty dollars in gold for the chair on which I sat and then went outside to turn it over to his protégé, the fellow he had molded in his own image throughout the war—George Armstrong Custer. Custer's widow no doubt has it today.

I took Lee's battle flag as my own prize—I later that day ripped it in half and gave the pieces to Orville Babcock and Horace Porter—and started back to headquarters, hoping for a bath. It was only when someone reminded me of the need to do so that I sat down on a rock by the side of the road and wrote to Stanton.

General Lee surrendered the Army of Northern Virginia this afternoon on terms proposed by myself.

The cause of human redemption had been won.

The willingness of the men on both sides to sit down with the enemy they'd vowed to kill the day before, as if they were long-lost brothers, was remarkable. This was particularly true among the officers, many of whom had been classmates or comrades earlier in life, particularly under Taylor and Scott. The underlying feeling of brotherhood Lincoln was relying on to produce an amicable reconciliation was at work, and there was no better example of it than the hulking silhouette that led the small delegation to my tent the next afternoon.

"Cousin Longstreet!" I cried. "Street, you ape, how the devil are you?" I said as I rose and clapped him on the arms.

"Sam!" he exclaimed, and grabbed me in a bearlike embrace and proceeded to bawl. "Sam, thank you for sparing all our lives! I can't believe we've gone through this!" He began to sob like a child. "I was wrong about you, Sam. I was wrong about you all these years."

I patted him on the back. "We don't have to dwell on that. It's behind us now," I said.

He sniffled and snorted and detached himself from me. "May God have pity on us all, Sam, for what we've done," he said, shaking his head.

"Enough of that," I told him. "Our souls deserve a rest before they're so thoroughly searched. Besides," I said, peering around Longstreet's massive frame, "I see you've brought company with you!" It was Wilcox and Pratte, the two fellows from the Jefferson Barracks who joined Longstreet as groomsmen at my wedding to Mrs. Grant, and with whom we played brag at the Planters House. "Well, it's only fair I see you gents surrender, since you saw me surrender to Mrs. Grant that day back in St. Louis."

Longstreet led us all in a laugh, and when he did, I knew the madness had finally passed.

I made my way to Washington with Mrs. Grant and the children on April 13—my interest now was in shutting down the war machine that feathered the nests of the contractors and other parasites who lived off it, including Orvil and Jesse Grant (but not Simpson, who died during the war). Mrs. Grant was also eager to depart City Point and visit our children, whom we had put in a school near Philadelphia.

I went to see Lincoln that Friday, April 14, 1865. He was in fine spirits.

"Grant," he exclaimed, rising from his desk as I entered his office. "You're the most popular fellow in the whole USA right now, Washington and Scott rolled up into one! Hell, you're a regular Julius Caesar, *Yoo-lisses*!" He smiled.

"I appreciate your flattery, as ever, Mr. President."

He waved his hands in front of me and directed me to a chair as he came around his desk. "Abe, please."

"My friends call me Sam," I said, smiling.

"Good! Now, listen up—we won the war, thanks to you, Sam, and now we have to win the peace. We got four million Freedmen on our hands, and it's going to be a god-awful mess! If I was one of these coloreds, first I'd shoot my old master, then I'd go roaming, looking for something to eat. And don't you think all these sanctimonious preachers up North, the abolitionists, are going to give them so much as the time of day! I know that type—they're all full of God's will, but don't do anything about cleanin' up God's *swill*, if you know what I mean," he said with a wink and a smile. He paused for a moment and then changed the subject. "Tell me about your buddy Sherman."

I smiled and nodded. "He's got Joe Johnston cornered in Carolina. I can't imagine it will go beyond the end of this month."

Lincoln leaned forward and spoke in a low, confidential tone. "Well, it won't be long at all, Sam, my friend," he said. "I know that because I had my *special dream* last night." His eyes were bright and he spoke as if he were sharing with me the most wonderful secret. "I get this dream regular, see? I'm not a spiritualist, but I know it's a dream fraught with meaning. I'm on an indescribable vessel, a singular curious-looking one, and I'm heading rapidly toward some distant shore," he said, extending his right hand toward an unseen horizon and losing himself in silence.

I regarded him curiously. "What does it mean?" I asked.

He turned to me with a perfectly tranquil, if not serene, expression, his homely features resting on his face with perfect grace. "I call it my *progress dream*," he said. "It means I'm moving on, going to where I'm supposed to go. I had this dream before Antietam, and then before Vicksburg, which is how I knew I was supposed to trust you. And now it means that Sherman's about to have himself a big battle, I suppose, and we can move on, go on to where we're all supposed to go." He smiled at me. "And I think I know where I'm going next," he said.

"Where is that?" I asked, curious.

"Well, first to a Cabinet meeting, and then to the theater tonight," he said with a laugh. "In fact, I would appreciate it most heartily if you and Mrs. Grant would join Mrs. Lincoln and me. They're playing *Our American Cousin*. I hear it's a pip! What do you say?"

"I'll ask Mrs. Grant," I said, thinking about spending an evening with Mrs. Lincoln and confident Mrs. Grant would say no.

"No," Mrs. Grant said when I saw her later that afternoon at our hotel. "I'd rather choke than sit in a theater box with that slatternly witch."

"I'm a little tired myself," I agreed. "We can skip it."

"And besides, I want us to get to Philadelphia and see the children."

"Let me send a message to the White House and tie up some loose ends, and I'll meet you at the station this evening," I suggested.

I met Mrs. Grant there and we boarded the private car that awaited us. We arrived in Philadelphia about midnight and were about to have a late supper at our hotel when a messenger entered with a telegram:

The president was assassinated at Ford's Theater at 10:30 tonight and cannot live.

Mrs. Grant cried. I went into a corner of the room to compose myself and recalled something else the President had told me only that afternoon.

"Listen here, Grant," Lincoln had said, his yokel smile now beaming only in my memory, "you stick with me and you can have my job when I move along in '68. It's like the carpenter said to his son," Lincoln said, grinning with unbridled satisfaction. "He said, 'Boy, one day this awl will be yers.'" He laughed, slapping his bony thigh with delight. "Hell, Grant. You're young and it's not too long to wait for this *awl*."

I remembered that I smiled politely. "I'm no politician, Mr. President. You can have your job and let me have mine."

"Sure, sure, that's what you say now," Lincoln said, chuckling. "But once those President grubs start burrowing in, they can't be driven out."

He was right, of course, the way he was right about everything. I thought of him, and his common manner and endless stream of homilies were suddenly displaced by my recognition of the wisdom and steadfastness that lay beneath them. I had been too distracted by his knobby gait, tinny voice, and backwoods roots to realize that he was the one man I truly looked up to. But there would be no more wisdom now. There would only be the silent vacuum he left behind. I folded the telegram in my fingers and lowered myself onto the sofa next to Mrs. Grant, and together we sat, stunned. As I reflected upon it, I would have spared his one life before I would have spared the lives of the hundreds of thousands who died to achieve the result he championed.

I returned to Washington in a private railcar, unable to sleep. Rawlins met me at Union Station and directed me to a small carriage waiting in a cobblestoned side alley. It was the middle of the night, but the city was awake, gripped by a nervous panic. Soldiers patrolled the streets. Occasional clumps of citizens roamed past, aspiring vigilantes searching for targets. "It was the South!" I heard many of them cry. "The Southerners did it!" A well-dressed gentleman stumbled past, bleary-eyed and disheveled. "Kill the Rebel scum!" he shouted. "Avenge Old Abe!" From windows and doorways came the wails of the anguished.

Rawlins and I made our way through the streets amid the anger and sorrow. "There is a wound here that must be healed," he said.

"If you expect me to heal it, you are mistaken," I said. "There is a new President now, and the job falls to him."

"Do you really think Andy Johnson is up to it?" Rawlins asked disdainfully. "Just because Lincoln made him Vice President in a moment of weakness? He's a drunken tailor!"

"You prefer a drunken clerk?"

"You know my meaning," Rawlins said. "Watch what happens at the funeral. All eyes will be on you. You are the only hero the nation has left."

The funeral was held in the East Room of the White House. Lincoln's coffin sat at the north end of the room, the flag draped over it, black bunting bordering it. Mrs. Lincoln had me stand at the catafalque's head, Johnson at its feet, facing each other. I knew Johnson, of course, going back to his time as military governor of Tennessee, but this was the first time I'd taken a good look at him. He seemed bitter and mean-spirited, and given his reputation as a drinker, I wondered if he had been drinking that day, just as so many there that day no doubt wondered about me. The eulogies flowed and the anguish in the room was overwhelming. Poor Lincoln, I thought. His dream did foretell the future, but not the way he thought.

And so I stood there, mourning Lincoln, in the stately East Room of the White House, where I had first met him, and cried, not just for him, but for me. I could no longer hide behind Lincoln's grand countenance and tell myself my destiny was limited to the field of battle. The real meaning of Mescalito's prophecy gripped me as I looked across Lincoln's coffin and watched Andy Johnson standing opposite me. I led great masses of men, but I was not done leading yet. I now had to confront the greater meaning of my destiny—like it or not, I would now no longer lead an army, but a nation. Just as at Donelson, Vicksburg, or Richmond, my time would come, I realized.

The old goat! I looked down at his coffin and was overwhelmed with a sadness. *Someday this awl will be yers.* He knew it even then. How I would miss him!

I looked over to the first row of mourners, to Mrs. Lincoln, her swollen, pugnacious face now ashen, her eyes reddened with tears. A hollow, blank gaze came over her as the eulogists droned on. I felt pity for her, imagining the grief and pain one must experience when one loses a loved one in so public a way and place and is not allowed the comfort of solitude in which to mourn. She now looked oddly beatified, as if in her grief and public pain she had acquired a kind of grace, or that the promise of grace lay ahead of her if her heart would only prove strong enough to bear this awful burden. I regarded her, flush with sympathy and compassion, when her eyes darted up and she saw me staring at her. Our gazes met and we shared for a moment an understanding of what had transpired and the way it would change not only her life and my own, but the course of history, forever.

Or so I thought until she winked at me.

CHAPTER XII

PRESIDENT ANDY JOHNSON—THE ENFRANCHISEMENT OF THE NEGRO— THE TENURE OF OFFICE ACT—THE COLONEL IN THE WHITE HOUSE—THE GOLD RING— BLACK FRIDAY

S PRING HAS RETURNED to the Adirondacks. The world I'll soon depart is being reborn all around me. We were living in the house Vanderbilt bought for me after my presidency, on Sixty-sixth Street in Manhattan. But a few weeks ago, as the weather got warmer, we moved to this cottage atop a mountain outside Saratoga. A developer is letting us use the place for as long as we like. He's hoping, I'm sure, I'll die here and his property will be transformed into a shrine and become that much more valuable for it.

I'll hold up my end of the deal, I'm sure of that.

With the better weather come the crowds—the tourists, the curious, the worshipers and medal hawkers. Each member of the deathwatch hopes to catch a glimpse of the old man before he departs. I sit out on the porch in the mornings if I can muster the strength, jotting down notes as I am now or reading the newspaper. A proper family, then a cluster of veterans in faded uniforms, then a gaggle of prayer jockeys, each of them files by in turn and regards me as I once regarded myself—*lo, the great man sits*. They won't see me later, in a chair in a darkened room, hoping Dr. Douglas and my morphine arrive before that simpering, piety-spewing fool Newman returns. I caught him the other day, preparing to splash me with water from his little bottle when he thought I was dozing off.

You don't think Newman would have splashed his water on General

Ulysses Grant in his prime, do you? Not a chance. But there isn't a liberty you can't take with a dying, broken old man like me.

And there wasn't a liberty that wasn't taken with me once I became President of the United States.

If I'd never been a general—only a President—I wouldn't be writing a book today. I'd be writing an apology. When a man succeeds, he is rewarded with new glory and new vistas until he stops succeeding. McClellan was a fine soldier who became a fine administrator and ended up a terrible commander. Halleck was a fine engineer who became a fine lawyer and then a lousy general. I was a fine commander who became a great general and then an abysmal President. The only man I ever saw escape the trap was Lincoln—he was a fine lawyer who became a jim-dandy President and is now a perfectly serviceable saint.

I used to wonder what they'll say about me when I go. Now that my going is imminent, I've ceased to care. All I ask is that they read my story and learn the truth before they decide.

And the truth is that I spent four years as a general and remember every moment and every detail—from the money I had to borrow to buy a colonel's uniform at Camp Yates to the sliced cucumbers I had for breakfast in the Wilderness to the look on Lee's face when I shook his hand in McLean's parlor.

And then I spent eight years as a President, and when I think back on it, it's all a blur. All I recall is being bounced from one crisis to the next, from each betrayal to its successor. Like a fellow on a merry-go-round, I traveled a great distance and ended up having gone nowhere.

If I'd known then what I do now, I'd have gone back to Galena instead.

President Andy Johnson was even more disagreeable than Vice President Andy Johnson. He was a hateful little man with a permanent snarl and a face furrowed with concern over everything and everybody. He grew up poor and never got over it, vowing revenge against all who had wronged him, a group that included everybody he ever met.

Lincoln picked Johnson as his Vice President because Johnson, a Tennessean, was the one remaining man in the country who was for slavery but against the rebel nation that fought to defend it. He hoped putting Johnson on his ticket would help him unite the country. But, instead, Johnson was distrusted by the North and considered a traitor by the South. His political base, therefore, consisted of Lincoln, and it died along with him.

Lincoln's body was carted off to Illinois, leaving Johnson behind in the White House. "I want you to know I'm going to continue Abe's good work," Johnson said to his Cabinet as they lounged disinterestedly around the ponderous cherrywood table in the Cabinet Room. If the Cabinet condescended to Lincoln, they were openly contemptuous of Johnson.

As general-in-chief of the army, I attended Cabinet meetings, although I reported to Stanton, who was still War Secretary. A more discouraging picture could not be imagined. The Cabinet Room was a mess. File drawers were overrun with papers, windows needed cleaning, and the wallpaper was peeling in the corners: After so many years of war, the White House was in disrepair. A dusty Bible sat open on a reader's stand. "I'm going to do everything Abe did," Johnson said to us from the head of the table.

"You could start by going to the theater," Stanton whispered to Seward behind a concealing hand.

"I heard that!" Johnson exclaimed, then turned to Welles, the Navy Secretary. "What did they say?" He turned back to Stanton and Seward, who sat together at the end of the table like mischievous schoolboys sitting in the back row. "I heard every word, you know!"

"I merely said, anybody who attains the Presidency and can still barely read is an inspiration to us all," Stanton said with a smile.

Seward nodded. "We are counting on you to lead our nation."

"Into our hands," Stanton whispered, sotto voce, and he and Seward once again shared a laugh behind their hands.

It didn't take long before they abandoned him, and he them. Johnson denounced the Lincoln program for reconciliation and the Radical Republican proposal for justice for the Freedmen, returning instead to his roots of bitterness, prejudice, and envy. The break between the two sides was now out in the open. Johnson had finally succeeded in uniting the nation: There was no one left who liked him.

"Lincoln was wrong," he raged at me during one of our regular meetings. "There'll be no mercy for the Rebels! I'll hang every single one of them!"

"Mr. President," I said dutifully, "I cannot help but recall Lincoln's words to me only a few short months ago: *Let 'em up easy*, he said."

"Let 'em *up* easy?" he scoffed. "Let 'em *down* easy, I say—*on ropes!*" Johnson's scowl became even more pronounced. "*Rape* is a crime, Grant! *Murder* is a crime!" His hateful eyes narrowed. "Well, *treason* is a crime, too, and traitors will hang for it, starting with Lee!"

I shook my head. "You know you can't do that, Mr. President," I reminded him. "The surrender terms make it clear every Confederate who goes home in peace is paroled. Including Lee." No one—least of all Johnson—was going to take my trophy away from me.

Johnson fell back in his chair, glowering in frustration. Meanwhile, Stanton and the Radicals—led by Ben Butler, a powerful congressman who had spent a brief hiatus as an inept general—had their own agenda. They were adamant that the Negro's enfranchisement was the prize the Union had won.

"What the hell's the point if the Freedmen don't vote?" Butler blustered when he came to seek my support.

"Shouldn't they be able to read and write first?" I asked.

"Read and write?" Butler exclaimed. "That idiot Johnson can barely read and write and he's the goddamned President, for Christ's sakes! I say the Freedman has a God-given right to vote, and in particular, a God-given right to vote Republican!"

"But the Negro can't vote in the North, either," I said. "Shouldn't we give the Northern Negro the same right to vote as the Southern one?"

Butler looked at me as if I had said the moon was made of cheese. "The North *won* this war, Grant," he explained laboriously. "Why the hell should *we* suffer? If the Negro wants to vote, let him, let him . . . hell, I don't know what to let him do. Let him stay down South and vote there!" He sat back and shook his head.

President Johnson, however, was just as adamant in his opposition. "Let 'em vote? My Lord, Grant, can you imagine the hell that would result if these pickaninnies *voted*? I've seen 'em up close, Grant. They're a heathen, lazy race, I can tell you. Let 'em *vote*? Not on your life!"

"But Mr. President," I pressed. "You don't want the Freedmen to vote, you don't want the Confederate soldier to vote, you're against giving women the vote—who is left in the South to vote?"

Johnson scowled. "Don't bother me with that now. I'm busy trying to stop these Radical nigger-lovers from ruining the country!"

As the months went by, the battle lines strengthened. On one side was Andy Johnson. On the other, everybody else, including his Cabinet and the Congress. It did not take long for those two bodies to conspire against him.

"Look at what they've done now!" Johnson exclaimed to me upon summoning me to the White House. He was slumped at a rolltop desk, a congressional bill in one hand, a glass of whiskey in the other. "Did you know this was going to happen—the Tenure of Office Act? Ben Butler and the Congress say I can't fire Stanton or any of these other Cabinet bums without getting the Senate's approval."

I stroked my chin pensively. "I had heard something to that effect, yes." Me and everybody else in Washington. Except, of course, Andy Johnson.

His face tightened into an expression of anger. "I'll show them a thing or two about politics! I'm going to fire Stanton and they won't do a thing to stop me!" He drained his glass and banged it down on the desk.

"How do you intend to do that?" I asked.

"Ha! I'm going to replace Stanton with *you*!" he said with a self-satisfied look.

Johnson and the Radicals might be at each other's throats, but I had no reason to step in the middle. "What makes you think I'll do it?" I asked quietly.

"Because if you don't," he said, leaning back in his chair, clearly delighted with the intricacies of his own thinking, "I'll ask *Sherman* to take the job—and *Sherman* will take it because he doesn't like niggers any more than *I* do! And if *Sherman* takes the job, you'll have to take orders from him," he exclaimed. "Hell! He might even decide to run for President and beat you to it!" he said, suddenly rocking forward and looking at me intently. "And don't deny you're thinking about it! Lincoln probably said that piece about the grubs to you, too, didn't he? Hell, he said that to everybody," he said, waving his hand in drunken dismissal. "You're not so damned special! You want to be President just like everybody else."

"I can take it or leave it," I said.

"Oh, I can take it or leave it," he said mockingly. "Well then, I'll just give the job to Sherman. Let's see if he turns me down!"

Drunk, stupid, and alone, Johnson could still handle himself. "Very well, then," I said. "Suppose I accept your offer. But what about the

Tenure of Office Act? According to the Congress, you can't fire Stanton. I can't take his job because it wouldn't be vacant."

He looked at me as if I were a child needing calming. "Well, all right, I'll tell you what. What if I make you *interim* Secretary of War? If you were *interim* Secretary of War, you could say you were really just helping your country out, not me. We could say you were only serving until I found a *real* Secretary." He looked up to see me frowning. "Or should I ask Sherman?"

I did not like being rolled by Johnson, but I wasn't going to let Sherman have the final say about the Negro, and I certainly wasn't going to let Sherman get ahead of me in the line to be President, even if he regularly denied interest. Just because Lincoln said that thing about the grubs to everybody didn't make it any less right. "So it would only be temporary?" I repeated.

"Only until I found somebody else—exactly!" Johnson swung his feet to the floor. "Do we have a deal?"

So I agreed. At first the Senate seemed to tolerate the situation, out of respect for me and the *interim* nature of my appointment. But all the while, I was wary. It was getting past time to plan my future.

Or so thought Mrs. Grant.

"I've been reading, Ulys," she said one night. We were living in Philadelphia then—a suitably quiet place to bring up children—and I was traveling to Washington during the week. "Do you know what the British did for Wellington after he defeated Napoleon? They fixed him for life! They gave him money, a home, a title—everything!"

"I have a fine job as general of the army," I told her. A grateful Congress gave me a fifth star when the war ended—even Garfield could not oppose it.

"Yes, but look at these," she said, and sat beside me bearing a packet of letters. Each bore an announcement of a new gift—Commodore Vanderbilt had headed a subscription committee in New York that had raised $100,000 for me, as much as my father had earned in a lifetime of bloodthirsty commerce! Alexander Stewart, a leading retail merchant of the day, and Daniel Butterfield, a young financier who had served under Sherman, chaired a subscription committee offering me a house in Washington—I later sold it to Sherman for $65,000. Jay Cooke, the leading financier of the war effort, raised a portfolio of bonds that gave me an annual income of $25,000 in perpetuity. The good people of Galena even purchased a house for us back in that city in the hopes that we would settle there. "I'll be damned if I ever go back to that place again," Mrs. Grant said, tossing that letter into the fireplace.

I regarded the letters somewhat incredulously. "Look at all of this!" I said, flabbergasted. "Do you think it's all right to take it?"

"*All right to take it?*" Mrs. Grant said, astonished. "Ulys, you're a great man now! It's your *obligation* to take it! It's your *destiny* to take it!

"Just like it's your destiny," she continued, "*to be President.*" She gathered up the letters she had been saving. "Besides," she said with finality, "what else are you going to do?"

Well, wasn't that exactly the point: *What else was I going to do?* Even forgetting the Great Master's prophecy, even putting aside the greatness for which I was destined, what else was I going to do? I knew how distastefully dull the peacetime army was, and I didn't care to do that again. And if Johnson and the Radicals continued to fight each other—there was talk of throwing Johnson out of office for trying to replace Stanton as War Secretary—the peace I'd delivered to the nation would be lost. Had I fought to save the Union only to watch it fall apart under these fellows? Not a chance.

So I went to New York and I made the rounds and let them all meet me—the Radical Republicans, the Wall Street traders, the moneyed class. I laugh now to think how I'd shown up in a plaid coat and a pair of brown pants. They quietly took me by the arm to Brooks Brothers, where they dressed me up to play the part that later came so naturally to me—dark suit, turned collar, black leather slippers, watch and chain. When I saw myself in the mirror I wondered whom the old Grant had been.

I had found the real me.

But as the weeks passed and no new nominee came forth from the White House, the Senate's mood began to turn. It was time to distance myself from the wreckage Johnson was about to become. I had stayed above this fray until now and had no intention of letting Johnson drag me into it.

"Why, look what we have here!" Johnson exclaimed when I went to him to press the issue. He sat behind his desk, his hair a mess and his tie undone. Yet another half-empty bottle of bourbon sat before him. "It looks like a New York banker, but it smells like Ulysses Grant!"

"This isn't working out," I said, ignoring his taunt. "You said this appointment was only temporary."

He rolled his eyes. "I said until I found somebody else," he said, "and I'm trying. Got anybody in mind?" He poured himself a camel's helping of liquor. "We have a deal, and you'll have to stick by it. Unless you want me to accuse you publicly of reneging on your pledge."

"But what of the law?" I asked. "As I read the Tenure of Office Act, if I serve as War Secretary illegally, I could be fined as much as five thousand dollars!"

Johnson smiled patronizingly. "Grant, Grant," he said, shaking his head at my lack of faith. "If the Congress dares to fine you so much as a penny, let alone five thousand dollars, I will pay it from my own pocket." *You put your share up and I'll stand up to the investment, Sam, that's how confident I feel,* Wallen had told me back in Vancouver, and so Johnson was telling me now. He rose from his desk and put an arm around me. "Don't let these Republicans stampede you, Grant. Go back to your office and honor the promise you made to me," he ordered.

I turned and walked out, dizzy with confusion, leaving Johnson sitting there, dizzy but not confused in the least. When I returned to our new home—we had accepted a house offered to us by the gentlemen's committee, 205 I Street, North West, was the address—I recall both Mrs. Grant and Rawlins were waiting for me.

"Well, what did he say?" Mrs. Grant asked as I entered our spacious parlor.

"Yes, give us all the details," Rawlins agreed. He let out a cough.

I recounted to them my conversation with Johnson.

"Johnson is completely isolated and will do everything he can to hide behind you," Rawlins said after a moment's consideration.

"It's time for a clean break," Mrs. Grant said as Rawlins's head bobbed up and down with emphatic agreement.

"Absolutely," Rawlins said, then coughed once again. I heard the sounds of fluids moving inside of him, just as I had heard in Simpson years before.

I rose the next morning and took a carriage to the War Secretary's office. I went inside, locked the windows and the side doors, then went out the front door, locking it as I departed, and proceeded across the city to find Stanton, whereupon I gave him the only set of keys. "There you go," I told him as I put victory in his hands. "I'm done with it. If you want Johnson, he's yours."

Stanton smiled and pocketed his prize. "Our friends in the Senate will be glad to hear you've finally come over to us," he said.

"Your friends in the Senate will hear from me soon," I told him pointedly.

He looked up at me with a broad grin. "Good," he said softly. "Your nation and our party await you."

They would not have to wait much longer. Johnson brayed like a drunken ass at what he saw as my betrayal and proceeded to relieve Stanton of his secretaryship once again. This time, the Senate was determined to assert their right to run the country as they saw fit, Johnson or no. By the spring of 1868, Johnson was being tried in the Senate for firing Stanton in violation of the Tenure of Office Act. He sat out the trial in a stupor in his office. The Senate fell one vote short of ridding the nation of him.

"All to the good," Mrs. Grant said as she read the newspaper in our parlor, turning to Rawlins to compare views.

"I agree," Rawlins said. "The longer the nation is stuck with Johnson, the more they'll want you as President to replace him."

Mrs. Grant smiled. "It's as if Fate were conspiring to deliver you," she said.

Rawlins coughed his agreement.

When I allowed my followers to put my name into the mix, the election was over. I didn't have to make speeches or excite crowds.

Speakers around the country lauded me, reciting a bit of doggerel:

> *And when asked what state he hails from*
> *Our sole response shall be*
> *He hails from Appomattox*
> *And its famous apple tree*

I simply sat at home and waited for the inevitable. Before I knew it, I was standing in front of the Capitol taking the oath of office in 1869, and addressing the crowd with what had become my campaign theme:

Let us have peace.

I made Rawlins Secretary of War, put Eli Parker in charge of Indian affairs, and took Horace Porter and Orville Babcock, my wartime assistants, with me as aides. I made Sherman general-in-chief. He was, after all, still my best friend, and I wanted him around. And if he had something to say, I wanted to hear it first. I assumed the Presidency with the same sense of prim efficiency with which I had won the war. I was where I was supposed to be—back in command.

Meanwhile, Mrs. Grant immediately went to work painting and papering the White House—she told me she would remake it in the image of the home she had always imagined. "You don't mind, do you, Ulys?" she asked, her coyest smile emerging.

"No, of course not," I said.

"I want it to be the picture of the home I wanted as a girl," she said. "I want it to have everything that home had, and more," she said eagerly. "Will that be all right?"

"Of course it will," I said, beaming at my wife's happiness.

"And I can have everything just as I wish it?" she said, her good eye wide with delight.

"Yes, my dear," I said, and kissed her on the forehead. Why wouldn't I want her to have what she wanted? It was finally mine to give.

And then I found out why I wouldn't. "Where the hell is everybody?" The Colonel's voice boomed through the White House a few short days later. I looked up, bewildered, from my desk on the second floor, wondering if I had just heard what I thought I'd heard. The echo had subsided when the peace was disturbed again. "I said, where the hell is everybody? Is there a goddamned soul in this godforsaken place?" he shouted.

I rose from my desk and proceeded out into the hall, where I saw Julia, Nellie, and Jesse—Fred (no longer the Little Dog) was already gone for West Point and Buck was about to attend Columbia University—scampering ahead of me. The old man was standing downstairs, suitcase at his feet, in the White House entrance hall.

"Where the hell is everybody?" he demanded again, even more disgruntled. "I'm tired and I'm thirsty, and I want to see my family," he hollered, when Julia came running down the stairs to greet him.

"Daddy!" she cried, throwing her arms around him. "You're finally here!"

I came down the marble steps to the entrance hall of the mansion to find her embracing him and the children circling delightedly around them. "Hello, Colonel," I said, maintaining an even expression. He was in my house now, I thought, and everything would be different. "Come to see us in our new home for a few days?"

"Hell, no!" the Colonel barked. "I'm here for the duration," he said, and smiled.

I turned to Mrs. Grant, who spoke before I could say a word. "But you *said*, Ulys," she insisted as he stood there, beaming. "You said I could have it just as I wished it, just as it was when I was a girl!"

My jaw dropped—I'd been had! "For heaven's sake!" I said when it had sunk in, "there were *slaves* when you were a girl, too. Should I expect to find slaves here next week?"

"Well, it's about time you came up with a good idea," the Colonel snapped. "And if there *aren't* any slaves around here, then who the hell's fault is that if not your own?" He snorted and turned to Mrs. Grant. "Can you believe this? The conqueror of the South now wants to know where all the slaves are!"

"That's not what I said! I meant—"

"I heard you just fine, Julius Caesar," the Colonel said dismissively. "Now let my little girl show me to my room so I can have myself a sit." He looked around to make sure everything was to his satisfaction. "At least you can finally afford a decent home of your own. I used to have to turn my head and look away when you built that ugly damned cabin you forced my girl to live in!"

"You mean *Hardscrabble*? Now see here!" I protested.

He ignored me. "I think I'm going to take myself a pipe on that *piazza* you have on the back of this place."

"It's called a *portico*," I said, barely restraining myself.

"Oh, a portico, is it?" he asked sarcastically. "You Yankees would come up with a new name for shit if you could think of one. Come now, Julia," he said, reaching down for his luggage. "Show me the insides of this here White Haven."

"White *House*," I corrected.

"Sure, sure," he said, and started up the staircase to the residence.

Mrs. Grant turned to me and ran her hands under my lapels. "Please don't be mad, Ulys. He won't be any bother at all. He just says these things, you know that. I'll make sure he stays out of your way," she said soothingly.

I sighed deeply. "Make sure he does," I said.

And stay out of my way he did. I spent my days in my office, while he spent his in the marbled entrance hall, which he decided he liked particularly well, smoking and spitting and holding forth for any and all who came to the home of the President, particularly the newspapermen, reminding them what a travesty it was that I, the subjugator of the Southern peoples, now presided as President to redouble their suffering. If I was still a general, I could have thrown him out of my district. But it's different when you're President.

When you're a general, you attack your problems.

When you're the President, your problems attack you.

Let us have peace, I had told America.

Thanks, America answered. *But how about a few dollars and a steady job?*

America's new economy—industrial capitalism, they called it—following the Civil War had its share of critics. That Marx fellow in Germany made quite a ruckus, although his twaddle led to nothing of consequence other than barricading the streets of Paris with furniture a few years back. There was no shortage of domestic harpers, either, all of them very perturbed about the oppressed masses rising up, which they saw as both desirable and inevitable, with a faith that rivaled my mother's in her impending trip to heaven.

All of it was bunk. None of them knew, or even suspected, the truth: Capitalism's greatest crisis and the suffering it led to was the direct result of my sister Jennie's inability to get married.

Clara, my oldest sister, died during the war, and Mary, the youngest, married a minister who needed work, so I made him minister to Denmark.

The middle sister was Virginia or, as we called her, Jennie. She was pleasant-looking and made adequate conversation, but nonetheless eluded Cupid's arrow and found herself a spinster at thirty-seven, when I became President.

It doesn't take a seer to predict a President's unmarried sister will attract an array of suitors who all share an absence of good intentions.

Had Jennie married a simple merchant or tradesman back in Ohio, we all would have been better off.

But instead she married a fellow named Abel Rathbone Corbin.

Two dozen years separated them; Corbin was sixty-one. But while his legs would no longer carry him far, his wallet would, particularly after his first wife died the year before and replenished it.

I can see it all now, of course, but then I could only see Corbin was one of those fellows who parlayed their ability to shake hands and nod knowingly into tangible wealth, the kind of fellow my father had once told me about and with whom I was only now becoming familiar.

"What do you make of him?" I asked Mrs. Grant.

"I think he's the kind of fellow you ought to be associating with. A rich, cultural type. Not like those ruffians Sherman and Sheridan."

I let that pass. "We don't know much about him. People say he's crooked."

"And people say you're a drunken butcher," she said matter-of-factly. "Besides, your sister is in love with him," she added.

She was right—Jennie had fallen for him, and once the union was made, I ceased to view him with a critical eye. He was a Washington insider at a time when I needed the advice insiders had to offer. Corbin wasted no time in offering me his.

He proposed, for example, that Daniel Butterfield—a fellow who had served in the South under Sherman and who handled the money for the gentlemen's committee that bought me my house on I Street— be appointed to manage the Treasury's gold, bonds, and so forth. Having no reason to object, nor any more trustworthy source of advice—he was, after all, now family—I concurred.

Money and its management was an area in which I was severely underinformed: I knew little about money, except for having come to admire, more and more, those who managed to have it. I decided to turn to Butterfield's new boss, my Treasury Secretary, George Boutwell, a former Massachusetts congressman, for some rudimentary lessons.

"Before the Civil War," Boutwell explained, "the government's money was always redeemable in gold. That means that you could always trade your dollars for gold. An ounce of gold was worth twenty dollars, so there was about an ounce of gold in a twenty-dollar gold coin."

"Yes, I recall. When I pawned my watch in '57, I got twenty-two bucks for it," I said, lighting a cigar.

"Yes," Boutwell said, nodding and waving away the smoke as he no doubt tried to understand my interjection, "exactly." He regarded me for a moment and continued. "But during the Civil War, we didn't have enough gold to pay for the men and the munitions and supplies, so we issued paper money, or 'greenbacks.' There are now almost half a billion dollars of this scrip floating around."

I absorbed this news but not its import. "Is that bad?"

Boutwell gave a small sigh. "Rather bad, Mr. President. Too much money floating around gets you inflation, which eats away at the economy."

"But not enough money gives you a depression, doesn't it? Isn't not having enough money the reason why people go broke?"

"In one sense, yes," Boutwell said, hesitating. "But inflation won't do, either. And the people who lent us money to fight the war now fear that though the money they lent the government was backed by gold, the money they'll get back won't be. Borrowing someone's gold and paying them back with paper is like borrowing a horse and returning it after it's had its leg broken—it still looks like a horse, and it still smells like a horse, but when it comes down to it, it's not really worth anything to anyone."

I paused to consider both my cigar and the newfound gravity of the matter. "Yes, I see," I said, stroking my beard to coax the thought along. "We certainly can't have that! You can't borrow a sound horse and return a lame one!"

"Exactly!" Boutwell said. "And that's not the end of it. The nation's enjoying a degree of prosperity right now. But all those jobs, and all those goods, are paid for with lame-horse dollars. It's not realistic. The whole economy is floating on an ocean of greenbacks that aren't backed by anything—their value could change at any moment. It lends our current prosperity a certain fictitiousness, wouldn't you say? The economy's expanded, but it's inflated like a bubble, a bubble that could pop tomorrow."

There *was* a certain fictitiousness to the economy's prosperity—I could see it plainly now—and I wasn't the man for that. "Then what shall we do?" I asked.

"We need to sell gold and lower its price," Boutwell explained.

I nodded sagaciously and again regarded my cigar, but no amount of ciphering allowed me to understand Boutwell's recommendation. "What the devil does that have to do with it?" I finally asked.

Boutwell leaned forward patiently. "It's simple. Let's say we sold gold and the price of gold goes down because more is available. When the price of gold goes down, the price of money goes up. Let's say it takes a hundred and forty dollars in greenback money to buy a hundred dollars in gold coins. Then the price of the gold falls to a hundred and thirty in paper. Do you follow?"

"Where?" I asked.

"The price of gold fell. You used to have to have a hundred and forty in greenbacks to buy an ounce of gold. But if the price of gold falls to a hundred and thirty, the same hundred and forty is worth an ounce of gold plus ten dollars. The greenbacks are worth more, see?"

"How can a dollar be worth more?" I demanded. "A dollar's a dollar!"

"If gold drops in price, then every greenback dollar you have buys more gold," Boutwell explained. "In fact, if we kept selling gold until a hundred dollars in gold coins was worth a hundred dollars in greenbacks, the problem would go away—greenbacks would be as 'good as gold.'"

This was beginning to make sense.

"So," Boutwell concluded, "we need to sell gold until the value of greenbacks goes up!"

Yes! I wasn't exactly sure why, but selling gold increased the value of paper money, until it was as good as gold—it was as if the lame horse could work again! I could see that now! So I told Boutwell to sell gold and my first Presidential decision was the subject of widespread support.

"You have taken an important step toward creating prosperity for generations to come," Commodore Vanderbilt came to Washington to tell me.

"What better word for money can there be but *sound*?" Jay Cooke—who had lent the government a good number of horses and wanted no lame ones in return—told me.

Of course, there were two other men who were eager to be my tutors on the subject.

"Now, I respect your ability to wage war," my father said over dinner one night, "but money is another matter." While Colonel Dent had moved right into the White House, my father took a more refined approach, taking a room at the Willard Hotel and dividing his time in retirement between Washington and Kentucky, sharing my Presidency with me as if his warfare transgressions deserved no mention. "But you are correct in thinking good money is hard, and hard money is good. Real good. In fact," he mused, "maybe I ought to buy some of those greenbacks before you do the right thing for your country and drive their price up."

"Typical Republican thinking," said the Colonel derisively from across the table. "More profiteering bleed-the-common-man talk from the nigger-loving Eastern banking interests," he spat, and fell back coughing into his chair at the table.

"Go ahead," my father snapped, "choke on your own words. What do you know about money aside from having lost most of yours?"

"Thieving mercantilist parasite!" the Colonel bellowed, then looked at me with scorn. "Forget what being broke was like, Grant? I suppose the apple doesn't fall far from the tree, does it?"

"Now, Daddy," Mrs. Grant cut in. "You mind yourself. And as for you, Jesse, it may interest you to know that nice Mr. Corbin, your new son-in-law, has some misgivings about the President's position on the gold question."

Corbin entered this debate in a sly way. When he learned Mrs. Grant and I were due to travel to Boston that summer—we traveled frequently as the White House was being remodeled—he arranged for us to do so on a luxury boat his friend James Fisk owned. We were lodged in a spacious suite and were served a fabulous dinner, after which cigars of the highest quality were offered. The conversation at the table turned to money, which struck me as wholly logical, given the prodigious sums of it possessed by Fisk and his equally admirable partner, Jay Gould.

Gould was a small, slight, intense man, with a rich, flowing black beard. In that regard he was like Rawlins, but where Rawlins was straightforward and open to a fault, Gould had a nervous, calculating air about him. Jim Fisk, in contrast, was heavyset, gregarious, and imposing, a bon-vivant with an eye to empty his pockets as well as your own, the distinct opposite of his more cautious friend, Gould.

Both Gould and Fisk knew I favored selling gold when they raised the issue after dinner that night. When the subject first came up, I looked up from lighting my cigar to see Gould leaning forward intently.

"Mr. President, have you considered the benefits to the economy if your administration were to *buy* gold?"

"*Buy* gold?" I asked, confused. "Mr. Gould, our policy is to *sell* it. If we sell gold, we lower its price relative to greenbacks. The cheaper gold becomes, the easier it will be to get rid of greenback notes. Why, my policy is endorsed by Commodore Vanderbilt himself!"

"Well, of course, that is the conventional thinking, just as the conventional thinking saw Missionary Ridge as unassailable," Gould said, undeterred. "But in a few months it will be harvest season, and the crops will come in. Foreigners pay for those crops in gold, not greenbacks. If you could get the price of gold up from, say, a hundred and thirty dollars to a hundred and forty, that would be ten more dollars in the pocket of the American farmer!"

He leaned yet farther toward me and grew more animated. "Consider that for a moment, Mr. President. The farmer will go out and buy more implements, more tools, all sorts of goods. And the manufacturers of all those goods will then have more capital to further add to this great, circular flow of spending, on and on, bringing ever more prosperity to all those it touches, and it will be to your credit, Mr. President—you and your administration."

I eyed him coolly. "And what about your interests?"

Fisk blew a cloud of smoke and drew my attention. "Why, our interests are those of the American working man, Mr. President!" he said. "When the farmer ships his grain to port, it moves in our railcar. And when it does, it brings greater prosperity to our engineers and our firemen and our brakemen and all our other workers. We've got forty thousand wives and families to look after, and we can't do it if our sidetracks are full of empties," he said, fingering a cigar of his own and winking at me as if we were sharing a joke.

"Prosperity is good for everybody, that's what Jim means," Gould said quickly. "And that's the point—prosperity!"

These were two rich ducks, to be sure, and I could see their point, but their theorizing was not enough to make me change my mind, particularly after I had worked so hard to learn my opinion in the first place. I measured my words carefully. "There is a certain fictitiousness to the prosperity of the country," I said. "And the bubble might as well be tapped in one way as another." I was learning Boutwell's sound money talk, even though I suspected I'd just said I didn't care if everybody went broke and to hell. Gould sat back in his chair, deflated, and Fisk gave him a look that seemed to say *I told you so,* and might have suggested to me that our after-dinner conversation was neither spontaneous or entirely hypothetical on the part of my two illustrious hosts, had I thought about it.

But I did not think about it. Instead, I went back to appreciating the very fine cigar I was smoking. To be sure, while Fisk and Gould disagreed with Boutwell, their cigars told me they were not really that bad at all, so when Fisk arrived at a hotel in New York where Mrs. Grant and I were staying later that summer, claiming to have a vital matter to discuss, I welcomed him in.

"Mr. President, I have important news," he began urgently, hardly pausing to sit down. "Three hundred ships have reportedly set sail from the Black Sea, bound for Liverpool with Russian grain."

I hoped that my look was more considered than blank. "And?" I asked.

"Mr. President, this is exactly what Gould warned you would happen. With gold at a hundred and thirty-two dollars an ounce, where it is right now, the U.S. farmer cannot compete with the Russian prices. The American crops will go unsold. But if we were to raise the price of gold, the American farmer could charge his British customer less gold per bushel and still have a profitable season."

Back during the war, my course of action would be clear—I would have sunk the Russian ships. But the endless subtleties of being President again confronted me. "I presume, Mr. Fisk," I said in measured tones, "you propose we buy gold to force its price up and cheapen the greenback dollar."

"Precisely! In the name of prosperity for all the American people!"

I'd never realized the American people would be so demanding, or their problems so complex. I would have hoped they'd be satisfied with peace. "Very well, then," I said. "When I return to Washington in a few weeks I shall discuss the matter with Boutwell." Fisk knew Boutwell held views opposite his own, but he'd made his case as best he could. He thanked me and departed.

Two weeks later, in Saratoga, on the next leg of our vacation, I came upon A. T. Stewart, one of my financial benefactors, at a private dinner. Stewart was the kind of self-made man who exemplified my ideas about what constituted success. He could talk rings around me.

I sat him down and asked him point-blank about this gold business.

"Mr. President," he said, "the market for gold is a nest of vipers. Boutwell's policy of selling gold favors the adders over the asps. Are you sure this is the particular serpent you wish to favor?"

I nodded slowly while taking in Stewart's good sense. Fisk and Gould certainly seemed like snakes of a sort, but Stewart had a point—why were the fellows who argued the matter the other way any different? If fellows such as Commodore Vanderbilt and my father liked a low price for gold, what made them better than Fisk and Gould, who liked a high price for gold?

"So long as you allow Boutwell to move the market in any one direction, you will open yourself to some charge of favoritism," Stewart continued. "My advice to you, sir, is to tell Mr. Boutwell to keep his gold in his vaults and his nose out of the market's business." He looked at me with great solemnity. "If you favor the adders, you'll be bitten by the asps."

Now, perhaps I should have taken into consideration the fact that Stewart and Corbin were old friends, or that Stewart might have resented Boutwell's being made Treasury Secretary instead of him, but here was a fellow of means in whom I had great faith. I found myself considering his arguments—and, by implication, Corbin's, Gould's, and Fisk's—in a new light as I boarded a train to return to Washington for a Cabinet meeting.

It was a warm summer day. The Cabinet room was in better repair than it had been in Johnson's day. The clutter was straightened away under Babcock's supervision, and the wallpaper changed. I walked in quite pleased to see the improvements and looked around the table to see every seat filled with the members of my Cabinet. I nodded hello to Rawlins as my eyes swept over him and noted that he looked unusually tired and pale. I then was suddenly appalled to notice that Boutwell was not there! Instead, sitting in his chair was Butterfield, Corbin's and Sherman's man.

"Good morning, Mr. President," he said politely as I glared across the Cabinet table at him. He was a young fellow who seemed concerned with making a good impression.

"Good morning my fanny, Butterfield," I barked. "Where in blazes is Boutwell?"

Butterfield shifted uncomfortably. "He is at his summer home in Gorton," he said quietly, meaning back in Massachusetts.

"Oh, is that right?" I asked with irritation. "Well, I came to this meeting from Saratoga, as long and grueling a trip as it is from Gorton."

"I understand that, sir," Butterfield responded.

"And, I might add, I came at the displeasure of Mrs. Grant, who is undertaking the Saratoga social season without me. Have you ever earned the displeasure of Mrs. Grant?" I asked caustically.

"No, sir, I haven't," Butterfield said, and squirmed uneasily.

"Be glad of it," I said, and sat down. "Now give me your report."

"If I may, Mr. President, Secretary Boutwell has ordered me to sell an extra four million to six million dollars of gold during September, triple the usual amount."

"Triple!" I choked, now enraged. "Who the devil does Boutwell think he is, sitting up in a seaside cottage, deciding how to run the country? Doesn't he know about the three hundred ships leaving Odessa for the world market?"

I reached for a tablet and began to write with all the conviction I had through the war. Boutwell's policy of selling gold was hereby changed, I ordered. Three hundred ships filled with the enemy's grain were making their way to England to cut off our farmers' hard-earned product, just as Lee had cut me off at Spotsylvania. Boutwell would keep his meddlesome gold in the vault and his traitorous hands in his pockets.

I gave the note to Butterfield and told him to wire Boutwell right away. He departed instantly, and I barely had time to reorient myself when I heard a cough turn into a gruesome rasp across the table.

It was Rawlins. He was hemorrhaging.

Fish, my Secretary of State, was sitting next to him and tried to assist, but up from Rawlins's chest came what seemed like a bucketful of blood. Rawlins was dying of consumption, just like my brother Simpson.

Several aides raced in and escorted Rawlins to another room where he could lie down. I ended the Cabinet meeting and went to his side.

"Rawlins," I said quietly, and then realized there was nothing else I could say.

"I'll be fine, Mr. President," he said in a whisper as his chest began to rumble once again, making it clear he would not. He smiled weakly and closed his eyes. In a moment he was asleep. Horace Porter came into the room and regarded Rawlins silently for a moment before he spoke. "You're due to board the train back to Saratoga, Mr. President," he said gently. "I've sent for Eli Parker," he said. "He'll make sure Rawlins is taken care of."

I nodded again and allowed Porter to lead me from the room. We boarded an overnight train for New York City. I joined Abel Corbin and my sister for breakfast in their new home, mentioning in passing my change of heart about gold as I did.

I returned to Saratoga that evening, but no sooner had I arrived than I learned that Rawlins was in his final hours. I would have to go straight back to Washington.

When I finally arrived at Union Station, Sherman was waiting for me—the four stars I used to wear sat uncomfortably on his bony shoulder. "Where were you?" he asked, agitated.

"There was trouble getting a train," I said, weakly. "Has he passed?"

"Yes," Sherman said, "and he was calling for you. I had to lie to him."

I've since learned firsthand that lying is the least of the liberties they take with a dying man, and I hoped Rawlins's end hadn't been too hard.

He'd been my greatest source of support. *Grant's never been beaten!* he said that night in the Wilderness. He believed in me from the moment we first met back in Galena, even if I was yet to believe in myself back then. In the months and years that followed, I kept him with me to make sure someone believed in me at all times.

But now I was up to the job of believing in myself—I had proved the great prophecy true in both war and peace. I would miss Rawlins and his fervent protectiveness. But I no longer needed him in order to be who I was. I no longer needed Rawlins in order to be Ulysses Grant.

Only now, as I look back, do I realize my real problems began the day I lost him.

I left Washington a few days later and rode the train north with Butterfield. I asked about the effect of my new gold policy.

"The price of gold has risen, sir. Almost five dollars per ounce."

I viewed this result with satisfaction. We would show these Russian grain merchants a thing or two.

"But I must mention to you, sir," Butterfield added, "the volume of activity, the total amount of trading, has recently risen quite substantially."

"Speculators, Butterfield," I said in dismissal. "They're adders and asps in a den of vipers. Let them bite and sting each other while we steer the nation out of harm's way."

"Of course, sir," he said. "But the speculation to which you refer is taking on the characteristics of a mania, almost an obsessive pursuit, and it reaches so far and wide, almost every individual one meets has become involved. One can't even look at, say, one's friends or relations without wondering what kind of a position they've taken in this market."

I remember thinking it was the kind of thing Rawlins would say. Well, I could handle myself. "Yes, Butterfield," I agreed, "that is how these manias play themselves out."

"Yes, and I've found that in the confusion of such a mania, one does well to take into account the particular interests of one's advisors. Even if they were, say, close friends or even family members."

"I see," I said, in as knowing a manner as I could manage, although in retrospect I'm appalled at how blind I was. The fellow had all but tattooed his message on my arm. Butterfield nodded sadly and let the subject drop. He had tried to come clean: I give him credit for that much.

It wasn't until the end of that summer, and far too late to avoid the consequences, that Butterfield's meaning became clear. I had taken the family on a late summer trip to the remote Pennsylvania countryside, where I could ride and fish. We were accompanied by Horace Porter. I recall I was enjoying a game of croquet with Porter when a well-appointed messenger from Wall Street arrived with a letter for me from Abel Corbin. I assumed the letter must address some matter of immediate concern, as the messenger treated it with great urgency.

But when I opened it, it was only another harangue about gold. Corbin wrote that gold prices were in danger of softening and we would have to recommit ourselves if we were to secure our objective of a high price. I shared with Porter the contents of the letter, and his face took on a concerned look. "There's something I need to mention,

General," he said, obviously troubled. "A few weeks ago, I received a letter from Jay Gould, saying an account for half a million in gold had been created in my name at his brokerage."

"Half a million!"

"I don't need to tell you I wrote back to him immediately, telling him I'd taken the greatest offense at his doing so," Porter assured me.

Wait a minute, I thought. Why had Corbin sent a messenger so far, so urgently, to deliver to me another lecture on gold policy? Why had Gould and Fisk tried to set Porter up in gold?

In fact, was it Corbin who sent the messenger, or was he doing all of this at somebody else's behalf?

Someone like Gould or Fisk?

Was this what Butterfield had been trying to tell me?

I suddenly felt as I did when Johnston came out of the woods at Shiloh—how could I not have seen it? "Get us a train to Washington immediately," I told Porter.

The next Friday, September 24, 1869, was "Black Friday," the day the gold market collapsed. Boutwell came to my office late that morning. He apologized for his absence at the last Cabinet meeting and then noted his concern with the unnatural rise in the price of gold since the Treasury had discontinued selling it.

"There is no need to discuss the matter further," I said, hoping Boutwell had not realized how my brother-in-law and his associates had played me like a fiddle. "How much gold do you want to sell?"

"Four million dollars' worth," he responded.

"Fine. Wire instructions to New York immediately."

Word that the government intended to sell four million dollars' worth of gold arrived there a few minutes after noon. Every speculator who had been assured by Fisk and Gould that the government stood on the side of higher gold prices was now confronted with evidence otherwise. The price of gold instantly fell from $160 an ounce back to $133, and fortunes were wiped out. The Gold Exchange closed.

Butterfield, despite his confession, had borrowed extensively to ride the gold wave. He was financially ruined and suffered a breakdown. Corbin also got cleaned out. And when he went to Gould and Fisk demanding to be bailed out, they told him to go to blazes. He ended up selling his home in New York and moving to New Jersey, where he and my sister could live within his now-limited means. Everybody seemed to be ruined except Fisk and Gould, who brazenly walked away from their debts and got away with it, and, of course, Commodore Vanderbilt, who watched the frenzy from the sidelines, sold when everybody else was buying, and then bought when everybody else sold at a loss.

The public was aghast at the scandal. Newspapers called me a fool. There were congressional investigations, and it would be fair to say I was not pleased to discover they would be headed by James Garfield, now a full-time congressman. It was no surprise that he turned out to be every bit the sanctimonious prig in civilian life that he was in the military.

"We'll have to probe this matter thoroughly," Garfield told me, with the same belligerence he demonstrated back in Chattanooga.

"There's nothing to probe," I said. "Corbin was in cahoots with Fisk and Gould, and we stopped them from working their scheme."

"I'll be a far better judge of that than you, Grant," he said, his chest puffing out. "Don't you read the newspapers? They have named me the Scourge of Corruption," he said pompously.

Garfield held his hearings, giving Fisk and Gould a chance to besmirch me, Porter, Mrs. Grant, and every other soul connected to me who had made the acquaintance of these conspirators. When it was done it was clear that we were guilty of nothing more than being too trusting, and we were exonerated.

The biggest losers turned out to be the very farmers whose welfare had been the pretense in the first place. Farm prices fell as surely as Fisk and Gould had first driven them up. But the farmers didn't just take their losses and go home; instead, they got mad. I wasn't to find out how mad they got till later, though.

And through it all, it didn't occur to me that my problems were just beginning.

CHAPTER XIII

THE SIOUX, THE SOUTH, AND THE SENATOR— THE LEADER OF THE AGRARIAN INSURRECTION—GARFIELD FIGHTS CORRUPTION—CUSTER'S LAST STAND

I HAD A DREAM, I recall, one night toward the end of my Presidency. I was sitting in my office when I looked up to see a throng of hostile visitors standing before me, each vociferously shouting his complaint. A newly emancipated Freedman demanded protection, enfranchisement, and opportunity for advancement. An Indian demanded restitution of the land that had been taken from him and the right to live in peace among his own people. A farmer demanded cheap money and freedom from economic peonage. A reformer demanded an end to graft, corruption, and incompetence. They all stood before me, shouting belligerently, pressing their cares, refusing to listen and unwilling to relent.

It was wholly unsettling.

But even more unsettling was the fact that when I awoke, they had not gone away.

"Get me my gun!" I heard the Colonel bellow one afternoon from his perch in the White House entrance hall. "We're under attack!"

I looked across my desk at Orville Babcock, on whom I relied more than ever with Rawlins gone, and we went out to see what the matter could be.

My father-in-law looked up from a settee by a front window to see us at the top of the stairs, his face red with agitation. "Don't worry, Grant! They're not going to get any of us while there's any fight left in me!" he shouted, pointing to something outside. "Not that you're worth it, of course," he continued loudly, "but I'm a loyal white American and these savages won't overrun the damned White House without hearing from me." We hastened down the stairs as the Colonel continued his diatribe, his pistol held closely by his side, peering out the window, where we joined him and saw a delegation of Oglala Sioux approaching the White House, in full native dress, which entailed both a great many feathers and a substantial degree of nakedness.

"The one in front is wearing a suit!" the Colonel shouted, alarmed and jeering at once. "He probably took it off a white man he killed on his way here!" He licked his lips and raised his gun. "My first bullet's for him!" he said as he squinted and tried to line up a shot.

I snatched the gun from his hand. "That is Eli Parker," I snapped, "the Commissioner of Indian Affairs, colonel of the United States Army, sachem of the Iroquois Nation, and thirty-second degree Mason," I told him.

The Colonel looked at me, dumbfounded. "That's some nigger," he finally said.

I took advantage of the Colonel's momentary shock to usher Parker and his companions into my office.

Parker introduced me to the Sioux, each of them a perfect physical specimen—lean and muscular, with graceful, athletic carriages, emphasized by the remarkable costumes they wore. They had come two thousand miles to see me, Parker said, because of a problem with the Northern Pacific Railroad.

"Congress gave Jay Cooke their land on which to build his railroad," Parker said.

"Yes, I remember," I said. "And what is the problem with that?"

"It was their land," Parker said. "They're upset."

"Well, it's Jay Cooke's land now. And you know he gave Mrs. Grant and I a substantial honorarium—certainly nothing like what Wellington got, but an appreciable sum nonetheless—and I can't very well take his land away. Ask the chief what he wants instead."

Parker translated as the Sioux leader spoke. "He says if they can't have their land back, a substantial honorarium sounds pretty good, particularly since it was good enough for the Great Father Grant," Parker said. "He says white men kill Indians without compunction and deserve to die like dogs, but for now money would be okay. He says

Cooke has plenty of money and he wants his people to get their cut. He says twenty-five thousand dollars would be a good start."

The Sioux nodded unflinchingly.

"Tell him we will give the Sioux a fine reservation in the Black Hills and the right to hunt in their ancestral grounds," I offered. Parker turned to the Sioux and translated, whereupon the chief responded emphatically, and then Parker turned to me again.

"He says to stick it up your ass."

I was quite taken aback to hear this and no doubt looked confused, whereupon the chief rose slightly in his seat and helpfully pointed to his hind parts.

I nodded to convey my understanding and sighed. "Ask him how he'd feel about twenty-five thousand dollars."

There was some more translation and then nods and smiles all around.

But, of course, the Sioux, like the farmers, would be back. Everybody came back. In war, when you whip your enemy, everybody agrees he's whipped and he has the courtesy to stay whipped. I paroled thirty-one thousand Rebels at Vicksburg and not one came back. In politics, when you whip your enemy, he takes it as an invitation to try again. Politics is like war without the physical violence or lasting resolution (which is unfortunate, as organizing violence and pursuing resolution were all I was ever good at).

There was, for example, no lasting resolution to the political situation of Negroes in the South. Reconstruction was a rude awakening for white Southerners. Negro legislatures appeared in such places as Mississippi and Georgia, and they were sometimes as corrupt as they were unsympathetic to their former oppressors. They ran down their states' treasuries, looted the railroad business as larcenously as Fisk, Gould, or Cooke ever did, and printed bonds that proved cream for the skimming. But white objections had less to do with the quality of Freedmen governing bodies than the need to keep the Negro race in submission. To this end, law be damned, Nathan Bedford Forrest founded the Ku Klux Klan in 1867. He had been known as a brilliant cavalry commander during the Civil War, but he had also been known for his refusal to take Negro prisoners, slaughtering on the spot those unfortunate enough to be captured, and peacetime had made him no more reasonable. Led by the Klan, the terror began to spread—the murders of

Negro political leaders, intimidation of Negro voters, brutalization of Negroes who sought to build businesses that would compete with white ones.

As a general, I had resolved the war and brought the nation together. In gratitude, the American people had made me President. As President, I would now have to divide the country again if the war's resolution was to stand. I sent the Congress the Klan Act, allowing the use of federal troops to shut the Klan down if necessary. I made Benjamin Bristow, an old associate of Lincoln's, the solicitor general, a job I created so somebody would prosecute Klan crime.

But it made little difference. All in all, my first term was a miserable four years, an endless parade of speculators, victimized Negroes, and displaced Indians. By 1872, Horace Porter quit, Eli Parker was forced out of his position by a Congress tired of seeing an Indian in a responsible position, and Rawlins was dead, leaving me with Orville Babcock as my last remaining aide from the war.

My reelection campaign immediately ran into trouble. My Vice President turned out to be on the take and had to be replaced. I did not like having a crooked Vice President, but I more strenuously objected to the way the news reached me.

"Vice President Colfax is a crook," Congressman Garfield announced as he swept into my office. "When he was a congressman, he accepted stock from the Crédit Mobilier company," the self-styled "Scourge of Corruption" said as he slid comfortably into a leather chair opposite me.

"Nonsense," I replied, looking up from the papers scattered atop my desk. "Colfax is an honest man. Besides, what the devil is the Crédit Mobilier company?"

"It's the company the Congress set up to supervise the construction of the Union Pacific Railroad," Garfield responded. "The government gave the Union Pacific the land, which was used to secure mortgages, which was used to issue stock, which was turned over to Crédit Mobilier, which was supposed to supervise the construction of the railroad. But Crédit Mobilier decided to hire itself to construct the railroad, and it charged itself too high a price, which made it very profitable, which drove the price of the stock up. By then it had already given large amounts of stock out to many members of Congress, Colfax among them."

This was far too circuitous to follow without a lesson from Boutwell, but it turned out his conclusion was correct—Colfax had to go. It wasn't until after the election that anyone bothered to note that Garfield had taken Crédit Mobilier stock, too. In fact, I later discovered that a road could not be paved in Washington without his getting a cut, but I suppose that was just a benefit of being the "Scourge of Corruption."

I won reelection in 1872, the year I turned fifty, despite that scandal, and despite the fact the farmers and the cheap-money types—the greenbackers—were still agitating. And when they weren't agitating about cheap money, they were agitating about the railroads, an issue that was upsetting Jay Cooke, as well. He had become one of my key supporters, using his considerable fortune to support both Republican causes and, after the war, me. He had a lovely home, a stone mansion just outside Philadelphia, which he graciously allowed Mrs. Grant and me to use when we passed through. I was there one night, enjoying a cigar with Cooke in his great room, when he shared a growing concern to me.

"This Northern Pacific business is proving troublesome," he said.

"You mean the Sioux?" I asked. "I gave them twenty-five thousand dollars," I told him, "and they went back to the Black Hills. That land will remain yours."

"No," he replied. "It's the farmers. They say they're charged too much for hauling their crops to market."

"Then let them take their business elsewhere," I said knowingly. "Take it from me—farmers don't need any help from the railroad to go broke."

"It's these farm insurrectionists!" Cooke lamented. "They're anarchists, I tell you! They're pressing the state governments to regulate rail rates—can you imagine that? Regulating the price a businessman can charge? Why, I've got bills to pay," he complained. "How can I provide a return to my investors if I can't make a profit?"

I clucked my tongue in dismayed agreement. It was a good question. It turned out he couldn't. After I left for Washington the next morning, Cooke's Northern Pacific went broke.

To say that the failure of the Northern Pacific was an economic calamity was like saying Cold Harbor was a setback. The stock market crashed. Depositors ran to their banks to get their money out before the next fellow.

Boutwell had gone home to New England for good, leaving me with a new Treasury Secretary—a fellow named Richardson—and a crisis on my hands. I determined the only way to avoid an outright economic collapse was to go to New York myself and meet with the bankers. After all, they were well heeled and well educated, and they knew how the world worked. I would go to them to find out what it cost to make the world work again.

It was Commodore Vanderbilt himself who organized their delegation, bringing us all to Delmonico's for a fine lunch and cigars. The Commodore was getting on in years, but he still had the best head for finance in the country. Surely he would know what a President was supposed to do.

"Money!" he said, facing me from across the table. "You must direct the Treasury to put more money into the system at once!"

"But I thought there was too much money already," I replied as I looked around at them. "How can the problem be too much money before and too little now?"

"Because now we don't have any," the Commodore said. "How much do you have on hand?"

I consulted with the new Treasury Secretary, and we agreed to put new money—$26 million of it—on the table to stem the crisis. It was a dramatic change of policy that had one predictable, compelling effect—it enraged those people who didn't get any.

The farmers howled. If I was willing to pump money into a small clique of Eastern banks, why wasn't I willing to pump some money their way? Farm prices were falling, railroad rates were rising, the low price of gold was hurting them on world markets, and the new mechanical reapers and threshers were forcing the small farmer to invest or get out of the way of those who did.

And so the lines were again drawn: on one hand, Commodore Vanderbilt and the lenders who wanted a sound currency; on the other, farmers and borrowers who wanted cheap money with which to pay Commodore Vanderbilt and the rest of the first group back. The Congress, under pressure from the farmers, passed a law called the Inflation Bill, which would force me to pump more money into the economy in the name of the farmers and debtors who needed it.

The only question was: Would I veto it?

"Hell, yes, you're going to veto it!" my father said—he had returned yet again to our dinner table during one of his regular visits. "I mean, they call it the Inflation Bill, don't they? Is that a good thing? If they passed a Measles Bill you'd veto that, wouldn't you? Well, why is inflation any better than measles?"

The Colonel leaned over his plate and shouted excitedly, "Sure, that's what the moneyed interests want! Well, one man's measles is another man's medicine, I say! Inflation ain't so bad if you've got nothing in your pocket to begin with!" He turned to me, his red nose flushed. "You were broke once, Grant, or don't you remember? All you ever grew on them sixty acres I gave you was children!"

The farmers, the merchants, the small businessmen, the workers, all of them led by the agrarian insurrectionists, came together against my hard-hearted refusal to be moved by their tales of woe. But just as it was my destiny to defeat Lee, it would be my destiny to put the nation's financial house in order, to save the Union economically, just as I saved it politically, to usher it into a new era in which all men could find wealth. So I did what I had to do. I vetoed the Inflation Bill and stopped the nation from slipping further down the slope of paper money into the abyss of inflation. Let the chips fall where they may.

Which they did, one morning shortly thereafter, when I awoke to find that the city was occupied by thousands of farmers, each with his team and wagon or buckboard, each carrying his tools and implements as emblems of his grievance.

"What the devil are they all doing here?" I demanded of Babcock when he arrived at my office.

"They are here to protest your veto of the Inflation Act. The city is overrun!" Babcock was saying, when Mrs. Grant suddenly burst in, pushing past him to hover angrily over my desk.

"The city is besieged!" she said with great agitation. "These farmers are everywhere! I can't get a carriage across town! You're the President! Do something!"

"They're farmers, protesters. They want cheap dollars," I said.

"Well, they can't have them!" Mrs. Grant said petulantly. She turned to Babcock. "We're for hard currency, sound money, and that's the end of it. Send them home!" She stared at Babcock as if he now had his instructions.

Babcock sighed. "I can't, Mrs. Grant. They're going to occupy the Capital until their demands for cheap money are met."

I rose from my desk and regarded the throngs covering the lawns beyond the White House fence. "Nonsense. They'll be gone when it's planting time," I announced, evaluating this new enemy as I would any other. "They'll leave before they sacrifice the year's crop."

Babcock bit his lip pensively. "But General," he said, "we are still left with the problem of keeping order in the interim."

"Very well," I told him. "Seek out their leader and tell him I wish to speak to them all. Let's see if a talk from General Grant isn't enough to move the situation along."

Babcock returned after arranging it. "The leader of the rebellion has agreed. They will come to the front of the White House this afternoon. You can address them from the steps by the front door."

"Good," I said. "We are doing the right thing—protecting the currency and putting the economy on a sound footing. I will explain it to them and they will see it is for their own good." I would conquer another army, this time with words.

At the appointed hour, I followed Babcock out of my office, down the carpeted hall, and down the marble staircase to the front hall. I could make out the outlines of a throng through the windows. A small knot of farmers stood in the hall. When we reached the group, they turned toward us, and Babcock introduced me to their leader. "Mr. President," he said, "this is Mr. Phipps, of Iowa."

I have been surprised in war, and I have been assailed in politics, but I have never been so shocked as I was that day when I saw this fellow, Mr. Phipps.

It was Useful Grant.

I studied his face. He had aged, but gracefully. His face was lined, yet now more gentle, and the look in his eyes had softened as if his rise and fall had mellowed him over time, the way rushing water smooths a stone. He was thinner than me now—or was I now more stout than him?—and had a look of resolve and focus that reminded me of the look I must once have had. Babcock, off to my side, looked puzzled by my stunned silence and cleared his throat loudly.

"Yes, yes. Mr. Phipps," I said, extending my hand. "It's a pleasure to receive you here in the White House."

Useful shook my hand forthrightly. "Mr. President, the farmers and workers of America have come to see you," he began.

"Well, that's quite a delegation," I said, chuckling. "But I am here on behalf of the farmers and workers of America as well." I extracted a cigar and offered Phipps one, which he declined. "Why don't you tell me something about yourself?" I asked, my eyes staying on him as I struck a match and watched him in disbelief through the smoke of my cigar.

"I am a farmer, sir, and a veteran, wounded at Shiloh. I returned home to farm after the war and found I was really working for the bankers and the railroads, for they kept more of my product than I did. So I have come here with thousands of my brothers to bring our case directly to you."

"And what case is that?"

"The case for more money," he said. "The case for enough money to buy seed, to plant crops, to keep our farms going. There is a depression in America, Mr. President, a depression not caused by us, but by the very same banks and railroads who seek an ever larger share of what we produce."

"There is a transition under way in America, Mr. Phipps," I responded, "a correction, a new direction. The economy once dragged by the draft animal is now propelled by the train and the farm machine. They are taking us to a new world. And there is the bill to be paid for the war we had to fight. That bill must be paid, and must be paid in gold if our credit is to be restored."

Phipps stared at me, his eyes hardening. "That is not a policy, sir, but a punishment! And it is we, the farmer and the workingman, whom you punish!"

"That is the speech of an insurrectionist!" I said.

"It is the speech of the farmer and workingman," Useful said, now the champion of the workingman, as his father had been the champion of the local oligarchs. "When Cooke's empire collapsed even as you slept in his guest room, and the bankers who financed him stood on the precipice of collapse—there were dollars for them, weren't there? Well, the farmer stands at the precipice of collapse, but your policies deny him the very same lifeblood you granted your friends the bankers."

I stood there impassively, setting aside my image of the Useful whose birthright I stole four decades before and confronting the Useful whose incendiary accusations now demanded a response. "You twist the facts, sir. I remember what life was like in a town where one man possessed all the wealth and made the law, I assure you," I said, allowing myself the satisfaction of saying it. "I am no handmaiden to oligarchs. I am pursuing the policies that will build our nation now that it is united once again. As I have said, Mr. Phipps, let us have peace."

We stared at each other for what seemed like an endless moment—he alive with the passion of his cause, I fathoming this last chapter in our intertwined stories. So this was his fate, to be a rabble-rouser, a traitor—in contrast to the mantle of greatness Mescalito had foretold—the destiny to lead great masses of men in the cause of their human redemption.

"Why don't I say my piece to your gathering and we can all proceed about our business?" I said, moving us along. Useful nodded and stepped aside. He and Babcock followed me as I walked through the lobby and emerged on the front porch, standing amid the pillars.

There were several thousand of them gathered, a throng of men in overalls and coats, their hands dirty and their expressions hard. They had taken the grind of poverty and turned it into rage against those who profited from their work. Perhaps each was to be commended for not being beaten down, but their actions together constituted insurrection against our nation. I would not permit it.

"My fellow citizens," I called out to them. "I appreciate seeing so many of you here, in the capital of a reformed United States during a time of peace. I know the suffering you endure and the challenges you face. I, too, have been a farmer and I, too, have known poverty. But poverty is an enemy with victims but no villains, and is conquered not by attacking another, but through the redemptive dignity of effort and determination."

"Effort and determination did nothing for you, Farmer Grant!" a voice shouted from the center of the crowd, followed by enthusiastic cheering.

"My vocation proved not to be farming," I said, unashamed of the facts.

"Then a lot you know!" shouted another.

I put up my hands for silence. "My countrymen, your situation is grim, I know, but it is not reason to rend the nation we fought to preserve. Go back to your homes and struggle on!"

There was a chorus of angry jeers in response. "We won't leave until you sign the Inflation Act!" one man exclaimed, and all his brothers shouted their agreement.

"The Inflation Act won't do you any good!" I shouted. "A fictitious bubble isn't real prosperity!"

"Go to hell, Grant!" I heard one say. "How would you know what's good for us?" There was another chorus of shouts and cries, this one louder and angrier than the first.

"You must listen to me!" I cried. "I was born one of you, I have tilled and sown, I have known a hard life! You must believe me—I act in no one's interest but your own. I am doing the right thing by vetoing this egregious legislation!"

"The right thing?" one shouted. "Just like you did the right thing at Shiloh and Cold Harbor?"

"You're every bit the fool they say you are, Grant!" shouted another. An irate roar began to build.

"No!" I shouted, when suddenly, from somewhere off toward my left, an object came flying at me. Only an instant before its impact could I make it out—a tomato! It landed against my shoulder and splattered everyone around me. "See here!" I bellowed.

"See this, Grant!" a man in the center of the crowd shouted back, then reared and let another tomato fly. A third let loose an egg. Suddenly, missiles were catapulted toward me, from each and every direction, just as the snowballs thrown by the Kentucky boys pelted Useful almost forty years before. A wiser man might have withdrawn, but I would be blamed if I ran from a mob, particularly from men whom, in all likelihood, I had led into the great *struggle for their human redemption*. I stood there, frozen by both determination and shock, when I felt two strong hands grasp me by the shoulders from behind.

It was Useful. "Get behind me," he whispered, and moved me to the side as he stepped to the front of the steps from which we faced the crowd. "My brothers!" he shouted. "You must desist at once!"

"Stuff it, Brother Phipps!" one of them replied, and a new barrage of objects flew from the crowd.

Useful herded me behind himself and called out, "Men! Men! How could we have come this far in search of our dignity, only to lose it at this rare moment?"

His remarks were met by a chorus of disgruntled shouts. "Grant's a stooge! Give him to us!" came a cry.

Useful turned quickly. "Get back inside," he said, quietly but directly. Babcock turned first and led me back in the front door of the White House as I heard Useful arguing with the crowd behind me. A hand towel was brought to me and I wiped the debris from my coat as Useful rejoined me in the front hall. "I appreciate your assistance," I said to Useful.

He addressed me uncomfortably. "I regret they treated you so, Mr. President. Regardless of their anger, none of us seeks to denigrate what you did for our nation. But even if the Civil War has been won, we are still divided in ways you never contemplated—haves and have-nots, the moneyed interest and the people who serve it. We are one country, Mr. President, but we are not yet one nation."

Useful sighed deeply. "It will be planting time soon, Mr. President. I am sure you have taken that into account—you did when you paroled Lee's army at Appomattox. You know we will leave Washington and return home, whether we have impressed upon you the merit of our cause or not. But you are not done with us, because we cannot be done away with. You will be forced to choose—which nation will you lead?"

We stared at each other for what seemed like an endless moment, and I thought once again of the two horses tethered to the millpole at my father's tannery—tied to each other, but constantly going in opposite directions. But now we each stood where the other had stood only a while before. Useful nodded to me and left, and I watched him walk away much as I did that afternoon in San Francisco, wondering where he was going next. One prophecy, two directions—the only difference was the Great Master's intent was now known.

In a few days Useful and his mob were gone and order restored. But if order was restored in Washington, it was not in the South. The Klan and the other white supremacists were engaged in an open insurrection against the government. In Texas and Arkansas, freely elected Negro officials were taken from their chambers at gunpoint. Negro political meetings were broken up and their attendees brutalized—sometimes taken out for summary execution. Negroes who refused to submit to sharecropping had their homes burned.

Fish, my patrician Secretary of State, was unmoved. "Yes, it's very disturbing, I know," he said, as Mrs. Grant and Mrs. Fish nodded empathetically from across the dinner table in the White House one evening. "But what would you have us do about it? I'm sure Sheridan"—Sheridan was now military commander of the Southern states—"would like to use his troops to restore order, but do you think the people of the North are willing to fight the Civil War a second time, and this time just for the damned Moors?"

Mrs. Grant snorted. "I should say not."

"Yes, but if we don't do anything, we might as well not have fought the first time," I said.

"Oh, come now," Fish said reproachingly. "Let's not be melodramatic. The Union is preserved, after all. The Freedmen will one day be full citizens. It's just that we need to keep our expectations realistic."

"What realistic expectations can be kept for men who are shot in the back of the head?" I demanded.

"Minimal ones," Fish said, shrugging. "But we have to start somewhere, don't we?"

Somewhere better than that, I thought, but I seemed to be alone in my misgivings. Rawlins was dead, Parker was gone, and Sheridan was far away—they were the only souls around me who had ever had any genuine sympathy for the Negro. Sherman still hoped we might send the Negroes to Santo Domingo or somewhere else far away, a solution then shared by a sizable faction who disliked the Negro but wanted to deprive the Southerner of the satisfaction of killing him. Mrs. Grant, at the other extreme, no doubt wished slavery might be reintroduced. Nonetheless, if the alternatives were a few Freedmen being murdered on the one hand and a second Civil War on the other, then perhaps Fish was right, even if the methodical killing of innocent men seemed so terribly wrong.

"Of course it's wrong," Fish agreed. "But that doesn't tell us what to do about it."

By 1875, the white insurrection was in full flower. Klan gangs roamed the South with impunity, murdering Negroes who put up resistance and leaving their bodies by the side of the road as a reminder for the rest.

I summoned Sherman and Sheridan to plan a response. Sheridan was ready to take up the challenge. "Fine," he said. "If they want to flaunt their refusal to subscribe to the law, let me whip them until they beg to change their minds. I'm ready."

"I don't care how badly Phil wants to fight," Sherman responded. "Whether you like it or not, we let these Southerners come back into the country. So unless you want to send a full-fledged army to kill a goodly number of them, Sam, you're going to have to live with it."

"Live with it? Isn't this why we fought the war? So we wouldn't have to live with it?"

"No," Sherman said sharply. "We fought so they would be Americans again. And we won by beating the enemy's army, not by changing his fucking mind."

"But letting them get away with this is tantamount to surrender," I argued.

"No, going to a fellow's parlor and handing your opponent your sword is tantamount to surrender," Sherman said with a laugh. "Stop being so fucking melodramatic, Grant," he said. "Lincoln couldn't get the country to fight a war if it was just for the niggers! Do you want to ask the country to fight a second war for them now? Ha!"

Sherman dissuaded me from acting then, and I let matters stand, but that didn't make the problem go away. In fact, the problem came to see me.

"There's a Senator Jones to see you," Babcock said as he entered my office one day.

"I don't know a Senator Jones," I said. "Where's he from?"

"Mississippi," Babcock said.

I dropped my pen down onto my desk. "Very well, I'll receive him downstairs." I rose from my seat and made my way down the stairs, through the entrance hallway where the Colonel usually held forth, into the Green Room, where I encountered: "William Jones!"

It was William, the Colonel's slave, whom I had freed in 1859.

"Yep, Grant, it's me, ol' William. Now a senator, much to my good fortune!" he said, rising perfunctorily from his chair and shaking my hand. He was older, balder and worn, but he retained a healthy, lean carriage and his keen, observant expression.

"William!" I exclaimed as I looked him over. "However did you get from St. Louis to Mississippi, and however did you get elected?"

"Oh, I been aroun'," my former slave replied. "I was in a Free'man's division in the war, became an officuh, and chose to stay in the South.

From there, it was my good luck more than anythin' else that put me here. That and a few of them carpetbaggers. Besides, if there is one thing more surprisin' than my bein' a senator, it's you in the White House, rather than the poorhouse!"

I managed a nod. "And did you ever write the book you imagined?"

William laughed. "Nah," he drawled. "Writin' books is for afterwards," he said, prophetically. "I'm all involved in politics now. I'm makin' a substantial livin' at it, too." He smiled. "I got the most respectable gemmin comin' to see me and offerin' me considerable sums for my allegiance."

My brow furrowed involuntarily. "William, what you're talking about is corruption!"

"Corruption?" he recoiled. "Grant, I watched the Crédit Mobil-yay, and I watched the most sanctimonious of the lot, Garfield, get his jest the same as the next fellow. So I say, sauce for the goose, Grant." He reached into his pocket and withdrew a sizable roll of large bills. "See this? It's worth more than I ever was! If I sell myself to a partic'lar interest, then I'm only doin' what passes for normal 'round here. Besides, I been sold various times in my life, Grant. The only difference is that now I get to keep the money!"

"But what about progress for the Freedmen?" I insisted. "Have you given any thought to that?"

William looked up, startled. "Have I given the Free'men any thought, Grant? Why yes, I have—it might not surprise you to know the problems of the Free'men been on my mind considerable. In fact, I've been thinkin' if I was President like yo'self, I'd send the troops down to the South to stop them Klan peoples from killin' any more of the Free'men—or, as I call 'em, *us*. That's what I been thinkin', Grant. Now, jest what have you been thinkin'?"

I shook my head. "William, William, please. Don't you think I appreciate the situation in the same terms as do you? But it's not that simple," I insisted. "We'd have to send an occupying army to the South, wage a second war against them. Right or wrong, William, the public would never stand for it."

"But you passed a law, Grant," William said. "You passed the Klan law back in '71—all you got to do is enforce it! What good is law if you don't enforce it?"

"Not much good at all," I confessed. "But my hands are tied."

William Jones snickered. "Grant, your tortured soul don't inspire any sympathy on my part. Back when you was poor, you somehow found your way to doin' the right thing. Now that you're the President, the right thing seems more elusive, don't it?"

The blasted, cursed *right thing*! It was a source of constant bedevilment! The farmers wanted me to do the right thing, the Oglala Sioux, William Jones and the Freedmen, all of them clamoring for the right thing to be done. When I was a general, the right thing was the work in front of me. If men died, if the wounded suffered, if lives were lost and human beings made expendable, it was all forgiven, for the right thing was victory. The wrong thing can be done in war, because the right thing is the ultimate objective. But in peace, when there is no ultimate objective, no duration and no suspension of hostilities, the *right thing* always comes at a cost.

I looked at William Jones and told him the truth. "I cannot start a second civil war," I said.

He shook his head. "Well, you needn't worry 'bout a second, Grant, 'cause the first ain't over yet." He slapped his palms on his knees and stood before me. "Grant, I didn't suspect I'd change yo' mind, but at least I thought I'd see the look in yo' eye of wantin' to do good, like the way you was proud the day you set me free back in '57. But you ain't that man no more, Grant. You is playin' the rich man's game."

"I'm different, yes, William, but the difference is I have a nation to lead," I told him sternly. "We may all want a better world, but somebody needs to be the one who guides us toward it, who leads us out of a time of suffering."

I watched him go, shaking his head, and found myself wondering if Sherman was satisfied. But while Sherman was a raging pacifist when it came to the South, it was a different story where the Indians were concerned.

"We've got trouble in the Black Hills," he announced to me one day.

"No we don't," I said, exasperated. "I met those half-naked fellows a few years ago and we made a deal. I gave them twenty-five thousand dollars and they moved to the Black Hills, the most godforsaken, inhospitable place in creation. What possible problem could I have in the Black Hills now?"

"They found fucking gold there," Sherman said, demonstrating his ability to reduce a situation to its essence. "I've dispatched Phil's boy Custer there."

Custer! I never liked that man. He rode around with Sheridan in the closing months of the war. Sheridan must have been taken with Custer's head of long blond hair, which he wore to such vain effect. Custer was a self-promoting showboat with an eye on a political career. "I'll tell you what Custer is trying to do," I told Sherman. "He's trying to stir up some trouble out there so he can kill Indians and run for President one day! We moved the Sioux to this land after Jay Cooke wanted their old land. The Sioux have a right to this land, even if there's gold on it. Custer's orders should be to protect them," I said plainly.

Sherman shook his head. "The job of the army is to keep the peace, Grant. It shouldn't mix into other peoples' quarrels. There are going to be thousands of prospectors streaming into the Black Hills, just like back in California. They're going to kill the Sioux and take their fucking land, gold and all, unless we keep the peace."

"Then what do you propose?" I asked.

"We've got to move the Sioux somewhere else or all hell's going to break loose."

"But if we try to move the Sioux somewhere else all hell *will* break loose."

Sherman snorted as he rose. "That kind of fucking hell," he said, "I can handle."

Oh, there was once a time when I would have had the energy and inclination to argue the point. Besides, as I've said, you can hire an architect, but the man with the hammer builds the house, and now Sherman had the hammer. If I told him not to attack the Sioux, he'd go observe them instead, the way Taylor observed the Mexicans. So Sherman's views prevailed: He sent an expedition out to give the Sioux hell.

While the bond between us could not be undone, this difference between us isolated me even more. Rawlins, Boutwell, Horace Porter, Eli Parker, even Fred and Buck were gone. My daughter Nellie married a British aristocrat, and even Jesse, our youngest, was now getting ready to go off to college. The only familiar faces left were my father and Colonel Dent, who held forth regularly in counterpoint in the front hall, one espousing enfranchisement of the Negro and sound money, the other white supremacy and cheap dollars.

"You're an ignorant, malevolent boor," my father reminded the Colonel one afternoon.

"You're a stone-hearted hypocrite," the Colonel retorted as he reached into his suit for a flask. He surprised himself by finding it and fumbled its top open. "You like your money close and your niggers far away," he said to my father, all the while regarding the flask, which he pivoted off his lips and turned upside down. He refreshed himself amply and ran his tongue over the droplets perched around his mouth. "You?" he asked my father, extending the chalice.

"Thanks," my father said, helping himself, albeit more politely. "And don't you tell me about how I like my niggers, you of all people, you slave driver."

The Colonel took the flask back and screwed it up. "It would take a Northern bloodsucker to worry about the rights of slaves while trampling on the Southern way of life."

"It would take a slave driver to see the misery of indentured servitude as a way of life," my father hurled back.

The Colonel sighed. "And so it was," he muttered as he slipped his flask back into his suit and pushed himself to his feet with his cane. "I feel the need for a nap," he announced.

My father put his hands on his knees and pushed himself upright as well. "I believe it's time for me to do the same at my hotel," he said.

"Very well. Tomorrow, then?"

"No, I'm going back to Covington tomorrow, but I'll be back in a few weeks. I'll see you then, you baboon."

The Colonel swung his cane against my father's rump with all the force he could muster, which was no force at all. "Fine, you parasite. I'll receive you here in the Executive Mansion when you return," and with that he walked away. My father left for Covington the next day and died there shortly thereafter. The Colonel followed that Christmas, 1873.

Which left me only Babcock and Mrs. Grant to advise me. I was now isolated and exposed, and vulnerable to my enemies, first among whom was the Scourge of Corruption himself, James Abram Garfield.

Garfield was becoming something of a national figure, the fiery opponent of all illegality with which he wasn't directly involved. Every scandal he exposed advanced him that much more. By 1874, you would think that he'd have thanked me for all the notoriety he'd gotten out of my administration.

"I have bad news, Mr. President," he told me one day, arriving at my White House office with a grim sense of purpose. "It appears our friend Congressman Butler has secured for one of his friends back in Massachusetts the job of tax bounty hunter. The fellow finds people who are delinquent on their taxes and receives a portion of whatever is collected."

"Well, that seems a perfectly fine arrangement to me," I said.

"It would be if the local tax authorities had not turned over their tax prosecution files to this fellow, Mr. President!" Garfield responded. "He's been skimming the tax system for hundreds of thousands of dollars! And he's done it with the Treasury Secretary's approval! If a thing like this gets out, it could cost us the Congress in the elections this fall!"

"Well, we'd better keep it from getting out, then," I said. That seemed simple enough to me.

"You can't conceal corruption!" Garfield drew back, aghast. "It would be corrupt!" He shook his head with a look of resolve. "I intend to have hearings!"

"And make it an issue with the election coming upon us?"

"We'll have to deal with that when the time comes, Mr. President. My first responsibility is to root out corruption!" He rose and made a little bow. "Each of us, I suppose, must in his own way make some sacrifice for the nation."

Garfield held his hearings and my Treasury Secretary was gone in the space of weeks, but the nation was up in arms over the tax scandal regardless. Newspapers wrote about it, drunk men in hotels debated it. And it gave Garfield a reason to come see me again.

"This tax scandal up in Massachusetts is costing us dearly," he now fretted. "Everybody knows about it! We're going to lose this election!"

"Maybe if you'd gone a little easier in your hearings," I suggested.

"It's too late for that kind of recrimination," Garfield said testily. "You've got to appoint a new Treasury Secretary, one people can trust."

"I suppose we can find one."

"What about Bristow?" Garfield asked.

Benjamin Bristow—Lincoln's old friend from Kentucky whom I had made solicitor general. If appointing Bristow would protect me on the corruption issue, then why not? In fact, if Bristow became Treasury Secretary, I could have Garfield go complain to him.

It seemed like a good solution. At least until the next scandal broke.

The Treasury was supposed to collect a tax on distilled spirits, but as will happen when small numbers of taxpayers and tax collectors do business over a long period of time, certain arrangements are made. The conspiracy of crooked tax collectors and their cronies came to be known as the Whiskey Ring. On a tip from a newspaperman, Bristow learned about such arrangements in the St. Louis area, where the tax collector was a fellow named MacDonald, a distinguished veteran of the Civil War whom I had appointed to the post for his honesty and bravery. At least I'd been right about his bravery—he no doubt needed it to amass over $100,000 in payoffs.

And it also helps to have friends in high places, or so Bristow told me. "This fellow MacDonald tells us he had a partner," Bristow said.

"They usually do," I agreed. "Who is it?"

"Orville Babcock," Bristow said.

"My Orville Babcock?" I asked.

"One and the same. He's in it up to his ears."

Well, I wouldn't believe a word of this. Babcock had been with me since the Virginia campaign, the picture of loyalty. Bristow was no better than Garfield, I thought—they were little yapping dogs, digging up the garden, looking for bones that weren't there and leaving nothing but holes behind. And so Bristow was off and running in pursuit of Babcock. And once Garfield got the scent, he was close behind—he wasn't about to let Bristow supplant him as the Scourge of Corruption!

"This Babcock matter is very serious," Garfield said gravely some time later as he let himself into my office. He had become an all-too-familiar fixture.

"You're not considering hearings, are you?" I asked, anticipating the worst.

"No," Garfield replied, and I sighed with relief. "We're too busy having hearings on the surveying scandal in the Interior Department," he added.

I sat back up. "What surveying scandal?"

"Your Interior Secretary had been awarding surveying contracts to people with political connections, people who can't do a lick of surveying, as it turns out."

I erupted. "Confound it, but I am tired of being hectored with these baseless allegations! First poor Babcock and now this!" I cried, my temper getting the better of me. "Name one soul who has been involved!" I challenged.

"How about Orvil Grant?" Garfield asked.

"My Orvil Grant?" I asked.

Garfield merely nodded.

Hearings into Orvil's surveying contracts went forward. He was truly our father's son, drawing ample pay for work never done. But the hearings into corruption in the Interior Department did not direct attention away from Bristow's competing investigation into corruption in the Treasury Department. Nor did it drown out the uproar over Babcock and whether he had been part of the Whiskey Ring. I now had conflicting scandals on my hands, and the Attorney General came to see me.

"You must address the Babcock matter," he said. "The public must have complete confidence you are not covering up criminal behavior."

"What am I supposed to do? Do you think he did it?" I asked, crestfallen.

The Attorney General nodded sadly. "The evidence suggests he did. You must release a statement to the press on the subject."

"A statement?" *No terms other than immediate and unconditional surrender can be accepted. I propose to move immediately upon your works.* Oh, I knew something about a good statement, I thought. "All right then," I said as I gathered myself. "Take this as my statement: *Let no guilty man escape.*"

The Attorney General made a brief note on his pad. "Very good, Mr. President," he said, with some relief, short and to the point. "*Let no guilty man escape.*"

"If it can be avoided," I added.

"If it can be avoided?" the Attorney General asked.

"Well, yes," I replied. "*Let no guilty man escape if it can be avoided.* That's my statement. We certainly don't want any guilty man to escape, and if Babcock's guilty, we certainly don't want him to escape, if it can be avoided. You know, if we can avoid his escaping, so to speak."

"How would it be avoided?" the Attorney General asked.

"I don't know," I equivocated. "Maybe the fellow makes a deal—

plenty of them do that, don't they? Don't many of them avoid prosecution by, say, giving up their superiors?"

The Attorney General looked at me sternly. "Is there a need for Babcock to give up his superior?"

I looked at him blankly until the meaning of his question occurred to me. "What? Me? Absolutely not!" I recoiled in my chair. "Why, that's preposterous!"

"So you had nothing to do with this?"

"Of course I didn't," I protested. "And neither did Babcock! All I'm saying is, let no guilty man escape, which Babcock isn't, and if it can't be helped, well, that's another story, that's all," I said, at which point the Attorney General left, but the sick feeling in my stomach did not.

Meanwhile, Garfield was not going to be outdone. "Our hearings on the surveying scandal have been concluded. Your Interior Secretary is a crook, and so is your brother. We shall now move on to this problem with Babcock, and from there we can go to the matter of Belknap, your War Secretary," he said, consulting his notes as if scheduling guests for tea.

"Belknap? What about Belknap?"

Garfield shook his head bitterly. "He's corrupt, of course. The War Department manages the trading exchanges found on every Indian reservation out West, and Belknap has been auctioning off these franchises in exchange for kickbacks."

"I don't believe it!" I said. "It's a smear, just like Babcock!"

"We have the checks and bank records to prove it. And I'm afraid it's worse than that."

"Worse? How can it be worse?"

Garfield sighed. "One of the parties providing the kickbacks was your own brother Orvil."

"Orvil!" I sighed. "Is there no end? One minute they're accusing him of securing shoddy surveying contracts, now this!"

Garfield nodded. "Yes, Orvil's been a busy fellow," he said, turning to his notes. "Also Babcock's brother, and your brother-in-law John Dent. All of them."

"But what *real* proof do you have? All that paperwork you mentioned could be forged, you know."

"Oh, we have testimony from people on the scene—we have testimony from the generals in command of the region!"

I folded my arms in front of my chest. No general would betray me so. "Name one!" I challenged confidently.

Garfield looked up from his notes. "Custer."

Custer! "Why, that little foppish yellow dog!" I shouted. "How dare he make such accusations!"

"Well, what if they're true?"

"They're not true!"

Garfield shrugged. "Well, we're voting to impeach Belknap, so we'll find out whether they're true when the Senate brings him to trial," he said indifferently.

Bristow was also indifferent. "If they want to impeach Belknap, it's their business. If I want to try him in court, it's mine. Besides, I've got my hands full with Schenck."

I sighed deeply and I rested my head in my hands. "Who's Schenck?"

"He's your ambassador to Great Britain," Bristow said. "He's been engaged in stock speculation over there, encouraging the Brits to buy shoddy silver mines, that sort of thing. As soon as we're done with Babcock's Whiskey Ring trial, we can get on to that."

But Babcock's trial was not over soon. Instead, it became a drawn-out circus. He came to see Mrs. Grant and me with a look of fear in his eyes. "They're after me!" he exclaimed nervously. "Bristow, Garfield, the whole lot of them! Just like they're after Belknap and Orvil! They won't be satisfied until they've torn down everyone associated with you!"

I nodded grimly. "So I sometimes think, Babcock. How is your trial going?"

"It's going poorly," he said, grimacing. "They have all this trumped-up evidence! Just because my name is on something doesn't mean I knew anything about it—like, say, a check!" He bit his lip. "They're a pack of jackals, I tell you!"

"Is there some way the General could help?" Mrs. Grant asked. She had always been fond of Babcock.

Babcock looked up as if he'd seen the light. "Why, yes! Yes, there is! A deposition!" he said, trying his best—but failing—to look as if he'd never considered it before. "Mr. President, what if you were to give the jury a deposition attesting to my honesty? Surely they would take that into account!"

I looked at Babcock uncertainly. I didn't know which was more disconcerting—that the man I had sent to bring Lee to McLean's parlor, the man to whom I had given half of Lee's battle flag, was reduced to begging me to help him avoid a criminal conviction, or my nagging suspicion that he deserved to be convicted.

"Of course he's telling the truth," Mrs. Grant said to me that night. "How long has he been of service to you? Think of the campaigns you fought together!"

"But what if—"

"What if Babcock goes to jail?" Mrs. Grant cut in. "How many more of those around you can we allow to be hauled away? You must take action at once!"

So I assented. It was February of 1876 when they came to take my deposition at the White House. I told them Babcock was an honest man, above reproach, a man known to me to have unimpeachable integrity, a fact on which I would stake my reputation.

The jury let him off. The lying, thieving scoundrel.

But if Babcock's integrity was unimpeachable, my Secretary of War's wasn't. Garfield made good on his promise to have Belknap tried in the Senate. Belknap came to the White House in tears one morning as I was heading out on business. "I need to talk to you," he said urgently.

"You don't need to talk to me," I said calmly.

"They're going to impeach me!" Belknap wailed.

"Good luck," I said.

"I need to explain."

"No, you don't," I said, trying to get by his right flank.

"Then what should I do?" he asked.

"You need to resign," I told him. "Go up to my office and write out a resignation letter. Make it short and sweet—trust me, I know about this kind of thing. Leave it on my desk."

He began to wail. "But I shall be disgraced!"

"Too late," I told him, "you're disgraced already. If you don't resign, *I'll* be disgraced, and you'll be impeached."

He sniffled and looked at me like a scolded child. "Very well."

The Senate decided to impeach Belknap anyway. "I thought the Senate wouldn't try Belknap if he resigned," I lamented to Garfield, who was making another of his periodic visits.

"Well, it is inconvenient, to be sure," Garfield agreed, "but the Senate's zeal to fight corruption is admirable. Besides, the Senate is so busy with Belknap they'll have no time for Robeson," Garfield added pleasantly.

I fell back into my seat yet again. "Who is Robeson?" I asked testily.

"He's your Navy Secretary," Garfield said.

Oh, yes, now the name seemed familiar. "And what's he done?" I asked peevishly. "Stock manipulation? Phony surveying? Tax skimming? Railroad bond graft? Auctioning of Indian exchanges? What is it?"

"Contract payoffs," Garfield said.

What else was I expected to bear? The Navy Secretary, a low-minded thief from Philadelphia named George Robeson, was shipping all of the navy's goods through a company that dispensed to him hundreds of thousands of dollars of kickbacks in the process.

"We'll investigate him," Garfield said, looking at his watch, "but we're pretty pressed." He shook his head wearily. "I think we can fit him in before Schenck."

They got around to all of them, sooner or later. Babcock was acquitted following my lying about him being a liar. Robeson resigned. Schenck disappeared. Orvil and John Dent got away with it. The Whiskey Ring was convicted. Vice President Colfax was dumped. The Senate acquitted Belknap since he no longer was a Cabinet member—I was right about that one! Eli Parker was railroaded.

By the time of the nation's Centennial, July 4, 1876, I assumed nothing else could go wrong in the Grant administration, as it seemed to me I was the only one left in it. It was time to enjoy the Centennial celebration.

I went to Philadelphia, where I spent a pleasant day. There was a great exhibition there, a colossal hall filled with every manner of machine and productive device. It was a testament to the truth I told Useful Grant and his fellow insurrectionists—the economy was changing, propelled into a new era of manufacturing that could not have been imagined before the war. I looked at the exhibits and considered what the moneyed class had wrought. My own Presidency would end, it occurred to me, with this new world coming into being.

But when I returned to Washington, Sherman was awaiting me, sitting outside my office with the gravest of expressions. "Grant, I have some bad news," he said, his head down.

I sat down apprehensively. "What is it?"

"Custer's been massacred by the Sioux. Custer's dead. They're all dead, every last man."

I gave Sherman the look of determination I saved for moments like Shiloh or Donelson. "Tell me what happened."

"Sheridan says he walked straight into Sitting Bull's main force," Sherman said, swallowing hard.

"What kind of resistance did they manage?" I asked, trying to construct an image of the scene.

Sherman swallowed hard. "Virtually none," he said softly.

"None!" I exclaimed. "Were they ambushed?"

"No," he said, "just overwhelmed. From what we can tell, most of their guns were unfired. They most likely fell to their knees and begged for mercy, but they were slaughtered." He looked down and shook his head. "Every one dead."

There was a long, silent moment as we both imagined the scene. Finally, I spoke. "The Sioux were getting even, Sherman," I said. "There have been more Indian massacres than I can count."

Sherman ignored my meaning. "We have to go after the Sioux, Grant. The public will cry for blood."

"Why? Because Custer was treated the way we treat the Indian? I've let too many innocent people die, Sherman. I won't have the Sioux killed!"

"It's too late for the fucking Sioux, Grant," Sherman snapped in response. "The public wants the Sioux dead, an eye for an eye. Either we send the army in now, resolve the matter, and move however many of them are left to somewhere away from white folk, or we leave them to fight with the settlers every day for the next twenty years until every one of them are dead. But if we don't go in now, then every time a farm family is killed, or a barn's set afire, or a train's robbed, every time a prospector is scalped or his throat is cut, it will be on your head, Grant. You can either let Sheridan and me bring the matter to a conclusion now or you can let it drag on, to the same effect. The choice is yours."

"I'm tired of these choices, Sherman," I replied angrily. "I'm tired of choosing between civil war and racist murder or between paper money inflation and throngs of starving farmers."

"You're the one who wanted to play this political game, Grant, not me. Now take your medicine and let me get on with business."

I sighed and knew better than to argue any longer. "Do what you must," I said, and watched Sherman leave, armed with my approval to transact his dirty business. It wasn't much, weighed against the thousands of Sioux I had no doubt just consigned to death, but at least I had the small consolation of knowing that Custer was finished, that strutting, self-promoting, long-haired dog. He had seen my success in battle lead to a political career, and so he'd tried to build his own on the backs of dead Indians. He got what was coming to him, although unlike most of the men he led to their deaths, he was lucky to be shot. I feel sorry for the poor Indian marksman who plugged Custer in the head from a distance before Sitting Bull could take his scalp. I'm sure that sorry brave got pulled out of formation that night.

And so my Presidency ended. It was as if I had emerged from a long, dark tunnel, as if time suddenly regained its cadence, as if the blur of events once again regained their clarity. My Presidency began with the challenge of reuniting the nation and bringing it peace. It ended with graft, oligarchism, and oppression. It was my fortune, or misfortune, that I was called to the office of the Chief Executive without any previous political training. Mistakes were made, as all can see and I admit, but my errors were errors of judgment, not of intent. Being a great man doesn't mean being an infallible one, I suppose, and being called to a great destiny doesn't mean answering every call. After all, even the great ballplayers like Cap Anson and King Kelly don't get a hit every time they're called to bat.

When I left the White House, though, I couldn't understand why I would have failed at a job I was destined to inherit.

Now, of course, I do.

CHAPTER XIV.

I TOUR THE WORLD—THE ELECTION OF 1880—GARFIELD'S REVELATION—GRANT AND WARD—A MEETING WITH VANDERBILT

WHAT WAS I GOING TO DO NOW? *I had led great masses of men in the glorious cause of their human redemption,* both as general and as President. I had fulfilled my destiny. But now, when I searched the horizon for a new destination, a new challenge, there was no mountain left to climb.

Moreover, how were Mrs. Grant and I to live?

We didn't even have a home in the true sense—the longest time Mrs. Grant and I spent in any one place was the eight years we lived in the White House, and now we were leaving. Kicked out, as Mrs. Grant saw it—from my perspective, escaped.

So there we were, the most important people in the world, with no home, no place to go, and nothing to do. It was then the newspaper people from Philadelphia came to me with an idea—a trip around the world, a voyage to each of the world's great ports of call! They would underwrite it in exchange for the exclusive opportunity to write about it.

"Bismarck's always said he admired you," Mrs. Grant said as we assessed. "Here's your chance to meet him. Besides, you're a great man, a citizen of the world, like Wellington was. Great men take trips like this."

But Mrs. Grant was wrong: There was never a trip like this. We departed Philadelphia in the spring of 1877, heading to Europe first. I met Queen Victoria (with whom Julia commiserated on being the wife of a great leader), visited Germany (where Bismarck cursed the French), visited France (where the French cursed Bismarck), saw

Venice (a nice place if they'd drain it), and went to Greece (where the statues wanted heads). We then traveled to Egypt (where slavery was put to better effect than in the South), Palestine (where a brass band marched behind me down the Villa de la Rosa), Turkey (where the Sultan gave me horses even better than those Banks had found for me—good country, Turkey), and India (where they thought me a coward because I would not go tiger hunting). I visited Singapore, China, Siam, and Japan and, after two and a half years of traveling, arrived to cheering crowds in San Francisco in the summer of 1879 and began a triumphant crossing of the continent, with testimonial dinners at every stop along the way. We returned to Philadelphia, from whence we had started, in December of that year. The mayor declared a holiday, and the schools, factories, and banks were closed—and they weren't the first or last banks to close because of me, as it turned out. Parades lasting the entire day were held in my honor—bands and spectacles in the daytime, choruses and torches in the night. On and on they went, thousands of marchers, hundreds of thousands of spectators, until the meaning of it all became clear, at least to Mrs. Grant.

"They want you to be President again," she said.

As amazing as it seemed, she was right. You would think I would have remembered the unpleasantness of being President, but now I was focused on the prospective unpleasantness of having nothing to do, and the need to stay in the public eye, where great men belonged. And you would think the *public* would have remembered the unpleasantness of my being President, but they didn't—they had forgotten about inflation and greenbacks and had put behind them Babcock and Robeson and Belknap and Colfax and Schenck and my brother Orvil—all of them—and they certainly didn't care about slaughtered Indians or murdered Freedmen. The economy had set itself aright again, and the public wanted an emblem, a symbol of better and less complicated days, and what better symbol was there than I? *Let us have peace.* I had unwittingly pursued exactly the right strategy for these past three years—I had skipped town. I had offered no opinions, taken no actions, offended no constituencies, nor riled any new enemies. I had washed myself in the waters of absence and emerged my old self, unstained.

Mrs. Grant, of course, also wanted a symbol of better days—the days when she was the center of Washington's social circle, with a mansion in the center of town and the attentive eyes of the world focused upon her. "All you need do is ask and it will be bestowed upon you," she said.

The only problem was that other prospective Presidents had emerged in the intervening four years, among them the reformer James Blaine, and my old champion, Congressman Washburne of Galena. The nomination would not be given to me, as it had been in 1868. This time, at the age of fifty-eight, I would have to win it.

I was not sure I could. In fact, I was hesitant about running because I feared a failed third attempt at the Presidency would tarnish my goods, so to speak, at precisely the point in life when I would have to begin amassing my fortune. But when Mrs. Grant began putting together a political machine to promote me—our friends in the Congress and around the country quickly rallied to the idea—I found myself in a campaign for the third term that even George Washington eschewed.

The 1880 Republican convention was held in Chicago, and Mrs. Grant shrewdly moved our household back to Galena. It was a nearby base among a loyal following, and because of our history, we could deny we had encamped there solely for political purposes. There I received visitors, campaigners, and hangers-on, while Mrs. Grant organized our supporters in every state. But when the convention began, the delegates were still evenly split between me, a representative of the old guard, and the reformer, Blaine.

The convention proceeded deadlocked between us for thirty-five ballots—I had a plurality, but could not muster the majority. And after these ballots, the coalition of reformers at the convention sought to open a second front against me by proposing to eliminate the "unit rule"—the rule that compelled an entire state's delegation to vote for the candidate favored by a majority of that delegation. Favored as I was in a handful of big states—New York, Illinois, Ohio, and the like—the unit rule was a favorable circumstance for me, and I was resolved to keep it.

We were unsurprised to learn who was leading the anti-unit-rule reformers.

"Garfield! That devil!" Mrs. Grant snapped when we were brought the news. She whirled at me, good eye ablaze. "You ought to crush him. Just like you crushed Lee."

"And what do you propose?" I asked.

"Ulys, this is just like battle," Mrs. Grant said, her voice firm. "You have the same compelling advantages you had when you crossed the Rapidan—strength and resources your opponents cannot match. The only question is whether you have the will to use them now as you did then. If you do, Ulys, we can win!"

She rose from her chair and paced the floor, sounding as much like a general as I ever had. "We must undertake a full frontal assault against the enemy!" she said. "We must attack! You must travel to Chicago and go out on the convention floor!"

"But it's just not done," I demurred. "It's tantamount to begging."

"Begging my arse," Mrs. Grant snapped back. "It's leadership! The moral courage to command! You're the one man in this country who can bring a gathering to its feet without so much as saying a word, the only man in America who can make a crowd weep uncontrollably simply by standing in place. You've got to go to the convention, go out on the floor, and simply *appear*. They will cheer until they cry, and then cry until you are nominated!" Her eyes were ablaze with vision. "What happens when Jim Blaine shows up somewhere? When Elihu Washburne shows up? Nothing! But if your friend Senator Conkling were to get up and recite that stupid little poem—" Here she stopped and put a hand on her breast as she looked upward with a reverent gaze:

> "And when asked what state he hails from
> Our sole response shall be
> He hails from Appomattox
> And its famous apple tree

"And then if Ulysses S. Grant were to arrive—the world would come to a halt!" She then paused, looking puzzled. "What apple tree are they talking about?"

"When they found Lee with my note telling him to meet me at Appomattox, he was sitting under an apple tree," I replied.

She pursed her lips. "That's good! Very picturesque. Now you must go and make it happen."

I sighed. "I am willing to be President again if you want me to, but I won't lower myself to begging to do it."

"You won't be *begging*—you're *offering* your services to your nation once again, that's all." Mrs. Grant smiled eagerly and sat beside me.

"Go and see Garfield," she said. "You're supposed to go to Milwaukee in a few days for a reunion of the Grand Army. Chicago's on the way, it's a natural place to stop. Garfield will be there at the convention. Just drop in and talk to him. It's a simple courtesy."

"What am I supposed to say to him?" I protested. "He hates me, and the feeling is mutual."

"Tell him you'll go to the floor of the convention if necessary to defeat the unit rule! Warn him he'll either have to surrender or fight you in the open, just like Lee was afraid to do. Show him you're willing to compromise: If he agrees to withdraw the rule without a fight, there will be someplace for him in the administration, maybe even as your running mate. But if he chooses to fight, his political career ends right there," she said with convincing vehemence.

Now, this wasn't a bad idea. I had no desire to make a public appearance, but a one-on-one discussion with Garfield in his Chicago hotel room could do no harm. And if Garfield gave me grave offense, I could always appear on the convention floor and finish him off, just as Mrs. Grant advised. So I wired Garfield and told him of my desire to meet, and a time was set for us to do so two days hence.

I took the train to Chicago and went to the hotel where Garfield was ensconced in an opulent suite decorated in burgundy velvet and mahogany—obviously, his resources went beyond his Crédit Mobilier stock. I was escorted into a parlor where he presided in a massive red velvet wing chair; the spacious room and enormous chair both accentuated his elongated frame.

He looked at me through his dark, narrow eyes. "Grant!" he said, welcoming me with feigned cordiality. "We are honored to be in your presence," he said in a manner that conveyed the contrary. He nodded without ever getting up, beckoning me toward a seat opposite him. His cronies lined the walls of the place—half a dozen of them, seated around the edges of the room, out of the conversation. I sat down and regarded them, then began to say my piece.

"Garfield, there has been bad blood between us, we both know that," I said, careful to sound gracious. "But your motion to eliminate the unit rule is no more than a brazen attempt to deny me this nomination." Garfield nodded passively, his hands folded in his lap, as I spoke. "I am obliged to defend myself, sir, but in the spirit of goodwill, I have come to give you warning.

"Before Scott took Veracruz," I continued, now sitting back comfortably in my chair and holding forth with all the confidence befitting a great man discussing other great men, "he sent in a note demanding capitulation, and only after receiving none did he begin his bombardment. I am doing the same with you. I insist you withdraw your motion regarding the unit rule. If you do, you shall be well placed in my administration—perhaps Secretary of War, or even the Vice Presidency." I waited a moment to let my words have their full effect. "But if you do not, I will go to the convention floor myself to defeat you, and I will put my considerable personal acclaim," I said, "on the line to do so. I will look every man there in the eye and defy him to vote against me."

Garfield answered without emotion. "The unit rule is antidemocratic, Grant. It denies the minorities in state delegations the right of fair representation."

"So does the Electoral College," I responded, "but I fail to see your agony over that. This is a matter of politics, Garfield, not reformism or Constitutionalism! And it is nothing more than a veiled attack against me!"

Garfield suddenly sprang forward in his chair, like a serpent striking. "Yes, it is, Grant! That's why I'm not giving up my motion—I can deny you the Presidency, and I have waited to pay you back for a very long time!"

I did not blink. "A man's desire for revenge can get the best of him. You proceed at great peril," I cautioned him, surprisingly calm now that I found myself at war again. The old feeling was returning to me now: I would crush him if I had to. *I propose to move immediately upon your works.*

"Great peril?" Garfield laughed derisively. "Of what? Your considerable personal acclaim?"

"Don't mock me, Garfield!"

"Mock you? I don't *have* to mock you. Listen to yourself speak of your faded reputation. You have become a tired old parody of yourself, Grant, a human souvenir! You mock yourself!" He leaned back and stared at me with cold contempt. "Your time has come and gone, Grant. Tomorrow you will withdraw your name from nomination and you will accede to my candidacy, not Blaine's. The nation wants honest government, and I am the man to deliver it—the Scourge of Corruption! You will support me or suffer the consequences!"

I drew back, barely in control of my anger. "The consequences! Of all the impudence! What consequence can you possibly visit upon me?"

Garfield broke into a hateful leer. "You'll find out, Grant! It will be my pleasure to destroy your great personal acclaim! I will see to it you are remembered only as the craven, drunken, whoremongering father of bastards you truly are!"

I sprang to my feet, flushed with rage. "You dog! You lying, hateful little cur! How dare you besmirch me! Have you gone so mad with your contempt for me you would spread such lies about a man who has served his nation so?"

He sat back in his chair and looked up at me smugly. "Do you deny it?" he said, smirking.

"Of course I deny it!" I answered hotly, planting myself squarely in front of him and jabbing the air as I spoke. "I have known but one woman in my life and my faithfulness to her will forever be unimpeached! If you do not retract this villainous, outrageous falsehood this very instant, I swear to you I will walk out on the convention floor tomorrow and lead the delegates in 'The Battle Hymn of the Republic,' I will recite that pap about the apple tree, I'll read my letter to Buckner at Donelson if I need to! I am Ulysses S. Grant, and don't you forget it!"

"You're a liar, Grant, and a five-star one at that," Garfield said, sneering. "A drunken, whoring liar. I have proof, and if you don't withdraw your nomination tomorrow, the rest of the nation will have it, too." He nodded to one of his cronies who got up and went through a door off the parlor and in a moment returned. Clinging to his arm was a woman, most likely in her late fifties, short and squat, with thin, plain hair pulled back into a small knot, wearing a red ruffled brocade dress that was both more elegant and daring than her dumpy frame warranted. Garfield's lackies placed her in front of me and turned her to face me—only then did I realize the woman was blind. For the life of me I could not place her. Who was this old woman and why were they dragging her out amid tales of whoremongering and bastardism?

"Say hello, madam," Garfield prompted.

The woman said, "Hello, Ulysses," and as I heard her voice, a second realization came to me.

She was my first Julia, whom I had last seen underneath Useful in his father's barn back in Georgetown, over forty years ago.

I gaped as I stood there—with my eyes wide and jaw slack, I must have looked like a marionette whose strings had been cut. Where had they found her? Did they know? Had they somehow found out about Useful, and my deception, so many years later? She stood there in an odd, disoriented posture, until both she and I were distracted by Garfield's voice.

"Well, then, Grant, my picture of virtue. Your reaction tells me all I need to know! You admit you know this woman, then?"

What was I to say? "Yes, I know her," I said tentatively, waiting to see where this would lead. "I knew her as a youth. And what of it?" I asked, probing for answers.

Garfield ignored my question. "And madam," he said, the leer in his tone unchecked, "you know Ulysses Grant, don't you?"

Her unfocused gaze turned back in the direction of my voice as she answered, "Yes, I do." Her voice was low and throaty, the voice of a hard life.

Garfield smiled at me with contempt. "And madam, did Ulysses Grant force himself upon you as a girl, disappear after you were de-flowered, and thereafter drive you into a life of prostitution and moral degradation?"

"Yes," she said impassively, "he did."

I shook my head as the scene unfolded around me. Julia was taking me to be Useful and, blind as she was, could not tell the difference! But to defend myself, to tell her the truth, would be to reveal every-thing—my spying upon her and Useful that night, our coming upon Judge Mayor Grant and his family, my entire life of deception—all be-fore my most hated political enemy!

Garfield smiled, confident he held the cards. "And madam, did you have Ulysses Grant's child?" he asked.

She stared blankly ahead. "Yes, I did. In 1838."

I buried my face in my hands. She had borne Useful's child and was now taking me to be the father! I slumped back into my chair as Garfield stared at me with satisfaction. "It goes without saying it was our good fortune to come across this poor woman, Grant," he said. "To her credit, and to soothe your tortured, exposed soul, she did not want to be involved in my passion play. But given her circumstances, she had very little in the way of choice, as you can see." He examined his suit coat for lint while I stared at Julia. "Very well, then, Grant," he said. "We have established who and what you really are. Now the only question is—shall we share our knowledge with the nation and with history, or will you throw your support to me and allow us to take this poor woman home in secrecy and avoid a public scandal?"

"Leave me alone with her," I said softly. "I will abide by your terms."

"You will?" he said, growing excited. "You'll withdraw and campaign for me?"

"Yes, yes, I will do so without reservation of any kind. Just end this nonsense right here, for everyone's sake."

Garfield rose from his chair with a self-satisfied look. "Then our deal is complete, Grant. I appreciate your coming this far to see me, given the circumstances, and I apologize for having stuck my *nose"*—he paused for a second to savor his revenge—"into your business. Let us leave these old friends to their reunion," he said to his lackies, before leading them out, laughing lewdly, into one of the rooms off the parlor.

The door finally closed and we were alone. "Julia!" I turned to her, flush with emotion. "Julia, what has become of you?"

She reached behind herself for the seat Garfield had vacated and lowered herself into it. "Well, Useful Grant, I declare!" she said in a withering tone. "I never thought I'd find you again—I didn't even think you were alive after they found your parents dead that day. Then, years later, suddenly, everyone in New Orleans was talking about you, about your victories at Henry and Donelson. I didn't know what I would ever say or do if I was to face you again!"

"What has become of you?" I asked again. "How did you lose your sight?"

"The lues took my sight," she said bitterly. "Syphilis! That's what left me blind! All these years I've whored to make my way."

I shook my head in disbelief. "Julia, how ever—"

She interrupted me. "How ever did I fall? How did I come to giving men their way for a few coins? Their few coins were more than I got from you!" She laughed contemptuously. "I have you to thank for everything, Useful. Wasn't that exactly what you said—I was a wanton little harlot, an easy mark, that you had me without a fight? Isn't that what you told me after you led me on that night? You pried me open with your fast talking, had me as artlessly as I've ever been had, led me to give up my innocence for the fantasy of being a rich man's wife, when I could have been the wife of the man I loved."

The man she loved. The ache in my heart came back after forty years: For an instant it was as fresh as the night I acquired it. "Hiram," she continued. "He was the man I loved." She pulled a handkerchief from the sleeve of her dress to wipe a tear as she thought of me. "What a mistake I made! I went home from your party and cried all night. I had let you take me when all I really wanted was the chance to make a life with him. I promised myself the next day I would find him, I would confess everything to him, no matter what pain it caused me, and I would promise myself to him for the rest of our lives, no matter what my father said, if Hiram would only forgive me." She shook her head in anguished memory. "But he was gone. It was the same day I first heard you had disappeared—a thief, they said, attacked your carriage, killed your parents, and you were missing. Oh, how I wished you dead."

"But—but what about Useless?" I asked, probing. "What happened to him?"

"His name is Hiram!" she shouted in my defense, just as she had that night forty-one years before, but this time there was conviction in her voice. "Don't ever call him Useless! He was a warm, sweet, caring boy, as useful as life itself. When I couldn't stand it any longer I went to his daddy's tannery and asked where Hiram had gone. His daddy said he was despondent over something—he didn't say what, but he gave me a look that scared me—and that Hiram had gone to live with some cousins in Kentucky to learn the tanning trade. I was afraid Hiram had somehow found out about us, about what you done to me, and took flight before I could explain. And then I realized he was never going to learn the truth." She sobbed a bit without ever softening her angry countenance.

"I'm sure he somehow did," I said.

"If he did, it was no thanks to you," she said. "By the end of that summer, I was with child—your child, Ulysses. I prayed to God to take the child away. But He didn't, and I didn't know how to do it myself. My father sent me from his house—drove me out, like a bad lamb from the flock, sent me away for the sin of licentiousness and told me never to return to his door, all thanks to the diddling you did on top of me."

Useful's child! I was overwhelmed with sympathy for her. "And what happened to the child?" I asked.

"*Your* child," she said pointedly, without getting to the point. "I had him in New Orleans, where I ended up finding the work." She looked down for a moment and rubbed her brow, then glared sightlessly in my direction. "And I named him Hiram! I named your child for everything you're not, and I named him for my struggles," she said, breaking down into speechlessness.

"Do you know where he is?" I asked.

"No," she said, staring sightlessly at a point on the wall. "I raised him in the house. When the war started, he said he was going up North, to fight for the Union—maybe he did. I was proud of him, but living down there, I had to keep quiet about it. But I never heard from him again, just like I never heard from Hiram himself," she said, her voice aching with regret. "And then the sickness began to catch up with me. I was bound to catch a dose sooner or later. I knew plenty of girls who got it and got by fine, but it took my eyes from me, maybe fifteen years back. When it did, I was glad Hiram wasn't there to see me."

She rubbed her brow with her palms. "For the longest time I had yearned to find Hiram and tell him the truth. I knew somehow that whatever had happened he'd find it in his heart to forgive me. I had a dream once that he was you and you were him, and he was rich and important, like you were, and he would be my child's daddy, instead of you," she said, smiling at the fantasy. "It would have been so perfect." She sighed and shook her head.

I stared at her with infinite sadness. If only I could have told her the truth. But it was too late for the truth, too late for me and for Mrs. Grant and our children, too late for the country that revered me and the history that would be written about me, too late to renounce my destiny. And it was too late for my first Julia, too. What would be the sense of telling her who I really was and what had become of Useful?

It was too late to tell anyone the truth. "Is there something I can do for you?" I asked.

She snorted. "Men! They ask questions like that after they degrade you! What gall! What infinite . . . paternalism, that's the word for it. Only a man offers to help after he's destroyed you. I've seen men, Useful. I've seen men as they really are, and I don't want help from any man. The night you had me was the night I decided I'd never be weak in front of another man again."

"Do you need money?" I asked. "Or medical treatment?"

She laughed out loud. "Don't worry about that, dearie. Garfield's given me as much money as I could ask for. I'll do fine now, for an old blind landlady." She put her hands on her knees and turned her head to the side. "Mr. Garfield!" she shouted into the air. "Get me out of here! I'm done with this gent!"

The door opened and Garfield reappeared, followed by his cronies. He smiled with satisfaction. "Have we had a pleasant reunion?"

I stood and looked at him bitterly. "We have an understanding, Garfield, and I will live by it. I will not bother you with the truth, which you would not believe anyway. I only warn you, if you ever come to break the terms we have agreed to—"

He put up a silencing hand. "Spare me," he said. "Our deal is struck." He then turned to his men. "Help this poor woman out before I show Grant the door."

Julia extended her arm and waited for one of the men to take it and escort her. When she felt a hand touch her arm, she turned toward me one last time. "Sad to see me go, Useful?" she asked.

"Sadder than you know," I said softly. She stopped, and from her look I thought for an instant that she might have realized there was a larger, more unspoken truth, but more likely that was just what I wanted to see. She nodded tentatively, and allowed herself to be ushered out of the parlor. I watched the door close. Garfield stood before me, gloating, but I was already a world away.

Mrs. Grant was a loyal wife and partner, to be sure: She had borne me four children and raised them dutifully when I was absent, drunk, and poor. She had not uttered a cross word to me until I was a success, by which time she had the right to utter as many as she did not when I was a failure. But the fate I had abandoned when I stole Useful's fate was not as I had imagined it. I would have been loved, the way a simple man was entitled to be loved—with simple devotion. Who knows what happiness I had abandoned?

I said a last good-bye to Garfield and headed for the door. I would think of something to tell Mrs. Grant later.

But if Fate had determined I would not be President again, I would prevail upon Fate to make me the next best thing—rich.

Ulysses Grant was now up for bid.

•　　•　　•

We moved into a nice home that was purchased for me by my rich patrons—it was in Manhattan, on Sixty-sixth Street off Fifth Avenue. I had a splendid office downtown, near Wall Street, with a bit of money coming in. But I was now upon my sixtieth birthday, and all the gifts of money and stocks and bonds from those same rich patrons, as well as my earnings as President, had been either spent or wiped out in the Crash of '73, and it was time to strike it big. There had to be something the man who saved his country could do profitably, and I was resolved to find it.

It was around then an opportunity came to me through the least likely of sources—my son Ulysses, Jr., Buck. After graduating from Harvard and Columbia, Buck married the daughter of a banker of considerable means. Buck went to work on Wall Street, where he ended up in partnership with a young fellow named Ferdinand Ward.

Ward was the most talked about young financier of his day, a second coming of Jay Cooke, everybody said. I would have done well then to remember that Cooke was planning his bankruptcy as I sat as a guest in his house.

Ward and Buck traded everything from agricultural commodities to the bonds of the elevated railway systems now flourishing in our cities, and they were a great success. I would not have gotten involved in their business, but in 1883 Buck visited me, half eager, half embarrassed, with Ferdinand Ward and a proposition.

Buck led Ward into my office—a pair of more prosperous-looking young gentlemen could not be imagined. "Father, thanks to Ferdinand here, I'm becoming a wealthy man," he told me. "My father-in-law gave me a hundred thousand dollars to invest in our firm—today it's worth almost a million! Ferdinand is the most sought-after trader and investor on Wall Street today!"

Ward was a dashing young fellow. He smiled confidently. "I'm only availing myself of the opportunities our remarkable economic system creates," he said modestly.

Buck nodded. "Father, I think you ought to sit down with Ferdinand and talk business."

"What makes you think there's a place for me in your enterprise?" I asked.

Buck's eyes opened wide and his smile came up like a sunrise. "For you, Dad?"

"For you, General Grant?" Ferdinand Ward echoed as he stepped forward and offered me a maduro double corona, a Cuban make with a perfect feel. "Why, General, I am only embarrassed we've never had this conversation before! I have always assumed it would be presumptuous on my part to suggest you join Ulysses and me in our enterprise! Of course there would be a place for you!" He struck a match and offered it in precisely the right spot to put a good red head on the cigar's end.

"Yes, but what is it I can contribute?" I asked as I puffed. I was wary of being sought as a purely ornamental figure.

"Your judgment, your dignity, your relationships with investors," Ward said, "your probity, your sense of strategy, your knowledge of the world and its ways, your instincts for command—you can contribute all of that," he finished with earnest admiration.

"I suppose I could," I said modestly.

"And a hundred thousand dollars," Ward added quickly.

My eyebrows shot up involuntarily, as they tended to do when such a sum was mentioned. "I suppose I could do that as well," I said, more tentatively.

"It's a fairly routine investment," Ward responded casually. "It just makes it easier for all concerned if you become a fully committed equity partner. After all, you don't want to look like an ornamental figure, do you?" *You put your share up and I'll stand up to the investment, Sam, that's how confident I feel.* "And any and all additions to our capital base help move us, all of us, forward. Our business, after all, involves investments. We buy securities, borrow against them, and then use the borrowings to buy other securities—"

"That's called hypothecation, Dad," Buck said, proud to show me his business savvy.

Ward nodded. "Yes, hypothecation, General Grant, as Ulysses has so ably defined it. It allows us to lever our base and make the kinds of returns for our investors we alone provide—forty percent in the last year!"

Ward went on to explain the workings of the operation. He bought simple, low-risk securities, such as the bonds of the government, and pledged them against loans he usually received from Marine Bank, which was one of the preeminent financial houses of New York, and whose president was the third partner in Grant and Ward. The proceeds of these loans were used to buy more securities, but of a more speculative sort—the elevated railroads, that sort of thing—and when these investments proved out and the bonds gained in value, they would be sold, the loan retired, the profits taken in, and the cycle begun again.

So I raised $100,000, selling all of our land in Missouri—abandoning the idea of retiring there one day—liquidating what was left of the trust funds established for us, mortgaging our home on Sixty-sixth Street, and putting all of the proceeds into Ward's hands, betting that Grant and Ward, as we called it, would be my big, final financial success. Then Ward went to work.

Ah, wealth! I've been drunk on liquor, and I've been drunk on hubris, but give me the sweet tonic of wealth every time. As the months rolled by I became a wealthy man at last, drawing a handsome salary while my capital burgeoned in value along with everybody else's. Ward had found Coronado, conquered Montezuma, sat on Midas's throne. His investments compounded as if by husbandry. I came in every morning to get Ward's reports, sign the mail he put in front of me, and read the letters of old associates who beseeched me to take their money. I didn't have to sell a one of them, didn't make a single visit or send a single telegram—they called me, begging to know if it was all true and how they could be a part of it.

And I told them what I knew to be true—Ward was as sound as a gold dollar. I recall one afternoon when an old veteran of the Army of the Tennessee came by. He had invested $50,000—his life's accumulation—in Grant and Ward and wanted to take his money out. Ward smiled politely at his request and left the room. He was gone far more than a few moments. The old fellow eyed me nervously as we sat there, but Ward soon returned with a check—for $250,000!

"But I've only placed fifty thousand on account," the old fellow said.

"Yes, but we have managed it prudently and it has grown to this amount," Ward said, smiling indulgently.

The codger fingered the check, his pale blue eyes watering and spotted hands trembling. "You have worked miracles!" he exclaimed, and then, drying his cheeks with his sleeve, he passed the check back to Ward. "No, you take it back. Put all of it back into the pot! Please!" he implored us, and I smiled benevolently as I watched Ward take the check back from the misty-eyed gent.

The old fool never saw a dime of his money again. Nor did any of us.

The end came on a Sunday morning in May 1884. Ward showed up unexpectedly at my home on Sixty-sixth Street. I had a study on the second floor, overlooking the street, cluttered with my war decorations—medals, uniforms, sashes, gifts of armor, weapons, and battle flags. I sat down on a leather armchair and bade him sit. "We are experiencing a cash flow problem, General," Ward began in a humble, self-deprecating way—*he hadn't seen it coming*, his demeanor seemed to suggest. "Our securities are all perfectly sound—we've not lost a dime on one of them. But we have deployed our capital so actively we simply do not have enough left in our bank account to meet the cash requirements of repayments and withdrawals one reasonably anticipates for a Monday morning," he continued, smiling in a pained way.

"We're out of money!"

"No, no," he corrected quickly. "We're far from out of money. Our assets total in the tens of millions! We simply have all of our money out working for us in securities, and not enough in cash. And I am hesitant to liquidate our assets on disadvantageous terms and reduce the returns we have been able to secure for our investors," he explained, leaning forward with a confidential air. "These financial traders are jackals of the lowest order, General! You have seen them all by now! They will tear us to shreds and give us pennies for our dollar if they get wind of our needs! We could lose everything we have amassed!"

I allowed his words to sink in—it all made sense to me. Our capital was at work, jackals would tear us to shreds, yes, this was a reasonable circumstance. And the risk—everything we had amassed! "I appreciate the situation we're in, Ferdinand, but as you know, I've not much more than a dollar in cash left myself. What course of action do you propose?"

Ward nodded solemnly. "We need three hundred thousand dollars tomorrow. I am confident, of course, I can raise my half," he said nonchalantly. "But do you think you'll be able to raise yours?"

It did not occur to me in the exigencies of the moment I had just been hoodwinked into raising $150,000. No, all I considered was Buck's future, and my own. I stroked my beard and considered the matter. From whom could I borrow such a sum? Fisk and Gould? No. Cooke? No. Stewart? Unlikely. And then it struck me.

"Vanderbilt!" While Commodore Vanderbilt himself had died in 1877, his son William had always continued the family's ongoing generosity toward me.

Ward looked up when he heard his name, as if savoring a fine aroma. "Vanderbilt! Why, that's a very good idea," he encouraged. "Do you suppose you'd be able to approach Vanderbilt for a short-term loan—simply a bridging device, to be sure—for the whole hundred and fifty thousand, say, this afternoon?"

I might have gulped a bit. "This afternoon?" I asked.

"Why, of course," Ward said matter-of-factly. "We'll need the money tomorrow. And if we could say that William Vanderbilt—the son of the great Commodore himself!—was providing us with financing, the markets would fall back from us entirely. Nobody would be concerned any longer about the safety of their investments or our ability to make our cash commitments. Why, that is an excellent idea, General!" Ward congratulated me. "And I urge you to have executed it when I return this evening, so I can bring the draft to our bankers at the earliest possible moment tomorrow."

Ward rose from his seat with such polish and poise I did not think to ask him how these people came to be concerned about the safety or security of their investments or our ability to make cash commitments in the first place. It all made sense, I told myself, and my own reputation, as well as Buck's, was on the line. I watched Ward leave and then put on my coat and hastened myself into my carriage for a short ride up Fifth Avenue to Vanderbilt's home.

My driver pulled up in front of Vanderbilt's mansion and I slowly descended the carriage and mounted the steps. A doorman met me and escorted me into Vanderbilt's library, and I sat there, alone, in the middle of that gigantic, vaulted space, feeling very small indeed. I was back where I had started from—*Papa says I may offer you twenty dollars for the colt, but if you don't take that, I am to offer twenty-two and a half, and if you won't take that, offer twenty-five.*

Vanderbilt walked in and gave me a puzzled but cordial greeting. He was wearing a purple silk robe and slippers, suggesting I had interrupted a quiet Sunday at home. He sat opposite me, the two of us now dwarfed in the enormous paneled room hung with hunting trophies, tapestries, and paintings by the masters.

"Good day, General," he said pleasantly, signaling over his shoulder for a butler to bring a silver serving tray with an assortment of liquors.

I allowed myself a brandy and Vanderbilt joined me, out of politeness, I suspected, but I drank mine without waiting. "Mr. Vanderbilt," I began, "I have come to ask your assistance in a business matter."

Vanderbilt's brow furrowed; he nodded and slowly lowered his drink onto the table next to him. "Yes?" he prompted.

I began to speak quickly, suddenly afraid I had little claim to his time. "As you know, I have had the good fortune to be involved in the firm of Grant and Ward these past several years, and we have produced what I believe is an exemplary record of investment on our own behalf and that of our clients. But our short-term cash flow requirements are currently in excess of our ability to service them," I said, imitating Ward as best I could, but to uncertain effect. Vanderbilt maintained a noncommittal expression. "We are concerned our clients and our lenders will misconstrue this situation and we will be forced to liquidate disadvantageously." I stopped and drew in some air—this was as much talking of this sort as I could do at one time.

Vanderbilt showed no response—not so much as a twitch.

I pressed ahead. "Given the extent of our assets and the underlying strength of our position, the amount of cash we will need at the opening of business tomorrow—one hundred and fifty thousand dollars—is well within our ability to service. But this being the Sabbath, we are hard-pressed to secure financing otherwise, and so I find myself here—"

At this point Vanderbilt nodded and raised a silencing hand. "My dear general," he said quietly. "Is Grant and Ward broke?"

"Why, no, of course not, nothing of the sort," I assured him. "Our problems are of a transient nature, a matter of—"

Here Vanderbilt raised his eyebrows in a way that demanded silence. "Perhaps I should begin another way," he said, cutting me off. "General, are you aware that Grant and Ward *is* broke?"

"Broke?" I faltered.

"General, are you familiar with the procedure known as *hypothecation*?"

"Why, of course," I replied, still playing at the man of the world. "It is the procedure by which securities are offered as collateral for loans that go toward the purchase—"

Vanderbilt cut me off again. "And are you familiar with the term *re-hypothecation*?"

I shook my head, bewildered.

"*Rehypothecation*," Vanderbilt continued, "is a situation in which a security already promised to one borrower is then promised to a second borrower without the first borrower's knowledge or consent. It is a form, sir, of fraud. Hypothecation is a procedure, General. Rehypothecation is a crime."

"But all of our dealings have been with the Marine Bank," I blurted. "The president of which is a partner in Grant and Ward. Surely he would be aware of any malfeasance on the part of Mr. Ward or our firm, were there to be any rehypothecation of the sort you are mentioning to me now," I said, babbling, until I had run out of words and breath.

Vanderbilt remained unmoved. "Unless," he said softly, "your bank president and your Mr. Ward were engaged in a conspiracy to defraud the Marine Bank by lending out its resources to Grant and Ward through such a scheme." His eyes bore into me. "*As is common knowledge in the financial community.* Surely you must have realized!"

While I knew he must be telling me the truth, it was too much for me to assimilate. "Mr. Vanderbilt, I am quite certain—"

"This reminds me of a story, General," he said, settling comfortably back into his chair. "Daniel Drew, President of the Erie Railroad, got caught being less than honest in his stock dealings back in '67. He wrote a poem about his experience. And it went like this:

> "*He that sells what isn't his'n*
> *Must buy it back, or go to prison.*"

He chortled lightly at this bit of doggerel before continuing in a tone of sad disbelief.

"General, surely you must have known! Surely you must have suspected these men were criminals. Even a babe in the woods such as yourself, sitting in your gilded cage of an office, wearing your finely appointed suit, must have looked up once and thought, *There is a certain fictitiousness about the prosperity around us.* Did you never once wonder where these magical piles of money came from?"

He rose from his seat and walked to the window, an ornate affair with leaded glass, and shook his head as he looked down at the street below. "General, you are an innocent lost in the world of men. You somehow think a nod, a gesture, a knowing look, can be translated into wealth." He turned to me and shook his head sadly. "Wealth does not come from the convivial handshake and the well-sipped drink. It comes from *power*," he said, his hand balled into a fist as he said the word. "It comes from a willingness to seize events and shape them, coax them, continually manage them, so they will produce one result— *the creation of more wealth.*

"That is how wealth is created, Grant. Not by knacks or tricks, but by an unwavering commitment to accumulate it regardless of the cost!" He walked toward me, the embodiment of the modern age's businesslike efficiency. "The cathedrals of Europe and the pyramids of Egypt, these monuments to dead social orders, will pale compared to what will be built in this new industrial age. We are entering an era, General, in which the engine of wealth will pull the train of America down the track of progress at a rate never before imagined. There is nothing more important today than progress. It is the *overriding objective*. If armed men must be sent to clear a railroad line, then so be it; if a Congress must be bought, so be it; if foreign nations and peoples must be subjugated, if boundaries must be moved, if history must be reconfigured, *so be it*. And if six hundred thousand men must die and a nation torn apart so there may be cheap cotton to weave and cheap labor to weave it, then so be it, so long as the overriding objective is met."

He reached for his brandy and took a short sip. "I admire—my father appreciated—what you have done for your country, Grant. Without you, the South's cotton and its African manpower would have been absorbed into the British sphere, British coffers fattened overseas, the British empire extended to this continent, and the positions of my family, and a few others like my own, compromised. We appreciate the sense of duty you have brought to your service to the nation, Grant. The world, you see, requires a balance—a balance between men of honor such as yourself and men who have no need of it such as me. Each of us has his place, sir, which is how you and I happen to be here today. I have need of men like you." He returned his glass to the table and crossed the room to a massive oak desk, where he extracted a ledger from its center drawer. "Just, of course," he said as he found his place among the ruled pages, "as you inevitably have need of men like me. You say you need a hundred fifty thousand?"

"Yes," I said, barely audible, even to myself.

"Fine," he said, and wrote out a draft. "But this is not a loan to Grant and Ward. It is my gift to you."

"No, no," I exclaimed. "I have come for a loan. I have collateral— my battle honors, medals, swords, flags, my entire collection."

He looked up at me, his head cocked quizzically, like a bird contemplating a seed. "A loan?" he asked, then paused. "Very well. Have these items brought here and we will store them, if you wish."

He put the ledger back into the drawer and walked back to where we sat. "I confess it is a pittance in the grand sense, General, ultimately small payment for the labor of gathering the nation's men to fight each other and then dispersing them when they reconvened as dissatisfied rabble. There are moments when I fear the trick of history will become clear to those on whom it is perpetrated, and we will all come tumbling down. There are moments when I fear some malcontent obsessed with life, fortune, and sacred honor will explain the trick," he said softly, "and the magic show will end. But thanks to you, that day has been deferred yet a little longer."

He handed me the bank draft. I looked down at it.

Pay to the order of Ulysses Grant.

The name stared back at me, the name spoken in the prophecy of the Great Master who visited me that night in Mexico four decades before, and I heard his words again: *Grantito, a magnificent destiny awaits. Ulysses Grant will lead great masses of men in the glorious cause of their human redemption. A great time of turmoil will come, and out of the suffering will come Ulysses Grant, who will become the champion of those who seek deliverance.*

I then understood for the first time what the Great Master meant. It was Useful who had fulfilled the prophecy. It was Useful who had led great masses of men in the cause of their human redemption— their liberation from oligarchy. It was Useful who became the champion who, in their time of suffering, led them toward deliverance. A magnificent destiny awaited him, and fate propelled him toward it. My usurpation of his birthright, his wanderings through the California goldfields, his life as a swindler, his brush with death on the field at Shiloh—none of it could stop him from fulfilling that destiny, the one the mighty apparition had communicated to me. His opposition to Vanderbilt and Vanderbilt's social order was what Mescalito had meant.

The Great Master—astride a steed of clouds, sunlike eyes blazing, crowned by moonlight, clothed in the colors of all living things—the dumb Indian had the wrong man!

I had lived a remarkable life—won great battles, overcome great adversity, displayed great perseverance. But the greatness I had achieved had blinded me to the Master's true meaning. I had not transacted the prophecy. I had transacted Vanderbilt's business instead, and like a dupe, a chump, I was being paid off with a pittance. A pittance in the grand sense, that's what he had just told me, compared to his wealth, and compared to the service I had rendered. That was ultimately what I was worth.

Mescalito had the wrong man. He had made a simple mistake. And why should I have been surprised? I had already seen the God of Israel make mistakes. I had seen our Lord let my men die in the Wilderness, in the trenches of Spotsylvania, at Cold Harbor. Theologists tied themselves in knots trying to discern God's plan in all of it, but I'll tell you what the plan was—there was no plan. The plan was as thought-out as the splatter on a boy's shirt when he spills his soup at dinner. It is all God's mistake. How could I have failed to anticipate a Mexican apparition would be no different?

I took Vanderbilt's draft and departed, delivering it to Ward that night. He dissembled to me about having obtained his half of the money, then pocketed Vanderbilt's gift and took off for parts unknown. His partner at the bank was apprehended and tried. Buck went back to his father-in-law to start again. I went home. I had a hundred dollars left to my name.

I had gone to sleep the night before a wealthy man, and went to sleep that night a pauper.

It could get no worse, I thought.

And then, a month later, I was eating a peach after lunch and recoiled from the pain in my throat as I swallowed. In the back of my mind, I knew instantly what it was.

And now the lump I couldn't swallow is swallowing me.

So this was how I would end—destitute, dying, writing this volume for Sam Clemens to publish in order to leave Mrs. Grant the means I had proved unable to provide otherwise, and also to tell the truth, both the truth I was afraid to speak all my life and the truth I finally learned at this late hour. The disease is quickly overwhelming me, and news of my condition has spread as rapidly as the condition itself. I write hurriedly, hoping to finish before I am finished.

I am now officially dying in public.

CHAPTER XV

A VISIT FROM SHERMAN—A SURPRISING LETTER—THE LAST UNION SOLDIER— REVEREND NEWMAN AND DOCTOR DOUGLAS

SHERMAN CAME TO CALL.

"Grant! You son of a bitch! As general of the army, I order you to get out of that fucking chair this instant!" he howled as he walked toward the cottage to find me sunning on the porch. A beautiful woman with long wavy tresses and a beckoning look walked along beside him. "What do you say, Grant? Can you get a croak out of that throat of yours?"

For all of my discomfort and for all of our disagreements, there was no one I would have rather seen.

"Sherman!" I answered in a hoarse whisper. "I'd offer you one of my cigars, but these doctors now rule my roost."

Sherman laughed and sat next to me on the porch, resting his strong hand on my frail one. His lady friend stood awkwardly a few steps from us. "Grant, this is my friend, Miss Vinnie Ream. Vinnie, this is Ulysses Grant himself," Sherman said with great theatricality.

"I'm very pleased, General," she said, stepping forward and looking down respectfully. Her voice was like poured honey, and she filled her loosely cut blouse and skirt in a way that reminded me of the girls of Mexico. She made a small curtsy of sorts and wandered off to the other end of the porch to give us some privacy.

Sherman leered at me. "Some kind of fucking fluff, that, eh, Grant?"

I strained to lean forward and get an eyeful of her. "How can you brazenly parade this girl around, Sherman?" I whispered painfully.

He grinned back at me. "What the hell, Grant. Ellen is old," he said, referring to his wife. "She suffers the boils, can't breathe. I've got some life left in me yet, Grant, and I'm going to give it away while I can!" We watched her look out over the porch rail. "She's a sculptress, this one is," Sherman continued. "I got her a commission for a statue of Farragut they put in a park in Washington. Ever think *you'd* be a statue, Grant?" Sherman smiled, then turned to admire his paramour's derriere. "And she knows how to make me hard as a sculpture, that's for fucking sure," he said, laughing. "Can't blame me for playing with that fire, can you, Grant?"

I shook my head and conceded with a small smile, "I suppose not."

Sherman sat back and sighed; we quietly stared out into the woods around us. "Not bad for a pair of failures, eh, Grant?" He tapped his feet nervously on the porch, not sure of what to say. "How's it going for you?" he then asked, finding the silence deafening. "How's about that book you're writing? I didn't take you for an author."

"I'm busy fighting poverty, Cump," I croaked. "How about you?"

He smiled as he shared the recollection. "I'm a dead cock in the pit, Sam," he replied.

"What did you think that afternoon back in St. Louis, Cump?" I asked, recalling the day in 1857 I encountered him as I sold my firewood.

Sherman shook his head. "I thought they'd put me in an asylum one day, Grant. I could barely live inside my own skin. And when they pretty much did in '61, I figured I was long overdue. When I wrote to you after Donelson and got back into the fight, I wasn't any better than I ever was. I just learned how to convince folks I had changed. No one ever changes, Grant."

I nodded—it was something I'd waited all my life to learn. "When I was floating the supply boats past Vicksburg," I rasped, "over your vociferous objection, I remember thinking it made as much sense to me as planting potatoes did in Vancouver, which was all the sense in the world. And I sat there and wondered how it would go wrong, just like planting those potatoes went wrong."

"You see?" Sherman said with new enthusiasm. "There's a destiny in each of us, Grant, whether we're crazy, or a failure, or whatever else. It comes out the way it comes out for a reason." He rested his hands on his spindly thighs and took a deep breath. "Although, for the life of me, I'll never figure out what the reason is."

I turned to him and looked him over. Forty-odd years later, the red hair was thin and white, the dark eyes lined, the strong voice cracking. "Sherman, did I ever tell you about what happened to me in Mexico?"

"Too often." He waved his hand and smiled.

"No, not that," I said. "When it was over, I was in Jalapa—"

Sherman shook his head and smiled. "I've heard all your stories, Grant. Spare both of us and save your precious breath."

I was about to interrupt him when it occurred to me he would find out soon enough, here in these pages. So we sat there together for the rest of the afternoon, saying as little as we had on the street in St. Louis. Back then we had nothing to say. Now we had no need to say it. It was already sunset. As I watched the reddening sky, I must have fallen asleep.

When I awoke, they were helping me to bed.

Sherman had gone. It was just as well. We were both spared saying good-bye.

I was lying in bed the next morning when my son Fred brought me a most remarkable letter. "I ought to read this to you, Father," he said. "It is from a fellow who was an assistant to Andy Johnson when he was military governor of Tennessee."

"Go ahead," I wheezed.

Fred looked down and read. "'*Dear General Grant,*'" the letter began. "'*I regret intruding during what must be a strenuous convalescence,*'"—a judicious choice of words, I thought—"'*but we are confronted here with an odd situation.*

"'*In the late autumn of the past year, a hunting party near the North Carolina border came upon signs of a hermit's dwelling in the nearby mountains, which is not unheard of in these parts. After some reconnaissance, the hunters were able to discern a solitary male figure, about fifty years of age, with long hair and beard, dressed in rags and animal skins haphazardly stitched together, and the remnants of the cap of a Federal soldier. When the hunters ventured closer, the hermit fired a shot over their heads and called them "Confederate scum."*

"'*The fellow has barricaded himself within a cave with a store of armaments and ammunition. He claims to be a corporal in the Army of the Tennessee, separated from his unit on the first day of Missionary Ridge. His wanderings took him deep behind enemy lines, and when winter set in, he discovered this cave and has since remained there. He has occasionally sighted men in Confederate uniforms, invariably on horseback and carrying firearms, which he took as a sign the C.S.A. had won the war. As a Federal soldier, he felt himself still in danger. When we explained to him the Union had won the war, and the men he had seen were former Confederate soldiers allowed to keep their horses and side arms when you paroled them at Appomattox, he refused to believe us. He said Unconditional Surrender Grant would never allow such a thing to happen, and he would not believe a word of it until he hears it from Grant himself.*

"'My most esteemed General, we do not expect you to come here, but we wonder if you might write a letter to convince this fellow to come out of his hiding place. We have found him in the military records of the Army of the Tennessee: Corporal Hiram Struggles. Our fear is that in his derangement, he might ultimately attack and kill someone. Nonetheless, we are, as I'm sure you understand, extremely hesitant to take a course of action that might lead to the death of a man who has needlessly sacrificed two decades of his life in the cause of the preservation of a Union already preserved.

"'We therefore turn to you for guidance, and look forward to hearing from you or your emissary. May God bless you, dear General.'" Fred looked up to assess my response. "He closes with salutations and wishes for your health," he concluded, before folding the letter.

I was silent. "Have you a reaction, Father?" he asked.

"Any number of them," I responded. *And I named him for my struggles.*

"Perhaps you might wish to dictate a letter," Fred suggested, "or have me write one."

I threw aside my bedclothes and tried to swing my feeble legs to the floor. "I must go visit this man immediately."

Fred rushed up to grab my feet and return me to a prone position. "Father, don't talk nonsense. Your health makes such a visit entirely impossible—"

"Not seeing this man would be entirely impossible," I rasped, and struggled with Fred over control of my limbs. A slap to the head, the best I could muster, convinced him of my intent to stand. "We can take a train from here to Washington, and then to Nashville, then Chattanooga. The railroad will provide us with the right accommodations—

Vanderbilt will see to that—and I can travel in a hospital bed in a private car with a doctor in attendance, much as I do here."

I had by now managed to get to my feet and was shedding my gown and shuffling to the armoire to get a suit of clothes. Fred ran from the room and in an instant returned with Mrs. Grant.

"Just where do you think you're going?" she demanded, arms folded over her stout breast in her best military manner.

"I'm going to take a train ride," I croaked, rummaging through my clothes. "Have the help pack my suitcase."

"I'll do no such thing, you tired old fool. Fred says you want to visit some sort of caveman."

"He needs me," I said.

"He probably needs a bath more than he needs you!" she shot back. "What good can you be to him? You're going back to bed."

"Julia, I must go see this man. How can I get you to agree?"

"I'm not about to let—" She stopped and brightened considerably. "Promise you'll let the Reverend Newman baptize you!"

I sighed deeply. "Very well."

"You'll do it?" she asked, surprised.

"Upon my return," I said. "And, preferably, upon my demise, so that I won't have to see him. And he must pray very quietly, in the hope God will not hear him." Perhaps the Lord would make another mistake and leave me be.

She considered this for a moment. "Agreed," she said, and then turned to Fred. "Get his clothes on him," she ordered, and hurried from the room to share the good news with my emissary to the next world.

We waited until nightfall to slip past the newspapermen and tourists encamped in a deathwatch around my cottage, and I found myself in short order on a train heading south. They dressed me in a black suit with a turned collar, a black tie, black silk slippers, and a black top hat, probably so I could readily lie in state if I happened to die on the way.

On the third day of our trip I arrived at Chattanooga, now a rebuilt, bustling city. A fine carriage had been turned into an ambulance to bring me near the secluded site. Once we were within a mile or so of our destination, the road ceased, and a sedan chair awaited me, a handsome black affair with a chamber trimmed in purple velvet, almost funereal in its aspect, which was not inappropriate. Eight strapping members of the local militia were on hand to bear me up a trail into the wilderness, and once I was comfortably situated in it, they lifted the entire affair into the air and carried me off.

I had been administered injections of morphine throughout the trip, and while the jostling was decidedly uncomfortable, I found myself being borne to the cave in a cloudy, dreamlike reverie.

We came to an abrupt stop at a small clearing hacked out of the forest. I peered through the curtains of the sedan chair. The mouth of the cave stood before me. A local official was waiting for me. He saluted with great emotion.

"General Grant," he said. "Words cannot express our appreciation—"

"Then don't bother," I said. "Where is Corporal Struggles?"

He looked at the mouth of the cave. "In there." He raised his voice and cupped his hands around his mouth. "Corporal Struggles!"

There was a moment of silence before a nervous, reedy voice emerged from the cave. "What is it?"

"General Grant is here!" the official responded, his eyes trained on the cave.

Another pause, then: "Send him in!"

"Come now, Corporal," the official shouted back. "Do you expect General Grant to crawl in the dirt here? Have you any idea of the distance he's—"

I reached out through the curtains and waved him off. "I will be fine," I wheezed uncomfortably, and then, under my breath, added, "if I live." I planted a cane in the dirt in front of the cave and slowly stepped out of the sedan chair, my slippered feet moving carefully until I felt both firmly under me. I nodded over my shoulder, dismissing everyone in the clearing, and waited until I was left alone. I faced the cave, standing as straight as I could, and shouted painfully, "Corporal Struggles! Fall in!"

My dim eyes and morphined mind could barely perceive him at first, but in a moment a small, thin, haggard man slowly made his way into the daylight. He had my first Julia's plain face, the simple look of an Ohio farmer. His Federal uniform was patched with animal skins and fragments of cloth he had gleaned from one place or another, and he wore a Federal soldier's cap, absent its brim, like a fez. He carried an old Enfield that had not seen a cleaning in some time. Nor had he: His hair was long and tangled as it fell down his back, and there were only one or two teeth in a mouth largely hidden behind his long, matted mustache and beard. His eyes opened wide and were suddenly filled with tears when he was sure it was me, and his spine stiffened until he was in an impossibly erect posture. "Corporal Struggles reporting, sir!" he exclaimed, and snapped off a salute.

"As you were, Corporal," I said, returning his gesture. "Have you a place a tired man might sit?" Corporal Struggles scampered, lizardlike, back into the cave and emerged with a stool he had fashioned out of a tree stump. He gave me a cup of springwater in a hollowed gourd— good handiwork, I noted. I sat down and we regarded each other for a moment, him in his rags and buckskin shoes, me in my black suit, silk slippers, and top hat, both of us showing more age than the past twenty years would have suggested.

He spoke first. "Is it really over, General?"

I nodded. "The war, you mean? Yes," I wheezed weakly.

"How did it end?" he asked quietly.

It would be my last chance to answer that question. "As I intended it to end," I said. "After we pushed Bragg and Longstreet off Lookout Mountain—"

"You charged up the mountain, sir?" he interrupted, disbelieving.

I sighed. "The men did. I had nothing to do with it. But I got the credit, of course. Shortly thereafter the President made me general-in-chief."

"President Lincoln or President McClellan, sir?"

"President McClellan!" I laughed through my discomfort. "Ha! No, Mac never got to be President, Corporal. Three months before the election, Sherman and your friends in the Army of the Tennessee took Atlanta and cut the South in half for good. Once they did, the people of the North saw victory was inevitable and reelected Lincoln. After that, all it took was for me to hunt down Bobby Lee, and I did."

"We all said you'd be the one to bag him, sir, if anyone could. You and Uncle Billy. When was that?"

"Spring of '65," I said.

He smiled broadly. "I had given up hope," he said. He reflected upon this news, then looked up inquisitively. "Then the Negro is free?"

I shook my head sadly, thinking of William Jones. "Oh, slavery is outlawed, to be sure. But once Sherman cut through the South, the slaves ran away from the plantations, and slavery ended then and there." Corporal Struggles nodded with quiet satisfaction. "And once the slaves ran away," I continued, "they ran back, for they found they were almost as free as were the poor whites who farmed next to them—free to be poor, free to be in debt, free to be broke," I explained, remembering as I spoke what being broke was like. "And they were free to be brutalized by their neighbors, free to be ripped from their beds and murdered, free to have their houses torched. It was my doing, or at least part of it was," I said sadly. "If I had been a more diligent President, then perhaps they'd have an easier time of it today. But I was unwilling to fight a second war to ensure the outcome of the first. I proved feckless, I suppose."

Corporal Struggles labored to comprehend the history he had missed. "When did you become President? Did you succeed President Lincoln?"

It had not occurred to me he could not have heard. "No. Lincoln was murdered, a few days after the surrender."

"Murdered? No! By whom?"

"Southerners," I said.

His cheeks flushed with rage. "Reb scum! Were they hung?"

I nodded. "Save the ringleader. He was shot, or so they say."

He leaned forward eagerly. "Did they hang Jeff Davis? And Lee? The whole lot of them?"

I shook my head. "No, once they surrendered, they were our countrymen again."

"But they were traitors!" He grumbled for a moment—he had been fighting them in his mind for twenty years, after all—then accepted it. "Well," he said finally, "at least we won, didn't we, General?"

"You and I certainly did, Corporal. The two of us are alive to talk about it, so we won."

"I mean our nation, General. At least the North won."

"Yes, the North won," I said, not without some pride.

"And the Union was preserved," Corporal Struggles said insistently.

"Preserved? Well, it's intact, yes," I conceded. "We became one nation again. But preserved? As what? Not as a nation of small towns where men of goodwill could congregate. Not as a place to raise a family and to farm. Our nation is an infernal place now. Railroads! Factories! Oligarchs who control the wealth! Our nation was preserved, to be sure—preserved as a place for industry to spread, for big cities to absorb thousands of people with no other place to go or jobs to do. The part of our nation that war best preserved was the people that own it. If that's what you mean by preserved, then the Union was preserved," I said.

Corporal Struggles shook his head slightly, and after a long silence spoke: "But if all that is true, then what did we die for?"

I leaned forward. "I'll tell you what we died for, Corporal," I croaked. "We died so there would be cheap cotton to feed the mills and cheap labor to run the machines. If you want a monument to our brave men's sacrifice, then go to the cities and look at the factories. Slavery's over and the Union's one again, but that's who won the war, Corporal. Vanderbilt and his ilk. The bullets flew and the blood flowed, and the Vanderbilts loaned the nation the money for the pleasure of letting them do so. And when it was all over, they duly thanked the participants and went back to what they were doing before the disruption.

"Oh, I beat Lee, Corporal. I whipped him good. No other soul could have done it. There's still some satisfaction in that. The history books will say I won the war, Corporal—they will say I led great masses of men in the cause of their human redemption. But what I ended up winning was the right to lead parades, to borrow against my good name, to live in the White House and then, when I was used up, to come and tell you it was over. So, did I win? I don't know if you'd call that winning or not. But as for you, Corporal, you have won the war— you're sitting here, alive."

He seemed suddenly filled with an uncertainty. "What should I do now, General?" he asked quietly.

I put a hand on his shoulder. "Are there people who miss you, Corporal?" I asked.

"Just my mother, sir, if she's still alive."

"Your mother loves you," I said. He looked up at me, confused. "You can believe me, son."

Tears came to his eyes. "I do, General. But all I have left in life is the cause we fought for. And if the cause is gone, then what am I to do now?"

I looked into Corporal Struggles's eyes—my first Julia's eyes—and was overwhelmed with the meaning of everything I had learned. From the moment my father and I had first come upon a dazed and confused Useful, to the Mexican War, to my days of impoverishment and then of glory, I had let the world define the terms on which I'd lived, let the events around me guide me as I groped toward what I thought to be my fate. But for Corporal Struggles, there was still hope—the hope that one man who clings fast could still define his own fate, that one man could become a fulcrum from which the earth could be moved. It was too late for me now—even as I sat there I could feel my insides wither and rot—but for Corporal Struggles, there was still this last hope. The war might have been over, but so long as Corporal Struggles travailed, its final outcome was still held at bay. There might be some who see life in a cave as an unendurable punishment, but for Corporal Struggles, each day he remained there would prove a great victory.

I rose slowly from my stool. "Go back to your cave, Corporal!" I exclaimed. "Go back and don't ever let them force you out! Don't ever let the war end, Corporal, because once it ends, everything I told you will happen. As long as you're in this cave, their victory isn't complete. As long as you're here, you're still fighting for the cause that was worth going to war for in the first place—the dignity of all people, the nobility of our country's spoken ideals. But the moment you step out of this cave, the things you and thousands of others held dearest will disappear and the cause will die. Don't do it, Corporal. You are the last man—it all depends on you."

He wrapped his hands around his weapon and a hard look came over him. "I won't, General! I swear it!"

"Good," I said, now standing before him. "Your nation needs you this one last time—one last soldier to stay on guard and fight the good fight. I will entrust you with this, Corporal! You are here to transact a great destiny." I raised my hand to my brow in salute. "Corporal Struggles, return to your post!"

"I won't fail you, General!" he replied, his expression one of great hope and resolve, and with that he returned my salute, executed a perfect about-face, and marched back into his cave. I could hear his footfalls for a few seconds more and then there was silence.

I turned, whistled sharply into the mountain air to summon my bearers, and shuffled back to the sedan chair. I stepped in and was dimly aware of being carried down the mountain. I awoke on the train, the morphine cruising through me, an image of Corporal Struggles coming through the drugged haze.

• • •

Mrs. Grant was waiting for me when I was returned to our cottage. They carried me into the house and laid me, exhausted, on my bed.

"Well, I hope you're satisfied," she said, as the household staff scurried away. "You look terrible!"

"I looked terrible before I left," I said, my voice ragged. Every movement sent pain through all my joints.

"Yes, but what about our deal? Reverend Newman is here, and you promised you'd let him—"

"I know, I know," I said. My tortured throat barely allowed me to whisper now. "First I need to tell you something."

She folded her arms and stood at the side of the bed impatiently. "What is it?"

"It's something I've needed to tell you all our lives. I was always too afraid, there was never a right time." I started to fade.

Mrs. Grant smiled. "That you love me?" she asked.

"No," I said, and she frowned. "Of course I love you, but it's something else." I wet my lips. "My name is not really Ulysses Grant."

Mrs. Grant shrugged. "Of course it's not. It's Hiram Grant, and they got it wrong at West Point, everybody—"

"No, no," I interrupted faintly. "There was a boy named Ulysses Grant, back in Ohio. They wanted him, not me."

Mrs. Grant regarded me with skepticism. "What boy?"

"There was another Grant boy in Ohio—Ulysses Grant. His parents were dead. I stole his trunk."

"You're not making sense, Ulys," she said, impatient and sad at the same time.

"I went in his place—he ran away. Give me some water," I said, fatiguing rapidly.

Mrs. Grant dutifully produced a glass of water and propped my head up so I could sip it. "You're delirious, Ulys. You need to rest."

"No," I croaked. "The other Grant, his son's in the cave."

"Dr. Douglas!" Mrs. Grant shouted, now frightened. "The general is delirious!"

The doctor raced in and began examining me furiously.

"I'm not delirious," I rasped. "I took his trunk. Mescalito meant him."

"You should rest, Ulys," Mrs. Grant said, tears beginning to fall from her eyes. Dr. Douglas took out a hypodermic needle and began preparing a solution.

"I'm giving him another dose of morphine in a solution of brandy," the doctor said. "It will have a sedative effect."

"Listen, please," I begged her. "It was in Mexico . . . the Great Master . . . told me my destiny—"

Mrs. Grant bawled openly. "Oh, no! Ulys, be quiet now, you must rest! Reverend Newman!" she shouted. "He's sinking quickly!"

The Reverend Newman came racing in like a dog who smells a table scrap. He quickly wrapped his little scarf around his neck and extracted a small vial of water from his satchel. "Listen, please," I gasped. "Great apparition . . . I would lead men . . ."

"There, there," Mrs. Grant said, patting my hand. I felt water being sprinkled about my head as the Reverend Newman began, "In the name of the Father, the Son . . ."

"Here we go," Dr. Douglas interrupted as he plunged the hypodermic. A wave of soft relief poured through me, as if springwater were now running through my veins and my limbs had lost their weight. "It's taking effect," he said.

"May the Lord forgive this man his sins, as he does all of us who accept His Kingdom and His Sacrament. All this is God's gift, offered to us without price," the Reverend Newman continued as he filled a nearby bowl with water and tried to guide my unwilling hands into it.

"Please . . . you must believe me . . ." I said.

"There, there, Ulys," Mrs. Grant said.

"Hiram," I said. "Call me Hiram."

"Yes, Hiram." She smiled as her eyes brimmed over once again. Dr. Douglas and the Reverend Newman stood behind her, and the last thing I remember is their three faces, looking down at me, before I fell asleep.

They were gone when I awoke—I had fooled them again and lived one more day.

I can face the end now. Maybe my mother was right and there is some great Other Side. If there is, then Lincoln is there, Rawlins, Taylor, and McPherson, too, the dead of Monterrey and of Little Big Horn, the men Meade sent to their ends at Cold Harbor, the men who filled the trenches at Spotsylvania. Maybe I will find Useful one last time there—maybe he will be gracious enough to give me his next life just as I took away this one. Maybe Lee and crazy Tom Jackson are there as well, the dead who covered the ground at Shiloh, the gasping cholera victims, the murdered Freedmen, all of them now most assuredly brothers in the vast fraternity of the departed. Maybe they will let me join them.

Or maybe my mother was wrong. Maybe there's nothing.

Or maybe the Hindus are right.

When I visited India, the Hindus told me of their beliefs. They believe a soul is endless and eternal, and it keeps coming back.

Maybe they're right. Maybe I'm coming back.

If I do, I want to come back as me.

AUTHOR'S NOTE

Grant was at once a great man, a human being, and a character in the pageant of history. I have tried to be faithful to the essence of each and to explore their interrelatedness in the context of what it means to have a destiny and to be an American.

I have taken liberties with some of the people around him, but the basic facts of Grant's life—personal, military, and historical—are as presented. While this is a work of fiction, the story you have just read is true: Grant's frustrated contemplation of his youthful prospects (and his nickname, "Useless"); his characteristically low-key heroism in the Mexican War; his failure in civilian life; his singular ability to perceive the gist of the Civil War around him despite its logistical and emotional cacophony, and the improvisational brilliance with which he acted upon that understanding; the tangled politics of the postwar period and his sense of being overwhelmed by the more amorphous role of President; and his fumbling search for a pot of gold at the end of his rainbow. Most of the specific incidents are factual, even if embellished—Sherman naming Grant "Sam" at West Point, the cholera epidemic in Panama, Grant's failed business ventures in the Northwest and the inebriated "camels," the manumission of William Jones, Grant's order regarding the Jews in Mississippi, the serial corruption in his Cabinet, or the knavery of Ferdinand Ward. I have superimposed over these facts people who did not exist (e.g., Useful Grant and the first Julia, Mescalito—although one never knows—and Hiram Struggles) or expanded upon some of the personalities around Grant (William Jones, Wallen, Lincoln, Lee, or Garfield) to develop Grant's search for the meaning of his life, but I have not changed or contorted the underlying historical reality. Instead, these characters have been added or expanded to develop the story of Grant's search within the context of historical facts.

I have attempted to use the actual exchanges attributed to Grant and his contemporaries by primary sources reported in a series of biographies and histories of great value. William McFeeley's *Grant* explores its subject's humanity with admirable sensitivity and reflects an understanding of the central role of the question of race in American history. Geoffrey Parret's *Ulysses S. Grant: Soldier and President* uses a finer sense of military history to explore Grant's singular ability as a soldier. Bruce Catton's two-volume chronicle of Grant's Civil War, *Grant Moves South* and *Grant Takes Command,* provides the best moment-to-moment experience of those four years. They follow Lloyd Lewis's 1950 biography, *Captain Sam Grant,* which follows its subject from his family's roots to the outbreak of the Civil War. Horace Porter's *Campaigning with Grant* and Sylvannus Cadwallader's *Three Years with Grant* are rich sources of anecdotage and context. Thomas Pitkin's *The Captain Departs* is an excellent description of Grant's final years. Nancy and Dwight Anderson's *The Generals* ably develops the personal stories of Grant and Lee. Among the many other sources I used often were John Marszalek's *Sherman: A Soldier's Passion for Order,* Catton's *A Stillness at Appomattox,* a fascinating appraisal of Grant written in 1920 by W. E. Woodward, a Southerner, titled *Meet General Grant,* John Keegan's classic *The Mask of Command,* Brooks Simpson's *Let Us Have Peace,* and James McPherson's *Drawn with the Sword* and his landmark *Battle Cry of Freedom,* the direct influence of which permeates many scenes, including the rants about the economics of slavery uttered by Jesse and the Colonel in Chapter V. Kenneth Ackerman's *The Gold Ring,* John Eisenhower's biography of Winfield Scott, *Agent of Destiny,* and K. Jack Bauer's *The Mexican War, 1846–1848* also provided important background for specific segments of the book.

And the Grant canon would not be complete without Thurber's famous *If Grant Had Been Drinking at Appomattox,* which is excerpted briefly in this work, on pages 253–54.

And there are then Grant's *Memoirs* itself, a magnificent book and the product of a methodical and composed mind. The straightforwardness and lucidity of his recollections stand out even more against the agony Grant was in as he wrote them. More than a literary master-piece, this is a great human triumph.

The Civil War reverberates through American history just as the Big Bang's rumbles can still be heard in the universe. I have taken my liberties with that conflict and its greatest characters, as well as other figures from what is now two centuries ago, in the hope of understanding "fate" and "greatness" and what it means to be an American, both then and now. I hope those liberties can be forgiven in the face of the larger goal.

ACKNOWLEDGMENTS

Writing did not make me preoccupied or self-absorbed; instead, it captured those tendencies for itself. My wife, Nancy, was continually gracious about my living in Grant's world as it unfolded around me, so much so that she occasionally came to visit me there. I appreciate now as then her reactions to my work, her sensitivities, and her support.

There were many people who shared my vision and helped me refine it. The eponymous Grant LaRouche, my research/editorial/administrative assistant and alter ego, ran alongside me from the first days of the project to the last, learning the history we would counterfeit, spinning out plot turns, choreographing wrestling moves, searching characters' souls, and abiding me with grace. Thanks, Smithers.

Stan Katz, Mark Lutin, David Moore, the Ranck family, and Maurie Warren all painstakingly read early drafts that only a friend would read, and their encouragement was as kind as it was soothing. Don Marks reeled in dangling antecedents, reviewed archaic scatology, and shared with me both his and Sherwood Anderson's insights into the common denominators of humanity, challenging and improving me as he did forty years ago. Thanks, Preacher.

I am grateful, once again, to the people who saw virtue in my work before there was either. David Chalfant of IMG Literary, ably assisted by Susan Lohman, provided not only the guidance and focus expected of one who plies his trade, but faith and friendship as well. Rick Horgan at Warner Books continually met me more than halfway in the process of perfecting—if that word may be used—the product for which he waited so patiently. And Howard Mittelmark has been a writing Zen master for me, delivering koans and slaps to the head as needed, clearing my mind so that it would have room to admit the writer's craft. Any deficiencies or lacunae are the fault of the student, not the teacher. Thanks, Coach.

And a last word of thanks to my three wonderful kids—Nick, Carl, and Alice—who persist in thinking that having an author for a father is exciting, as opposed to more trouble than it's worth.

ALSO AVAILABLE FROM WARNER BOOKS

BIG GOVERNMENT
by Ev Ehrlich

Snapshots from the nation's capital: A president demands a golden parachute from his wealthy backers in order to resign and devote himself to fishing...an airheaded academic becomes a rising superstar with a single campaign idea, Universal Daylight Savings Time...a 114-year-old congressman named Senior Younger, Jr., takes over the proceedings...Welcome to the world of *Big Government*, Clinton insider Ev Ehrlich's scathing, hilarious, and passionate novel about how big and bad our government really is—and how there just might be a little hope for us after all.

★ ★ ★

"Hilarious...a rollicking parody of current American political life."

—*Publishers Weekly*

★ ★ ★

LAST REFUGE OF SCOUNDRELS
by Paul Lussier

In this audacious and irreverent new novel, based on long overlooked facts of history, Paul Lussier blows the dust off the American Revolution and its icons and takes us on a you-are-there journey into a lunatic underworld. From the public relations ploy that was the Boston Massacre to the spiritual epiphany of the Boston Tea Party, from the preventable horrors at Valley Forge to the grotesque opulence of the court of Marie Antoinette, *The Last Refuge of Scoundrels* is at once a rollicking romp, a haunting love story, and a laugh-out-loud Dickensian epic that will stir passions as forceful as the Revolution itself.

more...

CITIZEN WASHINGTON
by William Martin

William Martin brings to life the flesh-and-blood man behind the frozen face on the dollar bill. A meticulously researched novel that intermingles extraordinary historical characters with brilliantly imagined fictional ones, Citizen Washington unfolds through the words of those who loved Washington, feared him, and tried to betray him. A story of war and peace, faith and doubt, public politics and personal secrets, it unravels the last riddles of Washington's life—and captures the essence of the man who changed the meaning of freedom.

★ ★ ★

"A deft, spicy, and exciting blend of fact and fiction."
—*USA Today*